The
LEGION
PROPHECY

Also by Mark A. Latham and available from Titan Books

The Lazarus Gate
The Iscariot Sanction

Sherlock Holmes: A Betrayal in Blood
Sherlock Holmes: The Red Tower (March 2018)

The
LEGION PROPHECY

MARK A. LATHAM

TITAN BOOKS

The Legion Prophecy
Print edition ISBN: 9781783296842
E-book edition ISBN: 9781783296859

Published by Titan Books
A division of Titan Publishing Group Ltd
144 Southwark Street, London SE1 0UP

First edition: September 2017
10 9 8 7 6 5 4 3 2 1

A CIP catalogue record for this title is available from the British Library.

Printed in the USA.

Did you enjoy this book? We love to hear from our readers.
Please email us at readerfeedback@titanemail.com or write to us at Reader
Feedback at the above address.

To receive advance information, news, competitions, and exclusive offers
online, please sign up for the Titan newsletter on our website:
www.titanbooks.com

The
LEGION
PROPHECY

To Mat, for, among other things,
saving me from death by headdesk.

PART ONE

Her words did gather thunder as they ran,
And as the lightning to the thunder
Which follows it, riving the spirit of man,
Making earth wonder,

So was their meaning to her words. No sword
Of wrath her right arm whirl'd,
But one poor poet's scroll, and with his word
She shook the world.

ALFRED, LORD TENNYSON

PROLOGUE

Monday, 12th May 1890, midnight

THE FURNIVAL ESTATE, WEST SUSSEX

Sir Arthur Furnival sat in his favourite armchair near the fireplace, swirling brandy around his glass thoughtfully. Jenkins prodded at the fire one last time. The night wasn't cold, but something about the flames seemed to bring cheer to the old house, and Jenkins wanted his master to cheer up more than anything, for he had been so terribly pained of late.

It had been an hour since the last of the dinner guests had left. Sir Arthur was notoriously reclusive, but lately he'd begun to host the occasional spiritualist gathering, whose exclusivity ensured they had become the envy of every medium in England. Arthur Furnival's powers, so long a closely guarded secret by the upper echelons of society, were on the cusp of becoming a sensation. He was a man possessed, it seemed, by some newfound enthusiasm, and had embraced his uncanny abilities afresh. Tonight's séance had enthralled his special invitees, but had left Sir Arthur deep in one of his troughs of despair.

'Thank you, Jenkins; that will be all.' The baronet sounded weary.

'If it's not too bold, sir, might I say something?' Jenkins asked.

'I know what you're going to say, Jenkins. But I can't stop, not yet.' Sir Arthur often talked to Jenkins in a manner too familiar for servant and employer. However, Jenkins liked to think he had proven himself a worthy confidant time and again, and over the years the baronet had come to rely on his valet as both trusted servant and, perhaps, moral compass.

The strain was showing; Sir Arthur grew more pale and gaunt with each passing day. He had dark rings around his eyes from lack of sleep, a consequence of the night terrors he experienced with increasing regularity.

'It's just that it's taking more out of you, sir, every time. I don't pretend to understand it, but I know it's dangerous. And these guests o' yours, they don't see what it does to you.'

'Enough, Jenkins,' said Sir Arthur, wearily rather than angrily. 'If I can bring peace to one poor, bereaved soul then it's worth the effort. Not that the séances really work that way... No, I have to keep at it, because there's something – *someone* – out there, trying to contact me. It's been getting clearer, stronger, ever since May Day, and it's close now. So very close...' He trailed off again.

'So you get them all here to help 'em contact the spirits, but really you're just doing it for yourself? If you don't mind me saying, sir...'

'Now you are being too bold, Jenkins,' Sir Arthur snapped.

'Sorry, sir.' Jenkins did not believe his master was a fraud, despite his fears. Jenkins was a down-to-earth man, but he'd seen Sir Arthur's uncanny abilities at play often enough to be convinced of life after death, though the knowledge was rarely as comforting as they made out in church.

'I'm fully aware of how it sounds,' Sir Arthur sighed. 'I know I risk turning into the very thing that I've always despised: a showman, a charlatan. I journey to the spirit realm, and try my best to interpret the portents, all the while telling my guests what they want to hear. They go home happy, my reputation grows, and I take one step nearer to unravelling this confounded mystery. It's so close, Jenkins... I have a part to play yet, and I must find out what it is. It's as though all my life I've been waiting for something, and now...'

Sir Arthur's eyes began to close even as he spoke, and his voice slowed as tiredness overcame him. Jenkins took the glass from his master's hand and placed it on the mantel, before hoisting Sir Arthur from the chair and helping the exhausted baronet upstairs. It was an increasingly regular occurrence; Jenkins was beginning to fear not only for his master's health, but for his frame of mind.

Sir Arthur woke abruptly. He'd been having his nightmare again, though this time it had been somewhat different. The pale young woman who so often haunted his dreams – the one with the fearful dark eyes – had seemed nearer somehow, her voice clearer. He had dreamt of her, saying over and over: *She is coming. Be ready. She is coming.* The sound of the shade's voice had been accompanied by the ticking of a clock, which had grown louder and louder until it almost deafened him, and this was what had shaken Sir Arthur from the bonds of slumber.

He looked around; it was dark, save for a narrow shaft of moonlight that fell across his bedclothes. Wind howled outside, and rain pattered in the gutters. A branch of the willow tree outside his window rapped rhythmically on the casement – the clock of his dreams, he realised. He rubbed at his face and reached for his candle. As he did, he heard a sigh. His skin prickled.

She is coming.

Sir Arthur scrabbled for a match and lit the candle. As the flame danced into life, he scanned the room nervously, and fancied that the retreating shadows harboured a pale, wasted woman, drifting from his vision like the afterthought of a dream. For a second he felt the fear of the nightmare returning, but as the candle flame grew stronger he saw he was alone.

The knock at his door almost made him jump out of his skin. He had not called out in his sleep this night, he was sure, and so he had not expected any servant to come to check on him.

'Who… who is it?' Sir Arthur called out.

'It's Jenkins, sir.'

Sir Arthur heaved himself out of bed, and when he opened the door, he found Jenkins wearing an anxious expression.

'What is it, man?'

'Begging your pardon, sir, but I thought I'd better fetch you right away. She won't rest until she's seen you.'

'What? Who won't rest?' Sir Arthur remembered the chill words of the dream-wraith with a shudder.

'Says she's your niece, sir. Come knocking at this ungodly hour, and she's in an awful state.'

Sir Arthur trusted enough in his own powers to know that this strange occurrence must not be put down to mere coincidence. He threw on a robe. Halfway down the stairs, he saw the shadow of a woman pacing the hall. A few more steps, and he saw her: skin pale, white dress muddied and torn. She was soaked through from rain. It dripped from her clothes, forming puddles on the tiles. She was so thin that when she stopped pacing and looked up at him, he half expected her eyes to be glassy and black, like the spirit of his nightmares made manifest. But these were not the eyes of some shade. They were human eyes, large and blue, pleading.

'Uncle Arthur,' she said in an unmistakeable American accent. 'It's me, Marie. I need your help.'

Sir Arthur realised he was holding his breath. He could not think that he knew a Marie, least of all a niece, although true enough she bore a familial resemblance. He had a very bad feeling about what this girl represented, but he heard the voice in the back of his mind: *She is coming. Be ready.*

'Please, Uncle,' she said. 'I didn't know where else to turn; I've come a long way to find you. A *very* long way.'

And as she fixed him with the most determined stare he'd ever seen from a young lady, he understood.

Sir Arthur looked to Jenkins, wondering if his valet would remember that the American Furnivals had no daughters that he knew of. For now, Sir Arthur would play along. 'My dear girl,' he said, 'let Jenkins get you a place by the fire, and some dry clothes. I shall go and dress, and be right with you. We have much to discuss.'

Saturday, 19th December 1891, 6.15 p.m.
PIMLICO, LONDON

'Where the devil are they?' Captain James Denny peered again through his eyeglass at the haulage yard across the road. Labourers came and went, but there was nothing out of the ordinary. Jim proffered the telescope to his fellow agent, Colonel John Hardwick, who refused it.

'They'll be here,' John said. 'Whittock knows what to do.'

Jim fidgeted. They'd been cramped up in the chilly, empty office for nearly an hour, waiting for any sign of their target: Otherside smugglers. Sergeant Whittock, one of John's group of chosen men, was working incognito with a street gang known to trade in esoteric wares.

'Well, they're deuced late, old boy,' Jim grumbled. 'I thought working with you would be more... eventful. Given the stories.'

'Nine tenths of this work is –'

'Observation,' Jim finished for him. 'So you always tell me.' Jim detected the hint of a smirk upon John's chiselled face.

'I thought you were seeing Jane earlier?' John said.

Jim fidgeted again, this time not entirely due to his numb muscles. 'Sadly I was otherwise engaged,' he said.

'Oh, Jim.' An admonishment – not for the first time. 'Do you forget that you are engaged? To her? Jane Pennyforth is a fine woman.'

'Again, so you always tell me. Honestly, John, you sound like my father. If you love her so much, perhaps you should –'

The door of the office flew open. The two agents spun about to see their compatriot, Lieutenant Bertrand, standing in the doorway red in the face, panting for breath.

'Change o' plan, sir,' Bertrand said, addressing his colonel. 'Something's got 'em spooked. They've fled north.'

'Bloody hell,' Jim said, levering himself to his feet.

John was already at the door. 'How could this have happened?' he demanded. 'We've been preparing this for weeks.'

'Whittock got a message to us, sir,' Bertrand replied. 'They got a tip-off we was here.'

John glowered, now looking every inch the man of his reputation, his eyepatch lending him a fearsome demeanour. He barged past Bertrand, leaving Jim and the dark-haired lieutenant to follow.

Half an hour later they were racing along New Oxford Street. The Apollo Lycea driver did not spare the lash, and the black coach-and-pair hurtled around bends, thundering dangerously through streets narrow and broad so that Jim's teeth jangled in his head. Twice they had caught a glimpse of a distant carriage, driving as recklessly as their own, and twice it had careened through traffic and along side-streets, scattering crowds, to evade them once more. John cursed to himself each time – he was the most fastidious agent on the Order's payroll, and Jim knew nothing irked the colonel more than plans upset.

'There, up ahead!' Bertrand called out. Another carriage hurtled around the next bend.

'What are they doing?' Jim asked.

'Escaping,' John growled. 'They have spent almost as long arranging this exchange as we have trying to catch them in the act. Whoever alerted them did it very recently. Now they bolt, probably to the buyer's new location.'

The carriage rocked onto two wheels as it took the next bend onto Shaftesbury Avenue.

John leaned out of the window, levered his American Winchester rifle, and cracked a round at the fleeing coach. There were screams in the street. The coach zigzagged across the road, slowed almost to a stop, and then took off again.

'They've abandoned the coach,' John said. 'The suspects are on foot, heading for the slums. Come on!'

Moments later Jim was pushing through a crowd of well-dressed onlookers, who clamoured about the entrance to an alleyway, as though setting foot in its shadow would give them a foul disease. It was not an unwarranted fear.

John came up beside him, helping to part the crowd, claiming that they were policemen. Up ahead, in the depths of the dark alleyway, Whittock lay stretched out on the cobbles, groaning.

'Whittock? Are you all right?' Jim asked.

The sergeant winced as he pulled himself upright, clutching a bloody wound at his thigh. He nodded.

'Had to give up my cover to slow them down, sir. Shot one – he crawled off over yon.' Whittock pointed to a back alley where a smear of blood on the frosty ground marked the trail. 'Two others, gone for the slum. Church Lane.'

'Come on,' John barked. 'If they get through the slums they'll disappear for good.'

The colonel was already dashing off as Whittock called to Jim.

'Smart-dressed fella, milksop like – he's the informant. And our old friend O'Keefe; he's still got the stash.'

'Good work, Sergeant,' Jim called back. Someone had to praise the men, for it was not John's style once the scent was in his nostrils.

Jim and John ploughed through a narrow side-street, leaping over the huddled forms of gin-addled vagrants as they went.

'Whittock said they still have it,' Jim panted.

'Then we won't find the buyer today,' John said. 'But we'll damned well find this informant.'

They emerged into a squalid court, of such unpleasant aspect and foul aroma that Jim pulled his scarf over his mouth and nose. Just a stone's throw from bustling promenades, theatres and shops, museums and churches, stood the remnants of the old St Giles rookeries, now islands of slums and high tenements packed with the most desperate, unfortunate and depraved individuals in this part of the city. Displaced, ignored by the smarter folk who walked nearby daily. And harbouring criminals.

John scanned every shadow, every face. Jim knew that Hardwick's one eye was just as keen as his two. After only a second's pause, he was off. Jim followed, pistol in hand, the sight of the weapon enough – for now – to persuade the more brazen louts to part the way at the agents' approach.

With almost preternatural senses, John chose a doorway, launched himself into the dosshouse beyond, and sprang up a set of spiralling, rickety stairs. Jim followed, leaping over shoeless beggars and pools of vomit as he went. At the top of the stairs John ploughed into a gang of rough-looking men, who tried to bar his path only to think better of it. John slapped one of them down, and the rest backed away as Jim arrived, pistol drawn.

'Which way?' he demanded.

A fat man pointed laggardly. John took off again, kicking down a door at the end of the corridor, racing through a tiny room where ten women huddled together on the floor for warmth.

Jim's lungs were fit to burst as they left the room behind them. A quick footfall on wooden stairs up ahead spurred him on. John was already following, and in moments they both emerged onto a flat roof, enclosed by taller tenements all around.

A black trouser-leg and shiny shoe vanished over a chimney stack above them. John climbed.

Jim followed. As he heaved himself over onto the roof a shot rang out. John's hat flew off, and the colonel fell to the ground. He still had the wherewithal to shoot back.

Jim saw two men ahead, one in a plaid suit and ill-fitting bowler, another all in black, with cape and hat. The man in the bowler fired again. The bullet struck barely a foot wide of Jim's head. Both suspects turned and ran across the rooftops, slipping as tiles skittered away from their tread. Jim was in the lead now, moving as fast as he could. He fired a warning shot, but the men did not stop.

The man in the bowler stopped and turned, aiming at Jim. It was a clear shot. Jim crouched, but knew he could not miss. The man in black caught up with the other, and Jim swore he nudged him. His arm jerked up, the gun fired, and the shot went high.

The two men exchanged some angry look, but Jim cared not. He returned fire. The bowler-hatted man spun around like a top, clutching his side. He collided with the man in black, who fell awkwardly, grabbing a spiked lead finial as he went, snagging his cape, and hanging on for dear life as his associate slid from the rooftop, stone dead. They were four storeys up, hard cobbles below. They had lost one suspect now, but there was no escape for the man in black.

Jim moved as quickly as he could, seeing the man's cape tear. He was indeed well dressed, with dark hair protruding beneath his hat, and a scarf pulled around his face like a bandit's mask. As Jim reached him, the man lost his grip, supported now only by his cape, which began at once to tear. The fugitive snatched again at the finial. It creaked, bent, and gave way. Jim grabbed the man's scarf, slipping on the roof tiles as he did.

The scarf came away in Jim's hand. He stared upon a pale face, one that he knew. Familiar, dark eyes stared back at him imploringly. Jim grabbed the man's hand, and for a moment feared they might both go over the edge. He felt the hand slipping from his grasp. And then, through disbelief, through anger, through fear; through a hundred emotions that defied definition, Jim slackened his grip. Those dark, handsome eyes widened in shock, hanging in the air just for a moment. Then the man fell.

Jim stood dumbly, the pale face etched on his mind. He had been betrayed. But it was more than that; much more. He let the black scarf fall from his hand, and it snaked away on the cold air, down to the street, where its owner lay dead.

* * *

SANDRINGHAM HOUSE

When death came to the young lion, it came not with a roar, but with a whine. Not his own, of course, for Albert Victor had long been rendered insensible by drugs before the end, even if his royal bearing had failed him. Nor was the whine that of his mother, Alexandra, who held a dignified silence by her son's bed, a slight moistening of the eyes the only betrayal of her feelings. No. The whine came from the prince's nursemaid, who had raised him from a cub, and now found herself outlasting her royal charge.

Sir Toby Fitzwilliam – right hand of Apollo, spear of the Empire – bowed respectfully, and left the room. There would be hell to pay for this, that much was certain. If only half of Sir Toby's suspicions proved accurate, rules writ in blood centuries ago had been disregarded; treaties as sacred to him as those carved upon tablets by the hand of God had been sundered.

Outside the open door, a line of aides and potentates waited solemnly for confirmation that the heir apparent was dead. Those near the front could see this for themselves, but in the royal household no one would accept a fact until it came by official declaration. Near the head of the queue, just five places down from the Queen's private secretary, Sir Henry Ponsonby, stood Lord Cherleten.

Sir Toby's eyes met Cherleten's, and the spymaster nodded to him. Sir Toby leaned forward, peering further down the line until he met the gaze of Sir Arthur Furnival. The psychic nodded also. They all knew what was to come.

Sir Toby closed the door of the private room quietly, and turned to his colleagues. Lord Cherleten's face shone a ghastly yellow momentarily in the flare from his match. He lit his cigar, took three good puffs on it, and shook out the lucifer.

'So it is true,' Sir Toby said.

'It is,' replied Cherleten. 'The prince did not die a natural death. Indeed, one could say his life was not altogether… natural.'

Sir Toby tried to ignore Cherleten's salacious tone, and the needling quality of the man's papery voice.

'Who sanctioned the operation?' Sir Toby asked. 'If this is your doing –'

'It certainly was not! And although the War Office and the Admiralty perhaps have cause, they would not be so bold. My informants tell me it was the Russians.'

'Russians? Why?'

'There has been increased activity from their agents in London. I believe they received the same intelligence regarding the prince that we did, and reached a similar conclusion. Do not do anything rash, Sir Toby – while this is the most likely explanation, we still cannot entirely rule out an… internal affair.'

Sir Toby had considered this. The prince had been involved in one too many scandals, and there were many within even his own family who had openly looked for a way to remove 'Young Eddy' from the line of succession. Some whispered he was engaged in immoral activities, and had unnatural appetites that extended even to murder. He had even called out the name of a former lover on his sickbed before finally being driven insensible, raising eyebrows in the royal household.

'The manner of the killing though…' Sir Toby said. 'I very much doubt one of the family would do such a thing.'

'Given the circumstances, they may have seen it as their only choice. Mercury poisoning is the only surety against… them. Unless of course one wishes to use more violent means. And remember, the prince was not… exactly dead when he was carried from this house. But our people have performed the necessary action to finish the job.'

'Decapitation, and burning,' Sir Toby muttered. He stared into the flames of the crackling fire beside his chair. He suddenly felt like an intruder at Sandringham at this delicate time, but there was no avoiding his duties to the family. 'If the Russians are behind this, there will be consequences.'

'My people are gathering evidence as we speak. If it is there, they will find it.'

'Good. Have the press been informed?'

'It is in hand. The Palace statement says that the prince died of influenza after a lengthy fever. There will be a period of national mourning, naturally. I put a few shillings in the apron-purses of the chambermaids. Some will spread rumours that the prince was syphilitic; others that he was assassinated due to fathering an illegitimate child while touring India last year. The usual stuff.'

Sir Toby glared at Cherleten.

'You know it is a necessary evil,' Cherleten shrugged. 'The more scandalous the theories, the less inclined anyone will be to investigate the truth, at least for as long as you and I live. And after that, who'll remember Alfred Victor enough to care?'

Sir Toby sighed. His own feelings towards the royal family made it impossible for him to besmirch the good name of even one such as Prince Albert Victor. Cherleten had no such qualms, which was just as well, because he was entirely right.

'You're sure the Queen has no idea?' Cherleten asked.

'I am certain. And it had better stay that way.' Sir Toby picked up his whisky. If the Queen had even an inkling of what Sir Toby had heard rumoured, she may well have given the order herself, had she not first died of shock. Sir Toby looked across at Sir Arthur Furnival. The noted clairvoyant had remained silent throughout the discussion. 'The warning we received, Sir Arthur. Do you now believe it to be genuine?'

Sir Arthur cleared his throat. 'There is no way to be certain, not yet. It could be that the Artist has returned – and given the prince's, *ahem*, "condition", we can no longer rule out any possibility, however fantastical it may appear.'

'He means the wily devil might have come back from the

dead,' Cherleten grinned. 'Bloody knew it, eh? You put too much stock in Hardwick, Sir Toby.'

'There is also the chance,' Sir Arthur continued, ignoring Cherleten, 'that whoever sent you that painting forewarning of the prince's death was also the person responsible for the crime. It is not prescience simply to foretell one's own deeds. And it's rather clever, if the killer knew no one would believe the warning.'

Sir Toby shifted uncomfortably, causing the leather of his armchair to creak. He had already considered this, but Sir Arthur's insightfulness served only to highlight his possible lapse of judgment.

'Now that we know for certain they are among us, these… creatures,' Sir Toby said. 'Now that we know what they are capable of… can you stop them, Sir Arthur?'

'Do not look to him!' Cherleten snapped. 'It is the armoury that has been developing the tools with which to fight them. You know as well as I that purebloods only come from one place. And where there is one, there will be others. There must be a portal, and you know what that means. We must divert more resources to Otherside research. Let me arm our agents, Sir Toby. We have the means –'

'No, Cherleten.' Sir Toby rubbed at his lined face. Cherleten had wanted this for a long time; to finally put to use the Otherside technology that he had spent over a year collecting and studying. If he had his way, he would build a gate of his own and start raiding the Otherside. Thankfully, the means to do so had thus far eluded Cherleten. 'I spoke with the Prime Minister on this matter only last week. We shall not turn our agency into an armed militia. We deal with this as we always have: quietly, and with guile. Sir Arthur, I asked you a question. Can you stop them?'

'I believe so,' Sir Arthur replied. 'My department is, as you know, uniquely equipped to deal with such threats. And if our man is indeed back from the grave, I believe my methods can counter him also. Or at least find him, which is half the problem.'

'The armoury will, naturally, assist Sir Arthur in every way possible, if that is what the Order decrees,' Cherleten said.

'For now, we have no choice,' Sir Toby agreed. 'Sir Arthur, when we leave here tomorrow you are to go directly to the facility at St Katharine Docks, and prepare your subjects for field trials.'

'Thank you, Sir Toby. And the... other matter?'

'It is in hand, Sir Arthur. Your ward has proven her value to the Order, and Lord Cherleten agrees that any potential threat she poses has been more than offset by her expert knowledge of the creatures we face. Given today's events... well, let us just say that her amnesty has been a long time coming, but it is granted at last.'

'You have my heartfelt thanks.'

'It is not your thanks we need right now, Sir Arthur; it is results,' Cherleten remarked with his customary indelicacy. 'We face the greatest threat since the Lazarus Gate, and it would appear that our best hope is your collection of freaks... your "Nightwatch". Let us pray they prove effective.'

ONE

Friday, 29th September 1893, 11.30 p.m.
ROYAL ALBERT DOCK, LONDON

'Right, lads, you know what to do.'

Jim Denny gave an encouraging grin to the policemen before him, who at once scattered in all directions across the deck of the clipper, *Glarus*, lanterns bobbing along in the darkness like fireflies.

The two constables nearest Jim immediately set about the largest crates on the deck with jemmies and hammers, prising nails and splintering wood with gusto. Jim winced as a box of fragile crockery fell from its protective layer of straw, and smashed upon lime-washed planks. A policeman looked at him for permission to carry on. Jim shrugged and nodded, and marched along the deck as pottery, machine parts and textiles spilled at his feet. If the intelligence were wrong, this would be an expensive night's work for Apollo Lycea. If it was correct, however, then someone would very likely hang. Jim's business was a grim one; there were no half-measures when dealing with smugglers in Otherside artefacts.

Jim had become accustomed to commanding the police rather

than his old cavalry battalion. Ever since a certain Special Branch copper named Boggis had betrayed the orders of John Hardwick three years ago, Apollo Lycea now took direct control of joint police operations. Special Branch weren't too happy about the arrangement, but with the Prime Minister on the side of Sir Toby, what could they do? Jim's transition from Horse Guards officer to agent of the Crown had been easier than John's; gradual, such that he had barely noticed it happening.

Jim hadn't thought of John Hardwick for a long while. Perhaps it was the setting that had triggered the memory; it was on a ship that Jim had almost died, and John Hardwick had saved his life. It was in a Thamesside warehouse such as those that he now looked upon that he had held Ambrose Hanlocke captive, and launched the opposition to the Otherside invasion. Those few who knew about it called it 'the Battle of the Thames', because apparently these things had to be named. The recollection caused a dull ache in Jim's left hand, which he exercised now, opening and clenching a fist. His leather glove creaked. The cold weather always played bally-ho with the hand, ever since Hardwick's sister – his Otherside sister – had impaled it with her boot heel.

With a shudder, Jim pushed the reminiscence from his mind. He turned the collar of his coat up against the cold, and took a long draw on his cigarette. Jim's eyes scanned the warehouses, still dark and quiet. Despite all signs to the contrary, Jim had a feeling he was being watched. It was an instinct that he'd learned to trust.

A police whistle trilled three times. Jim flicked his cigarette over the side of the ship, its ember arc flaring for the briefest moment. The whistle had come from below deck, and Jim hurried down steep iron-shod stairs into the dimly lit hold, ducking under joists and dangling ropes, where a group of three policemen stood around a large crate.

'This looks like the stuff, sir,' one of them said.

The crate had contained rolls of delicate lace, but beneath the fabric was something altogether more interesting.

Jim reached into the crate, and selected a glass phial from the many that were carefully lined up in a thinly padded tray. Poorly protected. Badly disguised. But unmistakeable.

He held up the tiny bottle to the lamplight, shaking the murky brown fluid. It was what the Othersiders called 'etherium'. There were many rumours in the club about what exactly the fluid was and where it came from, but the truth, if it were known, was guarded by those several steps above Jim's rank. All he knew was that Sir Arthur Furnival called it the most dangerous substance on earth; the very stuff that had accelerated the Otherside towards its inevitable doom.

He looked back at the broad tray. This was the largest cache he'd ever seen. He'd once recovered five small phials like this from a freight train travelling from Calais to Cologne, where the black market in Otherside artefacts from the Lazarus Gate – and refugees, at times – thrived. He'd been told that even such a modest haul had the potential to blow a very large hole in the fabric of reality. He counted perhaps two hundred here before him.

'Is this what we're looking for, sir?' the policeman asked.

Jim nodded.

'Some kind of foreign drug?'

'The worst kind.' Jim placed the phial back in its place, gingerly. He'd found etherium everywhere from spiritualist meeting halls to upmarket brothels. It was a drug that altered the senses far more dramatically than any opiate and, they said, allowed one to talk to the dead. This was the first time he'd found an outbound shipment. And the quantity... it had to be more than some wealthy buyer looking to add spice to a soirée.

This was the fourth raid Jim had been involved in this month. Each had turned up unusually large caches of Otherside contraband; everything from machine parts to electrical weapons, from strange tobacco to stranger pharmaceuticals. And the raids had been getting easier, more bountiful. It gnawed at Jim, had been gnawing at him for weeks. Something was pushing the black market to ever-riskier deals, and Jim wanted to know what was behind it. 'You've done well, Constable…?'

'Beresford, sir.'

'Very good, Beresford. Better see if there's any more of this stuff in the hold. And no need for kid gloves now. Take this ship apart if you have to.'

The policeman grinned. 'Right you are, sir.' Beresford turned, eager to break open more containers, but stopped abruptly, staring along the length of the dark hold, towards the prow of the clipper.

'Beresford?'

The policeman reached behind himself, slowly and without turning his gaze away from whatever he had spotted. He grasped his lantern and moved it out in front of him. The hairs on Jim's neck stood on end; the ache in his hand became more intense, as though his very bones were telling him that something was amiss.

Jim followed Beresford's gaze, squinting against the gloom. For a split second, he thought he saw two pinpricks of light, iridescent in the lamplight. He received the impression of a pair of bright, bestial eyes. Rats? They would have to be very large.

'Did you see that, sir?' Beresford whispered.

'See what?' Jim's fingers closed around the grip of the revolver in his pocket.

'I… an animal. Or maybe a man. Skulking over there.'

'If it's a man, Constable, then we'd better go and clap him in irons, hadn't we?' Something had spooked Beresford, and Jim needed to instil some confidence into the men. He'd seen enough esoteric oddities to know that they had to be faced, though not enough to inure him to the terrors that now lurked in the dark corners of the world. He stepped past the constable, drawing his gun from his jacket pocket, and strode steadily forwards.

'Bring that light, there's a good fellow,' he instructed.

The swaying yellow light shone over Jim's shoulder, causing black shadows to slide across wooden walls. Jim saw nothing, but over the creaking of the ship he fancied he heard a strange sound; sharp claws scratching rough wood.

Still rats, most likely.

All the same, the sound of scratching never failed now to set Jim's teeth on edge.

The light jerked away, plunging the area ahead back into gloom. A man cried out. A bestial growl preceded a horrid, gurgling croak of pain. Jim whipped around. A lantern rolled across the floor. Beresford's face was lit in its ghastly light, a mask of terror, glassy eyes bulging from his head in fear, the life almost gone from them. Blood oozed from his mangled throat.

Something bent over Beresford's body, something gangrel and foul, long of limb, red in tooth and claw. A face half-shrouded in shadow turned to Jim, eyes shining unnaturally in the half-light.

Jim fired his pistol twice. The first shot drew a rasping scream from the brute. The second hit thin air.

One constable stood quailing beside a stack of tethered crates. The other ran towards the stairs, heavy footfalls pounding the boards. Jim could barely see the man for the darkness, but he saw the thing drop from the beams overhead, falling heavily onto the policeman, tearing at him with clawed hands.

'Come on!' Jim shoved the frozen constable towards his compatriot. They could still save him. The men on deck would have heard the shots; they'd be coming.

Jim had taken barely three steps when he heard movement off to his right, from behind the ship's cargo. Crates toppled, the constable cried out and bolted towards the rear of the hold. Even as Jim fired his revolver, the creature barrelled into him, its momentum pushing him to ground. Blazing violet eyes stared into his, set within a snarling, bat-like face. Slavering jaws snapped hungrily. Putrid, maggoty breath assailed his senses.

Jim pulled the trigger over and over until the gun was empty. The thing screamed, then slumped on top of him, a dead weight. He pushed at it. The other creature was approaching. He heard its claws tapping on the boards. Its shadow drew closer, cautious and predatory. There was something familiar about the way it moved, the way it stalked. Something that reminded Jim of another encounter he'd had not so very long ago, aboard another ship – the *Helen B Jackson*. And those eyes... violet eyes.

The sudden memory spurred him to struggle harder against the pressing weight upon him. The thing that approached, whatever it was, limped, dragging one leg behind it. It was the one he'd shot previously. Jim shoved at the corpse on top of him again, with growing desperation.

It was close enough to smell. Stale sweat, rotting meat. With a final exertion, Jim pushed free. The new aggressor crouched, ready to pounce, uttering a low, guttural croak. Jim scrambled to his feet. The creature launched itself at him. Jim flicked his wrist to spring an Otherside derringer into his right hand, and pulled the trigger. The ship's hold was bathed in a momentary flash of blue-white light as electrical energy arced from the pocket pistol and wreathed the creature in crackling tendrils of energy. The beast screamed inhumanly, and dropped to the floor in a charred, sparking heap.

Jim blinked the spots of light from his eyes.

'What... what...'

The last policeman cowered beside the fallen lantern, muttering the word over and over as he struggled to comprehend what he had just seen. This was why Jim rarely used his secret weapon; and it was why he rarely revealed the nature of his assignments to the common constabulary. The man would have to be debriefed, and possibly paid off – even threatened – in order to keep the details of this encounter secret.

Jim's heart drummed in his chest. He picked up the lantern, and shone it about the floor. Two creatures – possibly human, though deformed beyond measure – now lay in the hold. One was charred and blistered. The other was pale and sickly, still twitching as it bled out from its gut. Upon its neck and part of its chest, a puckered red shape was burned into its flesh, like a cattle brand. Numerals – the number nine, and others either torn away or too indistinct in the dark. Two policemen lay nearby also, throats torn out, eyes glassy. Jim looked away, disgusted and angry, at himself as much as the enemy. He shook his head and muttered a curse. He had no idea what he was dealing with, but one thing was certain: it was not of this world.

He paused as he realised that no reinforcements had come. The silence from up on deck was telling.

Jim primed the derringer clumsily, with a trembling hand, reloaded his service revolver, and gave the constable a hard shove.

'Pull yourself together, man,' he said, quietly but sternly, summoning his best military tone. 'We're in a fix, but if we're to get out of here in one piece, I'll need you. Do you understand?'

The man turned his eyes upwards, questioningly, towards the deck where just minutes earlier he had seen more than a dozen of his colleagues confidently going about their business.

'I fear the worst,' Jim said. 'What's your name?'

'Butler, sir.'

'Alright, Butler. Bring that lantern, and arm yourself, just in case. Now come on.'

Jim had no idea what he would be facing. Smugglers, most likely. More of those strange creatures if tonight were destined to get any worse. The former he could stomach – it wouldn't be the first time he'd negotiated his way out of a tight spot. The latter case... that didn't really bear thinking about. Jim crept up the stairs, bracing himself for a fight, and the sight of a deck awash with the blood of London's finest.

What he saw instead was fifteen police constables, their hands held above their heads, standing in the middle of the deck in silence. On the jetty alongside the ship, ten or so rough-looking men trained rifles on the police. Above them, on the harbour wall, more men stood and watched, lined up beside a trio of beer wagons, painted with faded Charrington's Ales livery. Jim took a good look at the men. Most had their faces covered with scarves; the ones that did not were unmistakeably Chinese. This wasn't the first time the Chinese gangs had made a foray into the Otherside black market. Some of the substances the more illicit opium dens were said to add to their wares were as repulsive as they were infamous. But these men were far from their usual territory of Limehouse.

'So pleased that you could join us, Captain Denny.'

Jim spun around to face the owner of the heavily accented voice. Above him, on the quarterdeck, stood another group of men. At their head stood a stern-faced, yet surprisingly youthful celestial, arms folded behind his back. His eyes were fixed on Jim. His mouth was curved into a self-satisfied smile. At his signal, two of his men pushed a prisoner forwards through their number: a man, hands bound, a hood over his head. The celestial pulled off the hood, and Jim noticed two things simultaneously that made his stomach lurch.

First, the man had a rope around his neck. A noose.

Second, Jim knew him. It was Bertrand, the lieutenant of the Sixteenth Lancers who had been assigned to Apollo Lycea at the request of his former commanding officer, John Hardwick. The last Jim heard, Bertrand had been investigating rumours of 'doppelgangers' appearing in Belfast. It looked as though he had found more than he'd bargained for.

'Your coming was as clear as the rising of the sun, Captain,' crowed the celestial. 'It was foreseen.' At his nod, two of the men behind him heaved upon a rope, and with alarming rapidity, Lieutenant Bertrand was hoisted up by the neck, high into the rigging of the clipper. Jim cried out, and made to rush forwards, but a rifle report cut through the air, causing splinters of wood to erupt from the deck near Jim's feet. He slid to a halt, and could only look on in dismay as Bertrand kicked out, dancing the Tyburn jig.

The Chinamen laughed. Jim's blood burned hot with anger at the sound.

'His neck did not break,' the celestial declared with a grin. 'We will wait.'

And with mounting horror, they did. It took perhaps three or four minutes for Bertrand to stop kicking, his face purpling, then blackening, eyes bulging from his head, silent splutters escaping blue lips. The rifles of the Chinese stayed trained on Jim and the policemen the whole time. A copper heaved at the sight of it; a sight that burned itself into Jim's mind. He felt sick, and angry, and utterly helpless.

When it was over, the celestials' leader pulled back the sleeve of his tunic, and held out his forearm for Jim to see. It was tattooed with Chinese characters, punctuated by lines of neat dots which were unmistakeable as tong markings. But that was clearly not the significance of the revelation. Jim squinted to see the tattoos more clearly, gritting his teeth as he recognised them.

'You know what this says, yes?' the celestial said. 'My master sends his regards. Tell your people that this man was the first, but he will not be the last, unless they start to listen. And you may keep the etherium, for there is plenty more where that came from. The blood price you have paid tonight is sufficient.' He laughed again, and addressed his men in his own tongue.

The group proceeded to the gangway, not giving Jim and the constables another look. The gang on the jetty kept their rifles trained on the police, until finally all of the tong climbed the steps to the harbour wall, boarded the wagons, and left.

Jim breathed a sigh of relief as the sound of the wagons faded into the distance, leaving the night air silent, but for the tolling of buoy bells out on the river.

'You, and you,' Jim pointed to two constables, who looked about ready to quit the ship and abandon their duty. 'Get up there, and cut that man down. He deserves better than this.' The men set to the task reluctantly.

'Begging your pardon, sir.' It was Butler, who had been standing quietly behind Jim through the whole affair. 'What was that business with the tattoos? What did they say?'

'They said "*zhi ming*",' Jim replied. 'Or, as some would have it, *Zhengming*.' Jim turned to Butler, who looked confused. 'Best that you don't understand it, old boy; not if you want to sleep well at night.'

'No danger of that, sir,' Butler replied ruefully. 'Not any more…'

GEORGE STREET, LONDON

'Jane!'

Jim jumped awake with such violence he almost fell out of bed. The room was dark; a cold draught from the window chilled his sweat-slick skin and gave him gooseflesh. He shivered, though not entirely from the cold. For a moment he swore he saw the shadows of rigging and ratlines on the wall, of a hanged man kicking the air. They were gone as quickly as Jim imagined them.

He could still hear the scratching though, always, inside his head. It came at night, to remind him of what lay beyond the veil, hungering. The Other; the Riftborn. And something more. Ragged breaths, quiet sobs, fading away only gradually as wakefulness replaced painful memory.

Jim closed his eyes, but wished that he had not, for he could still see the images of the familiar nightmare, as though they were etched forever in his mind's eye. The pale girl on her deathbed. The judgmental glares of mourners at her funeral. His Jane, lost.

For a moment, Jim swore he was not alone. He swore he heard Jane, sobbing in the dark, begging Jim to be with her, even as she breathed her last.

Then she was gone, and Jim was alone, save for a faint odour of funerary wreaths.

And the scratching in his head.

TWO

Friday, 29th September 1893, 4.30 p.m.
THE APOLLONIAN CLUB, LONDON

Jim placed the phial carefully on Sir Toby Fitzwilliam's desk, and backed away as though it were a bomb. A satisfied smirk crossed Lord Cherleten's lips. Sir Arthur Furnival, by contrast, shifted uncomfortably in his seat. Sir Toby himself frowned, silver brows coming together to shade his piercing eyes.

The only person present who did not react at all was the young woman, Marie Furnival. Some agents, in less guarded moments, said there was more to her than met the eye. They said she was an authority on creatures from beyond the veil – creatures that few living men had ever seen. They said more outlandish things, to which Jim paid no mind, and he had not asked why Sir Arthur had brought his American niece along – he had learned that, in Apollo Lycea, if one was not given information freely, one was not meant to know it.

'Your report says that this is one of a hundred and eighty-eight identical bottles,' Sir Toby said.

It was not a question, but Jim felt the need to reply anyway. 'Yes, Sir Toby. But there was nothing else of interest aboard the *Glarus*.'

'I would not say that, Captain Denny,' the old man replied. 'The dead creatures you brought back for study are of singular importance to the Order. More than that, an agent of the Crown was killed aboard that vessel, and his killers are on the loose.'

'And two policemen, too. I only meant that –'

Sir Toby held up a hand to silence Jim, and then shuffled the papers before him, which comprised Jim's report, plus various memoranda from Lord Cherleten and Sir Arthur. Jim had never felt that Sir Toby had particularly warmed to him. The fact that he had been brought into the club by Cherleten had a lot to do with that. He was, like it or not, 'Cherleten's man', at least in the eyes of other agents. That came with advantages of its own, especially when requisitioning equipment from the armoury. But around the card tables and bars, where Jim would prefer to spend his time, he sometimes found himself a man apart from his fellows.

'You are certain that Bertrand's killer was from the Zhengming gang?' Sir Toby asked.

'I am,' Jim replied.

'And they specifically mentioned the etherium, making no effort to recover it?'

'That's right, Sir Toby. They said there was more where that came from. And they correctly used the word "etherium", too, which rather sets them apart from the average smuggler.'

'Quite.'

'The night's events cannot be viewed in isolation, sir,' Jim said. 'Someone has been moving contraband around in increasingly large quantities. I have apprehended more Otherside fugitives these past three weeks than in the last six months combined. The numbers simply make no sense – how could such quantities possibly be on the streets? Where are they coming from? In my view, this was a display of power. Someone knows we are tracking them. They wanted to send us a message.'

Sir Toby looked at Jim from beneath his flinty eyebrows, as if to question why Captain Denny had offered an opinion at all. 'A message to whom, I wonder?' he asked. 'The Order? Or a certain John Hardwick? It was he, after all, who killed the Artist. It says here that the celestial stated "my master sends his regards". A message of revenge from beyond the grave?'

'Perhaps the Artist used his... gifts... to make further predictions that we never discovered. Perhaps his men still follow his instructions even after his passing.' Jim was uncomfortable even discussing the possibility of the Artist's supernatural return; that monster, fused from the twin bodies of a criminal mastermind in both worlds. The man who had tortured John Hardwick, took his eye, and had later been assassinated by his would-be victim. Jim had never really understood if John had been acting under orders on that fateful night. He wouldn't have blamed Hardwick if not.

'Arrangements must be made to contact Colonel Hardwick,' Sir Toby said. 'Bertrand's death will be of singular interest to him; we cannot rule out the possibility that similar "revenge", or whatever this is, will be sought against him.'

'Do you think he'll come in, sir? Hardwick, I mean?' Jim did not believe for a moment that even the killing of a confidant would encourage John Hardwick back to the Apollonian.

'It remains to be seen whether he will have a choice in the matter,' Cherleten interrupted.

'And who would force him?' Sir Toby asked. 'He has more confirmed kills to his name than any agent in our history. A lighter touch is required, perhaps?'

'*Hmmph.*' Cherleten settled back into his chair.

'If he learns about the... Artist,' Jim offered, still incredulous, 'he may return of his own accord.'

'Nothing is certain with Hardwick,' Sir Toby said. Jim thought he detected a rueful tone.

'Perhaps these "tong" simply have a new master,' Lord Cherleten interrupted. 'One who wishes to take up where his predecessor left off.'

'That is, unfortunately, the more desirable of the possibilities,'

Sir Toby said. 'Pending further intelligence, we have no way to be sure what we are facing.'

'With all due respect, Sir Toby, might I ask what intelligence sent us to the *Glarus* in the first place?' Jim had no idea what Sir Toby and Cherleten were driving at. He was, however, eager to return to the field, though not if his superiors were to insist on keeping him in the dark.

'You might not.'

'I could have been killed,' Jim said.

'That is the risk all of our agents take daily,' Sir Toby said, matter-of-factly.

'And I accept that risk every time I take to the field,' Jim said, his colour rising. 'But what of my men? The common constabulary sent to support me do not expect to sell their lives in my service.'

'That's enough, Captain,' Lord Cherleten chided.

'You began by saying "with all due respect",' said Sir Toby. 'In my experience, those words are usually followed with a distinct lack of respect. It seems this occasion is no different.'

Jim stiffened. His eyes scanned the room quickly. Everyone was stony-faced, except for Marie Furnival. The ghost of a smirk vanished from her lips as his eyes met hers. That annoyed him further, though he would be damned if he'd let it show now.

'You are correct, however, in some respects,' said Sir Toby. 'You have served us well for three years, Captain Denny. You have rarely questioned your orders, and you have brought in more Otherside fugitives than any of your fellows. Your record is exemplary. And that is why you are here today. Lord Cherleten thinks you are ready for some answers, and I am inclined to agree with him.'

Jim stopped himself just in time from raising an incredulous eyebrow. Seeing Old Toby agree with Cherleten was like finding a dozen hen's teeth in his pocket.

'Our information network gathers hundreds of pieces of vital intelligence daily,' Sir Toby went on. 'Much of it is conflicting;

some of it is outright false. Traditionally, we have had trusted clerks and intelligencers working around the clock to decipher codes and correlate obtuse leads into practical guidance for our agents in the field. As a result, Apollo Lycea has often been accused of being slow to act – a great old wooden warship in an age of steam frigates. Since the Lazarus Gate opened in the heart of London, the world has changed at a rate far beyond that which anyone can keep up with. This is why the Order is exploring new methods of intelligence-gathering. Sir Arthur here is at the forefront of these methods. We thought he had hit upon great progress, given our recent run of fine results in the field, but it rather seems that we have suffered a minor setback.'

'I'm sorry, Sir Toby,' Jim said, looking at the pale face of Sir Arthur opposite. 'What are these new methods you speak of?'

'It is difficult to explain, Captain, although you shall be briefed presently, and in full. For now, let us just say that we have taken a more... esoteric approach. Sir Arthur, as I am sure you have heard, is uniquely versed in certain practices that would seem alien to most of us, but that were used to great effect by the Othersiders.'

'You mean... psychics? I was sent into an ambush on the say-so of some fortune-teller?'

'Mind your manners, Captain,' Sir Toby snapped. 'We do you a courtesy here, lest you forget it.'

Cherleten gave Jim the slightest nod, indicating that he should hold his tongue and listen. Sir Arthur remained silent, though a mild frown creased his large forehead.

'Sorry, sir, forgive me,' Jim offered. Much as he felt Cherleten relished seeing anyone reprimanded, the peer often helped guide Jim through prickly exchanges with the upper echelons, in his way.

'The Otherside technology that you have gathered over the years has enabled us to make great strides in this area, Captain Denny. Your actions have led directly to Sir Arthur's recent breakthroughs. Do not disparage his efforts – we have both seen enough with our own eyes to know that what men in our world call magic is rudimentary science to the Othersiders –'

'The difference, I should hope, is that our scientists practise their craft in the name of justice… and morality.' All eyes turned now to Miss Furnival, who had not only spoken for the first time, but had interrupted Sir Toby in the process.

'Quite so, dear lady,' Sir Toby said. If he was annoyed at her interjection, he did not show it. 'Miss Furnival references, no doubt, the strange science of the Othersiders that powered Marcus Hardwick's infamous gate.'

'I saw that with my own eyes, too,' said Jim, wincing at the memory. He kept the things he had seen on the Otherside from his thoughts as much as possible, though they plagued his dreams nightly. 'I saw people suspended from the arches of London Bridge; flesh and machinery functioning as one, like a vision of hell.'

'It was hell, for them,' Miss Furnival said. 'The Othersiders called them the Nightwatch. Psychics, enslaved by the government to serve as little more than cogs in a machine. Their deaths were a mercy.'

Jim tensed at those words. The 'Nightwatch' was whispered of in certain circles. Secret circles. Jim knew better than to ever ask, although he was privy to certain facts that other agents were blissfully unaware of. Miss Furnival, he was certain, should know nothing of the Nightwatch. He began to wonder now if she shared her uncle's fabled 'gifts'.

'Perhaps the Othersiders felt their cause was just enough to warrant their sacrifice,' Cherleten said. 'Or desperate enough.'

'By all accounts,' Marie said, her tone cooling as she addressed the red-headed lord before her, 'the Nightwatch merely sped the Othersiders on their path to ruin.'

'Our world is not their world. We do not have demons running amok here.'

'I imagine they once thought the same. Without psychics, the veil would not have torn. Without the tearing of the veil, there would be no Riftborn. Without the Riftborn, there would have been no Lazarus Gate.' The colour rose to Miss Furnival's cheeks, and she became animated, before checking herself.

Cherleten offered his most sardonic smile. 'The good lady is remarkably well versed in advanced science.'

'I have read the work of William James in this area,' she answered, quick as a flash.

'For a woman – and one of such tender years – to have grasped James' recondite theories so quickly… why, perhaps you should come and work for me. You've been keeping her quiet too long, Furnival, eh? Time to let her off the leash, perhaps.'

Sir Arthur gave Lord Cherleten the sharpest glare, and for once held his head high and defiant. Yet, he said nothing.

'We digress,' said Sir Toby, raising his voice a little. 'Thank you for your insight, Miss Furnival, we are most grateful. The exact workings of Sir Arthur's methods shall remain confidential for the time being. Captain Denny, know that we are working to resolve the problems you experienced, and that steps are being taken to ensure such mistakes do not happen again. I shall have to ask you to trust your orders, and to do your duty.'

'Always, sir,' Jim said. He rankled at the suggestion he might do otherwise. Jim had performed some questionable deeds under orders, and though he did not always like it, he never shirked his responsibility. 'Might I ask what my orders are?'

'All in good time, Captain. We are formulating a strategy, and when we are done you will return to the field. For now, you will await further instruction. These tong shall have to be dealt with, but we must plan our next move carefully, lest we walk headlong into another trap.'

Jim resented the use of the word 'we'; the loss of the constables under his command weighed heavily on his shoulders. The risks were borne by him and his men, no one else. He said simply, 'And the creatures, sir. What of them?'

'We have cadavers to study,' said Sir Toby. 'And we have the expert opinion of Miss Furnival here. Indeed, I would ask that Miss Furnival remain behind – we have much to discuss. Captain Denny, you are dismissed.'

Jim frowned, and glanced at the young woman. Her large blue eyes gave nothing away. He still could not understand what she was to contribute, or why he could not be privy to the discussion. Yet these were the least of his questions. 'Sir, I –'

'I said dismissed, Captain.'

Sir Toby was resolute. Lord Cherleten offered not so much as his customary smirk. All Jim could do was nod a bow, and leave his superiors – and the mysterious Miss Furnival – to their council.

THREE

Jim thrust his hands into his pockets as the first large raindrops splodged on the brim of his homburg, and a cold wind whistled along Jermyn Street. He caught himself thinking not of monsters, or of the tong, but of a warm fireplace and a mug of bitter in his favourite Regent Street tavern. He felt guilty for even entertaining the thought. He remembered Beresford lying dead in the hold of the *Glarus* – there'd be no warm fire for that poor policeman this night.

Jim tried to shake it off, reminding himself that time spent off-duty was infrequent – there would be opportunity to seek vengeance for the fallen in the very near future; his orders would probably come when he least wanted them.

Better to make a night of it now, because the next few weeks promised to be full of danger and toil. Supper at the Burlington, where he would undoubtedly bump into some of the West End set, would soon put a longing for danger out of his mind. Then it would be cards, followed by something deuced disreputable at a high-class parlour, if he was drunk enough and flush enough after the night's gambling. Jim managed a smile at the thought, even as the rain grew heavier and the wind more biting.

The streets were quieter than usual, given the inclement conditions. They'd still be thronging in Piccadilly and Regent

Street, but most sensible folk would be taking cabs to their destinations. Strange, then, that someone was following Jim. Stranger still that his shadow had followed him from St James's Square, staying with him despite his slightly unconventional route – a path he now took regularly, more out of habit than expedience. He had not taken a look behind him, but had concentrated instead on the pattern of the footsteps; a light tread, almost in perfect time with his own, neither drawing nearer, nor falling behind.

Jim waited until the Quadrant was in view, where a few people dashed about through the rain, and street-hawkers huddled miserably beneath lonely trees, too sodden even to call out their wares. Jim glanced over his shoulder, and glimpsed a dark figure vanishing into a doorway. He could not make out any detail through the drizzle, but it confirmed his suspicions. He knew he could turn around, but if his pursuer was an enemy he would likely flee or, worse, seize the initiative and lure Jim into a trap. No, he needed to break his habits and head somewhere unpredictable, set a trap of his own.

Jim moved on with purpose, determined not to betray his intent. His eyes darted left and right for some detour he could take, at last alighting on an alley, which led away from his original destination, in the direction of Berkeley Square. He walked as casually as he could, listening carefully for the footfalls behind him. Jim cursed under his breath, for there were too many niches and side-passages for a follower to conceal themselves. He knew that if he turned back to look, his shadow would slip down one such avenue, and would surely know that Jim was wise to his game.

Instead, Jim looked out for an open-ended alley, one that he could feasibly head down without raising his follower's suspicions. Spying one such passage, he turned along it, and immediately stopped, flattening himself against a damp wall. The footsteps drew nearer, hurrying just a little. When his pursuer turned the corner, Jim pounced, grabbing an arm, pulling the black-clad figure around and slamming her into a wall.

Her?

Jim stared into the face of Marie Furnival, instantly mortified that he had his forearm jammed firmly across her throat, her left wrist gripped in his other hand. He was too stupefied to withdraw immediately.

A crunching, burrowing pain spread across his stomach as Miss Furnival struck out. He released the woman's wrist, whereupon the arm that had barred her throat was twisted by small yet strong hands. Dagger-sharp pain shot along his wrist. Jim tried to speak, but could only gasp in pain. He saw Marie Furnival's determined scowl, before she, and the world, turned upside down.

Jim looked up at Miss Furnival from the flat of his back, rain pouring onto his face. His hat rolled to her feet. Miss Furnival picked it up, shook the mud from it, and held it out to him.

'Captain Denny, you appear to have dropped your hat,' she said. Her lips twitched upwards as she failed to suppress a rather self-satisfied smile.

Jim heaved himself from the cobbles, holding his breath so as not to wince and show any sign of weakness. It was rather too late for that, perhaps, but he felt suitably silly all the same. 'How careless of me. Thank you, Miss Furnival,' he said. He took the hat and patted it back onto his head. 'Might I ask what… brings you this way?'

'I was merely hoping to find somewhere to eat, and got caught out in the rain. When I saw you up ahead, I hoped I might persuade you to accompany me. As a chaperone, I mean.'

Jim narrowed his eyes. He could not glean any clue as to the woman's motives. That she had surprised him with her physical prowess was of no matter to him; a little dented pride was nothing in the grander scheme of things. Far more important to find out her game, and decide whether she was trustworthy.

Jim held out an arm. 'Miss Furnival, I, too, was hoping to find a dining room in which to shelter from this horrid weather. You are of course most welcome to join me, particularly in light of our… ahem… misunderstanding.' Jim offered his most practised smile.

Marie Furnival took his arm, nodded, and without a word walked with Jim back towards Regent Street. He would have to forego the tavern, given his present company, and find something more upmarket.

The dining room at Verey's had a somewhat more romantic ambience than Jim had hoped for, but he made do. A pianist in the corner played something blandly melodic and unidentifiable. The candles arranged in the centre of the table lent Miss Furnival an aura of comeliness that Jim was not sure she deserved. Her hair was brown, streaked with copper, somewhat tousled from the rain. Her eyes were large and cornflower-blue. Jim tried not to dwell on how slight she was, for she had thrown him about easily enough on the street.

Jim ordered for them both – Miss Furnival appearing apathetic towards anything on the menu – and once the waiter had poured their wine Jim turned immediately to business.

'Why are you here, Miss Furnival?'

'You mean, here now, with you? Or in England? Or is your question more philosophical?'

Her soft American burr gave the impression of playfulness, but Jim could not help but wonder if her retort was intended to be more barbed. 'Let's begin with the easier question,' he said. 'Why are you here with me?'

'That is not the easier question at all,' Miss Furnival sighed.

'We could pretend that you did not follow me intentionally. We could even pretend that you did not throw me to the ground as though I were a seven-stone weakling. But I doubt such a pretence would serve either of us well, beyond the simple pleasures of food, wine and music in the company of one another.'

'We are to be assigned together,' she said, simply.

Jim shuffled in his chair. 'When? I mean… how do you know?'

'I see you are as aware as I that even speaking of our next assignment is a matter for disciplinary action. I trust that you care about that as much as I do? That is, not at all.'

'I wouldn't say that... but sometimes consequences must be damned if an agent is to remain effective in the field. If you'll pardon my language.'

Miss Furnival laughed. Jim couldn't tell if she was laughing at him. He couldn't really tell much about her at all.

'Given my familial connections, Captain Denny, I sometimes come by information that perhaps I shouldn't. Sometimes I even seek out such information, if I think there to be an advantage in it. Does that make me wicked?' She took a sip of wine.

'That rather depends on what you discover, and about whom.' Jim wondered just how many secrets Sir Arthur Furnival was privy to, and just how many of them his niece had 'come by'.

'Not a great deal... this time. But you and I will receive our orders tomorrow. What concerns me is just how secretive Uncle Arthur is being. The inner circle will not reveal the source of their intelligence to anyone.'

'That will be the Nightwatch, surely?' Jim said.

Miss Furnival scowled at once. 'There is no Nightwatch. It is a failed experiment, nothing more.'

'I thought you were supposed to be telling me things. It appears that your intelligence is out of date, my dear.'

'What do you know about the Nightwatch?' Marie's tone was short. 'Tell me.'

Her insistence was a little too loud, drawing a brief look of disapproval from a greying, bejewelled matriarch at the next table.

'Keep your voice down,' Jim muttered. 'I know enough to face the noose if I say much more.'

'Don't be ridiculous.' Miss Furnival lowered her voice a touch.

Jim sat back as a waiter arrived with their first course. He waited until the man had gone, and took a mouthful of smoked salmon before leaning towards his companion again.

'I received the distinct impression that you already knew

about the Nightwatch,' Jim said. 'If that's not the case, it really isn't my place to tell you.'

'Oh, for heaven's sake, you men and your secrets,' Miss Furnival sighed. 'The Nightwatch is a theoretical department, based on the assumption that captured Otherside psychics might be employed in a fortune-telling capacity for the Crown. There are several reasons why it has not succeeded. Firstly, no one on this side has been able to fathom the technology used by the Othersiders to harness the cerebral potential of the psychic candidates. Secondly, no one on this side would risk using etherium to increase said potential, for that is the only conceivable way of making the system work. And finally, the effects on those psychics would be so dire as to make the entire process morally reprehensible.' Marie Furnival took a large gulp of wine, and looked defiantly at Jim.

Jim puffed out his cheeks, trying to take in what she had said. She appeared to have a grasp of the esoteric that was beyond his own. He wondered briefly if he should have spent more time paying attention to the armoury's scientists and less time chasing gunmen through dark alleyways.

'That's about the long and short of it,' he said at last. 'Though you made one glaring error.'

'Oh?'

'The Nightwatch is not a theoretical department. It's a fact.'

Miss Furnival's eyes widened. She dabbed delicately at her mouth with a napkin.

'I am afraid, Captain Denny, that you have been listening to tittle-tattle around the card tables. The Nightwatch was once a special department of the Crown – the *other* Crown – long since aborted. The Order toyed with the idea of initiating a similar programme here, but my uncle saw to it that such a folly was abandoned before it could begin.'

Miss Furnival's tone changed to one of defensiveness, and something more. Pride; admiration perhaps. Something told Jim that Miss Furnival would not like what he had to say about her uncle. And besides, he wasn't sure entirely why he should trust her with what he knew. 'I… ah,' he started, then paused a moment. 'It's just that, given the contradictory nature of the intelligence I received on my last assignment, I was led to believe that psychics were involved. Lord Cherleten said as much.' Jim knew he sounded guarded, despite his best efforts to the contrary.

'That's as may be. My uncle, as I am sure you're aware, has some small gifts in the area of mediumship, which he sometimes uses for the benefit of the Order. It is the very reason why he would never agree to the subjugation of his… "own kind", I suppose… no matter how noble the cause may appear. I hear, too, that Lord Cherleten places great stock in backstreet mediums and gypsy fortune-tellers. Psychics, Captain Denny, are becoming an increasing part of the Order's intelligence. But it is not an exact science.'

Jim had reached for his glass while Marie spoke, and almost dropped it at the mention of gypsies. He composed himself as quickly as he could, and took a sip of wine to buy some thinking time.

'Some might not call it a science at all,' he said, forcing a laugh.

'Some have not seen what we have seen,' Miss Furnival replied, stony-faced.

The waiter cleared away the plates, prompting another silence, a little more awkward.

'You mentioned our assignment,' Jim prompted, when they were alone again. 'That is why you're here, after all.'

'In a way. I prefer to work alone, Captain. When required to enter the field with an agent, I like to get the measure of him. See what he's made of. After all, we'll be required to risk our lives for each other.'

'You think it will come to that?'

'I know it. There is only one reason I would be sent along with you, Captain Denny.'

'The… monsters?' Jim speculated.

'Quite.'

'So it's true – you are the expert monster-hunter.' He could barely suppress a smirk. Miss Furnival's nose wrinkled at the implied slight.

'Do you even know what it was you saw on that ship?'

'Some kind of poor degenerates. Carnival freaks maybe, imprisoned since childhood by the tong and used to scare their enemies. Naked apes from the zoo, perhaps.' Jim shrugged. He knew the truth would be something to do with the Othersiders, and knew he would not like it. Not that it made any odds – how many times had he had to face an unpalatable truth in the execution of his duties? He steeled himself for Miss Furnival's explanation, knowing that whatever the creatures were, he would have to hunt them, and doubtless kill them, eventually.

'They are vampires, Captain Denny.'

Jim snorted laughter. He stopped immediately when he saw that Miss Furnival was in deadly earnest. 'Vampires? Blood-drinking nobles from the Orient? Those wretches were hardly Countess Báthory.'

'That's because Countess Báthory was a murderess given more sinful embellishment than she deserved by dime-novel writers. These creatures are real, not fictions devised by men who really ought to get out more.'

Jim blinked in mild surprise at her language. He was starting to like this rough-talking American.

'On the Otherside, vampires are a very real threat, and exist in great number,' Miss Furnival went on. 'An oblique mention of them appears in Colonel Hardwick's report of the Lazarus Gate – something Agent Hanlocke said to him when he confessed his crimes. You've read the report, of course? Good. The vampires – or "*wampyr*" as they call themselves – bartered themselves great positions of power on the Otherside when the Rift was torn open. Their innate ability to see – even fight – the demons known as "Riftborn" gave them a rather large bargaining chip. Of course, they weren't enamoured with the idea of the world dying in flames. After all, even if they survived the apocalypse, who would be left for them to feed upon? They are blood drinkers, first and foremost. And so, inevitably, a few found their way to this side when the Lazarus Gate opened, along with the countless other refugees whom you track each day.'

Jim rubbed at his chin. She explained the unbelievable as though it were elementary.

'You say "bartered",' Jim managed. 'The things I saw were incapable of rational thought, as far as I could tell.'

'What you saw were ghouls,' Miss Furnival said, finishing her glass of wine and refilling it herself. 'They are bestial degenerates, poor cousins of the true vampires, and probably more dangerous. You were lucky to escape.'

'You mean to say that there are... what? Intelligent versions of those creatures, loose here in London?'

'That's what we'll find out.'

Jim frowned. 'But if not, then who do the "ghouls" serve? If not their own kind, I mean?'

'I guess we'll find that out, too.' Marie Furnival smiled. There was a feline quality to her expression.

'So whoever controls these ghouls... they brand them, I take it, like cattle?'

'No, actually. I saw the one in the dead-room, Captain, and it got me mighty curious. Branded nine-seven-something. I've never seen its like.'

'How could you know all of this?' Jim asked. 'Of all the agents of the Order, I am the one usually tasked with tracking Othersiders. Why have I not heard of these vampires before?' He could barely believe he was accepting this as truth, but then, in the last few years he had seen mediums levitate five feet off the floor, ghostly manifestations, strange devices of fantastical application and, of course, refugees from another universe who were fleeing a horde of demons. Vampires were merely another facet of the ongoing madness.

'No, Captain Denny. You are the agent who is tasked with

tracking rogue artefacts, smugglers, etherium, and occasional escapees from justice. There are other, even more esoteric and terrifying things in the world these days. They seek ingress from the Otherside every waking hour. And when they find a way in, I am sent to hunt them, and kill them.'

'Sir; *Madame*.' The waiter placed the main courses on the table with a small flourish, giving Jim a moment to take in all he had been told.

Jim could not fathom how this young woman had come to such a role, especially within the Order, which was still ostensibly a gentlemen's club. He resolved to find out all he could about the enigmatic Miss Furnival later.

'You say you haven't heard of the vampires,' Miss Furnival said when the waiter was out of earshot. 'But of course you have. Yet the stories were doctored for the press. The involvement of Apollo Lycea expunged from all official records. You remember that business in Rotherhithe earlier this year?'

'The supposed return of the Ripper? I thought that was merely a hoax to sell a few newspapers. You mean to say…?'

'A nest of ghouls, living in a burrow beneath a mausoleum. They got tired of feasting on the dead, and forayed above ground to find living victims. Acting on instinct, you see, like dumb animals. There were even people in that district who knew about the creatures, and lured victims to their deaths at the hands of the ghouls. A good way to get rid of your enemies. And, of course, if a predator has a full belly, it's less likely to come a-hunting you and yours.'

'What happened?'

'I found the nest, burned them all alive. It's the surest way to destroy them. That's why your fancy little pistol is so effective – pretty much cooks them from the inside out, brains and all.'

'How many have you killed?' Jim asked.

'Too many to count. Not enough.' She looked absently at her food. Her tone was bitter.

'You hate them?'

'I do. I shall confess to you, Captain Denny, so that there are no secrets that may hinder our working relationship. There is a vampire nobleman whom I suspect to be at large here in England. His name is de Montfort. I do not know where he is, or how he got here, but he once hurt someone very close to me, and when I find him I will kill him without question.'

'I say... it's unlike an agent to take his work so personally. Especially the killing.'

'You kill for your country, do you not?'

'I have. But I can't say that I've ever enjoyed it. The Othersiders... sometimes they're wild, do you see? They are so intent on escaping the devil at their backs that they heap further danger upon our world.'

'They're desperate. They're scared,' Miss Furnival said. Was that compassion in her eyes? Jim could not understand this woman, so hard one moment, so gentle the next.

'They are dangerous. If they won't come quietly, it's best to put them down before they can enact whatever plans they might have. The Tesla weapons are testament to their ingenuity. My standing orders are to bring in every Othersider I find; "dead or alive", as your people would say.'

Something akin to a scowl crossed Miss Furnival's features. Jim wasn't sure if it was the jibe at the Americans, or something else.

'Are you always so obedient?' she asked. Her voice was unmistakeably cold.

'I... follow orders. I'm a soldier – or, I was. Are you always so rebellious?'

'I like to think I do some good in the world, Captain Denny. Didn't you leave soldiering behind you? I believe a good agent can question his orders now and again. How many frightened, otherwise innocent people have gone to their deaths by your hands, I wonder – even indirectly.'

Jim felt as though he were treading on thin ice with Miss Furnival. He scratched at his collar, irked by her accusation. More than irked. 'None, I'd like to think,' he said. 'If the

Othersiders are here, then they're already guilty of something. These are the very people who sought to kill every last one of us, and replace us. These are the people who infiltrated every tier of our society for ten years, while they built weapons of war to turn upon us. Even those who were not part of the military machine bring etherium and weapons into our midst. Some have psychic powers the likes of which are beyond we have ever seen, that could do to our world what they did to their own. You say they may be innocents? I say I'd rather see them hanged than let them threaten just one life in our world.'

'And what of their lives?' Marie snapped.

Jim's colour rose. They had strayed beyond barbed repartee, that was for certain. 'Their lives were forfeit as soon as they crossed over. They do not belong here. In truth, they do not even exist here, so what rights do they have?'

Marie's large eyes burned angrily; her lips pursed. 'There's another saying from back home – coined by a soldier like you – which I rather think you'd subscribe to, had you the chance.'

'Oh?'

'They say "the only good Indian's a dead Indian". It's how we justified driving a race to near-extinction. Or subjugation.'

'I must remind you, madam, that the Othersiders planned to do exactly that to us. Their extinction is not our doing, but their own. Their plan to replace us was barbaric. I am tasked with removing the last dregs of their race from our great country, and that I will do. It is no different from killing every last wolf in Scotland, and believe me when I say my quarry is every bit as dangerous. I wish to cause no offence, for you speak from a place of compassion, as a woman is wont to do; but compassion has little place in our line of work. Perhaps it is best that you hunt the monsters, and I hunt the humans. That way, neither of us shall be found wanting.'

The waiter approached with trepidation, noting the almost untouched plates. 'Sir; Madame. Is... everything in order with your meals?'

'I've lost my appetite,' Miss Furnival said. She stood, throwing her napkin to the table. Jim rose awkwardly, out of politeness. 'I'm sure the captain here will be able to finish. He doesn't strike me as the kind of man to lose either appetite or sleep over such a trifling disagreement.'

Even as Jim searched for some reconciliatory words, Marie Furnival turned on her heel and walked away, drawing a few surreptitious glances from bemused diners.

Jim slumped back into his chair and blew out his cheeks, not for the first time that evening. The waiter, face red, stood expectantly, waiting for some instruction.

'Take this away,' said Jim. 'And bring something stronger to drink. Scotch, I think. Better make it a large one.'

As the waiter scurried away, Jim checked his watch. The night was still young; he might just get away with a spot of debauchery after all. He'd need it to get over the whirlwind left in Marie Furnival's wake.

FOUR

Sunday, 1st October 1893

APOLLO LYCEA, ST KATHARINE DOCKS FACILITY

Sir Arthur Furnival led the way through the tight corridors of the docks facility, where the Order of Apollo Lycea stored Otherside technology and conducted its most secret research. Sir Arthur's little enterprise shared an uneasy cohabitation with Cherleten's armoury. Jim reported to the docks regularly, but was never permitted to venture into Sir Arthur's domain, which was reserved for 'special projects'.

Jim looked askance at Sir Arthur as they walked. The baronet's head always looked too large for his body, Jim thought. Pale blue veins stood proud at receding temples. Probably a result of all that mental exertion. The man was likely trying to read Jim's thoughts even now.

Sir Arthur turned his head, on cue, and Jim looked away quickly, pretending that he hadn't been staring. It was ridiculous of course; the Othersiders had psychics, but on this side of the veil – the real world – only freaks like the Artist had ever been proven to possess true psychic prowess.

Sir Arthur stopped at a door in a dimly lit passage, and rang a bell-pull. A moment later, a club servant appeared, bowed to Sir Arthur, and showed him in. Jim followed tentatively. Most of the St Katharine Docks headquarters was off-limits to field agents.

They now stepped through what looked and smelled like a hospital ward, though most of it was screened off from prying eyes by large curtains. Jim wondered just what took place down here – who the patients were – but could not stop to find out, as Sir Arthur had already hurried onwards.

Soon they reached a door, which the baronet opened with a key, and Jim followed him into a wood-panelled office. It was similar to Cherleten's room, on the other side of the dock, albeit smaller and tucked far away from the rest of the Order's inner circle.

Sir Arthur turned up the gaslights, and indicated a chair beside his desk. 'Please, take a seat,' he said. 'I had the electric lights removed from this room. Rather harsh on the eyes, don't you agree?'

'I... Sir Arthur, I was expecting to receive orders today. I perhaps should not tarry...'

'Do not worry, Captain Denny. I have your orders here.'

'You? I'm sorry, it's just that I expected Lord Cherleten to summon me.'

'No need to apologise. You are not used to receiving orders from me, and I am unused to issuing them. Since your discovery on Friday last, however, my little corner of Apollo Lycea has received renewed attention from the powers that be, and it has been decreed that agents assigned to work for me should do so directly... cut out the middle-man, so to speak.'

Jim nodded. It wasn't that he was particular about receiving his orders from Lord Cherleten. Indeed, like most agents of Apollo Lycea, he didn't really like Cherleten at all. Sir Arthur was an unknown quantity, and Jim was wary of him – more so, given the things people said about his 'talents'.

'I am not accustomed to the formality of command, Captain Denny, so forgive me if I break protocol on occasion,' Sir Arthur said. 'Indeed, before we get to business I must speak with you about a related, and yet rather personal matter.'

'Of course.' Jim tensed. He knew what this would concern.

'You will have a new partner on your next assignment. I'm sure you have guessed by now that my niece, Marie, is also on my staff.'

'I had made that assumption, yes,' Jim replied. He was cautious; he did not want to indicate that he was already acquainted with Miss Furnival outside of club meetings. He could not, however, tell an outright lie, in case Sir Arthur already suspected as much, and was testing him. For all Jim knew, the baronet could have read his mind.

'I know that working with a woman, especially on a dangerous mission, would not sit well with most agents. But I would very much like for you to extend her all the professional courtesy that you would any other agent. Marie's work has been largely conducted in secret, but believe me when I say that she has earned her position within the Order.'

'And what exactly is her position, Sir Arthur? She is certainly not a member of the club, and I note she is never referred to as "Agent" Furnival.'

Sir Arthur offered a mirthless smile. 'You are quick of mind, as Lord Cherleten said. No, Marie is not officially part of the Order. I employ her. She has no rank, and little authority, save what I can arrange for her. Through grave circumstance, however, she found herself embroiled in our secrets. She knows more about Othersiders than most agents of the Order, and works for us on a voluntary basis. Her skills have become rather invaluable.'

'Is she... like you?' Jim now wondered just what Marie might have gleaned from their liaison if she, too, was psychic.

Sir Arthur smiled. 'My abilities are exaggerated by the common agent. Marie is far more extraordinary than me, though not in the way you mean.'

'I see. So, might I ask... what are her skills?'

'Hope that you do not need to find out, Captain Denny, for if you do, things will surely have taken a dire turn. Now, I said that I wished to discuss a personal matter.'

'Of course, forgive me.'

'Not at all. There is much that Marie understands about our work, and indeed much that she has personally contributed to the cause of Apollo Lycea. But as you rightly point out, she is not an agent. What's more, she is a woman, and has certain... sensibilities... which do occasionally manifest themselves. Although I would ask that you encourage her in her work, and allow yourself to be guided by her expertise, you would do well to remember that there are certain secrets within the Order that we must never reveal to... outsiders. Am I making myself clear?'

'I understand, Sir Arthur. But if Miss Furnival has been working with the Order already, how am I to know what is beyond her clearance?'

'If you need explain it to her, Captain, then she should not know it. And there is one secret in particular that I would ask you to remain particularly tight-lipped about.'

'The Nightwatch?'

Sir Arthur raised an eyebrow.

'Miss Furnival's reaction on Saturday,' Jim said quickly. 'She was most agitated about the Nightwatch. I presume she objects to the project on some... sentimental level?'

'Ah, quite right. Yes, you really are quick, Captain Denny. Now, the Nightwatch. I am sure you understand what we are dealing with by now, so there's no point beating around the bush. In fact... oh, it is deuced hard to put into words, Captain Denny, for so much of my work here is based on intuition, you see?'

'Not really, Sir Arthur.'

'No, of course. You are a man of action, a practical man. Come with me, Captain, and let me show you exactly what I'm talking about.'

Sir Arthur strode purposefully from the office, and Jim hurried to catch up. He slackened his pace when he saw where they were going: the ward. Sir Arthur walked briskly along a wide aisle, between curtained hospital beds, behind which Jim heard the occasional moan or ragged, stertorous breath.

Once they reached the end of the aisle, Sir Arthur pulled out a heavy-looking ring of keys, identical to the set that Jim had seen in Cherleten's possession many times. The baronet unlocked a pair of metal-plated double doors. Within, Jim saw a large chamber, lit only by dim, flickering lamps, as opposed to the garish electrical lights that illuminated the ward. He felt some reluctance to enter, his limbs unwilling to move over the threshold. Sir Arthur seemed to sense it too, for as he stepped into the room he glanced over his shoulder and said, 'Come along, Captain Denny. Time and tide, and all that.'

Jim followed Sir Arthur into the room, which he saw now was another ward. In the far corner of the room, five beds were arranged in a circle, the heads of their resting incumbents pointing inwards. Jim shivered as he noted the wires, coils, and tubes of unknown liquid passing from subject to subject, and outwards to large machines, such as those Jim had once seen in an exhibition of galvanism. The machines hummed steadily with electrical current; Jim felt as though he had drifted into the story of *Frankenstein*.

At the approach of Sir Arthur's ringing footsteps, an attendant, who had been dozing in a rather uncomfortable-looking chair, now jerked awake. The man stood, revealing himself as a tall, blade-thin creature of singularly pronounced features. Jim had never laid eyes on him before, in all his time at the facility.

'Anything to report, Mr Amworth?' Sir Arthur asked.

The man stretched, long, skeletal limbs clicking. 'Nothing, Sir Arthur. Sleeping like babes.' He spoke softly, with pride and perhaps reverence for his charges.

'Good, good. Will you excuse us? I have some business to discuss with the captain here.'

The thin man nodded and left the ward, though not before looking back one last time with a smile for the sleepers, and a suspicious glance for Jim.

'Amworth is fond of our subjects,' Sir Arthur said quietly, explaining away the man's guarded behaviour. 'He cares for them like family.'

Sir Arthur approached the beds, and beckoned Jim towards him. Jim did as he was bid, but reluctantly, for he saw at the farthest bed a shock of long black hair around a pale face. His stomach twisted in knots. It was not just the vestiges of his recurring nightmare that gave him this fear, though he could not show it; he had long ago sworn never to reveal what he knew of John Hardwick's secrets. That the girl in the bed was surely the same girl Jim had seen here three years prior – a psychic from the Otherside, rescued from London Bridge. Elsbet, a gypsy girl, and the younger sister of John's lost love, Rosanna; or rather, the doppelganger of that girl. Her counterpart was dead in the real world at the hands of Otherside agents, but this wretched girl had been consigned to a life of slavery in the Nightwatch by the Othersiders. If Jim's suspicions were correct, and this was indeed Elsbet, then it was not merely the Othersiders who had enslaved her – she had, it seemed, traded one set of masters for another.

'This is the beginning of something that I hope will be far greater,' Sir Arthur said, his voice hushed. 'This is the Nightwatch. Oh, I know it's not much now – just five subjects, peaceful, dreaming of what may come to pass. But their predictions grow more accurate with each session. Soon, the likes of the Artist will be as nothing compared to this... this "divination engine", for want of a better phrase.'

'I...' Jim was at a loss. 'That is... are you saying that Miss Furnival's assertion was correct? These people are simply cogs in the machine?'

'Something like that.'

'But... I... Forgive my impertinence, Sir Arthur, but do you not also have abilities like theirs?'

'That is what people say, isn't it?'

Jim nodded.

'It is beside the point,' Sir Arthur said. He looked down at the nearest subject – a fair-haired man nearing middle age. Sir Arthur sighed. 'These people are fugitives from justice. Two of them were brought in by you, Captain, although given your many successes in that regard I doubt you would recognise them from the multitude. They cannot be sent back whence they came, and execution would be barbaric. So their options become imprisonment, or this. Here, they sleep, and dream, and have not a care in the world.'

'Then how do they… predict?'

'That is the key question. We are still learning much about the process, and it is awful strange to see, but the results speak for themselves. These machines – they keep the Nightwatch in a state of utmost tranquillity, and record every tiny variation in their brains' activity. When we are ready for them to make their predictions, we introduce a little of that etherium you've been gathering into their systems. Oh, don't fret, Captain Denny – it is a tiny amount, rationed most carefully so as not to cause any… disturbances, if you take my meaning.'

'Indeed I do,' said Jim, with a frown. He had seen many 'disturbances' in the past three years, usually as a direct result of pursuing psychics – what the Othersiders called 'Majestics' – and almost always after they had injected themselves with etherium out of sheer desperation to elude him. Sometimes the Majestics had managed to move things with their minds, which had at first seemed miraculous to Jim, but had surprised the culprits with how little power they possessed away from their own universe. Sometimes, however, during these confrontations, Jim had seen… things. Shadows moving unnaturally; echoes of the distant past or perhaps of other worlds, projected into a room like stage trickery. Once, he had seen – or rather, felt – something clawing beyond the veil, gazing hungrily towards a Majestic who knew not what he was conjuring. On that occasion, Jim had responded with deadly force, lest something evil break through into the world. Something he knew all too well.

'My people have calculated every variable to the most minute parameter, Captain,' Sir Arthur went on. 'We have seen nothing so far to indicate the slightest risk to our world, if that is what you fear.'

Sir Arthur moved around the arrangement of beds as he spoke, and came to a halt next to Elsbet. If he had any inkling of the girl's significance, he did not show it.

'Sir Toby dislikes being in here also,' Sir Arthur said, when Jim did not follow. 'He said that, when the Nightwatch make their predictions, it has the whiff of a parlour séance. He's perfectly correct – it is exactly like a séance. Each of these subjects possesses tremendous psychical power – far and away greater than any medium we know of from our own world. Except for Tsun Pen, but then he was not really one of us, was he?'

'So why do you need five of them?'

'I believe we'll need more before the experiment can be called a success,' Sir Arthur replied. 'You see, the future is uncertain – the skeins of fate are open to interpretation. Once the etherium takes hold of these sleeping subjects, they enter a trance, and begin to speak aloud what they see. They are guided towards particular subjects, their energies focused by our alienists, who gradually hone the Nightwatch until their visions are clear. You see?'

Jim didn't see at all, but said nothing.

'Sometimes, the five of them are not in agreement. Sometimes there is only one dissenting voice, who sees a different future, a different place or culprit. Sometimes all five speak at once, but differently, making the results almost impossible to decipher. That is where I come in, Captain. I have trained myself to interpret the Nightwatch's visions. I am arbiter of their clairvoyance – it falls to me to make the final judgment, if one can be made at all, on where to send our agents.'

'Ah.'

'You see now why I wanted to show you this, Captain? If it is my responsibility, then it falls upon my shoulders that you were steered false. If the answers were there, and I misinterpreted them, then it is to my shame. If the answers were not there, and

I sent you anyway, then perhaps it was my hubris and pride in this work that I did so. In either case, I wish to extend my most sincere apologies, Captain Denny. Measures have been taken to ensure this will not happen again.'

'What kind of measures, sir?'

'Robust ones.'

'Very well. And my next assignment... it comes from the Nightwatch, also?'

'It does, but as I said –'

'There are robust measures in place.' Jim hoped he did not sound as wary as he felt.

'Quite. I shall provide your written orders in full, as you would expect. Suffice it to say that we believe the tong to be within our reach. All of the intelligence provided by my subjects suggests that they will be moving their largest shipment of etherium yet tomorrow.'

'Larger than the haul from the *Glarus*? Good grief. And the... subjects... they are all in agreement this time?'

'As it happens, Captain, all but one. This one.'

Sir Arthur placed his hands either side of Elsbet's head. As he did so, Jim felt sure he saw the girl's eyes flicker beneath their dark lids. Then they opened.

Elsbet's back arched, her fingers curled like claws as she struggled against her restraints. A great hiss rose from the machinery behind her, like a pair of bellows suddenly compressing. Jim stepped back. Sir Arthur, having fair jumped out of his skin, now stroked the girl's hair and spoke soothingly to her.

'The... dark...' she croaked, her voice paper-thin. 'The lines. The lines lead to the dark. Monsters wait in the dark... They wait in the house of the dead.'

Sir Arthur put his ear close to the girl's lips as she spoke. Jim heard her perfectly well from where he stood, as though she were whispering directly in his ear.

'Tunnels. Once a place of healing. Now... the house of the dead.'

'Be still, girl. *Shh... shh...*' Sir Arthur muttered.

'Monster!' Elsbet shrieked. 'Red in tooth... red in claw... the Red Lord knocking at your door...'

The girl convulsed, rattling the metal-framed bed to which she was strapped. Foam spilled from the corner of her cracked blue lips. Jim winced, for with the girl's convulsions came a horrific sound; a skittering, scratching noise, as though a teeming swarm of insects were tearing at the inside of his skull, mandibles champing dryly behind his eyes. It was a noise Jim knew only he could hear. He heard it often, and mostly he could block it from his thoughts. But not now. He clutched at his head as the noise grew louder, and a sensation like daggers stabbed behind his eyes.

'Nurse! Nurse!' Sir Arthur called.

They were already on their way, heels pattering like raindrops on the polished floor. Soon they were holding Elsbet down. One took out a large syringe, and injected its contents into the girl's arm.

Elsbet's body relaxed almost at once, but she managed to turn her head towards Jim, fixing him with a blank stare, before her eyes rolled back into her head.

'We... are... one...' she groaned, and then fell back into a deep sleep.

Jim breathed a great sigh of relief as the discomfort subsided, and did his best to ignore the curious look Sir Arthur gave him.

'I am sorry you had to see that,' Sir Arthur said later, passing Jim a tumbler of brandy.

'I am not altogether sure what I just saw. Is that normal? Is that what passes for peaceful interment in the Nightwatch?' Jim was shaken, and he saw that Sir Arthur was too. The baronet's pale face had turned a sickly grey-green hue, and his eyes were full of sadness.

'No. Not at all. I have not seen such a thing... not since the earliest days of the experiment. Until just now I thought it impossible. They are heavily sedated when their abilities are not being put to the test.'

'And the things she said – they relate to the assignment?'

'Perhaps. I... I do not know. Sometimes, the visions come piecemeal. It sounded like a warning. But just as likely she was receiving some glimpse of another possible future; something painful and upsetting that caused her to wake from her dreams.'

'Or her nightmares,' Jim said.

'Who knows?' Sir Arthur put his brandy down, untouched. 'Is that what you saw, Captain? Your nightmares?'

'Perhaps she was not predicting the future at all,' Jim said, ignoring the question, and looking away from the baronet's inquisitive gaze. 'Perhaps she was remembering something from her past.' Jim had to be careful; fishing for information could easily expose his own knowledge of the girl. Whatever had passed between him and John, he had still made a promise not to reveal her identity, though heavens knew why John had stipulated it.

'A peculiar remark, Captain. Again you prove yourself astute. Sometimes the past of our Majestics does come back to haunt them, which is why we have alienists on the staff to placate them. That particular subject has always been one of the best. She's the only one to have graduated from the earliest experiments to where we are now. Many of the Majestics enslaved on the Otherside were subject to regimes far harsher than those we impose, and they simply could not adjust to even a sliver of comfort or kindness. She, however, endured it all, and now knows peace. Beyond her great mental fortitude, we know nothing about her. She may have been raised in captivity, for all we can glean. There was one thing the girl said that made me think she was indeed referring to your assignment,' Sir Arthur said.

'Oh? I hope you aren't going to say it was the "monsters".' Jim forced a smile.

Sir Arthur remained grave-faced. 'I am afraid I am, Captain Denny. The things you encountered aboard the *Glarus* will likely play some part in your fortunes yet. It is one aspect of this affair on which all of my Nightwatch agree. This is why I shall be sending my niece along with you. You understand why I do not wish Marie to know about any of this?' Sir Arthur gestured towards the door of the office. 'She may present a hardened – sometimes brash – persona to the likes of you, and her colonial manners only exacerbate the unfavourable impression some people form of her; but Marie is a Furnival. She is my niece – my ward. Underneath it all, she is a lady, and this operation would seem distasteful to her, at best. Women are wont not to understand the difficult actions men must take for the good of the Empire.'

'I understand entirely, Sir Arthur. You have my word that I shan't mention a word of this to Miss Furnival.'

'The Nightwatch represent hope, Captain Denny. But there are many, even within the Order, who might disagree. As far as anyone is concerned, this project was abandoned before it was really begun.'

Jim nodded.

'So now you know everything that I know, Captain Denny. As you can tell, I am not versed in espionage. I do not believe in withholding such information from an agent that may save their life in the field – which is why Lord Cherleten disapproves of my appointment as head of the Nightwatch.'

'I'm sure he's spitting feathers, Sir Arthur,' Jim said with a wry smile.

Sir Arthur returned the sentiment. 'I assure you, it gives me no pleasure to see Lord Cherleten put out,' he said, unconvincingly. 'Anyhow, I have already taken up too much of your time. Your orders, Captain.'

Sir Arthur took a small envelope from his breast pocket, bearing the Apollonian Club seal, and handed it to Jim. Mission specifics were never discussed openly. Jim would have to read them, memorise them, and burn them, as procedure dictated.

'Thank you, Sir Arthur. How long do I have to prepare?'

'Take the rest of the day. Happy hunting.' The baronet forced the pleasantry.

Jim extended a hand to Sir Arthur, then withdrew it awkwardly when he recalled that Sir Arthur never shook hands. Instead, the two men exchanged nods, and Jim went on his way, relieved to get out of the stifling ward, with its stupefied incumbents.

Jim was grateful when he returned to the more familiar parts of the facility. Dubbed 'the armoury' due to its experimental weapons division, more than half the facility was under Lord Cherleten's command. Jim passed by the peer's office, lightening his step as he went in the hopes of avoiding the notice of Cherleten, but to no avail. The door of the office swung open behind Jim, and he winced.

'Denny, just the man. Wait there.'

Jim turned. Cherleten ushered an unfamiliar man out of his office; a white-haired, mutton-chopped fellow, with a smart suit beneath an open white laboratory coat.

'Dr Crookes, this is Captain Denny. Told you about him earlier.'

The man bowed his head curtly. 'Pleased to make your acquaintance, Captain. I have you to thank for my latest specimen, I hear.'

'The creature from the *Glarus*?' Jim asked. 'Ah, you work in the mortuary.'

Crookes chuckled to himself, as though Jim had said something amusing. 'I suppose I do. Now if you gentlemen will excuse me, I must return to my work. My lord.'

As quickly as that, he was gone. Jim's interest was piqued, for there was something strangely clandestine about the interchange between Crookes and Cherleten, even for this place.

'I thought I knew all the doctors here,' Jim said. 'What does he do here?'

Cherleten smiled and patted Jim on the shoulder. 'Never you mind, my boy. There are some secrets I keep even from my most trusted agents. You met with Sir Arthur just now?'

'I did.'

'Well, I want you to remember that you're my man, Denny. You are seconded to the Nightwatch, but I want a full and frank report after the fact, as always.'

Jim frowned. 'Of course, sir. I see no reason to –'

'Full, and frank,' Cherleten repeated. 'I'm talking about the girl. There may be some activities you would rather withhold from Sir Arthur, for obvious reasons. Do not withhold them from me. Understood?'

Jim nodded.

'Good. Watch out for that one. I hear she's a wily little minx, eh?' He winked at Jim lasciviously, barked his silly little laugh, and stepped into his office. 'Happy hunting, Denny.' He closed the door, leaving Denny to wonder, as always, just how much Cherleten knew, and how he knew it.

FIVE

CHELSEA VESTRY WHARF

'**S**eems mighty audacious of them, don't you think?' Marie Furnival said, looking about the busy wharf, which rang to the sound of industry even at the crack of dawn. 'There are people working round the clock. Smuggling anything here would be difficult. And for a bunch of Chinamen, too… hardly inconspicuous.'

'Hmm?' Jim stared absently at the line of labourers coming in and out of the nearby warehouse, toiling under the watchful eye of police officers.

'I said, it's not the kind of place you'd expect to find Otherside smugglers.'

The annoyance in her tone pulled Jim from his woolgathering. 'You're right, but we have our orders. We start here and see where it leads.'

'You doubt the intelligence, too, don't you?' Her eyes brightened.

'I'm keeping an open mind.' Jim worked the stiffness from his hand. He did not want to encourage the rebellious Miss

Furnival by confessing his doubts. The Nightwatch had not been unanimous in their predictions, and there was nothing here at the wharf that reflected Elsbet's cryptic warning.

The lines lead to the dark. Monsters wait in the dark. They wait in the house of the dead.

A police sergeant approached, red in the face from lugging crates about all morning. Jim was impressed that the sergeant had got his hands dirty with his men, rather than delegate the work. It wasn't the kind of thing Jim would have done. Maybe Jim needed to take the lead more often, before he put more lives in danger. He knew it wouldn't have helped Beresford, but he felt the dagger-pang of guilt all the same. He tried to push such thoughts aside.

'Sergeant Craddock, what news?'

'Nothing here, sir; we've turned the place upside down.'

'No cellar... tunnels... that sort of thing?' Jim asked.

Craddock frowned. 'No, sir.'

'Right, we'd better speak to the foreman again.'

'Already have, begging your pardon, sir. He says if any other consignments have come in without his inspection, then they can only have been taken to the train sheds. There was some activity around No. 2 yesterday, but we'll need to speak to the gasworks men for access.'

'Yes. Oh, and, Sergeant? Good work. Very good work. Send one of your boys off to find a gasworks man, then. Maybe we'll strike it lucky over there.'

The policeman beamed at the compliment, doffed his hat, and hurried off.

'If the tong are working the river, as they always have,' Marie said, 'then surely this would be the most likely place to find the cargo. They'd be hard pressed to smuggle anything on a train here.'

'It depends. All of these warehouses are owned by different companies, some by private individuals. It would be deuced difficult to account for every crate coming and going between the railway yard and the barges. Look there – the rail tracks accommodate both passengers and freight, and they go on right across the city. Plenty of means to smuggle goods a bit at a time, if you have the right man in your pocket to turn a blind eye.'

'By that token the goods could just as easily be taken across the city in any cab or wagon,' Marie argued.

Jim sighed. 'The battle against the Othersiders is never-ending, for that very reason. But our orders are to start here.' He was repeating himself, but he saw no point in being defeatist. An agent went where he was sent, and did as he was bid. Jim was thankful when he heard a shout from over by the train sheds, and saw Craddock beckoning him. 'Come on, it looks like we've found our gasworks man.'

'Be careful with that –' Jim started, but too late.

The constables broke open the crate, splintering the sides and sending its contents spilling out of the freight wagon and onto the low concrete platform. Most of the phials were cushioned by the bundles of red silk that flowed out like the intestines of a stricken animal. Some rolled across the wagon floor. Others smashed, forming puddles of strange-smelling brown liquid all about them. Jim wiped his hand across his face.

'You god-damned idiot!' Marie snapped, stepping carefully over the pools of etherium, shoving the policemen out of the way.

'It's alright,' Jim said, keen to keep the coppers on side. 'Sergeant Craddock, have your men retrieve as many of these bottles as you can. Gloves only – don't get the stuff on your hands. Then I want this floor cleaned thoroughly. Trust me, you don't want to leave a drop of it behind; it's the very devil.'

Craddock presented a worried expression, his thick auburn eyebrows meeting beneath a furrowed brow. He nodded dutifully. 'Come on you lot, you heard the Captain. Dakin, go and find a mop and bucket. Jones, start picking these bottles up. Use the silk, wrap 'em up good and tight now.'

Jim hopped from the wagon, and helped Marie down.

She stepped close to Jim's side, scowling. 'How did you know?'

'The marks on the side of the crate. They're similar to the ones I found the other night. It could easily have been a coincidence... ah, hold on. Here's that foreman.'

Jim plucked a phial of etherium from the floor, and strode across the dimly lit aisle between the tracks, towards the tall man, who approached, flanked by two constables.

'Mr Gedge, I presume?' Jim asked.

'That I am.'

'Do you care to explain this?' Jim held up the phial so that it gleamed in the light of the gaslamp suspended overhead.

Gedge squinted. 'I'm sure I have no idea what that is.'

'It is a drug, sir. A very potent drug from foreign shores. It is so dangerous that possession of it carries a lengthy prison sentence. Smuggling and distribution of it... well, they say that hanging is considered too good for such immorality.'

Mr Gedge wiped his clammy palms across the front of his long warehouse coat. 'I don't know what you are implying, sir, but I will brook no threats. As I said, I have no idea what that is, or where it came from.'

'That part is simple – it came from a crate over there, amidst a pile of similar crates stored in one of *your* wagons. Tell me, is the gas company in the habit of shipping crates of Chinese silk to and from London?'

'Silk? No... I... that is to say...'

'Someone in the employ of the gasworks, Mr. Gedge, has obviously been making a bit of coin on the side, by indulging in some black-market work. And you are responsible for the men who work here, are you not? And for all of the trains that pass through this depot?'

'This shed houses thirty wagons and six locomotives at any given time! I cannot inspect every one of them.'

'Is that how your employers will see it, Mr Gedge? Do they not pay you to do just that?'

Gedge loosened his collar with his index finger; his mouth

tightened, already thin lips almost disappearing. 'I... Look here, what would you have me do? I may have missed a few inspections, but it's done now, isn't it? I'll extend every assistance I can.'

'Good. I need to find out when those crates arrived – if you have no records, I am sure someone will remember when they first saw them. I also need a list of every man in your employ, and their current shift patterns.' Jim held up a hand in anticipation of protest. 'I know this will take some time and no small effort on your part, Mr Gedge, but bearing in mind that you are the chief suspect, it would serve you well to be especially diligent.'

'Suspect...' Gedge paled, his voice cracked. He nodded sheepishly.

Jim, pleased with himself, glanced at Miss Furnival. Her face was, as ever, a blank slate, betraying nothing of her thoughts on the matter, approval or otherwise. He tried not to sigh. 'Miss Furnival,' he said instead. 'Shall we continue our search while Mr. Gedge finds us the records we require?'

'We'd better, before any more of these get smashed.'

Jim smirked to himself at Miss Furnival's cynicism, and followed her back towards the constables. Then she froze.

Miss Furnival held up a hand to stay him. She tilted her head, listening intently for... what?

A gunshot cracked, echoing around the vast shed, disturbing dozens of pigeons roosting in the roof space. Every policeman stopped what he was doing; boxes were dropped, shouts and cries rang out, a whistle blew. Miss Furnival dropped low to the ground and, seeming to pinpoint the direction of the shot, spun on her heels. Jim crouched down too, and followed her gaze.

Mr Gedge held a hand to his neck. Dark blood pumped between pale fingers, staining the front of his long coat red. Sergeant Craddock was already heaving the foreman into cover, but Gedge's prospects looked grim.

'There.' Miss Furnival had no sooner said it than she was up and running, boot-heels crunching on ballast, a .22 revolver already in hand.

Jim ran with her. Shadows slid across the far wall; a heavy

door slammed somewhere ahead.

'Come on!' Jim shouted, thankful when he saw several policemen following. The trilling of police whistles pierced the dusty air – neither use nor ornament, but somehow reassuring.

Jim overtook Miss Furnival, rounding a coal wagon only to hear another shot. The bullet whistled past, so close he felt the rush of air beside his cheek. He cried out involuntarily, skidding across the ground, colliding with the wall before rolling onto his front, pistol aimed at where his attacker had been. The outer door slammed again; the crack of daylight vanished.

Marie Furnival did not stop. 'No time for lying around, Denny,' she said as she passed.

With a huff, Jim pushed himself to his feet, and rejoined the chase, now flanked by three sturdy-looking constables.

When Jim and the policemen bundled out through the side-door into the biting cold morning, Miss Furnival was standing alert, panning across the loading yard with her pistol ready, one eye shut tight, the other scanning for movement.

'Which way did they go?' Jim asked. His breaths came sharp. It wasn't the most brisk exercise he'd had recently, but his narrow brush with death had rattled him more than he cared to admit.

'I don't know. It's like they just vanished.'

More policemen arrived, Craddock with them.

'Sergeant, where is Mr Gedge?' Jim asked.

'I've sent for help, sir. It looks bad.'

'Damn. Get your men to spread out across this yard. Keep to cover in case our gunmen are still about. Look for any signs of which way they went.'

The policemen set about their business at once. Jim moved beside Miss Furnival, and they both crouched beside a tall stack of loading pallets.

'We need to make haste,' Jim said, 'but we can't risk getting caught out in the open.'

'They've got rifles,' Miss Furnival said matter-of-factly. 'Martini-Henry I think.'

'How can you tell?'

'From the report,' she said, as though it were obvious.

'You sound like a cowboy, Miss Furnival,' Jim said.

'Cowboys don't know their guns half so well, except for Winchesters, six-guns and such, on account of them never travelling far from the plains.'

'Sir, over here!' The shout came from Craddock.

Jim and Marie joined Craddock at one of the yard gates.

'Here, sir,' he said. He stood over a constable, kneeling in the dirt beside a blood-splattered labourer, who groaned in agony. 'This fellow saw our men making their getaway, and tried to stop them. Not got too much out of him, except that they was Chinamen, and they went that way.' Craddock pointed along the northbound service track.

'Following the rails?' Jim asked.

'Aye, sir. Under the bridge he said.'

'Will he be all right?'

'I think so. Just a knock to the head. My men won't be long with the ambulance.'

'Then gather what men you can spare, Sergeant. We need some to stay behind with the wounded, and to protect that contraband. The rest are to come with us. We'll catch these devils yet.'

Craddock blew sharply on his whistle, and then ran back into the yard to signal his men. Jim started towards the tracks immediately, but checked his stride as Miss Furnival's hand caught his arm.

'These common gangsters have got the drop on you again,' she said, in a low voice. 'Either the intelligence coming into the club is false, or you got an informant in your midst.'

Jim thought on that. He could not say where the intelligence had come from, but he now had greater cause than ever to believe the Nightwatch was dangerously flawed. Sir Arthur himself said that the skeins of fate were open to interpretation – mayhap the poor souls beneath St Katharine Docks had come to different conclusions. Maybe the Othersiders couldn't be trusted even while sleeping in confinement. Or, worse still, perhaps the Artist really had returned from the grave, and was interfering with their visions somehow.

All of this went unsaid. Instead, Jim fired his best winning grin at Marie Furnival, and said, 'Given that the enemy is in our sights, Miss Furnival, I'd say that the Order's intelligence has led us right where we need to be.'

Miss Furnival's blue eyes narrowed. 'You must see that the only place we're being led is into a trap.'

'Whatever is the matter, ma'am? Afraid?'

She let go of Jim's arm. 'No. But if my suspicions are correct, we both will be before the day is done.'

'So now what?'

Jim ignored Miss Furnival's impatience, and the questioning gaze of the six policemen, and instead looked thoughtfully at their options. Ahead of them, the railway divided into two distinct lines. Passenger trains followed a downward slope, going down to a tunnel and thereafter joining the District Railway. The freight lines continued over-ground, northwards. Steep banks on either side of the freight line led up to rows of tenements and shops. The fences were difficult to climb, but not impossible for determined fugitives. Whichever way their quarry had fled, they would be hard to find.

'Sergeant Craddock,' Jim said. 'The time, please.'

Craddock checked his pocket-watch. 'Seven o'clock, sir.'

'The streets above us will be getting busy. I imagine the draymen have been about for over an hour already. There's a market up there, is there not?'

'There is.'

'Right, send one of your men that way. Climb the fence and start asking about. This is not an area of London where armed orientals would escape attention. If any trace of them is found, raise a hue and cry, send for help, and get word to us.'

'Where shall we be, sir?' Craddock asked, scratching at his thick red beard.

'The way I see it, Sergeant, our suspects have either taken to the tunnel, or have followed the freight line. If the latter, we have little chance of finding them on foot. If they've taken the tunnel, however, we may yet come across their destination. So that is where we shall go.'

Craddock slapped one of his men on the shoulder. 'You heard the captain. Get over that fence, lad. If you need to send word to us, we're following the line to West Brompton Station. Get some lads to delay the first train, just in case.'

The policeman looked reluctant as he eyed up the steep incline, but he nodded to his sergeant and jogged off dutifully. Jim repressed a shudder at the mention of following lines, remembering Elsbet's dire warning.

'For what it's worth, Captain Denny, I can't fault your logic,' Miss Furnival said.

'High praise, Miss Furnival. Now, shall we get on?'

Jim strode into the gloom, the crunch of ballast beneath his feet echoing through the tunnel. The stealthy approach would be difficult. Biting the bullet, he beckoned the others to follow. Jim had checked the trains running to and from the dock before setting out – there should be another half an hour at least until the first was due, and the police would now try to delay them further. Causing delays in London always brought vociferous complaints upon the heads of the Metropolitan Police, and those constables on the front line would not relish being on the receiving end.

He entered the shade of the tunnel, senses immediately assailed by the smell of mould, damp, and worse. A lukewarm breeze blew up from further down the tracks. The 'cut-and-cover' tunnel opened to the sky periodically, affording enough light to see by every few dozen yards, but not enough to spy potential threats or hiding places.

'Lamps!' Craddock shouted. Circles of yellowish light soon danced across the tracks as the policemen lit their hooded dark-lanterns.

Marie quickened her stride to walk beside Jim. 'No side-tunnels or service stairs,' she mused. 'If they came down here they're stuck for at least the next half a mile. Unless they're waiting around that bend yonder, in which case I guess we'll be shot at soon enough.'

Jim almost laughed. Miss Furnival's pessimistic quips were becoming almost reassuring. 'I'm sure you will "beat them to the draw", Miss Furnival,' he said.

'We'd better hope so.'

When they did reach the bend, there was no one to be seen. The air that wafted up the tunnel, however, was foul. The decline of the tracks had taken them beyond the open-roofed shaft, and into a pitch-dark stretch.

'Sergeant Craddock, this is your beat,' Jim said. 'Where exactly are we?'

'Mile or so from Brompton station,' the sergeant said. 'Must be fairly close to the Fulham Road.'

Jim squinted into the gloom ahead, but the lanterns provided scant illumination. 'Is there any access to this tunnel besides the station?'

'No idea, sir. Never had cause to come down here. But there's rumours, o' course.'

'What kind of rumours?' Something about Craddock's tone gave Jim the chills.

'Brompton's famed for two things, sir. Hospitals and graveyards. Some say there's dead-tunnels hidden round here, from the sixties. Never seen evidence of them, but heard enough to wonder.'

'Dead-tunnels?' Marie asked.

'Subterranean passages used for disposing of dead bodies discreetly,' Jim explained. 'They usually lead to and from morgues, to cemeteries. Or charnel pits, if you believe the stories.'

'If it's any more than a story,' Marie said, 'then we're in the right place. Stay sharp, Captain Denny. It seems to me that a certain enemy you faced recently would rather like one of these dead-tunnels to lurk in.'

The meaning was not lost on Jim, and now, in the darkness, he wondered if he had done the right thing bringing just half a dozen men down here. He remembered the pallid, naked half-men aboard the *Glarus*. The horrific sight of Constable Beresford dying in fear. The bestial grunts of the man's killer haunted Jim's dreams.

They forged ahead, Jim refusing to slow his step lest the men at his back detect his reluctance. He'd found the Metropolitan Police little different from the soldiers he used to command. Some of them, indeed, were former soldiers themselves – hardy men, used to following orders, and not shy of a fight. All qualities he needed now. Jim just hoped he wouldn't get any more of them killed. He'd lost more men on his so-called 'civilian duty' than he had during all his time in the cavalry.

The ground declined further. A hazy yellow light shone from somewhere ahead. Jim squinted, but the lamp was so dim he could make out no detail around it.

Something brushed past Jim's ankle. He stopped dead. Behind him, one of the policemen let out a half-stifled cry. A sound like loose gravel tumbling down a quarry bank grew louder, persistent. More things moved past Jim's feet. Soft, damp. Police lanterns were turned to the ground once more.

Rats. An amorphous mass of black and brown fur, matted and wet, tiny round eyes glowing like embers as the lamplight hit them. Their claws skittered on the rails. Their squeaks intensified as the light shone upon them. There were hundreds. Perhaps he imagined it, but Jim fancied they were disgusting, inbred things, covered in buboes, some with stumps for tails or missing legs; some as big as cats, some small as mice, but all scabrous and foul-smelling.

Jim spun about as he sensed growing panic behind him.

Constable Dakin was hopping up and down like a sailor dancing a jig, flailing comically at the vermin with his truncheon. The other policemen had the good sense to run to either side of the tunnel, allowing the undulating, living carpet to scurry and squirm past. Marie Furnival stood like a statue, unflustered by the creatures, her large eyes fixed ahead.

After an interminable time, the stragglers of the great swarm dashed past, chittering at their fellows like slow children left behind upon the playing fields. Jim shuddered, kicking out his legs as though the rats were climbing upon him. When his skin finally ceased crawling, he returned to Miss Furnival's side.

'I suppose you're going to say those rats were fleeing something?'

'Isn't it obvious?'

'Craddock,' Jim said, beckoning the sergeant who was fast becoming his linchpin.

'Sir?' The sergeant was beside Jim in an instant. If he had been shaken by the surge of vermin, he showed no sign of it.

'You said we were under Fulham Road – can you think where precisely?'

'Reckon we must have crossed the Fulham Road now, sir. Let me think now... above us are hospitals, as I said. There are more private 'stablishments along this stretch than enough. There's the cancer hospital... a mad-house, too. Might well be we're right under the grounds of one of 'em.'

'That light,' Marie interjected, pointing ahead to the yellow lamp. 'That is no train signal, so it must be there for a reason.'

'An exit?' Jim offered.

'Let's see. Sergeant, what do you suppose is above that section of tunnel?'

'It would be a guess... but for argument's sake, if we were under the cancer hospital now, then I suppose it would be Brompton Cemetery.'

When Jim's eyes met Miss Furnival's, he saw in them grim determination, as though she had acquired her target and was ready for battle.

'You think that's where we'll find our men?' Craddock asked.

'Something like that,' replied Miss Furnival. 'Shall we?'

She marched onwards at once. Jim swept his gaze across the line of policemen shuffling on their heels, looking somewhat confused at the determination of this slip of a girl. Jim jerked his head in Miss Furnival's direction to jolly along the men, and followed her.

The lamp came slowly into focus; a dim electric light in a filthy glass casing, set into the wall above a narrow doorway.

'Maintenance shaft?' Jim asked.

'Must be, sir,' said Craddock.

'Ah…' Jim stepped to the door, and pointed to a chain and broken padlock that lay in the gravel beside it.

Before he could pass further comment, Marie Furnival had reached past him, and shoved at the door. It groaned on hinges rusted from years of damp; the grating noise echoed through the tunnel. Lamplight danced as the men holding the lanterns flinched at the sudden sound.

Jim had his gun in hand at once, ducking to the side of the doorway. 'What do you think –' he hissed.

The American was through the door before he could finish, vanishing into blackness. Jim took a deep breath and went after her, hoping the men would follow, not blaming them in the slightest if they didn't.

The passage was not wide enough for two men abreast, and Jim found himself stuck behind Miss Furnival, ashamed at himself for letting her take the lead. His coat snagged on rough brick that in places dripped with slime. He had to stoop beneath the low, arched ceiling of the tunnel, which somehow managed to be hot and humid despite the cold season. The tunnel twisted so that it was almost parallel to the rail tracks, and continued some distance with no initial sign of an exit.

Judging by the cobwebs and slime-slick floor, the passage was not often used. Some ten yards ahead, another yellow light shone – someone was keeping the lights burning down here, though for what purpose who could say? When they reached the light, they found themselves at a crossroads. The narrow passage continued up a definite incline. Left and right, the passages were much wider. To the right, a shaft of daylight illuminated the end of a long tunnel, casting bars of deep shadow onto a set of stone stairs.

Craddock took a lamp from one of his men and held it out at arm's length.

'Told you, sir. That'll be the cemetery. Near forty acres. If they've gone that way, they'll be a bugger to catch.'

Jim cursed. He'd hoped to find his quarry caught in the tunnels like the rats they'd flushed out. In the open air, with the streets of London getting busy, the chance of catching the celestials was slim.

'So what's down here?' Miss Furnival asked, pointing to the left spur that yawned ominously.

'God, what's that smell?' Jim asked. The air that wafted from the tunnel was foul.

'Shh!' Miss Furnival hissed. 'Listen.'

Everyone was quiet. At first, there was no sound at all beyond the faint whistling of a breeze from the direction of the graveyard. But then a noise came from the pitch darkness of the left-hand passage. A scuff, and a scrape, followed by the squeal of metal hinges. The distant ring of a metal door closing.

'Craddock, bring up the light. Let's go!' Jim gave the order, and moved to the front of the group, grateful when Craddock took his lead and shone the lantern ahead. Jim had had quite enough of letting Marie Furnival lead them into danger half-cocked. He moved steadily, pistol at the ready, emboldened by the shuffling of the constables at his back. Miss Furnival stayed close, and silent.

The tunnel sloped upwards, until Jim was sure they must be nearing street level again. Before too long the ground underfoot became uneven, strewn about with detritus, and the tunnel at last terminated at a double door, bound in iron. One of the doors was ajar, and Craddock shone his light upon the doorstep, revealing an arc of scrape marks where the door had been forced open.

'Right, men,' Jim whispered. 'Arm yourselves, and take extra care.'

It was clear that none of the policemen relished the prospect of entering the dark room and potentially getting shot like poor Gedge at the warehouse.

Jim did not want to give the order, but he did so anyway. 'We need light in there, Sergeant Craddock. Two men either side, lamps high, truncheons ready. Miss Furnival and I will provide covering fire, have no fear. On the count of three...'

Jim counted down at once, before any man could argue. Craddock slapped the two men nearest him on their backs, indicating that they would be the ones to lead. When Jim reached three, the sergeant gave the men a shove to help them on their way, and the room beyond the doorway was at last illuminated.

A tiled floor and filthy walls materialised before them. A high ceiling and vaulted brickwork stretched until swallowed by impenetrable shadow.

No bullets rang from the darkness. No sound was to be heard but for the heavy footsteps and nervous breathing of the constables.

Jim and Marie entered next, followed by Craddock and Dakin.

'All clear,' Jim said. 'Keep going, through that arch, hurry.'

The men pressed on, sweeping through the arch and fanning out to either side of the room beyond. Young Dakin gasped.

By contrast to the narrow antechamber behind them, this room was much larger. Again, it was filthy, walls smeared with grease and grime. There appeared to be only one exit – a closed door in the left-hand wall – and no windows. The room was lined with counters, and metal-panelled cupboards. If it were not obvious from those that this was a dead-room, the two metal surgical tables in the centre of the room confirmed it. All around them, Jim now noticed surgical apparatus and jars of murky fluid, covered in thick cobwebs.

'I'll be blowed,' muttered Craddock. 'They was dead-tunnels after all, going to the cemetery. Never thought they really existed.'

'It seems you were right, Sergeant,' Jim said. 'This can't have been a poor hospital. If the bodies brought down here belonged merely to poor unfortunates, they would not need a Christian burial. They'd surely be burned.'

'As I said, sir, the cancer hospital, or the mad –'

Craddock fell silent. Jim turned to him, and was about to ask what was wrong, when he saw that the man was wiping some sort of fluid from his tunic. Craddock slowly turned his eyes upwards, as though it had dripped on him from above. Jim followed the man's gaze, and there, for a moment, against the dark vaulted ceiling a pair of sparkling violet eyes blinked, then vanished completely.

Jim could barely get any words out in time, and what feeble cry of alarm he raised was instantly drowned out by Craddock's scream.

A pair of pale, clawed hands reached down from the shadows, gripped Craddock's head, and twisted hard. The sergeant's head spun around, facing backwards, before the hands withdrew with half the man's face and great auburn beard hooked on yellowed claws.

Craddock's body fell to the floor. Jim squeezed off two rounds at the pallid creature that hung, bat-like from the ceiling. The sound of the revolver was deafening in the confines of the mortuary, but the screams of the creature pierced the air over the ringing in Jim's ears.

Another gunshot drummed, this time from Marie Furnival's gun. The creature fell from the ceiling in a crumpled heap.

Constable Dakin was by Craddock's side in a trice, trembling in fear when he saw the terrible state of his sergeant.

'What do we do?' he croaked. 'Oh, God… what is that thing?'

Before Jim could respond, a low growl echoed around the cold chamber. Another joined it, and soon there was a chorus of throaty, bestial snarls.

The other three policemen grouped together, shining their lanterns all about them in desperation. Marie Furnival stood apart from all of them, statue still, eyes scouring the darkness. Jim saw that she not only had a pistol, but now also a wicked-looking curved knife in her other hand.

'Dakin,' Jim hissed, 'make for that door. Quick as you like, lad.'

The young constable's eyes were wild, but he nodded, and looked to the door.

The screams began almost at once. Jim spun around to see two of the beasts drop from the ceiling into the midst of the constables. They clubbed at the creatures frantically, as claws tore at their uniforms and long teeth snapped at their throats. Miss Furnival leapt towards them, but her path was blocked by a third creature, darting as if from nowhere, slashing at her with a taloned hand. Miss Furnival ducked the blow. Jim aimed above her and emptied his revolver into the brute. It stumbled backwards, clattering into an operating table, but did not fall. Jim fumbled as he tried to reload, bullets pinging to the floor. The desperate cries of the other constables consumed his senses. The monster before him pulled itself to its full height once more, and staggered towards him, gaping wounds from the gunshots evident.

Jim cursed, finally pushing the last bullet into place and snapping shut the cylinder. He took aim, only in time to see the monster's head fly off, and its body drop to the tiles. Miss Furnival flicked dark ichor from her blade, and nodded grimly to Jim.

'Shoot them in the head, cut their throats, or burn them, Captain Denny.' With those words, she raced to the policemen, only one of whom still fought wildly against the two beasts. The other was trampled underfoot in a spreading pool of blood.

Marie plunged her knife into the base of a monster's skull. Her blade stuck fast, and was plucked from her grasp as the creature fell. Despite the American's intervention, the constable was overcome by the second ghoul. The creature bit deep into his throat, and was bathed in arterial spray. The constable gargled a hideous, wet scream.

Jim leapt forward, this time making no mistake; he placed the barrel of his gun to the creature's temple and squeezed the trigger, ending its feasting instantly.

Jim looked remorsefully to the policeman, who was still kicking involuntarily against his slain attackers. A banging noise drew Jim's attention towards the door. Dakin was flinging himself at it desperately, crying, 'It won't budge. Oh, God. It won't move. We're trapped.'

'Stand down, lad. It's over.'

'Captain...' Marie interrupted, her voice very quiet. 'Best help him get that door open.'

'What? I... oh.' Jim turned to the antechamber by which they had entered. At least five pairs of eyes gleamed hungrily from the darkness.

Jim pulled the young constable aside and fired twice at the lock. He opened the door with a sharp kick, and shoved the lad through it. Whatever danger lay ahead, Jim felt it could be no worse than being eaten alive.

'Smithy...' the constable said, feebly.

Jim looked back towards the dying policeman on the mortuary floor, but was himself pushed through the door by Marie.

'Leave him, he's dead,' she said. She fired into the advancing pack of ghouls, which seemed only to intensify their snarls and howls.

Marie slammed the door shut behind her, and threw herself against it as the ghouls began to hammer at it. So forceful was their pummelling that she was almost thrown to the floor; but she held her ground, her strength surprising. Jim put his weight against the door too. 'Dakin!' he shouted. 'Find something to block this door. Do it, man!'

The young constable snapped from some reverie, and set about searching what appeared to be the foot of a dark stairwell. He returned quickly, dragging behind him a battered old cupboard, and Jim helped him heave it into place.

'Any more where that came from?' Jim asked, as the pounding at the door redoubled.

'Aye, sir. A stash under them stairs.'

'Then jump to it.'

Miss Furnival went to help. 'Did you see the brands upon their necks?' she called back to Jim.

'I was somewhat preoccupied.'

'I counted a nineteen, and a one hundred and twenty-two. What was the one you found on the ship? Nine hundred and something?'

Jim frowned, and set about dragging furniture towards the door.

'I'm just saying, Captain,' Marie continued, 'if those numbers are significant, we're facing an army of those things. And there's surely only one place such numbers could come from.'

Jim silenced her with a look as Dakin began to take an unhealthy interest in Marie's terrifying observation. Together, they piled furniture high against the door, until there was not a stick remaining, and their limbs were weak from the exertion. Monstrous cries echoed from beyond the door, which rattled in its frame from the assault of the ghouls.

'It won't hold them for ever,' Marie said. 'They'll pound the door until it gives, or until their bones splinter to dust. We have to press on.'

'Three of us in a sorry state,' Jim said, 'with one lantern between us. Armed Chinamen waiting ahead, and perhaps more of these things, too? I don't like these odds.'

'Then we'd best take extra care, Captain,' she said. 'Because we don't have a choice in the proceedings.'

SIX

'**S**tay close, Dakin. We'll get out of this yet.' Jim peered around the corner, and quickly sprang back. He looked into Dakin's eyes – the boy was terrified.

'How many?' Miss Furnival asked.

'Two, I think,' he whispered. 'Although it's too damned dark to be sure.'

Dakin looked down at his lantern, which had been shuttered to cast only the tiniest sliver of light. Jim shook his head at the young policeman – the last thing they needed was to draw attention to themselves.

'There's nowhere else to go,' Miss Furnival whispered. 'We have to go through them.'

Jim nodded, and flicked his derringer from his sleeve. Miss Furnival reached beneath her jacket and took out a concealed pistol, all wood and brass, and gently primed the crank-handle on its side until a flicker of bluish light danced across the sights. Dakin's eyes almost popped out of his head.

'Not a word of this, Dakin,' Jim said. 'Top secret government artefacts.'

Dakin said nothing. In truth, Jim was almost as surprised as the constable that Miss Furnival had a full-sized Tesla pistol. He had been under the impression that no working examples had been recovered. The order, it seemed, always had its secrets.

'On the count of three,' Jim said. 'One… two… three!'

Both Jim and Marie swung around the corner. Jim found himself at once face-to-face with a wasted, ghoulish creature, which was momentarily lit by the flickering blue light of Marie's pistol as she fired at something further along the corridor. A distant scream indicated that the American had hit her target. The creature before Jim hissed, its breath rancid, and sprang into Jim before he could fire. Jim slammed hard into the wall of the hospital corridor, his breath escaping his lungs with the impact.

Dakin cried out. His light illuminated Jim's monstrous assailant. The creature raised an outstretched claw, ready to strike. Jim's own arms were pinned to the floor, and he knew he faced death, before the beast jerked backwards, and he was free. Miss Furnival shoved the ghoul away. That was the second time she'd saved his life today.

'Don't just stand there, Dakin!' she snapped. 'What are you, a man or a mouse?'

Dakin dithered still. Jim struggled to stand.

The creature leapt to its feet. Marie uttered an unladylike profanity. Jim felt as though he were wading through treacle; a growing sense of fear that he was about to see Sir Arthur's niece meet a grisly end gripped him.

Miss Furnival sidestepped the ghoul's slashing claws nimbly, drawing her conventional revolver in one fluid movement. Before it could turn, she fired a round into its eye, dashing its brains over the wall.

'Please feel free to cut in any time, gentlemen,' she said, glaring at her compatriots.

'Chastise us later,' Jim said. 'We have bigger problems.'

A chorus of growls broke out from along the corridor. Black silhouettes, gangrel, ape-like, swayed in crouching posture, perhaps only twenty yards away. Six pairs of eyes blazed like coals.

'Oh, this is too much…' Miss Furnival moaned.

'Come on, back the way we came.' Jim tugged Miss Furnival's

sleeve, and shoved Dakin away.

'To where?' Marie snapped. 'Every way is blocked. The only path leads upwards, and we can hardly escape from there.'

'We have no choice,' Jim retorted, dragging Marie along with him. 'We'll run out of ammunition before we kill them.'

'Speak for yourself…' Miss Furnival muttered, but relented regardless, picking up the pace as they raced back the way they had come. Dakin jogged ahead of them with the swaying light, following orders out of pure dumb compliance. 'Captain Denny, do you not think we're being… herded?' Marie asked.

'Who knows?'

'These creatures aren't normally so hesitant. Something is controlling these last ones – they're holding back.'

'That's good!' Jim tugged at Dakin's sleeve to direct him left down the passage towards the stairwell. He swore he saw another pair of ghoulish eyes for a second, waiting in the dark.

'How?'

'If they wanted us dead, they'd have let the beasts take us. If they're keeping us alive, it's for a reason.'

'That's what I'm afraid of,' she muttered.

They emerged onto the first-floor landing, in time to hear a tremendous crash, and a cacophonous screeching sound like a pack of apes was loose nearby. Dark shapes moved in the void below them.

'Up!' yelled Jim, dashing up the stairs two at a time.

The door at the top of the next flight was blocked by debris. Jim scrambled over piles of bricks and splintered wood, before helping Marie over. Dakin came next, almost falling in a panic when he heard the grunts and growls from below them.

'Good man,' Jim said, struggling to find words of encouragement to keep the lad's mind off his fear. 'Now come on, and hold that light steady. We won't get far without you.'

'Yes, sir; right, sir.' They were the first words he'd spoken for some time. Jim took that as some small progress.

They ran up another winding stair, pausing only at the sound of a loud metallic clang, and the ominous reverberation of the metal bars that encased the stairwell. Jim bade Dakin hang the lantern through the bars, and peered over cautiously to see a pair of wiry, pale arms clinging to the rails just a few yards below them. A grotesque, half-rotted face leered into view, teeth champing within an exposed jaw.

Jim only quickened his ascent. At the top of the next flight, the door was ajar. Beyond that was a short set of stairs leading to a heavy-looking door, chained and bolted. Jim presumed that was an attic, or even the roof – he did not want to be cornered there. At least on a main hospital floor there was a chance of another way out; a second stairway, an emergency exit. Clinging to that thought, he barged through the door, emerging into a single long corridor, littered with detritus, and cold as the grave. But that was not what made Jim shiver.

Near the end of the corridor, a pair of green Chinese lanterns blazed either side of a doorway.

'Like I said,' Marie Furnival purred in his ear. 'A trap.'

There was no way to bar the door behind them, and so Jim set off without reply, though cautiously. There was no sign of movement; no alcoves or junctions in which an enemy could hide. Jim passed two doors, both of which he tried, and both of which were locked. He wondered if their enemies had inhabited this building for long; whether they had keys to all the doors and might be lying in wait. He gripped his gun a little tighter.

Marie cranked her Tesla pistol. 'This is good for one more shot,' she said.

'Is that all?' Jim asked.

'This is practically a museum artefact. Unless you can find a certain Mr Tesla to make us new weapons – the *other* Tesla, I mean – this is the best I have.'

Jim nodded. He hadn't fired his derringer, and so he also had a charge remaining. It took too long to prepare in a prolonged firefight, but Jim had always found that most enemies were too afraid to continue a battle once he'd revealed the ace up his sleeve. Most enemies, however, were mere mortals.

They reached the paper lanterns, which they now saw were adorned with Chinese characters, peculiar to the House of Zhengming – the lair of the Artist, burned to the ground nearly three years prior, its proprietor put to the sword by John Hardwick.

Jim pushed at the door, which swung open easily, revealing not another darkened chamber, but what looked at first glance like rows of theatre seating, bathed in a rich crimson light as though a magic show was about to start.

Jim slipped into the room silently, sweeping his pistol about. The pretension of stealth and caution at least made him feel better, although he knew it was too late for all that. Marie followed. He felt the press of her back against his, and they moved as one along a narrow aisle, at the uppermost level of a medical lecture theatre.

The room was large and octagonal, with ten or so tiers of wooden pews sweeping around most of the upper space, separated by two narrow stairways that plunged steeply towards the circular stage below. Red paper lanterns hung overhead on long chains, bathing the chamber in a slaughterhouse hue, and singularly failing to illuminate the darkest corners, or the yawning, exposed rafters above, providing ample hiding places for crawling, scuttling ghouls.

The only exit from the room was below – past the staging area, in which an arrangement of objects were illuminated in the ruby light.

There was an operating table, which could once have been used by surgeons to dissect corpses in front of watching students. Now, it was laid out with several items, indistinct in the red glow. Behind the table, standing upon tall easels in a semi-circle, were five canvases – paintings of some dark and shadowy type – and these gave James Denny more cause for alarm than whatever lay on the table.

The central canvas was covered in a dustsheet. Jim kept his eyes fixed on it as he and Miss Furnival moved cautiously towards the nearest stairs; he leading the way, she covering his back.

'Dakin,' Miss Furnival hissed. 'Get in here.'

Jim heard tentative footsteps behind him, confirming that the policeman had followed the American's orders.

'I can't see anyone, but that doesn't mean they aren't here,' Marie whispered in Jim's ear. 'Ghouls can move unheard and unseen if they wish. Or if they're commanded to. And why the hell haven't the ones chasing us arrived yet?'

'As you said, they've forced us into a trap. I think we're being invited to look at that table down there.'

Miss Furnival peered over Jim's shoulder. 'And then what?' she asked.

'Then I suppose they'll either set us free, catch us, or kill us.'

'Wh... what?' Dakin quailed. Marie shushed him at once.

Jim led the way down the stairs, wincing as his boots crunched on brick dust and broken glass, his eyes darting to every shadow that slid across the walls in the flicker of blood-red lanterns.

When they reached the floor, Miss Furnival at once darted around the back of the canvases, gun raised, in case anyone lurked there. Satisfied, she rushed to the doors, rattling the handles futilely.

'Locked,' she said, returning to Jim's side.

Jim examined the operating table which, to his distaste, was stained with blood, not altogether dry enough to be old. He could smell its iron tang in the theatre's stale air.

The objects were neatly arranged. A small, corked glass phial of etherium stood upright in the centre of the table. On one side of it was a pile of papers and folios. On the other side of the phial was a cardboard box, mottled with blooms of black mould. At the far end of the table was a Tesla pistol, the exact type of which Jim could not recall seeing before. It was sleeker than Marie's, with a long silver barrel inscribed with ornate patterning. The loading capacity was larger, and the crank-handle had been replaced by a simple switch. Only the wooden body of the gun and the tiny coils, sitting flush with the sights, marked it out as a Tesla pistol at all. Marie went straight to it, snatching it up.

'Impossible!' she gasped.

'What?'

'This was... I mean, I haven't seen its like.'

She composed herself quickly enough, but Jim knew when someone was hiding information from him; he'd been in this game too long.

'Why would you have?'

'I've just... seen a fair few of these. Cherleten provides them for me; this looks more advanced than the ones we have.'

'Can you use it?' Jim asked.

'No – the priming cylinders are missing. The one in my pistol wouldn't fit.'

'You seem awfully sure of that.'

'I know my guns, Captain.'

Another lie. She could keep her secrets for now – he was used to that too, in Cherleten's employ. He shrugged, and examined the papers. 'Shipping manifests,' he mused. 'Good lord... this top one is the *Glarus*. Here... crates of lace, all paid for. Destinations... Oh no.' Jim sifted through the other papers with increasing alarm.

'What is it?' Miss Furnival asked.

'All of these manifests are dated this year. Dozens of ships, to ports all over Europe. Hundreds of crates.'

'Crates of what?'

'It has to be etherium. This is beyond anything I could have guessed. I thought we were curtailing the smuggling rings, but now...'

'Captain, compose yourself. This could easily be a fabrication meant to rattle us. Where would that amount of etherium even come from? Until our people have verified the information here, we can't get ahead of ourselves.' Miss Furnival placed her hands on the box lid. 'You don't suppose this is booby-trapped?'

'This is an elaborate show just to blow us up now, don't you think?'

'There are worse traps than explosives.'

'Unless you have a better suggestion… on the count of three?'

Miss Furnival opened the flaps of the box. 'Enough with your counts,' she said.

Jim flinched involuntarily. Miss Furnival stepped back, jaw clenched. Jim peered into the box.

The blood on the table was from the box. Or perhaps from the procedure that had created the box's contents.

A head.

Jim held out a hand automatically, to prevent Dakin from idling over to look. Swallowing bile and holding his breath, he forced himself to look at the head, which already crawled with maggots.

'Whittock,' he croaked through a dry throat.

'You know him?'

Jim nodded. 'Another of Hardwick's men. God, I only saw him a month ago…'

'This is starting to seem personal,' Miss Furnival said. 'And not for you or I.'

'You say that, but I'm Hardwick's man too, I suppose,' Jim said, closing the box gingerly, very glad he was wearing gloves. 'I fought with him at London Bridge. I was his friend.'

'Was?'

'A story for another time, if I live long enough to tell it. These paintings…'

Miss Furnival did Jim the courtesy of not pressing him. Instead, she squinted at the paintings, then went to the other side of the table to study them more closely.

The four small canvases were painted in different styles, as though not all by the same hand. Three were cityscapes – Jim recognised Paris and Moscow. The third he could not immediately identify until Marie whispered aloud, 'New York.'

The American looked a shade paler, perhaps queasy at the discovery of the decapitated Sergeant Whittock; perhaps ill at the sight of a city from her homeland depicted in such a horrific way. For all three cities were in flames – buildings toppled, citizens dying in streets of blood. Strange creatures poured into the streets in an endless procession of twisted forms. Legs ended in cantering hoofs or bloodied stumps; backs were hunched, or winged; faces ended in porcine snouts, or jutting jaws, with tusks or horns or tentacles where mouths should be. These creatures, bestial and demonic, cavorted amongst panic-stricken men and women, tearing them apart, torturing them like the very devils of hell.

Jim tore his eyes from the scene, though he could still see the creatures clearly in his mind. He collected himself, and nudged Dakin to hold up the light. It was not a trick of the Chinese lanterns – in all three of the pictures, from the most abstract to the most masterful, the sky was painted red. Indeed, it appeared to burn. Jim had seen that phenomenon once before, but not in any painting. He tried to swallow, but no moisture would come to his throat.

The fourth canvas was an enigma; it meant nothing at all to Jim, and Marie offered no comment. It was a black piece, almost Rembrandt-like in its use of light amidst utter darkness. Silvery cobwebs drew the eyes to the blazing eyes of an enormous, bloated spider, which was half-hidden in shadows. The spider sunk its fangs into a beauteous maiden, tangled in webs, her face stricken with… no, not terror, but ecstasy. Her yellow dress was dotted with blood – both her own, and the spider's, which bled from a great wound in its belly.

The painting was disturbing, and Jim stepped past it quickly, and yanked the sheet from the largest canvas. His eyes widened as he took in the painting beneath. The most realistic of all. A masterpiece of the grotesque.

London, in ruins, like the others. St Paul's burned. Violet-eyed vampires battled hunchbacked demons in the streets. Madmen tore at their own faces, eyes streaming with blood. The sky blazed red, the people died. And over it all, taking up perhaps three-quarters of the tall canvas, was a shadow, tentacular and yet claw-like, glistening and yet insubstantial, tearing gaping wounds in the burning firmament. Jim could almost hear it, picking, clawing, scratching in his mind. And then he realised he was touching a hand to his head, because he could hear it. And Marie Furnival heard it too. Both hands were clapped to her ears. She trembled like a child afraid of the monster beneath the bed.

She, too, had seen it.

Then the Chinese lanterns guttered, and died. The room became dark, save for Dakin's lantern.

Footsteps thudded rapidly in the gallery above the agents, from where they had entered; someone ran from one end of the aisle to the other. Laughter echoed around the room – a woman's laugh, cold and mocking.

Dakin swung the lantern this way and that, jumping at the shadows it cast. Jim expected to see those cruel violet eyes reflected in the light, but saw nothing but the thick grey darkness.

'Show yourself!' Jim called out.

Footsteps again, nearer. Perhaps from a lower tier.

Jim snatched the lantern from Dakin's grasp and shone it in the direction of the sound. A shadow moved swiftly away from the light – a swish of a dress or cape, perhaps; another laugh. This time it was followed by the report of Marie's revolver. Wood splintered as her shot struck the back of a pew; all fell silent again.

'That is no way to treat your host.' The cool, sardonic voice came seemingly from all around the auditorium. Jim panned the hooded lantern slowly, but could not fix upon the speaker's location.

'Who are you?' Jim shouted.

'Irrelevant. All you need to know is whom I represent.'

Jim detected the merest hint of an accent; he was certain she was no Englishwoman. Perhaps another celestial, although he fancied not. European? 'And who is that?' he asked.

'You know. The Artist has returned from the grave, bringing word of things seen in the afterlife. Bringing grim tidings for Apollo Lycea.'

Jim's blood ran cold. Yet there was something alluring, almost mesmerising about the voice. Jim felt his hand slacken on his gun, his arm lowering the weapon; he checked himself at once, as though waking from a daydream.

'The Artist's visions are displayed behind you,' the voice went on, now in another part of the room. Jim tracked it with the light, but saw nothing in its beam. 'The curse of the Otherside threatens to consume the world. The Order thinks it alone opposes this threat, but it is wrong. Britain's enemies are arming themselves against the coming storm. They gather etherium harvested from refugees, and amass weaponry to rival the power of your so-called "armoury". The Order thinks it has the ultimate weapon – a living weapon – but the greatest nations on earth are in secret developing their own. The girl denies the truth of it, but you know of what I speak, don't you, Captain James Denny?'

'What's she talking about?' Marie whispered. She had moved close to Jim's side.

'Tell her, Captain. Tell her about the Nightwatch.'

Jim sensed Marie tense, palpably.

Soft, mocking laughter. 'Great Britain has set foot on a dangerous path, to navigate the seas of prophecy, the skeins of fate. And to achieve this goal, to win the battle for intelligence, they resort to slavery, as surely as the traders of a hundred years past enslaved all they encountered. And in their arrogance, they think they are alone, but they are not. France, Russia, Austria and America are developing their own forms of the Nightwatch. Others are not far behind. They have no idea that the pursuit of these goals could damn the world to hell. The Artist has seen the possible outcomes. The Artist knows the danger of etherium, and has seen where it will lead.'

'Does he not supply the etherium?' Jim snapped. 'These manifests suggest that the House of Zhengming now deals in more than just opium.'

'The result would be the same. The Artist sees no harm in profiting from what is inevitable.'

'No harm? If the world is dragged to hell, as you say, will it not be in Tsun Pen's name?'

'Do not speak that name!' Footsteps thudded again. Marie aimed in their direction, but Jim stayed her hand.

'Why? He's returned, has he not?' Jim called.

There was a pause, and then the soft tones returned. 'The Artist wishes it known that there is still time to save this world from sharing the fate of the Otherside. It is foretold. But there is a price.'

'There always is. But he was defeated before, he'll be defeated again. He will receive not a penny from the Order.'

Laughter rang out from every shadow. 'Oh, the Artist is not interested in money. But you will want to pay this price before the end. The petty psychics in Furnival's laboratories are no match for the Artist's talents.'

'Liar!' Marie shouted.

'You, of all people, should be careful whom you accuse of lying. Or perhaps you can no longer distinguish the truth from the lie. You would not be the first. Perhaps it hurts too much... You have my sympathy, dear girl.'

'What's she talking about?' Jim whispered. Marie gave no reply.

'Know this, agents of the Crown: your efforts so far have been in vain. The veil thins daily, and the horrors of the Rift are closer to this world than even your Nightwatch could ever predict. How could they? They are a part of the sickness that threatens to tip all you hold dear into madness, and death, and fire. Only the Artist can restore balance to the world. Only the Artist can save you.'

'So what does he want?'

'Apollo Lycea will be contacted in good time. The Artist's terms will be made clear then. For now, take what scraps you can carry from the Artist's table, and go.'

At those words, the doors behind the companions clicked softly open.

'You will be sure to give the Artist's regards to your friend Hardwick,' the voice added. 'Now, I advise you not to tarry, for I cannot control these servants indefinitely.'

Jim was about to ask about Hardwick, when he heard a door creak open – the one atop the stairs. Scratching and shuffling noises sounded above; bumping and thudding along the upper tier.

'Get everything you can carry,' Jim hissed to Marie. 'Dakin, help her.'

He shone the light around as the others began gathering the objects from the table. The light reflected dozens of beady purple eyes. They blinked from every corner, blazed from the rafters overhead.

A woman's voice whispered in his ear, cold and crisp as a winter's breeze through a graveyard.

'Run.'

Jim turned to see only darkness beside him, but the word triggered movement all around. The clattering and thudding of a press of ghouls loping down the stairs; the scratching of claws as more of them clambered over wooden pews. Growls and hisses echoed around the chamber.

'Go!' Jim shouted. 'Go now!'

They threw themselves through the door, and raced down long, winding corridors as baying and howling rose up behind them. They ran until they saw a shaft of daylight ahead, probing feebly through grimy glass. None of them paused to look back at the things upon their heels.

Moments later, Jim, Marie and Dakin tumbled through a door, into a walled courtyard. Dakin tripped and fell. Marie dropped armfuls of papers. The phial of etherium smashed on a mossy flagstone.

Jim turned and aimed his gun at the doors behind them, but nothing came through. He flung the door open and trained his weapon along the corridor. It was still and quiet.

Around them, dark broken windows looked down upon the courtyard. Pigeons fluttered between the brown-stone hospital buildings, disturbed for perhaps the first time in years. Jim finally allowed himself to catch his breath.

'We need to get out of here,' he said. 'But first... Constable Dakin, you're going to round up a bloody army of policemen, heavily armed, and come back here. Tell them about your comrades. Tell them about Craddock. I want them angry, and in numbers, do you hear? Exterminate anything you find in this hospital, and secure those paintings. And then, Miss Furnival, you and I are going to have a long talk.'

SEVEN

Jim followed Marie into an empty lounge at the Apollonian Club. The American had said nothing on the journey – indeed, she had resisted all attempts at conversation – but had palpably seethed the whole way. Now she stormed across the room, turning on her heels, rumpling the Turkish rug beneath her feet.

'What did she mean about the Nightwatch?' Marie Furnival's eyes blazed, her cheeks blushed hot.

Jim, taken aback by the woman's sudden fury, shoved the door closed.

'I'll ask the questions, I think,' Jim said, firmly.

'The hell you will!' The more angry she grew, the less ladylike she sounded; the more American. 'What's this about the Nightwatch? Is it true? Are you and my uncle in cahoots?'

Miss Furnival stepped towards Jim, her face close to his. He grabbed her firmly by the shoulders just in case she was tempted to strike him.

'I advise you to ask your uncle in regards to confidential information,' he said. 'But perhaps you'd care to explain the things you have clearly withheld from me. Like where exactly you came from, for a start.'

Miss Furnival shrugged Jim off angrily, and took a step

backwards. 'Don't lay your hands on me, sir,' she seethed. 'Remember the last time?'

'Quite. I remember how surprised I was that a young woman had become so accomplished in the martial arts. How surprised I was that a young woman was accepted into the Order, on even an honorary basis. And, of course, how surprised I was at your knowledge of these "ghouls" and "vampires". You seem to have trained for a long time to fight them, seeing as how the first time you encountered them was three years ago, after the Battle of the Thames.'

'You don't know what you're talking about.'

'Really?' Jim raised an eyebrow. 'Not many agents have seen the Otherside for themselves, or know the effect it can have on a person. That... thing in the sky. The way it calls to you, calls to your very soul. But you've seen it, madam. I would stake my oath on it. Yet there were no female agents back in '90, and no one but my men could have crossed over during that fight. So when did you see the shadow? When did you see the sky that burned?'

'You're talking like a fool. Perhaps you are unmanned, Captain Denny. The Artist's doxy got you rattled?'

'On the contrary, I think I see things most clearly now. This is twice I've been led into a trap, Miss Furnival, despite all the Order's intelligence.'

'And where did this "intelligence" come from, Captain Denny?' Marie snapped. 'That woman back there said you've been following the Nightwatch. I ask you again: is my uncle involved in this madness?'

'Oh, I rather think you already know the answer to that.'

'What do you mean?'

'I mean you have unprecedented access to a senior member of Apollo Lycea. It's absurd that you did not know, or even suspect that Sir Arthur was running the Nightwatch. That you could have learned about the Nightwatch's predictions, and planned accordingly, certainly gives me great cause for concern.'

'What?' Miss Furnival faltered. 'Are you suggesting that I tried to sabotage the mission?'

'I never said "sabotage", Miss Furnival. But I am suggesting that you are not who you appear. That you are one of *them*.'

Marie Furnival's eyes narrowed. She made to speak, but apparently thought better of it.

'I shall take your silence as an admission of guilt. I do not know whether your uncle is party to this deception, but I plan to find out. For now, Miss Furnival, you will come with me. I am arresting you in –'

'You certainly are not, Captain Denny.' A stern voice from behind Jim cut him short. Jim turned to see Lord Cherleten standing in the doorway. 'And keep your voices down; this is a club room. There are ordinary members passing by regularly – I should not have to remind you of our need for discretion.'

'Sir,' Jim nodded. Miss Furnival said nothing.

'Miss Furnival,' Lord Cherleten said, 'kindly return your weapons to the armoury, and then repair to the ladies' waiting room. And you should know better, Captain Denny. Make yourself presentable, man. You're in the Apollonian Club, not some Hackney chop-house. Black tie. Both of you will meet me and Sir Toby in his office in half an hour, and there will be no repeat of your outbursts here, do I make myself clear? Good. You are dismissed.'

When Sir Toby Fitzwilliam was displeased – which seemed to Jim to be most of the time – the ticking of the clock in his office felt like some form of torture. Why a man would have a clock so loud was beyond Jim. It certainly did not feel conducive to quiet contemplation. Jim could think of nothing but the clock, in fact, until Sir Toby stopped writing and gave him a fixed stare.

'Where are the paintings now?' Sir Toby asked. It was not the first question Jim had expected after recounting the details of the morning's exploits.

'The police have orders to deliver them to St Katharine, sir.'

'Do they? And you thought it wise to leave the constabulary to this task?'

'When I left, Sir Toby, there were almost fifty constables making a search of the hospital, although the... creatures... were gone. I believed that was more than enough men to secure the evidence.'

Sir Toby stood bolt upright, and pounded his fist upon the desk. 'And what if I told you, Captain, that those paintings, which are of singular import to the Crown, were stolen shortly after leaving the hospital?'

'Stolen? How? By whom?' Jim had expected neither the news nor the outburst, and his stomach tied itself in knots.

'By whom, we know not. How? A simple matter of a hold-up, as Miss Furnival might say. Highway robbery, here in London. Three of the constabulary, whom you purport to care so much about, slain in cold blood for a cargo that you should have secured personally. Shall I tell you their names?'

Jim rubbed his face with a trembling hand.

'Constable Herbert Briggs,' Sir Toby went on, reading from his notes. 'Constable Jacob Leese; Constable Robert Dakin.'

Jim could hardly breathe. Was this what he had kept Dakin alive for? To survive a hellish threat only to meet a sudden end in the company of his fellows...

'If that were not enough, Captain, you tell us "almost fifty" common policemen saw the evidence in that room, because you found the task of delivering it beneath you. Or perhaps you deemed an unseemly argument in the first-floor lounge of greater import?'

'That's not what –'

Jim stopped short as Sir Toby's brow furrowed. He cursed inwardly; he had been so intent on sending men back into the hospital to kill whatever lurked there, and, he had to admit, on saying his piece to Marie Furnival, that he'd quite overlooked normal procedure. That mistake had borne a greater cost than he could have imagined.

'And then there is the etherium recovered from the docks,' Sir Toby said. 'Also now in the hands of Scotland Yard.'

'Sir, I am sorry. Truly sorry,' Jim said. He could barely look the Lord Justice in the eye.

Sir Toby sank back into his chair, and sighed. His expression of anger turned to one of bitter disappointment, which Jim found worse still. 'What is done is done. This mishap could prove costly, but it is beyond our control.' His eyes flicked briefly to the door behind Jim and Miss Furnival. Jim glanced over his shoulder and saw a club steward nod curtly, and slip from the room. The man wasn't merely a steward, of course, but one of the Order's trusted servants. Jim expected he was going to arrange for the safe return of the etherium, and again cursed his own sloppiness.

'Also beyond our control,' Sir Toby went on, 'is the regulation of the black market in Otherside artefacts. If what this mysterious woman told you is true, we have enemies across the globe arming themselves with technology they cannot possibly understand.'

'Do any of us understand it?' Lord Cherleten scoffed. 'Even Sir Arthur's great experiment is a leap into the unknown; its results are too unpredictable, as has now been proven.'

'The results are open to interpretation,' Sir Arthur said. It was the first time he had spoken; his voice was quiet. Jim fancied that the baronet stared very deliberately into the middle distance, scrupulously avoiding the gaze of his niece, who glared at him intently. 'If there is a fault with the intelligence received from the subjects, perhaps the fault is mine. It does not mean the experiment is a failure.'

'Uncle!' Miss Furnival gasped, and then collected herself at once as all eyes turned to her. 'It is just… I'm sorry. I have explained my feelings about the Nightwatch previously.'

'And we do not need to hear your objections again,' Lord Cherleten said. 'We listened, and we chose to follow a different course from the one you would advise, as is our right. These are desperate times, my dear, and they call for desperate measures.'

'These measures aren't merely desperate,' Miss Furnival said coolly. 'They're foolhardy. And dangerous.'

Cherleten met the American's gaze, and smirked in his usual, infuriating manner.

'Might I say something?' Jim asked. Now everyone looked at him, and he squirmed in his seat.

'Do enlighten us,' said Cherleten.

'It seems to me that the intelligence we have received both for this morning's assignment and the raid on the *Glarus* was not just incorrect, but deliberately false. I believe we have been manipulated into a trap.'

'A serious allegation, Captain,' said Sir Toby. 'But, under the circumstances, I would hear your theory.'

'When I saw the Nightwatch with my own eyes, there seemed to be no true consensus between the subjects. As Sir Arthur has told us, their predictions must be interpreted, and I am sure that there is no finer mind in England to undertake such a task. However, if there is a viper in the nest, then the Nightwatch would surely be the best place to strike. We are becoming reliant on intelligence from esoteric sources, it seems. It is possible, given all that we know, that Tsun Pen may be able to manipulate the Nightwatch from afar, but it is far more likely – in my view – that the interference comes from a source closer to home.'

'Just come out and say it!' Marie snapped. Jim faced her, and saw her face flushed, her eyes like coals.

'Yes, Captain Denny, let's clear the air,' Cherleten said. 'You were ready to arrest the lady when I saw you upstairs. I assume that's what all of this is about.'

'It is, my lord,' Jim said.

He turned away from Miss Furnival; he hardly knew the girl, but there was enough anger and indignation in her eyes to make him doubt his conclusions already. Jim took a breath – he knew better than most how convincing the Othersiders could be; how they could play a role so well it was impossible to unpick the truth from the lie. He remembered Ambrose Hanlocke. Jim had never liked the rogue, but never in a million years would he have suspected Hanlocke of being an Othersider. There was another, too, in Jim's past, whom he did not wish to think about, even now. Jim steeled himself for the inevitable furore he was about to cause.

'Miss Furnival is not who she claims. Perhaps she truly is the niece of Sir Arthur, but not the real niece. I suggest to you, gentlemen, that she is an Otherside agent, perhaps the last vestige of our counterparts still operating in London for some unknown ends.'

Jim's great revelation was met with stony silence. There was no incredulity, no outrage, and no resistance from Miss Furnival. Only Cherleten looked anything but nonplussed, his lips twitching as though he struggled to keep his familiar smirk from becoming outright mockery.

'Captain Denny,' Sir Toby said, after an unbearable delay. 'Perhaps it was remiss of us to keep you ignorant of all the facts – not that it is our custom to furnish mere field agents with the private details of one another. What if I told you that your discovery is a surprise only to yourself? Miss Furnival's history is known to us, and as such, her character is vouched for by us.'

'Sir? I... You mean to say we have Othersiders in our midst?' Jim felt his colour rise. Though he'd had many encounters with Sir Toby and Lord Cherleten that had left him exasperated, this was the first time he had been truly angered by it.

'Just one, actually,' Sir Toby replied. 'Miss Furnival's history is quite unique amongst those from the other universe that we have encountered. She is not one of those agents you battled against three years ago. Indeed, Miss Furnival was opposed to them then, as she is now.'

Jim looked to Miss Furnival, who glared at him defiantly, and then to Sir Arthur, who avoided his gaze entirely.

'Don't look so confused, Captain Denny,' Lord Cherleten said, almost coughing with laughter. 'Sir Arthur's one of us, eh! The Furnivals who emigrated to the United States never had a daughter – but on the Otherside, they had two, Miss Furnival being the younger and sprightlier of them. You see?'

'No, Lord Cherleten, I do not.' Jim stood. 'I have no reason to doubt any of you gentlemen, but I have never encountered an Othersider who could be trusted. They have spent their lives learning how to infiltrate us... Even if Miss Furnival has no superiors to report to on the Otherside, that does not make her trustworthy.'

'Explain yourself,' said Sir Toby. 'And take my advice: you had better make it good. You are on thin ice.'

'It is clear in the short time that I have known her that Miss Furnival mistrusts – no, hates – the very idea of the Nightwatch. I believe that she would do anything to put a stop to the experiment.'

'That's true,' Miss Furnival interjected, her words hot and angry. 'But I didn't even know about the experiment until now, not for sure. I didn't think anyone here would be fool enough to do it.'

'That's quite enough, Miss Furnival,' Sir Toby said. 'You shall have your chance – let Captain Denny say his piece.'

'Thank you, Sir Toby,' Jim said. 'Miss Furnival may claim she knew nothing about the Nightwatch, but she seems privy to other secrets ostensibly known only to Sir Arthur, so it seems reasonable to assume she also discovered this one.'

'A bold claim,' Sir Arthur interrupted.

'Indeed it is,' said Sir Toby. 'What proof do you have that Miss Furnival has had access to confidential information?'

'No proof, Sir Toby, except the confession from her own lips.'

'She told you this?'

'She did. Miss Furnival met me the evening of Saturday last, and told me as much.'

'Why, you snake!' Marie Furnival leapt to her feet, and glowered at the side of Jim's head. He did not meet her gaze this time. 'To think I saved your life today.'

'Sit down!' Sir Toby snapped.

'Sit down be damned,' she snarled. 'The cat's out of the bag now; no point playing these games any more. I'm not some delicate English rose to be ordered around.'

Sir Toby rose slowly, placing his fists upon the leather top of his desk as he leaned forward. 'No, you certainly are not,' he said. 'But in this place, you will do me the common decency of obeying my command, or I shall have you removed.'

'I am no traitor, to my people or to yours,' Miss Furnival said, remaining on her feet. 'I've fought my own battles in my own way while the war was raging. If anyone should feel betrayed, it's me.'

'How so?' Jim asked, facing the girl at last.

'Because I've been lied to by a man I treated as blood kin. Who *is* blood kin, in a roundabout sort of way.' She turned to Sir Arthur. 'Uncle, you can't pursue these experiments with the Nightwatch. You'll damn us all.'

'The proper measures are in place to prevent any repeat of what happened on the Otherside,' Sir Arthur said.

There was a tremor to his voice; Jim could not work out if the baronet was afraid of his niece, or ashamed at what he had done.

'The measures won't be enough,' she said. 'I warned you... and you lied to me.'

'Sir Toby,' Jim said, still unconvinced. 'Miss Furnival does not deny gathering classified information from her uncle, or attempting to discuss that information with me outside the permitted disclosure of an assignment. Ambrose Hanlocke was an agent here for six years, with no one realising his true nature... can we really be sure that Miss Furnival is to be trusted? She probably understands the Nightwatch better than Sir Arthur, or any of our best scientists. It would be easy for her to falsify –'

The slap took Jim by surprise, so hard and sharp that he staggered sideways. He turned to see tears in Miss Furnival's eyes, her cheeks rose-pink with ire.

'You cur,' she snarled.

Sir Arthur and Lord Cherleten were soon on their feet, each with hands on Miss Furnival's arms, though not roughly.

'I...' Jim started. 'It's alright, gentlemen. Time will tell whether or not I deserved that.'

'Damn right you deserved it,' the woman scowled.

'Well, well,' mocked Cherleten. 'Striking an officer. If this was the army she'd be up for court martial, right, Captain Denny? It is unheard of in these hallowed halls for sure... Perhaps we should place the girl under arrest after all. I have cells in the armoury that could hold her.'

'This is no time for jests, Lord Cherleten,' Sir Toby said, appearing exasperated at the turn proceedings had taken.

'Only half a jest, Sir Toby.'

'Miss Furnival,' Sir Toby said sternly. 'A serious allegation has been made against you, and must be investigated. Despite my learned colleague's opinion, you will not be placed under arrest, given your exemplary record in service to the Crown. However, I ask that you return home with Sir Arthur and remain there. Consider it confinement if you will, but for your own good. Sir Arthur – you shall see to it that Miss Furnival does not wander before we have the opportunity to speak further.'

'I will, Sir Toby.'

'Very good.'

Miss Furnival shrugged Sir Arthur and Lord Cherleten away, and wiped her eyes on her sleeve. With no further word, she allowed Sir Arthur to guide her gently from the room.

Only when she had gone were Lord Cherleten and Sir Toby seated once more.

'Sit down, Captain Denny,' Sir Toby said, his tone one of supreme annoyance. 'Now, I shall say this to you but once, so pay attention. You are an agent of Apollo Lycea, and a man of honour, and as such we shall investigate your claims thoroughly and by the fullest extent of the rules of the Order. But, and I say this as fair warning, I do not believe for one moment that Miss Furnival is guilty of the accusations you have levelled at her.'

'But –'

'I told you to pay attention, Captain, and that means you will listen without interrupting.'

'Yes, sir. Sorry, sir.'

'Shall I tell you how Miss Furnival came to be in our employ? While the Othersiders were plotting to take over our world, Marie Furnival was fighting a war of her own. Not against us, but against these... vampires. She was trained as an agent by Apollo Lycea on the Otherside, but turned her back on the Order when she discovered that they themselves were making peace with the vampires. A step too far, in her eyes. You see, in her world, Sir Arthur Furnival was slain in a most brutal manner by one particular vampire, and Miss Furnival has been hunting that creature ever since. Ah, I can see this strikes a chord.

'As the Lazarus Gate opened, she came by intelligence to suggest that the monster had crossed to our side in secret, and so she followed. That creature, she believes, is still at large today, here, in our world. If there is any evidence to support the theory, it can be found in the nests of ghouls that on occasion spring up in the city.

'The girl turned herself over to her uncle almost as soon as she arrived. She has been interrogated by the army, studied by the finest alienists in London, tested by physicians. She has endured, Captain Denny, rather severe treatment, after which we could only ascertain that she told the truth. Eventually we gave her an assignment to test her loyalty, and ever since she has passed every such test. The only thing that would ever seem to shake her fealty to the Order is the matter of the Nightwatch. Thanks to you, that particular bugbear has been revealed, for good or ill.'

Once Jim was sure Sir Toby had finished, he ventured a reply. 'Sir, if my accusations prove false, I shall offer Miss Furnival a full and sincere apology.' He doubted his own mind now. The creeping sensation he felt rising from the pit of his stomach was, he was certain, shame. It was a feeling with which he was not unacquainted.

'At the very least,' Sir Toby scolded.

'But, might I say, it was not I who revealed Sir Arthur's experiment to her. Even when she asked me outright, sir, you have my word as a gentleman that I said nothing.'

'Ah. Tsun Pen – or, rather, his mysterious lackey.'

Jim nodded.

'Is there nothing else you remember that might help us to identify this woman?' Sir Toby asked.

'She had a foreign accent – not much of one. I could not even identify it, so I'd guess she's lived in England for a long time. I don't think she was from the Far East, sir, but beyond that I could not say.'

'One of the European enemies that she warned you about, perhaps? Russian?'

'Perhaps so. Come to think of it, yes, she could have been Russian.'

Sir Toby exchanged a strange glance with Cherleten.

'It would explain how she knew so much,' Jim went on, unsure what was passing between the aged spymasters. 'If Tsun Pen is now working with a foreign power, as suggested –'

'If Tsun Pen is alive at all,' Cherleten interrupted. 'We have not seen him. These paintings Denny saw could very easily be fabrications... Besides, it is very easy to make "predictions" when you have engineered what is about to happen, is it not? If the tong are arming Britain's rivals with etherium, then war becomes inevitable, not prophecy to be averted.'

'With all due respect, Lord Cherleten,' Jim replied, 'our encounters with Tsun Pen's men so far have seemed rather... personal.'

'As though he is taking revenge on his killers from beyond the grave?' Sir Toby asked.

'Something like that, sir, yes.'

'Not the Artist's style, if you ask me,' Cherleten scoffed. 'He never was one for vendettas – say what you like about Tsun Pen, but he always went after the biggest catch. Further evidence that it's not him, eh?'

Sir Toby stood, and paced across the floor, passing back and forth in front of the large window of the office. The carpet beneath the window was almost threadbare, so engrained was his habit. Lord Cherleten offered Jim the slightest of shrugs. At last Sir Toby spoke. 'What if it is not John Hardwick he is after, but me?' he asked.

'Sir?' Jim asked, uncertain whom Sir Toby was addressing.

'Nonsense!' Cherleten said. 'Denny, this does not leave this room, understand? Czar Alexander is not well disposed towards us at this present time. Russian assassins were involved in a sticky business here in England last year, and Sir Toby exposed them for it to the embassy. Sanctions were issued, heads rolled, so on and so forth. The czar made Sir Toby *persona non grata*, eh?' He chuckled, even at such serious business.

'But, sir,' Jim said, 'if this was a plot to rattle Sir Toby, why start with common soldiers? Surely they would go for Hardwick and be damned, if they even had reason to suspect that John meant...' he checked himself, 'that Sir Toby sponsored Colonel Hardwick.'

'There you go, Lord Justice,' Cherleten grinned. 'Told you Denny was just as good a detective as Hardwick. It's damned fortunate he doesn't go poking around learning all our secrets.'

Sir Toby pursed his lips in contemplation, ignoring Cherleten as was his custom. Finally, he spoke directly to Jim. 'I suppose there is no escaping what must be done, Captain Denny. Regardless of the enemy's target, it would seem that John Hardwick is in very real danger. After the murder of Lieutenant Bertrand, we sent a telegram to Colonel Hardwick to establish whether or not he was safe. We received no reply, but that is not unusual given his... shall we say, "lapsed" status? Now with the murder of poor Sergeant Whittock, we must force the issue. I have decided to heed Lord Cherleten's advice and send some men to bring Hardwick in, whether he's willing or not.'

'Returning John Hardwick to duty... is that wise?' Jim asked, tentatively.

Sir Toby raised a bushy eyebrow. 'It is what I have ordered, Captain Denny.'

'Very well, sir. But...' Jim hesitated. What he wanted to say filled him with dread. 'If it would enable me to make amends, even in part, for my lapse of judgment today, I would like to volunteer to fetch Colonel Hardwick personally. I believe I have the best chance to bring him in without any unpleasantness.'

'You sure about that?' Cherleten asked. 'Didn't you come to blows last time he was in London? Surprised you survived that one, eh!'

'I was once his friend. His only friend, some say. And it was I who discovered the deaths of his men. It is true, I... I have not spoken with Colonel Hardwick in some time. I should like to see that he is well.'

EIGHT

Marie ducked. The sailor's wild haymaker flew harmlessly over her head. She shoved the barrel of her revolver into the man's gut and pulled the trigger. Over the mayhem all around, no one heard. The man died with a look of surprise etched on his face.

Marie ran silently across the deck of the Russian cruiser *Varna*, dodging behind a capstan as a dozen sailors raced past her towards the forward guns. If they saw her, they paid her no heed. Risking discovery, Marie stood, and looked along the length of the deck to where the sailors now hurried.

Before them, London Bridge was in flames. Black smoke twisted into the air, the very mirror of the great shadow flickering against the red sky. Sparks flew from the Tesla-engineered power couplings that adorned every inch of the bridge. The amber glow of the Lazarus Gate flashed ominously. Something was very wrong.

Behind them, more ships of the flotilla drew perilously close as the invasion fleet slowed to a crawl. Marines opened fire skywards at tatter-winged Riftborn – those ragged, shadow-like carrion that had plagued the city this past decade. The creatures swooped low, encouraged by the sight of stricken ships and men drowning in the blood-coloured waters of the Thames.

The *Varna*'s engines groaned their last. The boards beneath Marie's feet juddered as the ship creaked to a dead stop. Men shouted. A foghorn blared.

To starboard, HMS *Aurora* careened into the supports of the bridge, deliberately crashing to avoid pushing through the failing portal. Tesla coils flashed bright. Dislodged by mast and spar, machinery fell from the arches of London Bridge onto the deck of the *Aurora*, drawing panicked screams. Not just machinery – people. Cadaverous psychics, withered husks of the Nightwatch, lashed to the infernal devices powering the gate, fell to their deaths. Marie winced. She thought of her uncle. If he had lived to see this day, he would likely be one of those unfortunates, for the time of free Majestics had long passed. The thought of Sir Arthur brought with it a surge of renewed vigour and purpose.

Through the fire and smoke beyond that vessel, Marie saw USS *Helen B Jackson* – half of it, at least, listing awkwardly as it sank. Howitzers roared, though she could not tell whose guns they were, or what they fired upon. Her heart came to her throat. She had never wanted any of this. She had argued against the madness of an invasion. And yet now, at the end, she could not bear to see it fail. Lazarus had called this the last throw of the dice; if that were truly the case, then Marie and everyone she knew were as good as dead.

But there was one aboard this ship who would die before she did. Marie would at least have that satisfaction. She swallowed her despair, and looked to the upper deck. If de Montfort was here, he would be in the control room with the captain.

Marie checked her pistol, and ran to the midsection. She took the iron-shod stairs to the control room two at a time. Reaching a narrow gantry, she raced along a short corridor towards a bulkhead door. As she approached, the door swung open. A man stepped out, puzzlement spreading across his heavyset face when he saw the slip of a girl before him. Marie did not hesitate. She cracked off a revolver round into the man's leg and hopped over his crumpling form, through the door to the control room.

A bearded captain confronted her, shouting something in Russian, quickly backing away when he saw Marie's pistol. Another man stood with his back to Marie, silhouetted in red light as he gazed from the porthole at the Lazarus Gate. Marie's heart lurched. He was tall and slender, crow-black hair hanging loose past his collar. Her hand tightened on the grip of her revolver.

'You speak English?' she demanded of the captain. The bearded man nodded. 'Good. I'm not here for you. I'm here for *him*. Stay out of my way.'

She took out a second weapon, her favoured Tesla pistol. Its ornate silver barrel gleamed in the red light, its mahogany handle reassuring in her hand. She flicked the switch, and the weapon hummed, tiny copper coils priming with energy. She aimed it at the dark man's back.

'De Montfort. It's taken me a while to find you. Turn around, so I can look you in the eye, you cowardly –'

The man turned before she could finish, and Marie's heart sank. He was *wampyr*, that much was certain, but it was not de Montfort. His features were broad, his nose hooked. His violet eyes gleamed from his olive-skinned face, not yet turned to the porcelain death-mask typical of his kind. So he was young – one of de Montfort's blasphemous creations, not as powerful as his first – Agent Hardwick – but dangerous enough. Probably some sycophant recruited to the vampire ranks purely to act as a decoy, or to fulfil a lucrative contract to the Russians. Most of the ships in the flotilla had a vampire on board, to protect against the Riftborn. It was the only thing they were good for.

'As you can see,' the vampire purred, his voice heavily accented with the promise of far Arabia, 'Lord de Montfort is not here. My name is Orsini.'

'I...' Marie faltered.

'My lord left a message for you, however,' the *wampyr* said with a smile.

'A message?' She had come close to finding de Montfort several times, but she had never been sure if her quarry was even aware of her existence.

For a second, she dropped her guard. In that second, the door behind her flew open, and someone barrelled into her. She twisted; her revolver went off, punching a hole in the viewport glass. Two Russian sailors wrestled with her, tearing the Tesla pistol from her grip. The captain joined the fray, wrenching her revolver from her, before grabbing a fistful of hair, yanking back her head.

'Witch!' he cried. 'On this day, when we see Lazarus fall and all hope destroyed, you dare raise arms against the Russian Empire?'

The vampire stepped forward, and the captain shrank back at his approach, as though he could not stand to be near the creature. The vampire peered into Marie's eyes. Her nostrils flared, assailed by the mingled smell of chemicals and sickly corruption.

'Lord de Montfort has already crossed over, child. His influence is great; he was first through the breach. Though this world falls to ruin, he goes now to bring the Iscariot Sanction to another universe. The mirror world will belong to our kind, as surely as this one belongs to the Rift. But as I said – he left a message for you. He asked me to tell you that your uncle died in agony, like a stuck pig, and the sacrifice of his blood was the only contribution of note he ever made to the world.'

Marie struggled, but to no avail. Two pairs of strong arms held her fast. That it should end like this, with de Montfort far beyond her reach, was the ultimate insult. She hung her head in despair.

'Are we done here?' the ship's captain growled. 'Throw the girl in the brig.'

'No,' the vampire said. 'Kill her.'

The captain looked reluctant, but nodded and cocked Marie's revolver. 'Madam, in the name of the Russian Empire I –'

A great bang cut him short, and the entire vessel shook with singular force. One of the sailors staggered, the captain looked around in surprise. Marie flicked her wrist, and a slender punch-dagger slid into her hand. She jabbed it under the chin of the other sailor. As he gargled his last, she threw the man into Orsini, and ran from the control room, along the corridor and onto the gantry. Outside, everything was aflame. Men fought shadowy, indistinct figures that defied description, but slaughtered with impunity.

Bullets rang against the railings at Marie's side. She glanced back; the captain and Orsini were after her. The captain aimed again. Marie took a breath, and jumped the rail. She landed awkwardly on the hard deck. A marine looked at her with shock. She kicked him hard in the groin, and took his rifle from him. Orsini was above her, and now leapt down beside her. Marie fell backwards and fired a shot, tearing into the side of Orsini's neck, drawing an enraged snarl, but sending him wheeling away. Sailors all around became aware of Marie's presence, and rushed towards her. The captain shouted something in Russian, and fired again. Marie felt a bullet rip her tunic, draw blood. A flesh wound, but it appeared her luck was running out.

Men approached from all sides. Orsini staggered to his feet. Marie looked forward at the flickering gate and the hissing waters of the Thames around it. She'd have to take her chances.

She limped to the gunwales, and leapt over the side of the ship, into the blood-red river.

NINE

A young man, eyes dark, skin dry as parchment, reached out with trembling, spindle-fingered hands. Jim thought the youth had been beautiful, once, but certainly no more. Jim remembered loving him once. He remembered letting him die.

'Why?' the youth rasped, voice like the creaking of a gallows rope.

Jim pulled back, unable to reply. He saw a light appear behind the youth, a crackling, fizzing golden light, that drew closer, and larger. It enveloped the corpse-like man, and those dark, pleading eyes vanished into the Otherside. The outstretched hand went last, light rippling in its wake.

Jim staggered away. All-too-familiar shadows flickered behind the shimmering pool. Squamous tentacles and raking claws drove sparks from the surface of the rippling mirror; dark things sought egress from their foul realm.

Scrit-scratch.

The noise tore through Jim's mind. Long talons picked at the meat inside his skull; rusty nails hammering their way out of his head. The Other came.

Jim stumbled away, then ran as fast as he could, though he knew he could never outrun the shadow of his past. He reached a door in the darkness, and plunged through it.

The four-poster bed before him smelt of sickly blooms. The sound of quiet sobbing surrounded him. Something pale and awful lay in that bed. Jim was drawn inexorably towards it, not wanting to look, unable to stop himself. He reached out to pull back silk sheets, hand trembling with fear and grief.

'End of the line!'

A call from the train conductor woke Jim before the familiar nightmare could take hold. Cold sweat evaporated on Jim's brow. Freezing air rushing through the gaps around the rattling carriage windows. Jim shuddered. He stared out at the rolling Kentish countryside. He took small comfort from the rustling newspapers of his fellow passengers; the vanilla aroma of pipe-smoke.

'End of the line. All change please.'

The rhythmic clunk of the tracks slowed along with Jim's heartbeat, becoming steadier, sidings and train sheds rolling into view. Jim took a deep breath, burying the memory of the dream deep. The mission had revived old memories. He knew he could not let the ghosts of the past best him.

Wednesday, 4th October 1893
NR. FAVERSHAM, KENT

It was almost two o'clock when Jim finally came upon Bluebell Cottage. It had proved remarkably hard to find, being situated some way from the beaten track. At least the walk had not been unpleasant. He had trodden the narrow lanes that wound between patchwork fields and wild meadow, over which plumes of smoke from the oast-houses carried the rich smell of drying hops. Jim had become lost in the quiet beauty of the Kentish environs quite willingly, little relishing the task ahead.

He found himself now at the end of a broad path, looking towards the home of John Hardwick. The house itself, despite the name, was not a cottage at all, but a well-proportioned farmhouse, with a thatched roof, and rather too much ivy covering what might once have been a handsome north-facing prospect, now suffering neglect.

Jim took a deep breath, and marched up the path. He rapped smartly on the door, and waited. On the lintel above him was a weatherworn stone shield, upon which a heraldic dragon stared down at him, unwelcoming. Jim rapped again. There was no answer, and no sound of any kind from within. He tried the door, but it was locked.

Jim had come too far to give up easily. Instead, he took the cart-track at the side of the house, tutting as he picked his way through long grass, trouser-legs snagging upon stray brambles. A small stable and a row of sheds greeted him at the end of the track, and a gate leading to the back of the house, where at last he heard some sounds of occupation; the splintering of logs beneath an axe.

Jim stepped through the gate, and followed a narrow path. Beyond, a leaf-covered lawn sloped gently upwards towards a sundered brick wall – little more than piles of rubble – which marked the boundary to fields and forest beyond. Was this the fabled gate through which his doppelganger had once emerged? Jim remembered that much from those days when he and John Hardwick had been more companionable. He paused, morbidly picturing his own double lying dead upon that lawn, at John's hands.

Chop!

Jim shook these foolish thoughts away, and continued through the garden, past a tumbledown woodshed. There, at last, was John Hardwick, bringing an axe down upon a great log, splitting it expertly in a single blow.

Chop!

Hardwick toiled in shirtsleeves, the muscles of his scarred arms like knotted cords. His face looked gaunt, older than Jim remembered from only a year past. He was bearded, and his left side was turned to Jim, revealing the unmistakeable eyepatch, doubtless masking Jim's approach. Hardwick placed another log upon his chopping block. Jim paused, wondering how best to reveal his presence.

A low growl sounded behind him. Jim jumped, turning to see a black, wolf-like dog, with a pointed muzzle and keen eyes. It hunkered low, baring large white teeth.

'Did you forget your manners, Denny?' Hardwick said. 'No need to stand there like some kind of ghost.' He brought his axe down once more.

Chop!

Hardwick left the axe embedded deep in the block and wiped his brow. Only then did he approach, fixing Jim with his one good eye.

'You are here on club business, I take it?' Hardwick asked.

Jim glanced to the dog, and cleared his throat. 'Yes.'

Hardwick whistled, and the dog ceased its growling. Its posture relaxed, from attack dog to faithful pet, and it trotted to its master with a wag of its tail. Hardwick patted the dog on the head, and said, almost in a growl himself, 'Then you'd best come inside.'

Jim sat in silence as Hardwick lit the fire in the dingy sitting-room. He politely refused the offer of brandy, but accepted a glass of water. Hardwick poured himself a brandy, and sat in the armchair opposite Jim. The dog lay down in the corner, licking at a bone.

'Funny,' Hardwick said. 'The last time I saw you in my yard, you tried to kill me.'

'I thought about that very thing as I passed by the garden. The wall at the top of the hill there… was that…?'

Hardwick nodded. 'I hear you have become quite the agent since I last saw you, Captain Denny,' he said. 'Your record is exemplary.'

'I do my part.' Jim wondered how Hardwick had heard anything about him at all, living out here.

'And you do it well. Britain needs men like you. The world

needs you. These Othersiders… they eat away at society, and plot its destruction from within. They are a disease, Captain Denny. You, I suppose, are the cure. It is a heavy burden, is it not?'

'It is.'

Another silence fell. The fire spat, something pinging against the iron guard.

'Have you heard from Mrs Whitinger of late?' Hardwick asked.

'Oh, yes, she sends her regards,' Jim answered a little too quickly, glad of a chance to overcome the awkwardness. 'In fact, I'm staying at the boarding house now. Right above your old rooms.'

'Why so?'

Jim struggled to ignore Hardwick's brusqueness. 'As you know, after I left the army, well, in a manner of speaking, you know… let's just say my father did not approve.'

'I trust you bring no trouble to Mrs Whitinger's door,' Hardwick said, too fiercely. 'Or disrepute.'

Jim girded himself. He would simply have to come straight down to business, for it seemed that chit-chat was now beyond both of them.

'I received the note from Sir Toby,' Hardwick said at last, saving Jim the trouble. 'Regarding Bertrand. Said you were the one who found him?'

'I did,' Jim said, somewhat relieved to be down to business, despite the uncomfortable subject. 'Although, not "found" exactly… more like "witnessed". And there is more, I am afraid. Much more.'

'Another?'

'Sergeant Whittock.'

At that, Hardwick's expression darkened. He drained his brandy in one swig, and stood abruptly. Turning away, he placed his hands on the mantelpiece, head bowed, shoulders hunched. 'How?'

'I'm sorry, old boy.'

'How did he die?'

Jim paused; there was no easy way to say that a man John had great affection for had been brutally murdered; decapitated. 'We... we don't know the exact cause of death. I'm afraid we do not have the whole... that is to say, the body has not been recovered.'

'I must hear everything – every detail.' Hardwick stalked to the sideboard where his decanter sat, poured another, larger brandy, and returned to his seat. 'Spare me nothing.'

Jim nodded. He began with his mission aboard the *Glarus*, the hideous creatures he'd fought in the hold, the deaths of the policemen under his command, and Bertrand's murder. He related the search of the docks, and of the old Fulham Road hospital; of the horde of ghouls, the Chinese tong, the mysterious woman who had taunted them. Hardwick's brow furrowed at mention of the paintings. When Jim told him of the gruesome find in the cardboard box, the knuckles of Hardwick's clenched fist whitened.

'This American – Miss Furnival,' Hardwick said, when at last Jim had finished his tale. 'She sounds a singular sort.'

'Indeed she is.' There was only one thing Jim had not revealed during his narrative, and that was the nature of Marie Furnival. Until he had himself been convinced of her innocence or guilt, it seemed ungentlemanly to prejudice Hardwick. But it seemed that Hardwick suspected already.

'How did she come to be an expert on these "ghouls"?'

Jim decided to take no chances. 'Some experience abroad, I shouldn't wonder. London is not peculiar in its contact with the Othersiders. At any rate, she is a rare thing indeed. She fights as well as any man I know. A fine shot, too.'

'Sounds as though I might like her,' Hardwick said, though mirthlessly. 'Very well, I have the facts. I understand there is a risk to my person. So why not tell me exactly why you are here, Captain Denny.'

'Still "Captain Denny" is it? Look, old boy...' Jim paused.

Hardwick stared into his glass a little ruefully. 'We are different people now, you and I.'

'Only because you chose this path. You could have stayed.'

'I did stay. Long enough to become a killer, a mercenary, a spy. I did my duty and more besides. And in my darkest hours, when I most needed a friend, I do not recall seeing you overmuch.'

Jim felt anger – old resentments – rise within his breast. He had not been prepared for any reprimand, much less an argument. 'You recall the reason for my absence, I suppose?'

'I do. Jane was a fine woman. I mourned your loss.'

The words came like a slap to the face. Jane Pennyforth had taken ill with fever just months before their wedding day. Jim had been a somewhat inconstant fiancé throughout their brief courtship, barely noticing the severity of Jane's illness until it was far too late.

'You know as well as I that she was not the reason. The cause, perhaps, but not the reason.'

'I know. I confided in you my greatest shame, because I thought perhaps our loss would unite us. Instead you chose to stand in judgment over me. Me!'

'*Our* loss was not the same,' Jim snapped. 'You surrendered the love of your life to the Crown. Mine was taken from me.'

'The love of your life? You didn't know what you had until it slipped through your fingers. That girl was not cold in her grave when I dragged you from a molly-house with the police at the door.'

That stung. Jim's many transgressions had been born of shame – a shame he still felt. He had not, at first, loved Jane, as he had once confided in John Hardwick – and only in John – but she had been a fine woman, beautiful, clever, and rich. A smart match, so everyone said. Only after she died had Jim realised the extent of his feelings for the girl. He never thought of her now without wondering if she truly had been the love of his life; without wondering what might have been.

'And I seem to recall likewise dragging you from every opium den in the East End after the Battle of the Thames.' The words sounded petty even as Jim spoke them.

'I overcame my addiction.'

'Addiction?' Jim shook with indignation.

'Did I ever judge you for yours?'

'It rather seems you did.' Jim's throat was tight with anger. The words stuck there.

'Good Christ, Denny. Even now... You know what Rosanna meant to me, you must know it. Do you think you could judge me more harshly than I judge myself? Let me tell you of that day. I was so convinced of the rightness of it. My own father had betrayed his country – the world – for the love of his daughter. Or, rather, the pale shadow of his daughter. Sir Toby's implication was clear – like father, like son. Perhaps I would be willing to betray the Order for the sake of Rosanna. I had a duty to prove myself.'

'It is always "duty" with you. Duty and honour; how comforting that must have been for you, knowing that the woman you loved had been made fugitive by your actions.' At last, Jim gave voice to the crux of the matter; the real reason he had allowed his friendship with Hardwick to sour. Jim had never felt such grief as when Jane Pennyforth had passed, so close on the heels of another tragedy in his life. He wondered, every day, if things would have been different had he been there for her, had he kept his appointments. He had sunk into the depths of despair, from his grief and guilt, and in that despair Jim came to realise the extent of John Hardwick's betrayal of the gypsy woman, Rosanna. The magnitude of it. And he had increasingly come to find that betrayal unforgiveable.

The dog, which had lain quietly in the corner so far, let out a low, rumbling growl. Hardwick's face purpled. For a moment, Jim feared Hardwick might strike him, and that his mission must end in failure. But his former friend turned away.

'It was no comfort at all,' Hardwick said, quietly. 'How many fugitives have you brought to justice, Denny? How many of these "Majestics" have you captured, or even killed? You have seen only a fraction of what they can do. Rosanna and her sisters, with no machinery, no Lazarus Gate, no etherium... they tore the veil. I saw the evil of the Othersiders; the way they enslaved their own people, their psychics – and what they would surely do to us. And I saw, too, the demons – the Riftborn – ravening at the edge of sanity. I believed I was saving not just our world, but Rosanna also, for only in the care of the Order could she be protected from those… things.'

Jim had never heard Hardwick be so forthcoming. Perhaps the isolation had changed him. Perhaps Jim's presence had merely disturbed those memories that had been allowed to lurk too long beneath the surface.

'You speak as though something has changed your mind,' Jim said. 'About the rightness of it all, I mean.'

'When I saw what Sir Arthur had planned… I knew what I had done. I knew then that we were little better than the Othersiders.'

'The Nightwatch. So you know?' Jim asked.

John nodded. 'I would have taken Elsbet out of there, had I anywhere to take her where she would not be found. And so I abandoned her. I lost myself to bitterness; to rage. I used that rage to exact my revenge upon the Artist, but even that victory, it seems, was fleeting. I am lost, Denny, just as surely as if I'd been stranded on the Otherside. In truth, I wish I'd stayed there, and watched the world burn.'

'And now? What do you believe now?'

'It hardly matters. I am Colonel Hardwick, of Apollo Lycea. When the Order calls upon me, which these days is rarely if they know what is good for them, I…' He paused, and gave a rueful smile. 'As you said. I do my duty.'

For a moment, Hardwick looked ashamed, but then his shoulders squared again, his head lifted, and he was the grizzled, resolute soldier once more. Jim noted, for the first time in their turbulent acquaintanceship, how very much John Hardwick looked like Lazarus.

'So will you tell me now, Captain,' Hardwick said, 'what your instructions are? Why are you here?'

Jim knew not what to say. His deepest secrets were Hardwick's to keep, just as Hardwick's were his. Their past friendship had allowed them to say, finally, that which had for so long gone unsaid; and yet it had made no difference. There would be no reconciliation, not here.

'I am to escort you back to London... Colonel Hardwick.'

'To what end?'

'To ensure your safety, until the nature of this new threat is ascertained.'

'The Artist, back from the dead?'

'We have no evidence that it is any more than a new gang lord bearing Tsun Pen's name,' Jim said. 'But the threat is real nevertheless.'

'I can't possibly come to London at such short notice. What will happen to Gregor?' Hardwick nodded to the dog.

'For pity's sake...' Jim muttered. 'He can stay at Horse Guards if it's so important to you, with the regimental hounds.'

Gregor cocked his head to one side, as though he knew he was being talked about. Jim fancied that the brute was well suited to its master. Alert, dutiful, and dangerous.

'Very well. But there is really no need for an escort.'

Jim fished an envelope from his breast pocket, and handed it over. 'I have my orders, and now you have yours. Sir Toby thought perhaps you could not ignore them if I handed them to you in person. I don't intend to leave Kent without you... sir.'

Hardwick gave a sardonic glance to Jim, before tearing open the envelope. He skimmed the contents of the letter, crumpled up both note and envelope, and tossed them into the fire.

'It appears Sir Toby is more certain than you about what we face,' Hardwick said. 'Trust me, Captain, I am not summoned to London for my safety.'

'Oh?'

'These days I am summoned only when someone needs to be killed, and our people lack the means to see it done. This is the first time, however, that I have had to execute a man twice. Wait here, Captain Denny. I shall pack a bag.'

TEN

Saturday, 19th December 1891
HAMPSTEAD, LONDON

Jim half-rolled, half-crawled out of bed, rubbing at his head that felt full of mush. He grasped about the bedside table for his pocket-watch, and groaned when he flicked open the case and saw that it was almost noon.

'What's the matter?'

Jim felt the hand at his back, followed by a tug at his arm. 'I'm late, old boy. Very, very late,' he replied.

'Ah, for your next tryst? You're positively awful. They will call you a cad.'

'They should call me worse than that if they knew,' Jim said, turning to gaze into Algie's dark eyes. 'So they'd better not find out.' He pulled away from Algie's embrace, and began rifling through the pile of clothes on the hotel room floor.

'Oh, God,' Algie groaned. 'You are at her beck and call. Come back to bed and be done with it.'

'In case it had escaped your attention,' Jim said, pulling on his creased trousers, 'this is no tryst. Jane is my fiancée.'

Algie touched the back of his hand to his head and said

theatrically, '*Cherchez la femme,*' before collapsing back onto the pillows.

'Besides, it is almost Christmas and she will be expecting my undivided attention. That means no more of… this.'

Algie sat bolt upright. 'Don't be preposterous! Married life won't suit you.'

'How would you know what suits me?' Jim snapped. Algie's endless hedonism had a surprising way of becoming monotonous.

'I know you better than you know yourself. I know, for instance, that you are not going to spend the afternoon with Jane Pennyforth at all. You will offer her some lie about being called back to barracks, when really you are going to work for that stuffy old club of yours. The lovely Jane is the excuse you give to me, the army is the excuse you give to her, and the club is the real subject of your devotion. You break both our hearts, James Denny.'

Jim fastened his cufflinks. 'You knew the rules of this game when you got involved, old boy.'

'Ah yes, the romantic life of a spy's lover.' He reclined on one elbow, languidly. 'How lucky I am to know the dashing Captain Denny, with a girl in every port, and a youth in every alley. The things I have heard of you – let alone the things I've seen – would curl poor Miss Pennyforth's delicate toes.'

Jim flew to the bed and grabbed Algie by the jaw, squeezing his chiselled face into unflattering jowls. 'But you would not tell her, would you? Because we both dance with the devil here, you and I. If my life is ruined by the word of a mandrake, you will face two years' hard labour also. I would ensure that much.' He kissed Algie hard on the mouth, and pulled away.

Algie laughed, somewhat fiendishly. 'You know, James, I could make you a better offer than the club today.'

'I doubt that, Algie. Duty to the Queen, and all that.'

'I don't doubt it. But Brennan has one of his games on tonight, and I know how you love a roll of the dice. Lucius will be there, and that French strumpet with the enviable taste in wine. *Marga-reet.*'

Jim sighed. 'Not tonight. My business may delay me too long. Only... Where is it?'

'A secret. I am expecting a missive this afternoon with the gory details.'

'Then that's settled. You will have to count me out.'

'Preposterous! Where will you be later... say seven o'clock? I'll meet you in a cab.'

'I can't tell you that, Algie.' Jim felt the pull of the gaming tables, and struggled against their call.

'You can count on my discretion, James. Heaven knows, we've been playing this game long enough. Name a place you can get to easily. Finish your business, and I shall be there. Then it's off to the secret den, and a night of music and merriment and getting filthy rich.'

Jim sighed. He knew he could not resist; this was not to be the first time, and it wouldn't be the last. 'You know the St George on Belgrave Road?'

'The Pimlico cabaret!' Algie cried with glee.

'That's the one. My duty takes me to the vicinity. I shall do my best to meet you, but if I'm not there by half-past seven, go on without me, and take temptation with you.'

LETTER, CPT. JAMES DENNY TO MISS JANE PENNYFORTH

Dearest Jane,
Again, and with a heavy heart, I am afraid I must cancel
our engagement for afternoon tea today. It is beastly of me,
I know, and I wish there were some way to circumvent the
commitments that keep me from your presence. The Army
is an unforgiving master, it seems, and I must attend to
business that will detain me well into the evening.

I shall send word tomorrow, and doubt not that we shall
make fresh arrangements, for every second away from you
is a chore.

With eternal fondness,
James

LETTER, MISS JANE PENNYFORTH TO CPT. JAMES DENNY

Darling James,
Of course, you must do as duty dictates – your devotion
to Queen and country is one of the things that drew me
to you after all. It may even be for the best, for I have not
been feeling quite myself of late. Mother thinks I should
send for the doctor, but really it is nothing more than a
chill. I shall be right as rain when next you call. And, my
love, do not make me wait too long, for my heart aches
when we are parted.

Your ever loving,

Jane

Jim woke covered in cold sweat, alone in a Knightsbridge hotel room. He was still clothed. His head pounded.

Ever since London Bridge, he'd had nightmares, but nothing like this. Now the demons of his mind's eye heralded new terrors. They showed him the last moments of his betrothed, sick and desperate in her bed, calling out for a fiancé who would never come. And they showed him the dark eyes of a beautiful youth, his Algie, falling backwards from a rooftop as Jim had tried in vain to save him.

But had he? Had he really tried? Jim asked himself that question every time the nightmare fug cleared. Algie had played him for a fool, yes. But he had also held incriminating evidence over Jim. There was no scenario in which Jim's erstwhile lover could have escaped that rooftop without Jim finding himself either imprisoned, or in thrall to the Othersiders by means of blackmail.

He told himself that he had done everything he could. He told himself a good many things these days; not all of them were true.

Jim rolled out of bed. He patted down his waistcoat, which was damp from sweat and reeked of gin, and checked his pocket-watch. It was past ten.

He groaned. He had scant time to go home and dress, hopefully avoiding his father into the bargain. He had a funeral to attend.

Snow fell, slowly, settling upon the ridges of tombstones and the boughs of skeletal trees, and over the shoulders and hats of the circle of mourners beside the grave. The vicar commended the soul of Jane Pennyforth to God, and yet Jim knew the tear-raw eyes of the flock were not on the coffin, but on him. He could not look up. He felt their eyes boring into him, turning his insides to knots. He could barely focus on the service. The words became a drone. Jim thought he might faint.

'…We therefore commit her body to the ground: earth to earth, ashes to ashes, dust to dust, in sure and certain hope of the resurrection to…'

Frozen dirt scratched upon the coffin-top. It sounded like skittering claws. Jim wanted to be sick.

'…Who died, was buried, and rose again for us. To Him be glory for ever.'

'Amen,' all said in unison.

The chorus of voices brought Jim to some semblance of lucidity. He turned about in a daze, mumbling condolences to those around him, despairing as people turned their back upon him.

He saw Jane's younger brother, Samuel; thirteen years old, the boy had idolised Jim from the first visit, dressed in uniform like one of his tin soldiers. Jim made for the boy, and offered his hand. He did not really know why. Samuel looked up to him; perhaps Jim's favour might lend him strength at this difficult time. Other mourners shuffled away. Samuel looked shaken, angry.

'Get away,' the boy said.

'Sam, come now. I'm so sorry –'

'Get away. If I were a man I would fight you, Captain Denny. I would fight you.'

Tears welled in Sam's eyes. His father placed a hand on his shoulder and pulled him away. Samuel Pennyforth the elder had never looked more stern. Gone was the beaming face of the prospective father-in-law. Now he looked hawk-like and austere, his sharp features pecking from beneath a black hat, eyes full of weariness, and bitterness.

'You heard my son, Captain,' he said quietly, seething. 'If only half of what we have heard is true, you bring shame to my daughter's graveside. The absentee lover, the gallivanter, they say. The shame should be on you! My daughter worshipped the ground you walked on, and yet you did not…' He could not get the words out. He visibly shook.

Jim tried to speak; the words would not come. He was still holding out his hand, stupidly, in some hope of reconciliation. He saw Jane's mother over Samuel's shoulder. Eyes ringed with red, heartbreak writ large upon her aspect. Jim wished a second grave would open up beneath him and swallow him. There was no such mercy.

'Do not stand there and gawp,' Dr Pennyforth said. 'Do not stand before me as a friend. You should not be here. You are not welcome here.' The pitch and volume of his voice began to rise. Jim stepped away. Mourners who had been on their way to the chapel turned to see who had antagonised the bereaved family on this of all days. 'You are not welcome at my house again,' Dr Pennyforth said. 'Never again –'

He stopped as Jim's father came between them. Colonel Denny, craggy and imposing as ever, turned Jim away from the family, and muttered some words to Pennyforth that seemed to calm him. Jim let himself be led away. He did not have it in him to resist.

By the time he came to his senses, he was standing on the pavement outside the wrought-iron cemetery gates, and his father was waving for a cab.

'I'm sorry. Father, I am so very sorry,' Jim managed.

'It's too late for that, boy,' the colonel said. 'Listen to me. You are to go straight home, pack your things, and leave my house. This very day. I am going back in there, and I am going to make things right. Later, I shall call in some small favours to see that the rumours going around about you are nipped in the bud. It is the last favour I shall do for you. You are a bloody disgrace. That club has... No. Perhaps it is not the Apollonian. Perhaps this is who you are. I had hoped the barracks would make an officer and a gentleman of you, but you turned your back on Horse Guards just as you turned your back on that girl. Well, I hope you are happy. You are free.'

'Father... that is not what I wanted. None of this is. I did love her.' Jim's words sounded feeble to his own ears. He could not help it. He only knew what he had lost now it was gone. The wounds of Algie's betrayal had barely healed, and yet they paled in comparison to this. He had failed Jane at the very end. What kind of man did that make him?

'Do not speak of love now, like some doe-eyed schoolboy,' his father growled. 'It is too late. Far too late. Go and drown your sorrows; it's what you are good at. It is all you're good for! And when I return home tonight, I had better not find you there, or so help me I shall have you thrown out on your ear.'

Jim tried to protest, but his words were lost in thickening snow, and were spoken only to the vanishing back of his father.

He half staggered to the hansom. He felt the questioning eyes of the cabbie upon him. In the end, he could do nothing but climb aboard.

'Drive,' he said to the cabbie.

'Where to, guv?'

'I don't care. Anywhere. Just away from here.'

ELEVEN

Wednesday, 4th October 1893
NR. FAVERSHAM, KENT

I t was dark by the time the hansom swept around St James's Square, coming to a stop outside the Apollonian Club. The streets were busy, with the smart set out en masse despite the bracing cold of the evening.

John Hardwick alighted onto a frost-glistening pavement, leaving Denny to pay the cabbie. He looked up at the noble façade of the club, recalling how in awe he had been the first time he had been admitted. That was just three years ago, when he had felt undeserving of any place on the membership list of such a famous gentlemen's club; now he was wary of it. Now, he could see this place as nothing more than a headquarters for the Order; a den of lies. He almost envied the old clubmen who moved, shadow-like, behind those great windows, knowing little if anything of Apollo Lycea; of the many secrets it harboured behind the walls of this estimable establishment. Of the many lives it ruined.

John ascended the steps, and the doors swung open for him. A servant took John's small bag and his rifle case.

The familiar figure of Holdsworth stood before John, and

nodded respectfully. 'It is good to see you, Colonel. Am I to make up a room for your stay?'

John thought there was some sincerity to the head porter's greeting, though it cheered him little to see the man, who had always in John's mind represented the secret functions of the club.

'No, thank you, Holdsworth. I imagine I shall stay at the Army & Navy tonight.'

'Very good, sir.' Holdsworth nodded to a servant to take John's hat and coat, and Captain Denny's too. 'You are expected, sir. If you and Captain Denny would care to follow me.'

Holdsworth acted as though John had simply returned from a short holiday. For John, however, it had been too long. It felt strange. He felt like a dog left too long in the wild, returned home and expected to behave as it always had. He knew what he must look like to these fine people, the great and the good. He saw it in their eyes – furtive glances flicked his way from finely dressed gentlemen; whispered rumours echoed in John's ears, deafening. He swore he heard the refrain, 'The last honest man in London,' the nickname given him by Agent Hanlocke. The nickname that had followed him, picked away at him, ever since. For a moment, the bright lights of the electric chandelier and the surreptitious attentions of the assembled clubmen conspired to overwhelm John's senses. He had grown unused to attention, to society. He had tried to remove himself from the world, but the world, it seemed, was not done with him.

'Colonel Hardwick?'

John realised his eyes had been closed tight. He opened them to see a young woman. The owner of the voice that had interrupted his thoughts. An American voice.

The intense light that had clouded John's vision subsided. The whispers that had become like an incessant buzzing in his head were gone. The clubmen seemed to be chattering about other business.

'Colonel?' The woman spoke again, a look of concern on her face.

'I... Yes,' John managed, and at last composed himself. 'You must be Miss Furnival. Captain Denny here has told me much about you.'

'Has he? Nothing bad, I hope.' The comment was in jest, but barbed, as was the look she flashed over John's shoulder at Denny.

'Not at all,' John said. 'Nothing at all, really, though he said that you are an exceptionally fine shot, and a rather expert hunter.'

Marie Furnival afforded him a slight smile. 'I hear you are a fine marksman yourself, Colonel. Perhaps we could hunt together some time.'

'That depends on how long I am in London, I'm sure,' John said. As he spoke, a strange sense began to creep up his spine, spreading out like pins and needles. It was a sense he had long learned not to ignore. Not a sixth sense, as the girl's eccentric uncle would surely have it, but certainly an intuition. He stared at Miss Furnival perhaps more fixedly than he intended. There was an air of familiarity about her, and yet one of extreme... oddness. Only when she shifted uncomfortably did John check himself. 'You are joining us, I presume?'

'Unfortunately, Miss Furnival is not privy to tonight's business,' Holdsworth answered for her. The man had waited patiently while John had been momentarily disorientated. 'Indeed, Miss Furnival, your uncle requests that you find entertainment in the ladies' waiting room until his business is concluded.'

John saw the young woman's nose wrinkle almost petulantly, just for a moment, and then she smiled sweetly at Holdsworth. 'Of course, Holdsworth, I merely wished to make the Colonel's acquaintance – his reputation precedes him.' She turned back to John and gave a curt bow. 'Colonel.'

'Madam,' John bowed in return, and watched Miss Furnival make her way to those club rooms that were reserved for the wives and family of ordinary members.

Denny stepped forward, and nudged John's arm. 'Best not keep Old Toby waiting.'

'Keep an eye on that one,' John said.

Denny only nodded.

'It will doubtless come as little surprise that events have moved on in your absence, Captain Denny,' Sir Toby said.

Pleasantries had been brief, which was how John preferred them. He glanced at Denny, who appeared confused.

'Moved on, sir?' Denny asked. 'I've been gone less than a day.'

'Our enemies do not wait on you, my boy,' Lord Cherleten barked. He sat in a shadowed corner, as had always been his wont, wreathed in cigar smoke that Sir Arthur Furnival, seated by his side, periodically made a show of waving away. 'While you were in Kent, a delivery was received. A letter, signed allegedly by Tsun Pen, and a package containing one of the Artist's customary paintings. It appears, Colonel Hardwick, that our enemies know that you are here. Whatever their plans, they involve you. We were right to recall you to active duty.'

'Or perhaps you have brought me into the lion's den,' John said. 'These objects have been inspected? By Sir Arthur, I mean.'

All eyes fell upon Arthur Furnival.

'They have, and by more skilled hands than mine, Colonel,' Sir Arthur replied. 'Each of the Nightwatch returned a singular phrase when shown the painting.'

'Go on,' John prompted. He knew what Sir Arthur was about to say, just as surely as if he were psychic himself.

'The house of the dead,' said Sir Arthur, confirming John's suspicion. 'They said it over and over; there were no dissenting voices, and sadly no further clarification.'

'Then it is of little use,' said John. 'While it may point to Tsun Pen's return, or merely the rise of the organisation he once led, the house of the dead is gone. That is, the House of Zhengming. If the tong have founded another base of operations in this name, we must uncover it.'

'All in good time, Colonel,' said Sir Toby. 'For argument's sake, let us assume this really is the Artist, or at least someone using his name. First, we must decide what to do about his demands. He has given us much intelligence that remains somewhat unpalatable. He claims that our enemies close in on us even now, and have already opened negotiations with this Zhengming gang regarding the control of Otherside artefacts and considerable quantities of etherium.'

'Enemies?' John asked.

'Russians, primarily. The letters contained the name and address of a certain Russian agent operating here in London – the details are being ratified as we speak. But there are twelve others, supposedly, along with unknown numbers of agents from other nations, all seeking the same prize.'

'How could the Artist possibly have this much etherium, sir?' Denny interrupted. 'We've scarcely seen this quantity in all the time we've been operating. Even the wreckage from the Thames could not have yielded as much.'

Sir Toby glanced sidelong at Cherleten, then stood and strolled to his customary place beside the tall sash window, hands folded behind his back.

'We have known for some time that stockpiles of etherium exist beyond what was seized at the Thames,' Sir Toby said. 'Either it was placed here by the Othersiders before the attempted invasion, or it has been somehow transported here since.'

'Since?' Jim gasped. 'Then you believe there is still a threat from the Othersiders?'

'This is what I have been afraid of for some time,' Cherleten interrupted. 'The Othersiders were defeated at London Bridge, yes, but they still outclass us in technology if not in numbers. This is why my armoury should be –'

'Please, Lord Cherleten,' Sir Toby said. 'Time will tell if you will be proved correct. But this is not the time for us to re-tread this ground. The Prime Minister will not tolerate the militarism of Apollo Lycea without far more tangible evidence for the Othersiders' return. Besides, everything we know – everything that we are able to glean from the Nightwatch, at least, suggests that such a thing is impossible. More likely it was stored secretly by their agents to pave the way for their invasion of our world, then left to gather dust.'

'And anything that can be kept secret can be uncovered by Tsun Pen,' John mused.

Sir Toby sighed resignedly, and turned about to face John. 'Colonel Hardwick, we await permission from Gladstone to proceed with our plan, but I am certain it will be forthcoming, for the stakes are too high.'

'Permission for what, sir?'

'As I said previously, Tsun Pen has made a list of demands. Grotesque demands, really. If he truly has the leverage he claims, then we must answer those demands, for fear of what might happen to us, to the world at large. If he does not… then perhaps making a show of appeasing him will at least draw him out. It is not without regret, however, that I even entertain the thought of –'

A sharp crack interrupted Sir Toby mid-sentence. Glass exploded from the window-pane. Blood burst from Sir Toby's chest, dark claret. The Lord Justice made a sharp cry, and fell. John was beside Sir Toby before he even hit the floor.

'Stay down!' John snapped, his hands already pressing on the wound to staunch the flow of blood. The bullet had struck close to the heart. Perhaps too close. The old man groaned.

Denny crouched by the window. 'I see him!' he cried. 'The Carlton Club – on the roof.'

'Sir Arthur, take a handkerchief and press down on this wound,' John barked.

The baronet did as he was told, almost in a daze, and John was away and through the door the next instant. He raced along the corridor, shoving clubmen out of the way. Holdsworth was rushing towards the office, but turned at once to run alongside John, waving members and servants aside to speed John's passage. John took the stairs three at a time. He emerged onto the great balcony, saw the stairs filled with gentlemen who gawped at his approach, and leapt instead at the curved handrail, sliding rapidly to the marble hall and continuing towards the doors without breaking stride.

'You. My gun,' John shouted at a confused-looking servant as he bore down on the lad. Behind him, fingers clicked; Holdsworth, presumably, signalling the boy to obey.

Mere seconds had elapsed. John was now out on the street, discarding the leather case of his Winchester rifle, his ragged breaths misting on the frosty air. He heard a cry from the Carlton Club, saw shadowy figures pushing through a crowd, and leaping into a waiting carriage, black, unmarked. Reins cracked, the horses were away, terrified pedestrians leaping aside as they realised the carriage was not about to stop.

John's heart pounded in his chest. He'd had time to load only two rounds into the repeater, and fired one off immediately. He swore as the shot went wide; cursed his one eye and flustered aim. He took a deep breath and worked the lever of the rifle. The coach was almost out of range. Someone across the road screamed.

And then the rifle was pulled from his hands. John was ready to fight or die, until he saw the slender form of Marie Furnival beside him on the street corner. She raised the rifle to her shoulder in a fluid motion; her eye flickered, her finger squeezed the trigger.

John squinted. At the extreme of the weapon's range, in the dark, she had struck home. The vague silhouette of the coachman slumped forward; the carriage careened into the middle of the road, drawing distant shouts of alarm.

Captain Denny ran past John and Miss Furnival, feet pounding the cobblestones. He tore along the street in pursuit, but not fast enough. The shadowy coachman straightened, the carriage righted its course, and in moments it had disappeared around the next corner. Denny stopped running, his shoulders sank.

'Damn.' Marie Furnival handed the Winchester back to John, a look of dismay on her face.

'Devil of a shot,' John muttered. 'Nearly two hundred yards.'

'Two-ten,' she said. 'But it wasn't good enough.'

Denny returned, red in the face, and crestfallen. A few Apollonian servants and members of the Order had already taken to the streets, spinning some tale about a police operation and burglars at the Carlton Club; anything to stop the crowd of influential gentlemen of clubland asking awkward questions about young ladies firing Winchester rifles in the street. Once all attention had been drawn to the Order's people, John passed the rifle to a nearby servant, and strode towards the Carlton.

'Come on,' he said to Denny. 'You too, Miss Furnival. We have work to do.'

John pushed through the crowds that gathered still, bolstered by onlookers now spilling out of the neighbouring Reform Club. He drew some attention as he got closer, until his way was physically barred by stewards on the front steps. John fixed them a glare from his one eye, but it was Jim Denny who stepped forwards, touching John's arm, indicating he should stand down.

Denny flashed his card to the stewards, and spoke quietly to them, remonstrating only gently when he met resistance, nodding patiently as they explained the situation at the club in discreet half-whispers. Soon, the stewards stood aside, allowing the agents to pass, looking with some suspicion at John, but reserving their most disdainful expressions for Miss Furnival.

'I've dealt with these chaps before,' Jim said quietly as they crossed the threshold. 'Being officious is the best form of attack. And well dressed. You look like a merchant seaman in a suit, if you don't mind me saying.'

John recalled how Denny had often taken advantage of his newfound status, using his club privileges to stay in the best hotels, hire cabs so that he never had to ride the omnibus again, dine well and dress smartly. He recalled once being concerned with appearances a little too much himself, but that seemed like a lifetime ago.

'He's got a point,' Miss Furnival said. She strode past him, and cast a look upwards.

From the entrance hall, more opulent than the Apollonian's, two staircases led to a mezzanine balcony, which swept around three sides of the building, drawing the eye to a great glass atrium, glowing deep blue in the moonlight.

'The chaps outside said the intruder was mistaken for a member at first, due to his attire,' Jim said. 'All of this commotion started because, in his hurry, he bumped into the wife of Lord Dalmeny, and knocked her to the ground. A hue and cry went up and that's when the servants saw the man had a gun case. Unlike the Apollonian, that sort of thing isn't the norm here. They followed cautiously, and saw him jump into an unmarked carriage. The rest, we already know.'

Denny summoned the nearest servant and quietly explained that the intruder had been seen on the roof of the building. The servant pointed to the north-east corner of the balcony, mumbling directions to the roof, and Denny led the way. From the first floor, where angry discussions were being held in the library about the intrusion on the club's sanctity, the agents took another set of stairs to the less grand environs of the private chambers and offices, and then up once more, squeezing up a narrow access stair to the roof.

'Where was he?' John asked.

'Over here, I think.' Denny led the way to a stone balustrade, cold wind whistling through its embrasures.

John looked over the edge, down onto Pall Mall, where police constables now arrived, doffing their helmets to the great and good who all had a piece to say. John did not envy the common constabulary, having to calm a crowd of solicitors, judges, peers and politicians, all of whom felt they had a right to know what was happening; most of whom would be disappointed in that regard. Across the road, on the corner of St James's Square, the upper windows of the Apollonian were dark. On the street outside, a carriage driver took direction from Holdsworth, and then drove slowly by, doubtless circling around to the concealed rear entrance.

'Oh God,' Denny said. 'Sir Toby... I mean, that carriage...'

'I don't know,' said John, a sense of inexplicable emptiness growing within him at the prospect of Sir Toby's passing. 'Let us hope it is the doctor, and not the undertaker.' John cast his eye carefully across the rooftop around the balustrade. 'Here,' he said, kneeling to indicate what he had found.

The stub of a cigarette, and a tiny mound of ash. He picked up the stub carefully, examined it, and sniffed at it. He passed it to Denny.

'Smells a bit off,' Denny said.

'Foreign, and not one of the more common brands. Wouldn't be a stretch to guess at Russian,' John said.

'Oh, really,' said Miss Furnival. 'How could you possibly –'

She stopped as both John and Denny turned to stare at her.

'You said yourself his reputation preceded him,' Denny said. 'Colonel Hardwick is a veritable Dupin.'

'He knelt here,' John said. 'There are three scuff marks on the balustrade, the rearmost one more pronounced than the others. A small tripod. The trajectory of the shot would confirm this as the gunman's position. The shot was quiet, but powerful. The bullet went right through Sir Toby and into the wall behind me.'

'Could the shot have been meant for you?' Miss Furnival asked.

'No, I wasn't standing in line at the time. But the gun has to be something unusual, definitely a rifle with a strong recoil, and quiet report.'

'Mauser.'

'Very good, Miss Furnival. We shall need to inspect the round to be certain. Regardless, it raises the question of how long this has been planned.' John stood, casting his eye around the roof once more, before looking back across at the Apollonian. 'Someone has infiltrated the Carlton Club. A well-dressed man, yes? So someone posing as a club member managed to bring a rifle and tripod up here, and wait God knows how long for Sir Toby to stand by his window.'

'He often stands by his window,' Denny pointed out.

'But I doubt he can be seen doing so from the street. Someone had to observe his habits. Someone had to know precisely when he would be at the club – why not strike at his home, or at

149

chambers? Our enemies sent that package to the club today to ensure Sir Toby would be there. Whoever did it knows that important meetings are frequently held in his office. And as they seem rather keen to involve me, they doubtless timed their assassination attempt to coincide with my presence.'

'I wish I could say you were being conceited, old boy, but I think you have a point.'

'You say "assassination",' Miss Furnival said. 'You're sure they meant to kill Sir Toby... not just send a message?'

'The bullet was mere inches from his heart,' John said. 'The gunman could not have been certain of merely wounding him – he could be dead now, for all we know. Even you, Miss Furnival, could not have made that shot with the certainty of the target surviving.'

'Well... with an optical sight...' she moved her head from side to side as she weighed up the possibility.

'Now you're being conceited,' Denny said. John noted a sharp edge to the reprimand, which Miss Furnival ignored with grace. 'Besides, even if the shot was not fatal, Sir Toby could die from his wound. That being the case, we should get back across the road and find Lord Cherleten.'

'Very well,' said John. 'But remember: speak to no one in this club. At best it is compromised. At worst, someone here is complicit in the crime.'

John led the way back downstairs and onto the street, pushing again through the throng. They were plucked from the crowd by Holdsworth, who fell into step with John, his face pale and pinched. John saw the normally unflappable steward's moistening eyes, and feared the worst.

'Where is he?' John asked.

'They're taking him to an ambulance carriage, sir, at the back doors to avoid a fuss. It... it does not look good, sir.'

'Take me there at once.'

Holdsworth led the way, past the kitchens, through the servants' hall, and outside into a frosty courtyard surrounded by tall buildings. Cherleten stood outside overseeing the loading of the carriage, puffing on a cigar. A man was about to close the rear doors, when John strode forward, bade him stop, and hopped aboard.

Sir Toby lay still, face ashen. He looked suddenly smaller, shrunken and frail.

The ambulance man at his side said, 'You can come with us, sir, but we must away.'

'No!' Sir Toby spoke, some strength still in his voice. With a great effort he pawed the man away, and beckoned John close.

'We must away,' the man repeated.

'You will wait,' Sir Toby wheezed.

John nodded to the man to move aside. 'Sir, I –'

The baronet held up his hand, and John was silent. The hand fell to Sir Toby's side, and the old man took a ragged breath. 'I am done,' he said. 'You will do me the duty of writing to my wife. Madeleine... she thought such days were long past. Tell her... oh, tell her whatever men should tell the women who have suffered much out of love. You always were... the writer.' He coughed, wincing in pain at the effort.

'The hospital, Sir Toby. There may yet be time.'

'No. No time. Listen – I am glad it was you here... at the... the end. There was so much I needed to say. The things I have asked you to do... they were for the good. I want you to know that. I suppose I needed your father still, and hoped there was just the right amount... of the man I knew living on in his son. I was right, I think. But this life I have given you... it is not the life your mother would have wanted for you. Dear Dora... I hope she would forgive me, knowing the stakes. I hope you will too, in time.'

John was unsure how to respond. He felt a lump in his throat rise at mention of his departed mother, but refused to let it show. Even now it was hard to reconcile Sir Toby Fitzwilliam, spymaster and Lord Justice, with Old Toby the family friend. Old Toby who was slipping away. 'There is nothing to forgive,'

John managed. 'We have all done our duty, and nothing more could be asked of a man.'

Some vague expression crossed Sir Toby's face. John had tried to offer some words of comfort, but could not help but feel the look was one of disappointment. Sir Toby's grip slackened on John's arm. He tried to say something more, but only a rattling wheeze escaped his lips. The life went from his eyes. A grey shadow crossed his features. John put a hand to Sir Toby Fitzwilliam's face, and closed the old man's eyes.

TWELVE

Tuesday, 3rd May 1892

Sir Toby rubbed his hand across a gnarled brow, stood from behind his desk, and gulped the last of his scotch before pacing the floor beside his office window. John waited patiently; it was how the old man pondered things, and John had given him plenty to think about.

'Almost two years to the day! You know, Colonel, that this is most inconvenient,' Sir Toby said at last.

'Yes, sir.'

'And embarrassing. You are turning down a knighthood, which I went to some pains to arrange for you.'

'I am sorry, Sir Toby, but –'

Sir Toby raised a hand, as he so often did, and John fell silent. Finally, the old man turned around and fixed John with his steeliest gaze. John remembered with some ruefulness how once that look had made him fumble. Now, Colonel John Hardwick was a different man. He remained unmoved.

'When you ask for an "extended leave of absence", just how long do you think you will be gone?'

'I do not know, Sir Toby. That is the honest truth... indefinitely, perhaps.'

'Indefinitely.' Sir Toby repeated the word, and sucked at his teeth. 'And you think that the Order is done with you, Colonel? Do you think that we gave you the position you have only to throw away our investment? A not inconsiderable investment, I might add.'

'Sir Toby, I am through with it,' John snapped, drawing a sharp glare from the old man. 'I will not kill another soul for the Order. I will not take another penny from the Crown's coffers. You played to my naivety when you persuaded me to enlist, and I see now that you expected me to carry on even after I'd seen the truth; that somehow the facts of life in Apollo Lycea would inure me to the suffering that I myself must cause at your behest. For a time, that was true. I have followed my orders to the letter, to distract myself from my own failings. I think perhaps it is time to face those failings, and pray forgiveness for them.'

'No man has ever spoken to me thus, in this place,' Sir Toby said. 'Not even Cherleten, though I'm damned sure he's thought worse.'

'Perhaps a little honesty is long overdue, sir,' John said, through gritted teeth.

'And these failings... you speak of the gypsies? I'd have thought you had long since seen sense over that matter.'

'Sense?' John almost rose to the bait, but thought better of it. 'So had I,' he said instead.

Sir Toby sighed. 'One does not walk away from the Order. You know that. If I agree to this, Colonel, it will be with conditions.'

'I would expect nothing less.'

'The Order will need to know where you are at all times. That means regular contact. We also reserve the right to re-establish our... agreement... should it be deemed necessary. This is non-negotiable.'

'Sir Toby... it rather sounds as if you are agreeing to my request.'

'Are you giving me a choice?'

John gave a bitter laugh. 'The Order always finds a way to stack the deck, Sir Toby. Believe me, I've stacked it more than once on its behalf since London Bridge.'

'Not this time, Colonel. I have seen this day coming for some time. Oh, do not look at me like that, I am no fool. I know you have suffered; I know that the role you play is not the life you had hoped for, and that can do strange things to a man. You know, your father set me on this path. I would have died at Kandahar were it not for him. Instead, I returned home wounded, my military career over. I would have been content to serve as a simple soldier all my days, were it not for circumstance. My predecessor in the Order prepared me for the life of a spymaster. Under his tutelage I took some... questionable actions, which hardened me to this life. I tried to prepare you the same way, but it was obvious that it was not to be.'

'You saw me as... your successor?' Sir Toby never failed to surprise John.

'I did. And why not? Your father was my equal in the running of the Order. He was the vital link between the army and the Order of Apollo, and I rather hoped you would take on that role. Now, all I have is Cherleten, and we both know he does not wish to share power.'

'You have Denny,' John said.

'No, Cherleten has Denny. Besides, he has not served, not really. I know they don't receive you kindly at the War Office, in no small part due to your employment here, but they respect you. You have seen more action than most of the men in the barracks, and they damn well know it.'

John nodded. He was wary of Sir Toby's flattery, but it had the ring of truth. He had let his current feelings towards Denny show at the Army & Navy Club once, and had felt a general air of approval from the clubmen of 'The Rag'. James Denny had many fine qualities, but they had not been tested in the forges of battle, and thus his honorary captaincy was greeted with some resentment in certain quarters. John's retention of rank, by contrast – even his promotion to colonel – had never been begrudged.

'I am not my father's son,' John said. 'As I have told you more than once.'

'Quite, quite. Where will you go?'

'Back to Kent, I should think. Take over the old house, run the estate. I cannot be idle.'

'You have done good work, you know,' Sir Toby said, with utmost sincerity. 'It may appear otherwise at times, but the Empire prevails thanks to your efforts.'

John only nodded. He was no longer certain if the Empire prevailing was a good thing, if it did so at such a terrible human cost as he had seen these past two years. He waited for the catch; surely Sir Toby Fitzwilliam would not let John go without some last revelation, or some contractual bonds hitherto unknown. But instead, Sir Toby stepped forward and shook John's hand.

'I shall have the arrangements made, papers drawn up,' he said. 'We expect certain secrets to go with you to your grave. Remember, too, that you are always a member of the Apollonian. I would hope to see you from time to time.'

'I would hope to stay away from London for some time to come. Goodbye, sir.'

'John…'

'Yes, sir?' There was a queer look in Sir Toby's eyes – some look of fellowship for John that had never previously been expressed.

'Just… live a life, Colonel Hardwick. Go and live a life, so you have nothing to regret when the time of judgment comes.'

John considered this. 'I'm afraid it is too late for that, sir.'

THIRTEEN

The boardroom was too large for the needs of such a small gathering, but it was windowless, and private, much like the office that Cherleten kept at St Katharine Docks. Jim was unused to seeing his commander openly rattled. There was something about his manner that made Jim feel this large, cheerless room was now a bolthole, and Jim was not one for hiding.

Hardwick sat in silence. The death of Sir Toby had taken some toll on him. Jim could not tell if he was about to descend into a pit of despair, or explode with pent-up rage, but some storm certainly brewed in the colonel's mind.

'What has happened this night will have grave repercussions,' Lord Cherleten said. He held a whisky glass in a trembling hand, ice rattling. 'Very grave. Nothing will ever be the same again.'

'How could this happen?' Hardwick asked, his voice quiet, but there now was the edge of threat that had made him so feared. 'We are the foremost agency of intelligence in the land, are we not? Who could have done it?'

'That is what we must establish,' said Cherleten. 'Believe me, we all have our part to play in bringing Sir Toby's killers to justice.' He downed his whisky in one gulp.

There was something about Cherleten's tone that bothered Jim immensely. He sounded insincere, as though he were not at all concerned for Sir Toby. Were his nerves born out of fear for his own safety, perhaps?

'Let us not dwell solely on this tragedy, Lord Cherleten,' Sir Arthur said. He had eschewed his usual timidity for an air of resoluteness. 'Rather, we should brief our agents, for they will face great peril in the coming days. It is only right, under the circumstances, that they should know why.'

Cherleten frowned at Sir Arthur. 'You think we should go ahead with Sir Toby's plan? Even after this?'

'Especially after this. Before, we gave lie to Tsun Pen's claims. I rather imagine he expected we would. And so we dithered, again as he expected we would. And then he arranged for the murder of our commander. There is no doubt in my mind as to why, Lord Cherleten. He wishes to demonstrate that he is serious; that he indeed wields the power and influence that he claims; that we are not safe even here, behind the hallowed walls of the Order of Apollo. And so we must assume that he is deadly serious indeed, and that all of his claims, therefore, must also be true.'

'And you would bow to his demands?' Cherleten sneered. 'You? Despite the cost?'

'If I am willing to bear the burden,' Sir Arthur said, 'then you should also. No victory is worth winning without sacrifice. Sir Toby told me that.'

'Would anyone care to explain what is going on?' Colonel Hardwick asked. Jim was glad he had – neither he nor even Miss Furnival would dare. Yet John Hardwick had positioned himself uniquely within the Order – an agent rarely called upon, afforded great freedoms by Sir Toby, and yet still trusted with secrets that would curl the toes of most operatives. It crossed Jim's mind that, in light of the night's events, Hardwick might find his various liberties rescinded. The look Cherleten gave Hardwick certainly suggested as much, although if the colonel was cowed in the slightest, he did not show it.

'Blunt as ever, Colonel Hardwick,' Cherleten said.

'Colonel, you have every right to know what is going on, for it affects you directly,' Sir Arthur said. 'Captain Denny, Lord Cherleten and I believe that you will have a part to play also. And you, Marie,' he gestured to his niece, who had positioned herself a few seats away from the rest of them, so quiet one might hardly know she was there. 'My dear, I have no great wish to see you set upon a more dangerous course than the one you have already forged. And I have less wish to instigate any development that may estrange us. But for all that, you have seen tonight with your own eyes the peril in which we find ourselves. If, after hearing what we have to say, you wish to walk away from the Apollonian, and from the bosom of your family, then I certainly could not blame you. However, if you will stand with us, then I promise to set right that which has made you doubt me.'

'No time for sentimentality, Furnival,' Cherleten snapped.

'It is precisely the time, Lord Cherleten – there may be no other time.'

'Uncle... what are you saying?' Marie looked worried.

'He is saying, my girl, that we are about to send these two agents on an assignment that may result in their deaths; and that you are invited to accompany them.' Cherleten had a face that always looked as though he were smirking at one's expense. *Perhaps he is*, Jim thought.

'The assignment, then,' Hardwick demanded.

'Very well, Colonel,' Cherleten relented. 'Sir Toby told you earlier of the Artist's potential deal with the Russians. It is clear now that the Artist was telling the truth – he is indeed conspiring with our rivals, and therefore we can conclude that he does indeed hold the Otherside contraband that he claims. And a fine claim it is – he says he has enough etherium to tear a rift in the fabric of reality the likes of which would make Lazarus weep. Yet he has no qualms about selling it to the highest bidder, along with weapons and other devices captured from the Othersiders' secret caches... unless, of course, we give in to his demands.

'First and foremost, the Artist wants amnesty for himself and his most loyal followers, so that they may return to London in a legal place of business. It seems he wishes a return to the old status quo; to be once more of service to government despite his many transgressions.'

'Outrageous!' Jim cried.

'It is. Oddly, however, before that happens he has made another request. He wishes a member of the Nightwatch to be delivered into his hands, to aid him with his prophecies. Not only that, but he has specified a particular subject – one that he could not possibly have known about, and yet has identified as being of singular talent.'

Jim's stomach knotted, for he knew what was to come. He glanced first at John Hardwick, and then at Miss Furnival, who was already scowling at the mention of the Nightwatch. He wondered again if Miss Furnival could be trusted.

Sir Arthur spoke up. 'We can only put the Artist's great knowledge of our Nightwatch subjects down to his own uncanny powers. The one he has singled out is indeed our best. Her predictions, in fact, have been consistently more accurate than those of her fellows, even when she has disagreed with the consensus entirely, though unfortunately it is only with hindsight that this was ascertained. Captain Denny has seen her incredible abilities at first hand.'

Jim felt Marie Furnival's eyes boring a hole in the back of his head.

Cherleten picked up where he had left off. 'The Artist has requested that Colonel Hardwick deliver the subject to a remote location in Essex. It is a stretch of woodland in a place called Mundon, far removed from town or train station. Crucially, it is near the coast, and Sir Toby had already begun making inquiries at the Admiralty. It would seem logical, given our recent dockside discoveries, that the Artist may be planning to move the cargo by boat.'

'Sir Toby also mentioned the Prime Minister earlier,' Jim said.

'Yes,' Cherleten said. 'Given the unusually high stakes, we need Gladstone's approval, but I am confident it will be given. Gladstone is a God-fearing man. He has little tolerance where psychics and prophecies are concerned – sees them as blasphemy. But especially now, after the assassination of a ranking intelligence officer by a foreign agent on British soil… The Prime Minister is not a weak man. He will want a reckoning of Biblical proportions. I shall provide one.'

'When Sir Toby wrote to the Prime Minister, he advised caution,' Sir Arthur interjected. 'Lest the Artist was merely bluffing.'

'Well, it appears he was not!' Cherleten snapped. 'After that awful business with Prince Albert Victor, Sir Toby made an enemy of the Russians. Against my better judgment, I might add. It stands to reason that they allied themselves with the Artist in order to take revenge on him. However, in exchange for meeting his demands, the Artist has promised us the full list of spies that he alluded to in his earlier message, along with lists of all the stockpiles of Otherside artefacts they were planning to purchase. If Sir Toby's killer is on that list, he'll bloody well hang, diplomacy or no.'

'Why would he give up the ace in his hand?' Hardwick asked.

'I doubt very much he will give us everything, unless his desire for revenge upon you is so powerful it has caused him to lose all reason. Regardless, Colonel Hardwick, you will deliver the cargo to the Artist tomorrow.'

'You speak of cargo,' Marie Furnival spoke up before Hardwick could reply. 'This is a human being.'

Hardwick gave Miss Furnival a curious look, and then turned back to Cherleten. 'Miss Furnival is right, Lord Cherleten. Who is this subject in which the Artist is so interested?'

'A gypsy. Your kind of girl, all told,' Cherleten said, barbed smile returning. 'More than that, we do not know, for she has not spoken lucidly since she came to us.'

Hardwick's jaw tightened. Jim wondered if he knew that Elsbet had been inducted into the Nightwatch. If not, he certainly did now – John Hardwick was no fool. He had seen the girl three years ago, alive at St Katharine Docks. He had told Jim all about her, and sworn him to secrecy. And now he was being asked to deliver the girl into the hands of his most hated enemy. Jim could already foresee the myriad things that could go wrong, and yet honour dictated that he could say nothing still about Elsbet – at least not to Cherleten and Sir Arthur.

'Lord Cherleten,' Jim said, acutely aware that John was on the verge of giving away his vested interest in the girl. 'Miss Furnival and I were summoned also; what, might I ask, is our role?'

'There was no stipulation that Colonel Hardwick had to travel to Essex alone. You are to follow, and to observe,' Cherleten said. 'That is, if you can set aside your differences for long enough.'

'I...' Jim saw that Hardwick was now staring at him. He had not mentioned his mistrust of Miss Furnival, let alone the cause of it. 'Of course, sir. Will we have men?'

'Every agent of the Order presently on these shores has been recalled to the club. We expect to have naval support along the coast, and the Essex constabulary on side by morning. We cannot act rashly, however much we may desire revenge. It is unlikely that the Artist will himself be at the rendezvous point; and so his men must be followed if we are to find and capture him.'

'Capture?' Hardwick said, with some of the surprise that Jim also felt. 'The man plans to sell catastrophic amounts of etherium to our enemies, yet you seek to double-cross him, and let him live?'

'Look here, Colonel Hardwick. As far as we are concerned, the Artist is the most dangerous man alive. You were once sent to kill him for that very reason, and unless this creature is playing a damned silly game with us, there's a good chance you failed. Tsun Pen or no, he will be captured and interrogated, and when we have scooped every ounce of knowledge from his evil little brain, we shall hang him. With any luck, we shall avert a war in the process, but I'll be damned if I shall give in to his demands.'

'Sir Toby –' Sir Arthur began.

'Sir Toby is not here!' snapped Cherleten.

'It is not a war against the Russians or anyone else that should concern us,' Hardwick said. 'If that etherium is put to use, you know what will follow.' As he spoke, Hardwick glanced furtively over his shoulder. Jim noticed that Sir Arthur was staring at Hardwick. Or, rather, past Hardwick, also over the colonel's shoulder, though there was nothing there but darkness. Jim tried to ignore it – who knew what things Sir Arthur saw, or imagined he saw, in the shadows.

'It will not come to that,' Cherleten went on. 'The Artist is by his nature craven – he no more wishes to die at the hands of these... "Riftborn" and more than the rest of us. He will turn over all he knows of these foreign spies, and every drop of etherium, in a desperate bid to save his own skin.'

'And what will you do with the etherium?' Miss Furnival's continued impertinence again drew a cold glare from Cherleten.

'Why, use it for the Nightwatch, of course. Or, if Sir Arthur's experiment continues to prove fruitless – as it has so far – we shall destroy it.'

Jim saw Sir Arthur look downcast, and wondered what the true plans of the inner circle were. They would not be revealed here – certainly not to Miss Furnival.

'We have little time to prepare,' Cherleten said. 'The exchange will take place tomorrow. The psychic for the list. Once the Artist is happy that we have delivered on our other promises, he will give us what contraband he has... but all things being well, he will be in our custody before that happens.'

'It rather seems as though I am being sent into a trap,' Hardwick said. 'A sacrificial lamb.'

'We do not yet have enough intelligence to ensure your safety, Colonel Hardwick, it is true,' Sir Arthur said. 'But the Artist has given us this night, at least. We have means at our disposal to second-guess him, and we shall explore every avenue, you have my word. Sir Toby was adamant that you should be afforded every protection if this plan was to proceed, and we shall stay true to his wishes.'

There came a knock at the door. Holdsworth entered without being summoned, moving noiselessly to Lord Cherleten's side. He whispered something in Cherleten's ear, and then left as discreetly as he had come.

'I think we have done all we can do here,' Cherleten announced, 'and said all we can say without further intelligence upon which to act. I suggest we reconvene tomorrow, when our plans are more concrete. I am still to speak with the Prime Minister, and Sir Arthur has much to prepare.' No one looked happy about leaving with no plan of action.

'That's it?' Hardwick asked. 'Our commander is slain, and we are ordered to sleep on it?'

'Yes, Colonel. And speaking of which, you and Denny have been secured lodgings here tonight. We have men outside and snipers on surrounding roofs. I would strongly advise that you do not leave the club.'

'What about me?' Miss Furnival said.

'The ordinary members would object to having a lady on the premises overnight. You will go straight home and return first thing. An escort will be provided – we cannot be too careful. Any of us.'

Chelsea Embankment, London, 1.30 a.m.

Sir Arthur stamped his feet against the cold, and handed his overcoat to Jenkins. His London home afforded almost as many comforts as the Sussex estate, though tonight he found it singularly devoid of cheer. He had dark work to do; work that led him to steal away from the sanctuary of the club like a thief in the night.

'I took the precaution of lighting the fire in your study, sir,' Jenkins said.

'What? Oh… yes. Good fellow. I shall go up now.'

'Will you be down for some dinner, sir? Only, Miss Marie was asking earlier.'

'No, I don't think so. I shall ring if I need anything. I… I am not to be disturbed. For any reason.'

Sir Arthur trudged upstairs, mind churning over the failure of his Nightwatch. Cherleten's sneers still stung.

He took a glance along the hall towards Marie's room; all was quiet. She was probably asleep after a tumultuous evening. Sir Arthur was glad of that. He entered his study, clicked the door closed, and turned the key in the lock.

This was his sanctuary. A room of good proportions, unfavourable as a bedroom because of its single, small window overlooking the river that made it somewhat gloomy. It was perfect for Sir Arthur's needs. Two walls lined with his books of esoterica, a large writing bureau, a comfortable chair. Here, Sir Arthur often meditated. Sometimes, he would pull back the rug in the centre of the room and mark a circle of salt, in an effort to commune with the darker entities detailed in his books of occult philosophy. He had met with no tangible results in that regard, despite several attempts.

By the glow of the fire Arthur found his candles, tall and black, and lit five of them, positioning them in a rough circle around the room. He placed a small box on the table beside his armchair, and sat down. He rolled up his shirtsleeve, opened the case, and took out a syringe. Sir Arthur looked warily at the needle, uncertain whether or not to proceed. He had attempted this only once before, in a small, controlled dose, with doctors present. The results of the experiment had surprised him, but they were not as spectacular as those achieved by the Nightwatch. And yet he had achieved a greater degree of control over the visions, possibly due to the mundane nature of this world compared to the hell-stricken realm of the Othersiders. The after-effects of the etherium, on the other hand, had been unpleasant, even though the dose had been minuscule.

He remembered the last time he had done this, years ago. He had seen the girl, Elsbet, before he had ever met her. But at the same time, it had not been her at all, for in his visions – and his nightmares – she was dead, pale, soaked through as though drowned. That was how he'd known, from the minute he'd set eyes on the gypsy girl in St Katharine Docks, that she was special. Well, he could not rely on her now. He could rely on none of them.

'Courage, Arthur,' he muttered to himself.

He had to be certain. He had to explore every avenue, as he'd promised. Lives depended upon his success or failure. The Nightwatch was compromised, but Arthur knew that he still had strength left. Was it strength enough to navigate the Eternal Dark? To discern the skeins of fate even more clearly than his Nightwatch? He would soon find out, for there was no one else to trust; no other recourse. And so he took up the small phial of etherium, and drew its entire contents into the syringe. He stared at the needle for a moment; at the brown-gold liquid that must have come at the cost of several lives. Perhaps, just perhaps, he wanted this. He'd missed it.

Arthur did his best to clear his thoughts, to quell his nerves and prepare himself to commune with the mighty dead. To learn their secrets.

Snip – Crack!

It was the worst sound Sir Arthur could imagine, simultaneously heard and *felt*. The slapping of a headmaster's cane across a schoolboy's palms; the twisting of a leg from a chicken carcass; the wet champing of a hunting-hound's jaws around the neck of a fox.

Snip – Crack!

Again. The sound of a neck breaking at the end of a rope.

Arthur stood upon the deck of a ship. The air was freezing. Men stood around him, ghostly white faces turned upwards.

They were motionless, indistinct as figures in fog. Tiny glowing lights drifted all about, motes of iridescent dust, like snowflakes gently falling beneath yellow gaslamps. Sir Arthur looked up, where the motes gathered and swirled in greater quantity, where Lieutenant Bertrand's body twitched, the hangman's noose about his neck, trailing up to the rigging of the *Glarus*.

Why are you showing me this?

The mists gathered, thickening in great tendrils, until all was silver-grey. When they again parted, Sir Arthur was standing upon the harbour wall, the *Glarus* floating silent by the quay. A sound behind him signalled the arrival of wagons. He approached them as they drew up – three beer wagons, the gold livery of Charrington's Ales painted upon their sides. Arthur looked down at himself; he was dressed in a grey tunic, after the Chinese style. A dagger hung by his waist – he saw through the eyes of another.

More celestials leapt down from the wagons, bearing arms. They dragged a prisoner from the back of the nearest cart, hooded and trembling. Bertrand. Sir Arthur moved backwards through time it seemed. No; he was being guided by some unseen force.

Snip – Crack!

Sir Arthur searched for the source of the hateful sound. He saw only the enfolding mists, obscuring the black river and distant lamplight. Yet he knew something was lurking in the strange fog; some unseen predator that caused his hackles to rise.

The wagons departed, wheels rolling not along the cobbled harbour, but through thick mud and damp sand. They trailed towards a narrow causeway that rose from an inky sea. Soon they were gone, the last of their lamps vanishing into gloom, and Arthur was alone.

Snip – Crack!

He spun around. The sound echoed, impossible to place. For a moment he thought he saw a pair of eyes blazing in the darkness, but they were gone in an instant. He was on an island, overgrown and rugged. In the distance he saw the black outline of a large house. Between here and there, however, lay crumbling ruins, an expanse of overgrown pasture, tumbledown gravestones. A trail wound its way towards the house, and he followed...

...until he stood instead at the mouth of a tumbledown mausoleum, jagged and ruinous, surrounded by skeletal trees like cracks upon a painted canvas of the night sky. He was uncertain he could truly feel anything, but he fancied it was bitterly cold. The battered doors were weathered and rotten. Arthur stepped forward, hand outstretched as though he were impelled to do so by some unseen force. The doors swung open; for a second he thought he saw movement in the shadows beyond – the impression of large white teeth grinning, of eyes dancing like distant lanterns, of sinewy limbs reaching towards him.

Come, little blood-sack. Show us the way...

The voice reverberated like grinding millstones, rising as a deep, guttural quake within Arthur's belly. Hungry lips smacked beside his ear. Something alighted on his shoulder, pressing hard; bony fingers. Claws scratched at his shoulder, impossibly sharp, picking away the fabric of his jacket, slicing flesh with the precision of a surgeon's blade.

Snip – Crack!

Arthur could not move, try as he might. He shut his eyes tight, prayed it was merely a figment of his imagination in this dark place, this endless night. In all his experience, he had never found a spirit that could do him harm, even when it displayed malevolence. He held on to that thought. The thing at his shoulder was gone. The whispers within him subsided.

Arthur opened his eyes. He stood now in a large chamber, bedecked with bizarre machinery and apparatus. Flickers of electrical energy undulated along copper cabling, illuminating the chamber in sporadic flashes. Arthur recognised the design at once, for it resembled closely the Otherside technology locked away by Lord Cherleten. There was an inlet in the chamber's centre. Black water lapped gently at aged stonework. But this was not St Katharine Docks. A boathouse, perhaps?

Before him, a man worked frantically, hoisting at pulleys, winding handles to power his machines, dashing from pillar to post, examining gauges and muttering to himself giddily. He was thin, with scruffy, dark hair and a large moustache. His face was swollen, black and blue from some accident, or recent beatings.

Arthur turned his attentions to the room. He had little time, for the visions came thick and fast, beyond his control. He had to discern every possible detail. In the water, something stirred. Riveted metal bobbed just beneath the surface, like the fins of some huge artificial sea-creature. He heard a voice say something in a strange language, and then the words 'storm hunter'.

A system of pulleys held the strange vessel fast, by means of chains that led to thick rafters overhead. As Sir Arthur's eyes followed the chains, he caught sight of something moving in those rafters. He heard the beating of leathery wings, the scraping of claws on aged wood.

The room was gone. The mist drew in again, swirling orange, flickering with ghost-light. Arthur felt a sense of something vast and empty beyond the mists; or perhaps there was nothing but mist. He could feel nothing beneath his feet, his hands touched only thin air before him. The sense of endless emptiness all around was dizzying.

Arthur was not alone.

Snip – Crack!

Something – several somethings – flitted around him, circling, predatory vultures lurking in the shadow and uncanny fog.

We will snip-crack your bones, little blood-sack.

Arthur knew what it was. The Nightwatch cried out in their sleep sometimes. They feared it more than anything. They called it the Other.

Yesss… Show us the way. Show usss…

A great shadow erupted from the mist, tearing through even this void with a rapidity and violence that made Arthur scream involuntarily. He shook until he thought he might be shaken free of his earthly shackles and his astral form cursed to roam the darkness for ever. All around him, vast, undulating tendrils snapped like whips. Beneath him, he saw nothing, but he sensed it – a gaping maw; endless rows of pin-sharp teeth, so hungry they could swallow the world.

'Uncle! Uncle Arthur!'

Marie pounded on the door again. No sound came from within. She had heard nothing since the scream, which had made her blood run cold.

Footsteps pounded the landing behind her, and Jenkins was by her side. He rattled the doorknob furiously, to no avail, and lent his voice to Marie's, calling to his master.

'Break it down,' Marie commanded. 'Do it, man.'

Jenkins heaved his shoulder against the door, once, twice. At the third attempt the lock cracked and the frame splintered. Jenkins tumbled into the study. Marie barged past him into the room. Sir Arthur lay face down on the hearthrug, beside a dying fire. And for a dreadful moment, Marie thought they were not alone. Something stooped beside him, stroking his head with long black fingernails.

Marie flung herself towards her uncle, candles guttering in her wake. As the dim light flickered, the thing, the shadow, was gone.

'Oh no...' Marie knelt by her uncle's side. 'Light. Jenkins, bring light!'

Jenkins was already turning a paraffin lamp to its fullest, and brought it quickly. His face was ashen.

Sir Arthur's right shoulder was wet with blood, his shirt and waistcoat crimson. He groaned, and moved gingerly, and Marie helped him turn over, only then realising the extent of his injuries. A row of prick-marks pierced his forehead, and blood trickled from the wounds, his nostrils, the corners of his eyes, and from the blue veins that bulged at his temples, now burst as if from great pressure. Great scratches ran down his throat, and bloody gouges encircled his heart. He was limp and weak, his breathing ragged.

Marie tried to ignore the syringe upon the small side-table, but she knew at a glance what it contained. She knew also that the thing she had seen was not a mere trick of the light. In that knowledge, she fought every instinct to run, as she had learned to do on the Otherside as a girl. She would be safe here, in this universe, she told herself. The Riftborn could not gain a foothold here, not permanently. And right now, Sir Arthur needed her.

'Call for Mrs Bennett,' Marie ordered. 'Tell her to bring fresh water. And send for a doctor.'

With an unlikely show of vitality, Sir Arthur grabbed out at Jenkins' ankle, stopping him in his tracks. 'No. No... doctor.'

'Uncle, you're hurt. You need medical attention.'

'McGrath. At the club... No other.'

Marie looked up at Jenkins. 'Do you know who he's talking about?'

'Yes, ma'am. Mr McGrath is a surgeon. He is a member of Sir Arthur's... club.' He emphasised the word 'club' so that Marie would take his meaning, and she resisted the urge not to chide Jenkins for treating her like an idiot.

'Then find him.'

As soon as Jenkins' footsteps had receded across the landing, Marie cradled Sir Arthur's head, and hissed, 'What were you thinking? What have you done?'

He coughed. He looked sicklier by the second. 'I have... seen it. By God... you were right.'

'Uncle, if you have brought it into this world... Do you have any idea what you have done?'

'It... showed me... things. Listen, Marie. You must listen...' He broke into a violent fit of coughing, chest heaving, limbs contorting. Marie held him close.

'You should have listened to me,' she whispered, tears stinging her eyes. He was so much like the uncle she had known in her own world. Less assured, perhaps, and with a certain frailty, but just as stubborn, just as heedless of danger.

'Damn it, Marie!' he spluttered. 'Listen. Charrington. Charrington's... Ales. Find it.'

'What?'

'And an island.' More coughing, followed by a dreadful wheezing. 'He is on... an island. With a causeway. And a... a machine. A floating machine. No! A submarine. But... beware.'

He spluttered. Marie cradled his head. 'Be still,' she said. 'Help is coming.'

'No... time. Take these.' He fumbled in his jacket, and withdrew a ring of keys, dropping them on the floor as strength left his fingers. 'If I... die...'

'Uncle?'

Sir Arthur grew limp in Marie's arms, his eyes appearing almost glassy. He fought for every breath.

'Beware... the house of the dead,' he gasped. 'It... it is... foretold.'

'The good Lord preserve us!' Mrs Bennett's shrill tones announced her arrival, and the housekeeper almost dropped her bowl of water when she saw Sir Arthur lying on the floor in tatters.

Marie cradled his head as his eyes closed. He breathed but weakly.

'Hold on, Uncle,' she whispered. 'Please. I can't lose you again.'

Sir Arthur's eyes opened once more, and a look of violent horror seized him. He shielded his eyes as though something was at the small window of his study, before collapsing into unconsciousness.

Marie turned to look, but there was nothing, save for the black mirror of the window, and the distant chiming of buoy bells upon the Thames.

FOURTEEN

Monday, 16th July 1888

THE OTHERSIDE

'No! Again!'

Marie gritted her teeth as the Japanese instructor's words were accompanied by the thwack of her cane on Marie's behind. Mrs Ito must have been over a hundred years old, and for all of the old woman's fierce reputation, it was only her venerable years that stopped Marie throttling the life out of her.

Mrs Ito shuffled away, climbing the steps to her podium. Marie, breathing raggedly, wiped blood and sweat from her eyes, tried to slow her pulse in preparation for the next wave. She glanced back to see Mrs. Ito take her seat, well out of harm's way, beneath the only lamp in the training room. Agent Hardwick stood beside the old woman's throne, face pale and impassive as porcelain, hair immaculately coiffured. Beautiful, like a doll.

Mrs Ito clapped her gnarled old hands, and Marie turned back to face the darkness. She saw the violet eyes bobbing towards her, heard the low, throaty growls. She tightened her grip on her two curved blades. The ghouls were more wary this time, as though they sensed what had happened to their predecessors.

They fanned out across the tunnel mouth, hugging the walls. Marie could have sworn they were learning, forming a strategy, though that was surely impossible.

The last wave had been almost too much. Marie's heart pounded, blood racing, anger threatening to overcome her. Her armour was stifling. It was alright for the other agents – they'd had years of training. Marie had only turned seventeen last Wednesday, and she was exhausted. She knew she'd been too eager to show what she could do in the first few tests. She hadn't held anything back. She hadn't expected more. And now here they were, more ghouls, walking cadavers come to tear at her.

Her vision blurred – tears of hot rage mingling blood and sweat. Each pair of violet eyes that blinked into view was another object of her vitriol. She would slaughter them all or be damned.

The first came, pouncing from her right. She darted beneath it, catching its inner thigh with the first blade, swirling about as it landed behind her, and stabbing the second knife through its temple. She snapped a kick at an onrushing ghoul covered in pustules, grimacing as something fleshy burst upon impact. She ducked beneath the flailing claws of two others. Her limbs burned with fatigue, but anger drove her on.

Rolling beneath attacks, springing over the bodies of the slain, slashing and stabbing, she went on. Two more fell, one with a slice across the throat, another disembowelled, the beast fighting on for a few seconds before it realised the extent of the wound and fell.

At once, Marie was aware of some new attacker. Her instincts screamed to leap aside, and she did. That sixth sense saved her life; a ghoul dropped from the arched ceiling of the cellar, raking its ragged claws down her back. They tore through her padded doublet, slicing flesh. Marie cried out. The armour was next to useless. This thought gripped Marie; knowing that she had been protected from the ghouls' claws had lent her confidence. That confidence was misplaced. Knowing that the ghouls could not attack from above had likewise emboldened her. The ceiling was covered in an electrified mesh to stop this from happening – Mrs Ito had turned it off. Marie knew it, and the hard lesson felt like a betrayal.

She lashed out, slicing the creature across the belly, though not deep enough. It knocked the blade from her hand, and for a moment Marie stared into a face almost devoid of flesh, just a skull with sharpened teeth and burning eyes. It leapt forward, knocking the wind from her. She hit the flagstones, rolled over as the creature leapt on top of her. She slashed blindly, taking off two of its fingers, before jamming the knife hard into its throat. The skull-faced monster hissed and fell, then another ghoul dropped from the ceiling, its weight almost crushing Marie. She could barely see. In a moment of panic, she realised she could die here, in a training exercise.

The new attacker punched at Marie's helmet. She batted its claws away from her eyes instinctively. With a flick of her wrist, a small blade sprang from her sleeve, and she punched it repeatedly into the creature's flesh. It roared, then wrenched her arm aside. With its other clawed hand it tore off her helmet. Its distended, mutated face hung an inch from hers. She was powerless to stop its great fanged mouth descending. It was barely an inch from her throat when some dark force hoisted the creature away. A lithe, deadly shadow whirled amidst the remaining ghouls, and all of them retreated in fear from the pureblood before them.

From Lillian Hardwick, Apollo Lycea's *wampyr* assassin.

Marie lay in shock among stinking carcasses. She heard the cell doors close, and knew it was over.

Lillian Hardwick dragged Marie to her feet. Marie wiped more blood and dirt from her eyes, and sniffed away her tears. She was half blind and hurt all over.

'Never let them claw you, Miss Furnival,' Lillian said, her voice like distant bells carried on a cold wind. 'If you do that in the field, you would betray your mind and body to one such as me. Do you have any idea what it is like to have the *wampyr* in your head? To have them see through your eyes? To hear their honeyed whispers? Pray you never find out.'

'She… she cheated,' Marie gasped. Her legs were like jelly; she wanted to collapse to the floor and not move.

A walking stick rapped loudly on brick, three times. 'Too emotional!' Mrs Ito shouted from the podium. 'If the girl not so blind by her anger, she would have seen the danger sooner. The girl is not ready for the field. You tell them she need more work. Much more.'

'I shall tell them, Mrs Ito.' Lillian bowed to the podium. The old woman nodded back.

Lillian Hardwick led Marie away, holding her up with great strength.

'Do not fall, girl,' Agent Hardwick said, quietly. 'If she sees you fall, you'll never get out in the field.' Agent Hardwick led Marie through a reinforced door and into a corridor, where bright lights stung her eyes. 'You have skill – more than the old woman would care to admit. But you're reckless. More so than I ever was. If you wish to avenge your uncle, you have a lot to learn beside strength and speed. You need guile, and finesse. Above all, you must be fearless. Your anger was born not just of vengeful thoughts, but of fear. Fear will get you killed. Tomorrow, you train with me.'

'Th… thank you,' Marie croaked hoarsely.

'Oh, do not thank me. I intend to break you, and remake you. The next time Mrs Ito sees you, you will either be a warrior, or a corpse.'

FIFTEEN

OLD NICHOL, LONDON

John crashed shoulder-first through the stud wall of the dilapidated rookery, plaster exploding to dust beneath his charge. He hit the floor, rolling beneath the grasping arms of a huge bearded man, half-naked and full of rage. A woman screamed; she tumbled from a bed, covering her modesty with filthy, greying sheets.

The bearded man looked for a weapon. John was up and running. He leapt through the air, putting all of his weight into one herculean punch. John's fist connected with the man's temple, and he fell to the bare floorboards in a heap.

John looked for another way out. A dog barked upstairs. He marched for the door, his men already filing into the room behind him. John registered the sound of a knife on flesh as one of them slit the big man's throat. The woman stopped screaming, and fell to quiet sobbing instead.

John threw the door open, dashed down the next corridor. The element of surprise was lost. A thug in a bowler hat flew from a side-room, swinging a truncheon in a vicious arc. John blocked with his forearm, grunting at the momentary flash of pain. His right hand spun his blade outwards and punched it into his assailant's ribs in swift, darting jabs; three times, four. The man's face was a mask of surprise and disbelief at the swiftness and ignominy of his demise. The life drained from his eyes and he dropped to the floor like so much butchered meat.

Like all the men in this den of iniquity – these Old Nichol Street men – he had probably thought himself beyond the reach of law. That may have been true, but the Nichol Street Gang had begun dabbling in more esoteric crimes than trafficking, cash-carrying and petty extortion. Now they had drawn the eye of Apollo, and John had been dispatched to clean up the mess created by this gang of ne'er-do-wells.

John nodded to Bertrand, who at once entered the side-room. John himself dashed up the rickety stairs at the end of the corridor, three at a time, with Whittock, Clements and Raynor close at heel. He kicked down the door at the top of the stairs, darting away as a dog leapt at his throat, teeth gnashing and spittle flying. Whittock raised a firearm, but John stayed his hand. The dumb brute was at the end of its chain, and had seen better days. Its black-and-tan fur was matted with dirt and excrement, plastered to its skeletal frame. John gave the creature a fierce glare with his one eye, and it ceased straining at the chain, backing away warily. John sidestepped the dog, staying clear of its radius, and signalled his men to do the same.

A set of double doors burst open and two men took aim. John and his men scattered as a shotgun roared. Whittock was first to respond, twin revolvers blazing away. One of the attackers stumbled back into the room; the man who had fired the shotgun convulsed as three rounds turned his chest into a bloom of crimson before he fell.

John leapt to his feet, unslung his trusty Winchester and strode through the doors. The second gunman, wounded, scrabbled for a weapon. John shot him through the neck and levered another round into the breech. There were murmurs, cries, shouts of alarm. A stench of excrement, sweat and decay assailed him.

Before him, a long room stretched outwards, three, perhaps four slums, all knocked into one huge attic space, now a workshop for the Nichol Street operation. A few windows, covered in newspaper, let in slivers of sickly yellow light. On filthy mattresses arranged in two neat rows, like a hospital ward, emaciated bodies lay languid, dead or dying, some chained to ironwork, others rotting in open air.

The attendants to these poor souls shrank away into the corners of the room, whimpering, knowing full well that a righteous judgment had arrived to punish them for the cruelty they had inflicted. But John's attention was not on them, not now. The hair at the back of his neck prickled. His flesh numbed with cold; each breath felt like icy daggers plunging into his chest.

Walking away from him, sweeping slow and silent along the shadowed aisle, was a girl. Her white dress billowed softly, as though she were underwater. Her hair was black, dark and shimmering, similarly drifting like seaweed in shallows. Her small hands and feet were white as her raiment. All of John's guilt flooded back to him. He wanted to cry out, to tell her to leave him be, to end this accursed haunting. But he knew his men were near; he could not show weakness in front of them.

'Sir?' Whittock was by John's side, doubtless wondering why his commanding officer had stopped. But John could say nothing; he could only watch dumbly as the shade – this ghost – walked away from him. The ghost of Elsbet stopped at the foot of one of the mattresses, and extended a slender arm towards the makeshift bed, fingers pointing to the wretch upon it. There was a woman on the bed, wasted and grey-skinned, lying in her own filth. Beside her sat a man, trembling with fear, fingers still curled about a syringe, the needle probing deep into the woman's forehead, between the eyebrows. The 'third eye', mediums called it. Brownish fluid bubbled into the syringe, unpurified, impregnated with swirls of blood. John knew what it contained. He knew what Elsbet wanted from him.

Mercy. Mercy for the lost. For the ones like her.

'Sir!' Whittock snapped.

John blinked. Warmth returned to his bones. Elsbet was gone.

His men had seized the attendants, holding them now at gunpoint. Seven men and women, the youngest perhaps twenty, the oldest in their last winters. All were sallow-skinned and haunted about the eyes. They were low commoners, East End dregs, doubtless brought into this foul business against their will. They had performed the darkest deeds out of fear, perhaps out of ignorance. But they were now complicit in what the Order deemed a capital crime: the harvesting of etherium from Otherside refugees. They knew too much, and had become just as guilty as their paymasters.

John told himself this thrice more, steeling himself for what was to come. He trod the creaking floorboards, to the mattress where Elsbet had stood, and gazed down at the woman. The attendant dropped the syringe, which leaked its contents onto the floor, and stared up at John, and then to Raynor, who aimed a revolver at the scrawny man's head. The woman on the bed breathed weakly. She would never recover.

'Interrogation, sir?' Whittock asked.

'No,' John said, grimly. 'We shall get more out of the Old Nichol boys. These petty servants can give us nothing that we need.' He hesitated. 'We have our orders.'

Gunfire. Screams. And then silence.

As his men composed themselves after their grim work, John took a sodden, dirty pillow from the floor and pushed it over the face of the frail woman on the bed, holding it there until her weak resistance ceased, and she was at peace. He stood and wiped his brow with his sleeve.

'Sir...' Whittock had a strong stomach for killing, but John had broken orders. 'Should we not take them alive?' He was hesitant.

'Check them all,' John said. 'If they are too weak to survive the trip, give them mercy. Otherwise... load them up.' For the first time in a long time, John hated saying it. His reasons for smothering the girl were nothing to do with her physical state, although Whittock seemed to accept it, and went about his work.

John walked from the room, unable to look at the poor souls his men had so casually dispatched. How had it come to this? When had he become a contract killer for the Order? He could no longer reckon the butcher's bill. It was necessary, he knew it. But did it have to be him?

Have I not done my duty ten times over?

A low growl, then a whimper.

John looked down at the skinny dog, cowed and whale-eyed.

'Best let me kill the mutt, sir,' Bertrand said, appearing at the door, wiping blood from his knife. 'It'll only starve to death here. Be a mercy, I reckon.'

Mercy.

John looked at the dog again. 'No,' he said. John stepped forward, ignoring the increasing intensity of the dog's growls. He unhooked the chain from its anchor, and looked sternly into the dog's eyes. 'You're coming with me.' John touched his hand to the dog's head, without fear, and the growls ceased. A twitch of its tail; perhaps this was the first kindness the brute had ever been shown. And it came with the last cruelty John would ever oversee. He swore it to himself.

No more.

PART TWO

O this world's curse – beloved but hated – came
Like Death betwixt thy dear embrace and mine,
And crying, 'Who is this? Behold thy bride,'
She push'd me from thee.

ALFRED, LORD TENNYSON

SIXTEEN

Jim dreamed of madness, always.

Chaos reigned upon the streets outside his window. Naked lunatics ran barefoot over blood-slick cobblestones, beneath a sky that burned with liquid fire. They fell upon each other, shrieking and cackling as they tore out each other's throats, poked out eyes, rutted like animals in the gutters. Other things cavorted with them; formless shadows dancing to an inaudible tune, cantering on sharp hooves, slicing flesh with blade-like claws of metal and bone. Over it all was the shadow on the sky. That cyclopean, many-tentacled thing that picked at the roiling red clouds like the hand of some ancient god rising from the earth. Winged creatures of nightmare swooped and swirled on eddies of fire like crows around a steeple. Like some hellish rainbow, the shadow seemed both near and far, but when a man looked upon it, it could always be heard. It scratched inside Jim's mind, until the scratching drowned out all other sound and thought. Even the sound of…

No. He recognised the room. He knew where he was, and he would rather be anywhere else.

'Jim?' The scratching subsided long enough for Jim to hear her – his Jane. The shadow allowed him to hear, for her voice was more a torture than anything the Other could conjure.

Jim turned slowly. He had no choice in the matter, though he did not want to see.

The wasted girl on the deathbed; garlands of sickly-sweet flowers hung all about; sweat-slick flesh, mottled with the marks of contagion. She reached out with a hand that was far too thin. Sunken eyes implored him to be by her side. Jim's heart broke all over again; he had never been there at the end, yet he was forced to relive her final moments, night after night.

He went to her, knelt by the bed. He closed his eyes, and took her cold, weak hand in his. But when he opened his eyes, Jane was gone, and instead he looked upon Algie, his lover, dead and pale, neck snapped from the impact of his fall. His eyes were alive. They stared at Jim, full of accusation.

Jim snatched his hands away from the corpse, and raced from the room. Beyond the door, an opulent lounge of silk and velvet and red lanterns stretched as far as the eye could see. Men, young and old, lay languidly, half-naked on sofas and beds, drinking absinthe and luxuriating in each other's arms. Mandrakes with painted faces pawed at Jim as he hurried past. Even as he approached the door, a great pounding came upon it, causing it to bulge in its frame. The unmistakeable 'copper's knock', signalling the arrival of the law.

Jim looked in all directions. Men pushed past him, scrambling for an exit. Jim was blind with grief; he wanted nothing more than to be clapped in irons, to court the judgment of his father, and Lord Cherleten, and anyone else who would come to crow at his downfall. He deserved it.

And then someone seized him firmly by the shoulders. Jim wanted to cry out, 'Yes! Take me away. Lock me up and throw away the key!' But he looked up, and saw John Hardwick, ever dependable, ever dutiful. Jim allowed himself to be steered through the labyrinthine house, too large, too winding to be real, until he was outside in the hot air that smelled of brimstone, under the shadow of ravening demons that scratched in his skull.

NR. MUNDON, ESSEX

The coach rattled along unkempt roads, the flat, misty fields of the Essex countryside rolling by. Jim's nightmare had again robbed him of precious rest; again reminded him of his moral failings, and how to this day he had failed to make amends for them.

Jim looked across to Miss Furnival, the dark rings about her eyes betraying the tumultuous night she'd had. The woman was dressed in a mannish fashion, with trousers, shirt and overcoat, and her hair tucked up into a soft cap. Better, everyone had agreed, if she tried to pass for a lad for her own safety. Better, she had said, that she be dressed ready for a fight.

'I'm not sure why Cherleten sent you,' Jim said to Marie, as she stretched and yawned once more. His own tiredness subsided, and the nightmare with it, and Jim wanted nothing more than to make conversation, as though words were a spell with which to lay the ghosts of his conscience.

'You still don't trust me?'

'That's not what I meant,' Jim sighed. 'But with your uncle and all... maybe you should be with him. We'd have understood.'

'He knew the risks, and there's really nothing I can do. Better that I come along and make sure his efforts weren't in vain.'

Jim looked to John Hardwick, who had remained silent for most of the journey. Hardwick gave them both a sideways glance.

In accordance with precise instructions sent to Cherleten by the Artist in the early hours, they had alighted the train at Maldon East, with seven other agents in tow, as well as two members of Special Branch. Five agents had ridden north, to scout the lay of the land around what was suspected to be the Artist's lair: Osea Island. The presence of Charrington's Ales' wagons at the docks had all but confirmed that this was the island of Sir Arthur's vision – Osea was owned by the heir to that business, Frederick Charrington, though if Sir Arthur's intuition was correct, Charrington now had some less than desirable tenants. The man himself was proving impossible to reach, provoking fears for his safety.

Jim, Miss Furnival and Colonel Hardwick travelled to the rendezvous point at the head of the small convoy. The other two agents brought up the rear, travelling in a hired fly. The Special Branch men sat on the wagon between them, guarding their precious cargo – Elsbet – who slept within the confines of a large crate, little more than livestock. It was like transporting a corpse in a casket. Jim considered that appropriate; the girl spent more time communing with spirits than with the living.

Now, the three vehicles rolled towards the remote woodland of the Mundon Furze. There had been scant time for preparation, though Jim remained confident that Lord Cherleten would not leave them at the mercy of the Artist. And Sir Arthur's foray into the spirit world had given them more to go on than they had previously hoped.

'Your uncle's efforts are appreciated, of course,' Jim said. 'I can't begin to understand the risk he took.'

'I can,' Hardwick said. Jim and Miss Furnival had become so unaccustomed to the sound of his voice that they both turned to him in surprise. 'Three years ago, I saw exactly the threat our world faced. I thought I'd defeated it. Sir Arthur Furnival was the man who told me that I had not. He told me the fate that had befallen the Otherside could still befall us. He showed me how to prevent that from ever coming to pass. And yet now he has done the very thing he advised me against. His actions may well have damned us all.'

There was an uncomfortable silence, before Jim spoke. 'Hopefully it will not come to that. There is no proof that Sir Arthur has caused lasting harm. In fact, it seems unlikely that someone from our side could summon the power required to open the Rift.'

Hardwick glared at Jim. 'I have seen it done, by a group of mere gypsy girls, all of them from "our side". And they did not have the benefit of dangerous doses of etherium.'

'We've got to trust he knew what he was doing,' Miss Furnival said. She was visibly upset, but kept some semblance of calm. 'Perhaps my uncle saw what the Artist had in store, and decided it was worth the price.'

'Meddling in the future always comes at a price,' Hardwick replied. 'Perhaps by attempting to second-guess the Artist, Sir Arthur has sped along his plans. Perhaps we shall never know.'

'We will after today,' Jim intervened, seeing from Miss Furnival's expression that the conversation would soon turn ugly. 'Cherleten said that the Nightwatch had been sending conflicting messages to the Artist to mask our intentions.'

'More truthfully, he meant that a group of Otherside test-subjects have been thinking very hard about false plans, in the hope that the Artist might somehow divine them mistakenly,' Hardwick grumbled. 'I may have seen many fantastical things in my time, but Cherleten's plan sounds very much like wishful thinking to me.'

'Better hope it's not wishful thinking, old boy,' Jim said, himself bridling at John's tone. 'We have five men on their way to Osea, and a flotilla of navy chaps on standby. If the Artist knows our plan –'

'Or if Sir Arthur was wrong and he's not on Osea at all...' John interrupted.

Jim sighed. 'We have our orders.' It was the best retort he could think of.

Hardwick nodded. 'As you know, I always follow my orders,' he said. 'Even into certain death.'

'I like your style,' Miss Furnival said. She looked askance at Hardwick, and he at her. Did a whisper of a smile pass between them?

Jim shook his head in disbelief.

* * *

Daylight was fading even before the convoy took the winding road through the forest. It was hardly a welcome change of scenery from the flatlands that stretched to the coast on the Dengie Peninsula. The woods lined either side of the road, which rapidly became little more than a bumpy track; great gnarled boughs of ancient oaks reached overhead, bare branches thick enough to blot out the dying light. And then the woods began to thin a little, and the trees became stranger, twisted, until the coaches entered the furze itself – an unusual tract of petrified trees, impossibly ancient, standing sentry, black and ominous, against the approach of these strangers.

The road ahead was blocked by wagons. The silhouettes of men stood, not just with the blockade, but all around. More of them materialised from the cover of the forest like ghosts, watching the agents intently. They flanked the trail, perhaps a hundred yards on either side, shadows barely visible through the clearing.

The coach drew to a halt at the blockade.

'No heroics,' Hardwick said. 'They may try to take me down, but if it's a fight we cannot win, you must let them. If they try to renege on the deal, on the other hand, then we do what we must to protect our country. Understood?'

Jim nodded reluctantly. Marie Furnival was impassive. Hardwick checked the Webley revolver at his breast, ensuring his overcoat obscured it. He took up his cane – the one once carried by Ambrose Hanlocke, with which Hardwick had once stabbed the Artist – and exited the coach. Jim disembarked on the other side.

'Stay here,' Jim said to Miss Furnival. She considered this for a fraction of a second, before pulling her cap down to hide her eyes and hopping out behind Hardwick.

Jim looked towards the vehicles behind him. The Special Branch officers clutched rifles, and looked about sternly from beneath the brims of their black bowlers. The other agents – Carr and Fearnley – made their way forward, eyes alert to the danger all around.

'That is far enough,' a man at the blockade called out. His face was covered by hat and scarf, but his accent was unmistakeably Chinese. Jim thought he recognised the voice as the leader of the tong he had met aboard the *Glarus*. 'Which one of you is Colonel Hardwick?'

'I am.' Hardwick took a step forward, with no hesitation.

'I send to you my master's regards,' the man said. 'You have the cargo, as requested?'

'We do.'

'Show us.' He gestured to his men, and six of them, shadowy figures all, marched towards the wagon.

Hardwick turned and nodded to the Special Branch men. One of them climbed onto the wagon, removed the tarpaulin, and took the lid from the crate. One of the celestial's men hopped up too, and checked Elsbet's breathing. He stood upright and signalled to his master that all was well.

'Elsbet, that is her name,' the leader said. 'You once caused her death, and now you offer her a better life. How many men can say they had a second chance in such circumstances?'

Jim looked nervously to Hardwick. He saw the colonel's fists bunch.

'There has been a change of plan,' the celestial said loudly. 'The Artist wishes to treat with Colonel Hardwick personally, to discuss with him the price of betrayal.'

'That was not the agreement,' Jim called back. Hardwick held out a hand to prevent him saying more.

'It is now,' the celestial said. He held up a thick envelope. 'In here is all that you were promised. The Russians – including a certain assassin you will be keen to locate. The addresses of several warehouses storing black-market goods. All here. And to sweeten the pot for you, we offer something extra. The wagons behind me contain salvage from the Lazarus Gate itself. Salvage that your scientists would give anything to see. We offer them to you.'

'In exchange for Colonel Hardwick?' Jim asked.

The man shrugged.

'How is it possible that you have components from the gate?' Hardwick said.

'It does not matter. What matters is that we have them. And we offer them to you.'

Hardwick stepped close to Jim and Marie, and Fearnley and Carr drew in also.

'We are outgunned, and we need that information. I should go with them,' Hardwick said.

'We cannot allow that,' Jim replied.

'I doubt they will give you a choice. You must ensure the goods reach London. I suppose we shall just have to hope that Sir Arthur was right – if he was, perhaps I shall see you at Osea.'

'And if he was wrong?'

'Then perhaps the Artist and I shall have one last dance before the end.'

'Come, enough talk!' the celestial shouted. 'Colonel Hardwick comes with us. You take this wagon, we take yours. It is a simple offer; one that might expire if there is further delay.'

'Expire?' Jim broke away from the group and glowered at the man.

'Yes. Decide now, or we take Colonel Hardwick anyway.'

'Try it, and you'll be the first to die.'

The celestial pulled his scarf away, revealing the familiar face of Bertrand's killer. He smiled wickedly.

Jim felt a firm hand on his shoulder. Hardwick eased him back towards the others.

'We accept your terms,' Hardwick said. 'But I insist on seeing my people safely away from here before I go anywhere with you.'

'You are in no position to make further demands, Colonel.'

'If you agree, I shall come quietly. Believe me, sir, you do not want the alternative.'

There was a tense silence. Jim could scarce believe Hardwick's audacity, or the steely nerve with which he held himself now. This was barely the same man that Jim had met on the dockside more than three years ago, emaciated and wide-eyed. But Jim was not the same either, he reminded himself. The Order had a way of changing people, hammering them like iron in a forge.

The celestial laughed; quietly at first, then louder, his shoulders rising and falling. The men around him laughed, too, and more joined in, jeering.

'You are lucky I am more generous than the Artist, Colonel John Hardwick,' the man said at last, making a show of wiping away a tear of laughter. 'Very well.'

He gestured to his men, who began to turn the nearest wagon about. The two men who had inspected Elsbet's casket now took the reins of that wagon also, at the muted protests of Special Branch. Hardwick signalled the driver to turn their carriage around, which was not an easy task on a single track. The agents of Apollo Lycea stood to one side, seething, while the manoeuvring was conducted, until eventually both parties were ready to go their separate ways.

Jim insisted briefly on inspecting the wagon that the celestial had presented them, and discovered a veritable mountain of steel, copper and brass devices, and several crates containing complex machine parts, instruments and even weapons. Some of it was at least vaguely familiar to him, but the rest would no doubt be puzzled over by Cherleten's engineers for some time.

The armed men who had stood silently in the petrified wood now advanced. Two dozen, with more hanging further back. They were not all Chinese, indeed the majority were white, hard-faced, stern and haggard. Jim hoped they were Englishmen in the Artist's employ, and not foreign agents – if the latter, the ramifications of the transaction they were now completing would be too horrible to consider.

When it came to it, the agents, policemen and coach-drivers were ordered to their own convoy, which now pointed in the direction of home. For good or ill, Elsbet was taken by the celestials and loaded onto one of their wagons – not, Jim noted, painted in the Charrington's livery this time. Jim was the last to obey, instead turning to Hardwick.

'We shall see you again, Colonel,' he said. 'Depend upon it.'

Hardwick only nodded.

Jim stepped back solemnly, and the colonel was led away.

'Listen, agents,' the celestial called as he walked backwards towards his wagons. 'Go straight back to London. I warn you, do not try to follow. My master has ordered me to shoot Colonel Hardwick if you do.'

Jim gritted his teeth, and climbed into the coach. He did not know if there would truly be reconciliation if indeed John got out of this scrape, but he liked to think so. He would move heaven and earth to make it so.

The reins cracked, and the coach moved off.

'What's the plan, Captain?' Miss Furnival asked.

For a moment, Jim entertained the thought that Miss Furnival was behind everything, or somehow involved. He wanted to give her short shrift; to send her back to London. But there was something about her that he could not dislike, something that he trusted despite himself. 'We get to the next village, make sure we aren't being followed, then you and I find some horses and double back,' he said. 'We head for the coast as planned; with any luck we can rendezvous with the Navy, and put the fear into these scoundrels. Besides, I'll be damned if I entrust the life of our most celebrated agent to the vision of a psychic.'

'Uncanny,' Miss Furnival said, with a wry smile.

'Why?'

'That's exactly what I was thinking. It's like you read my mind.'

SEVENTEEN

John sat on the back of a wagon, a sack over his head, hands tied behind his back. He had submitted to these indignities, though not without some guile; he had slipped similar bonds in his time, and could do so again if he wished.

The men beside him rarely spoke, and when they did they exchanged coarse words in Mandarin Chinese. John had a smattering of the language, though he could discern nothing that gave him any clues as to their plans. He gleaned that their leader – their 'headman' – was named Xiang, and that he had been summoned from exile in the United States to serve the Artist. The men were afraid of him, but that was not so uncommon in these gangs. Before the hood had been put over his head, John had counted five wagons, with Elsbet being loaded on the front-most of the convoy. He was certain at least one other wagon had joined them a few miles along the road, adding its clattering wheels to the throng. Perhaps a third of the men he had seen at Mundon Furze had clambered aboard the wagons – he knew not where the rest had gone. He hoped they had not gone after Jim and the others.

They had been travelling for nearly an hour, along uneven roads, and the bench upon which John sat was unforgiving. If they were going to Osea, they should be nearing the causeway by now. There was a tang of salt on the air. A bitter wind blew at them, suggestive of coastal roads. But he also heard the wind rustle through trees. He had heard no sounds of civilisation, nor had the wagons moved over any metalled road – the north road to Osea passed through the town of Maldon. Likely that the celestials would take back roads, away from prying eyes, which would add considerable delay to the journey. If they were going to Osea at all.

Soon, with pitched calls and whistles, the wagons came to a halt. John heard voices from the head of the column. There was some kind of exchange occurring; it was difficult to hear. He thought he could discern thick accents, not Chinese, or oriental at all.

'This is he?' The voice was nearer. It sounded familiar. What was that accent? Turkish perhaps?

'Leave him be.' That was the celestial, Xiang.

John sensed they were talking about him.

'Maybe I kill him now, and save you the trouble.' The new man again.

John felt a more certain glimmer of recognition this time. The accent was Romani. John's heart beat that much faster.

Rifles were cocked. 'You have your orders,' said Xiang.

'You won't kill me. She would not allow it.'

'Are you so certain? And what about your men?'

'Maybe it would be worth it to gut this dog.'

Raised voices, heavy footsteps; a hand jerked at the back of John's coat; he felt himself almost topple over the side of the wagon.

With a flick of his wrists, John's hands were free. He let himself fall, landing on his feet, lashing out blind at his assailant who cried out in surprise. John tore the bag from his head.

A gleam of torchlight shone from a blade. John ducked as the knife thudded against the side of the wagon. He drove hooking blows into his attacker's ribs, a quick flurry, *one-two-three*. The man fell to the ground. A celestial leapt forwards, and John ducked, then jerked upwards, connecting with a blistering uppercut. Another man came, and another, not just celestials, but Romani – he recognised their curses, their outlandish dress. He twisted, blocked, countered, realised his foes were fighting each other as well as him.

Xiang strode into the fray, hacking aside a gypsy with a fierce blow to the temple, aiming a kick at John. Before John could even brace himself, he flew backwards five yards, vivid pain in his chest where Xiang's heel connected. John fell into the arms of more men, who held him fast. The gypsy who had pulled him from the wagon was similarly restrained, and John stared into the man's hate-filled eyes.

Andre. The leader of a gypsy troupe John had long thought fled abroad. Andre had loved Rosanna once, had treated the 'Five Sisters' like family. But he had lost her heart to John, and his resentment of that fact had never been more clear.

'What is it the English say?' sneered Xiang. 'There is no love lost between you?'

'Dog!' spat Andre, struggling against the men who now held him. The other gypsies held back. John wondered how many of them also recognised him, and harboured him ill will. He felt sick to his stomach.

'What are you doing here? Why do you work with these men?' John demanded.

'How dare you ask anything of me? I owe you nothing, treacherous worm!'

'Rosanna? Is she with you?' John asked, a glimmer of hope filling him as he realised the significance of it all. If Andre had anything to do with securing Elsbet, then Rosanna must be behind it.

'She is lost to you,' Andre growled. 'And to me.'

'What does that mean? Does she live?'

A hand snatched at John's throat before he could say more. The tong leader stood before him.

'That is enough. You promised not to resist – a man who breaks his word does not last long amongst our kind.'

Xiang released John's throat, and planted a clubbing right hook into his stomach. John gasped, the breath forced from his lungs, bile rising in his throat. The bag was placed over John's head once more, and his hands tied, more tightly than before. His ankles were bound this time, too, and he found himself hoisted upwards, and thrown unceremoniously onto the wagon.

John heard another exchange between Xiang and Andre. 'The girl is yours, gypsy,' the celestial barked. 'Take her away, far away, and never return. Do not test us again. The prisoner belongs to the Artist. The debt to you is now paid, you understand?'

There was a harsh exchange, but Andre relented, and eventually cartwheels crunched through piles of fallen leaves, and receded into the distance. Before John had been bound, he had barely had time to take in his surroundings in the dark and confusion. He was sure they were near the coast, with a forest at their backs, but that was all.

As his own wagon lurched on, John wondered just what deal the gypsies had done with the Artist, and just what Andre had meant when he had said Rosanna was lost.

EIGHTEEN

John had stood in darkness for nearly half an hour, or so he estimated. He could smell sea air. The ground beneath his feet was soft, sandy. The sound of nesting gulls nearby scraped through him, like the cries of a discomfited baby. His legs were numb, but no longer bound. His hands were tied behind his back. Cold wind bit at his fingers. He was almost thankful for the hessian sack over his head, which protected him from the elements. Each time he had tried to move from the spot, he had received a hard slap to the head, or a jab in the ribs with a rifle butt.

The sound of the last wagon wheels began to fade, clattering and splashing, along what John assumed was the causeway by which they had come.

Finally, the hood was removed from John's head. He blinked, freezing air making his one eye water. The only light came from six burning torches, held aloft by his guards, flanking a path ahead that wound some distance before fading into a thin, silvery mist. An austere house with lightless windows loomed at the periphery of this fog, black and square. If this was Osea, as he was almost certain it was, then that would be the Charrington house.

John looked around. The sea surrounded them, rough waves crashing, their peaks whitened by the light of a low, waning moon. More fog, thicker now, billowed towards the island across the dark water. He could make out the faintest impression of the causeway to his left, and only by the coach-lamps that swayed their way towards the dark mainland.

A sharp jab to the kidneys caused John to grunt in pain, spinning to see the grinning features of a guard, a rifle pointed directly at him. A second man grabbed John, and cut the bonds from his wrists. He took up John's cane, and presented it to him. John glowered at the man warily, and took the concealed sword. He half expected to be beaten again once he had placed hands upon the weapon, but he was not. Instead, the man before him merely grinned, and the man with the rifle shouted an order: 'Go now. Go, to house.'

John scanned the faces around him. Xiang was gone, leaving just his minions behind. Enough to subdue one prisoner perhaps. John sized them up all the same.

'Where is your headman? I would speak with him,' John said.

The man at his back jabbed him again, harder. John stumbled to one knee, rising angrily. Mocking smiles crossed the faces of the men around him. John recalled such a smile on the face of Maung, his gaoler in Burma. He recalled, too, a similar smile on the face of Tsun Pen when his lackey, Hu, had taken John's eye. Rage grew inside of him, but not for these mere hirelings. The prospect of coming face-to-face with the Artist once more became not so daunting. Indeed, he began to wonder if he really had made a terrible hash of executing the tyrant of the dockyards; perhaps tonight he would have the opportunity to atone for that error. The celestials had made a mistake of their own in giving John his cane. Surely they knew it contained the very sword that had once slain Tsun Pen? He knew not what games they played, but they would regret it.

John nodded, more to himself than to the guards, and began the walk. He shivered – they had not returned his coat.

As he trudged the gravel path towards the house, John became increasingly aware that there was movement around him. He glanced over his shoulder; the guards had not followed. They stood in a close group, holding their torches high. To the right of the path, large, thorny bushes hid the rest of the island from view. To the left, rocky outcrops dropped sharply to a spit of beach, to which the fog clung tenaciously.

There came a rustling through the bushes. John turned sharply, scouring the darkness for any sign of a hidden foe. For a moment, he swore he heard a low growl, as of some stalking hound nearby, but the sound was quickly carried off by the whistling wind coming in off the sea. He quickened his pace a notch. The sound came again, more distinctly. John looked all around, trying to pinpoint it. He felt sure he saw some dark shape move along the rocky bank to his left, scree tumbling down to the beach at its advance. The briefest shadow, nothing more – an animal perhaps. Then he heard grating breaths nearby. He stared into the bushes, and for a second a pair of beady, shining eyes stared back at him.

Something ran across the path behind him. John spun as gravel crunched beneath skittering feet. The men at the bottom of the path were almost out of sight now, but John heard their laughter. There was a nervous quality to it. They were frightened, and that meant John should not loiter. He knew not what the enemy was for sure, but he could guess, and even the hint that the island was occupied by these 'ghouls' was reason enough not to stray from the path.

Jim stood on the foredeck of the Royal Navy sloop *Daphne*, observing Osea across the Blackwater through his field-glasses. It was a long, thin island, divided almost equally between farmland and marsh, mostly uninhabited bar the one house. That house would be visible, were it not for the darkness and gathering mist conspiring to hide it. Other than two jetties, north and south, the only way onto the island was via a narrow causeway, along which a line of wagons now departed the island, their dim lamps giving away their position.

'There they go, back to the mainland,' he said.

'Tide's coming in, and more fog with it,' Captain Abrams said. 'If they're not gone in the next half an hour, they're stuck there 'til morning.'

'Any sign of Colonel Hardwick?' Miss Furnival asked.

'No,' Jim replied. 'This fog is deuced inconvenient. We have to get closer, but we can't risk it yet. Captain, would you be so good as to signal ashore? I want those wagons followed.'

'That I will.'

The captain went to organise his men. A party of marines was already ashore at the bluff east of St Lawrence, awaiting orders. The remainder from the *Daphne* were readying the boats, along with twenty more men aboard HMS *Sparrow*, hanging further back.

'So far so good,' said Jim. 'It looks as though your uncle was right.'

'I hope not entirely,' Miss Furnival said. 'It sounded like there'd be terrible danger on that island.'

'Then we should make haste, because Colonel Hardwick is alone there.'

'You seem most concerned about him. Yet I sensed there was some... hostility between you.'

'More a... difference of opinion. Our old ties have become somewhat strained. Perhaps that can be rectified, if we get out of this.'

'And what of me, Captain Denny? May I take our current state of cooperation as a sign that you trust me at last?'

Jim thought for a moment. He looked over his shoulder to see where the seamen were. Confident that there was no one in earshot, he turned to Miss Furnival. 'In honesty, I am not sure. There is much about you that I do not know, and what I do know does not instil confidence within me. Do I think you would try to harm me directly? No. I think I am a good enough judge of character for that, at least. Do I trust you implicitly...?

I am afraid it is too early for that. Miss Furnival, I have spent several years rooting out your kind, and bringing them to justice. I cannot take it on faith that you are the exception to the rule.'

'The rule?'

'That the Othersiders mean us ill; that they are trained to deceive us. Even at the start of all this, Colonel Hardwick and I were taken in by an Otherside agent. He turned us against each other expertly. He evaded detection for six years, all told.'

'Whatever Ambrose Hanlocke was, I hear that if he hadn't seen the light at the end, you'd likely be dead. In any case, judging all of us by his standards is hardly fair.'

'No, it's not. But I've seen the Othersiders' treachery up close many times since then. One of my own men – hand-picked – at the Battle of the Thames... he turned out to be in the employ of Lazarus; that is, Marcus Hardwick. And then there were the agents who were only revealed after Lazarus was gone. I counted friends amongst them – men I had known for years, and in whose hands I would have placed my life. Yet I know now that my life would have been forfeit if I had. There was one...' Jim almost choked on the words, and realised he was about to confide too much in the girl. 'Let us just say that John Hardwick was not the only man who lost someone he cared about in the line of duty.'

Marie frowned. 'Who was she?'

'Please, do not press me. Accept that I had reason for my prejudice, and be done with it.'

'Captain Denny, I think I know of what you speak, and let me say you have some nerve to stand before me and talk of prejudice. That night we dined together... do you think I didn't follow you further after you left the restaurant?'

Jim felt his colour rise. 'What?'

'I saw where you went, Captain. What you did there is hardly difficult to guess.'

'I do not know what you think, I'm quite sure. But be careful what you say.'

'Does Colonel Hardwick know? Is that what passed so unpleasantly between you?'

'No! I mean...' Jim bit his tongue. For all he knew, Miss Furnival could be playing games with him even now; she could have pulled the wool over the eyes of Sir Arthur, Sir Toby... even Cherleten. Yet he did not think her false. He had become a veritable inquisitor these past three years. If he had any faith in his own ability to root out deception, then he had to listen to his instinct. 'John knows. But he never held it against me, as far as I could tell.' It was something of a confession. A weight that he had barely known he carried lifted from his shoulders.

Miss Furnival nodded thoughtfully. 'So he knows your most intimate secret – a secret that most men would spurn you for, or even have you arrested for – and yet he doesn't judge you?'

'I... suppose you could say that, yes.'

'A pity you could not extend him that same regard. You sit up there on your high horse, cutting off your friend for not living up to some moral standard that you set, passing sentence on the likes of me. It seems to me that you and the colonel have more in common than you might think. It would be remiss of me not to help reunite such soul-mates.'

Jim was about to conjure some retort, when they were interrupted by Abrams.

'The men are ready for you, Captain Denny,' he said.

'Thank you, Captain. Miss Furnival, you do not have to come with us, and I cannot ask you to risk your life again.'

'Wild horses couldn't drag me away. Do lead on.'

The door was open. Wisps of drifting fog felt their way inside the house, into a dark, cold hallway. The low, rumbling growls at John's back intensified as he paused on the threshold, encouraging him inside. He went, but reluctantly, and closed the door behind him, feeling for a bolt and throwing it shut to keep the creatures at bay. He did not think it would make a difference, but the small act made him feel better.

John fumbled about in the dark, until at last he found a candlestick upon the hall table, and a book of matches beside it. They must have been left on purpose, but he was not so foolish as to refuse this one small comfort. He struck a match, squinting against its bright flare, and lit the candle, slipping the matches back into his pocket. It took a moment for his sight to adjust, but gradually the house solidified into focus.

John stood in a narrow space, with wood panelling extending from floor to ceiling on both sides. There was a door beside him, locked. Another door lay ahead, half open, revealing pitch darkness beyond. John realised that he had passed the stairs while searching for his candle, and now backed along the hall, peering upwards into a black void, lined by peeling walls and redolent with the smell of mould. He hesitated. Up the stairs, or forwards? There seemed no favourable prospect. In the end, he pocketed the remainder of the matches and strode purposefully forward, determined to scour the ground floor for other exits in case he had the opportunity to mount an escape later.

He pushed the door with the tip of his cane. It swung open too noisily, hinges grating. John could see nothing; there might as well have been a black curtain hanging over the doorway. Through this veil of darkness, John pushed forward, holding the candle out before him. By its cold light, a large kitchen swam into view. Dark stains covered every surface. Mould bloomed overhead and underfoot. John's heels crunched on broken glass and chipped tiles. A long workbench divided the kitchen in two. A large table stood against the wall on one side, an oven and more benches on the other. The windows, which lined one entire wall, were boarded over, planks screwed tight into window-frames.

John was sure he saw a reflection at the far end of the room, of light on glass. He felt his way around the table. At times like these, he mourned the loss of his eye, for he could not focus well in poor light, or judge distances accurately. He stumbled over an upturned stool on the kitchen floor. When he righted himself, he hit his head on a brace of saucepans hanging from a rack. He started at the sudden noise they made; it made him realise just how deathly silent the house had been.

When the ringing subsided, John ventured forward again, more stealthily. He reached a door, with a panel of begrimed frosted glass set into it. It was locked. John wiped the dirt from the glass and tried to peer through. Nothing. He held up the candle, and detected no draught. He did not think this way led outside. Perhaps that was why there were no guards. He had made up his mind to go back to the hall when he saw reflected by candlelight a figure, distorted in the dimpled surface of the glass. Feminine. Long, dark hair. A yellow dress…

John spun about. There was no one behind him, and no sign of anyone in the kitchen, although there were plenty of places to hide. He chanced a look back at the glass to see if it was a trick of the light. There was nothing but his own fractured visage.

With a jolting thud, something threw itself at the glass. The door rattled in its frame. John leapt backwards.

Hands pawed at the pane of glass. A pair of purplish eyes shone from the gloom. The creature sniffed the air loudly, and then it was gone.

John turned back to the kitchen; there was no way out beyond that door.

Something moved ahead of him. A dark shape lurched from one bench to the next. John gripped the candlestick more firmly, held it out towards the movement. He suppressed a flinch as the moving light caused all of the shadows to push their way around the room like the figures in a magic lantern. He hefted his cane in the other hand, its weighted, monogrammed pommel a fine weapon even before the blade was drawn.

There was no further movement, so John crept towards where he had seen it last. He managed perhaps half the length of the kitchen before he heard a scuff behind him. This time, when he held the light towards the source of the noise, he was met by the sound of dull, thudding footsteps, like a large animal moving away from him on the other side of the bench. Or, John could not help but think, someone moving spiderlike, on all fours, bare feet and palms of hands slapping against tiles. So vivid was this image that John gave up all thought of investigation, and instead raced to the door by which he had entered. He checked himself for a second when he saw that, in the hall beyond, several candles had been lit in his absence.

The hairs on the back of his neck stood on end. He heard a sound, like claws scratching against damp wood. He heard more slapping palms and thudding feet, and knew, in his mind's eye at least, that something hideous and naked and bestial had dragged itself up onto a workbench, and was now glaring at him hungrily. Slowly, he set the candlestick down on the floor. He stood, gripping the pommel of the cane-sword, listening intently. He heard its wheezing, phlegmy breaths. It moved, gathering pace, barrelling towards John's back. He held his nerve, waited as long as he dared, until he visualised the thing at the end of the long bench, leaping from it towards him.

John spun around, drawing the sword from the cane, slashing outwards in a lethal arc. The creature twisted in the air, the blade slicing it across the belly. John leapt sideways to avoid the brute's momentum, only just keeping to his feet as the ghoul clattered to the floor, toppling his candlestick over, very nearly tearing the sword from John's hand with its sheer weight.

It rolled, springing to all fours. Blood dripped from a gaping wound. A pair of bright, gleaming eyes fixed on John; the creature hissed.

Something pounded on the door at the other end of the kitchen, and the suddenness of it threw off John's concentration. He afforded a glance in that direction, and in a heartbeat the ghoul had pounced at him. John flung himself sideways, parrying slashing claws with blade and ebony cane. It came on, relentless, until John bumped into the large kitchen table. He dropped low, beneath the talon-like claws, and thrust the sword outwards, beneath the creature's ribs and out the other side. It screamed, an ear-piercing, equine cry. It began to flail uncontrollably. John twisted the blade, felt blood pump onto his hand, and then grunted as intense pain flared through his shoulder.

The creature had latched onto him, its claws pushed into his flesh. With all his strength, John thrust the sword upwards, gouging into the beast's organs until it slackened its grip. He forced himself upright, throwing the ghoul from him. Pain screamed through John's shoulder, shooting down his arm. It made him sluggish as the beast pounced again, this time clamping onto the same shoulder with its great yellow teeth. He felt a tongue slurping at his blood. John roared with pain and fury, kicking and hacking at the creature until again it relented. He pushed it away, and as it launched yet another attack, John stepped aside and swung his blade in a heavy, diagonal slash.

For a moment, the creature stopped, and blinked. And then its head began to slide apart – one eye, an ear, half a nose – falling to the ground, the rest of the ghoul's body collapsing in a heap after it.

John staggered away, clutching at his shoulder. The only sound he heard beyond his own breathing and heartbeat was the pounding at the far door. The creature could surely break through if it wished; John wondered why it had not. It appeared as though the Artist was willing to kill him after all, if it would send such a creature after him. Or perhaps Tsun Pen had not expected John to make a stand here?

John's shoulder throbbed. A wave of nausea threatened to overwhelm him, and he staggered out of the kitchen, away from the stifling darkness. He felt peculiar. His head swam.

He sheathed his sword and picked up the candlestick again, moving down the corridor. He passed the side-door, and realised it was no longer locked, but slightly ajar. Something whispered to him, words carried on an icy draught.

We are one.

John stood, indecisive, until he heard from the room a girlish laugh, playful and yet mocking. A smell of lavender drifted about him, so strong, so poignant to his memories that he was overpowered by it. He knew he should enter, and yet some great fear seized him; he had the strongest sense that whatever was there, in the darkness, was not to be confronted. He knew that, if there was anything there at all, it was likely another ghoul; a flesh-and-blood opponent that he could face. And yet his skull seemed to freeze and crackle at the very thought of entering. He could not explain this sudden fear.

You swore. You swore to repay a debt of blood.

John baulked as the whispers caressed him, entered his head, filled his thoughts entirely. They had to be his own memories, haunting him now at the behest of the house's dreadful master. He had to stand fast; he could not become unmanned. He grabbed the doorknob and slammed the door shut.

The great sense of dread subsided. John felt foolish, and cowardly. He half considered investigating the room after all, and running through whatever, whomever, he encountered. But he heard creaking floorboards over his head: footsteps upstairs. Whatever servant of his enemy lurked behind the door, John knew he would only get answers if he played along with this infernal game.

He went to the stairs, and peered up into the darkness, the candlelight too weak to even illuminate the landing above. He heard the laughter again, though he knew not where it came from. Cautiously, he ascended.

At the fourth step, the tread gave a mournful creak. With it, a voice like a sigh whispered in his ear, in his mind.

It is a dark path that you tread.

At the seventh step, it came again.

You will bring about their destruction. It is foreseen.

John faltered. With each step he felt weaker. And the words he heard... did he imagine them? They were too painful to hear. They had to come from within. He could only guess that the Artist was using his own mind against him.

He climbed further, a landing now paling into view.

You are a fly, and you have flown into the wrong web.

Tsun Pen had said that, on the night he died. By the time John reached the top of the stairs, his head was filled with whispers. His own voice, Rosanna's, others. Each clamoured for his attention.

Last honest man in London... A fitting tribute... The destroyer of worlds and the healer of worlds... You will burn them...

...Burn them!

When John removed his hands from his ears, he did not know how he had come to be on his knees, or when he had closed his eyes, or even how many times he had repeated the words in his head aloud. But now, at last, the whispers faded, until they became nothing more than waves crashing outside, on the Blackwater. At least the unnatural silence had been broken.

John was in pitch darkness again. He fumbled around on the floor, and found the candlestick, the candle fallen from it. He pushed them together again, and lit the candle.

The blood from his wounded shoulder had dripped upon the floorboards, where it now glistened in candlelight. It was smeared, forming words traced by fingers upon the floor. John held up the light, and read the message scrawled in his own blood.

We are one.

Anger burned. Someone was playing games with him, reaping his memories in a search for his weakness. They would soon discover that John Hardwick's weaknesses had long since been crushed.

John wiped the sweat from his brow. He took up his sword and used it to tear strips from his waistcoat, binding up his arm as tightly as he could. Who knew what foul disease that ghoul carried? He determined to find his tormentor quickly, and put an end to this one way or another.

He dragged himself to his feet, and pushed onwards.

* * *

The boat slipped noiselessly through the inky water, oars raised. The jetty was only a few yards away, the fog masking their approach, but Jim held his breath all the same. A guard walked idly along the wooden jetty, lantern shining, cigarette flaring. When he reached the end, he turned and walked back, near enough to hear his boot-heels tapping on the planks. When he was gone, Jim raised a hand.

As one, the marines dipped their oars, and the boat pushed to the jetty. Nine men hopped from the boat in a silent, practised manoeuvre. Two hunched low, bayonets drawn, and vanished into the mist. A minute later, a whistle, like a bird call, trilled in the night. The lieutenant, who had stayed in the boat, now gave the all-clear, and left the boat himself, extending a hand to Miss Furnival. The two marines returned, dragging the body of the guard with them. Rifles were checked. Another pair of marines went ahead, taking up firing positions. Jim was impressed by their grim efficiency.

Lieutenant Stanbridge made another bird call, different this time, and the second boat appeared behind them, gliding across the water towards their position.

'The jetty is secure, sir,' the lieutenant said. 'Awaiting your orders.'

Jim never ceased to be amazed at the cooperation he received from serving men who would normally have baulked at the thought of assisting an army officer, or a policeman. The Order of Apollo opened doors that normal rank and station could not.

'According to the map,' Jim said, 'there should be a path from here leading to the Charrington house. It is little more than half a mile away. We must proceed with caution. If we can reach the house without being discovered, so much the better – we have no idea just how many guards are on this island.'

The other unit of marines arrived, their ensign saluting Jim and Stanbridge.

After a brief exchange with the new arrivals, Stanbridge suggested splitting the group into three parts. 'The two smaller groups spread out either side of the trail, skirmish order,' he explained. 'They're marked good at infiltration. They will subdue any guard they meet, and ensure the coast is clear. We shall take the largest group to the house, and judge the best course of attack.'

'A fine plan, Lieutenant. We are in your hands.'

Stanbridge doffed his cap to Jim and to Miss Furnival, before forming his men into three groups. Jim recalled how a certain police sergeant had been similarly emboldened by his words recently, before walking to his death. Jim took some solace in the fact that these were hardened men, about to engage in the very type of action they had been trained for. Besides, there was no nebulous prize at the end of this mission: they had a man's life to save.

Two groups of eight marines took off, soon disappearing into the foggy night. Jim lit a dark-lantern, using its narrow beam to illuminate the ground beneath his feet as the fog began to thicken.

'We shall be mostly without light,' he said. 'But this is to our advantage. If you see lights out there, they belong to an enemy.'

They moved out, treading a path so muddy as to be almost impassable in places; the men had to spread out either side along broad grass verges. The mist ahead thinned at their advance, although visibility remained poor. At their backs, however, it thickened, rolling inexorably from the estuary, a great steel-grey curtain pushing them onwards. They had barely proceeded for ten minutes when the sound of gunfire cracked dully from the darkness.

'One of yours?' Jim hissed to Stanbridge.

'Sounds like.' The lieutenant cocked his head, listening for further reports. When it came, he pointed off to the right, eastwards. 'One of ours all right. That way, sir.'

'The bloody fools!'

'They are not nervous men, sir. If there's shooting, it will be for good reason. Should we assist?'

'We must. We cannot risk letting the flanking party become

overwhelmed, or we'll have the enemy at our backs soon after. Come on!'

The marines dashed to and from what meagre cover the island offered. Those men on the peripheries of the formation were soon engulfed by fog, and Jim could see no more than three or four men to his left or right, and perhaps only ten yards ahead. He bade Miss Furnival remain close by his side.

Another gunshot, closer now. Then something else, a gurgled cry, the death-rattle of a scream. It was too close for comfort.

Stanbridge peeled off, rifle readied. Two men formed up beside him unbidden, like clockwork soldiers. Jim reached them in time to see two dark, gangrel shapes charge silently from the fog, eyes blazing with infernal violet light. The marines opened fire as one; the creatures fell, snarling.

'Fire again!' Miss Furnival called. 'Aim for the heads.'

One of the marines backed away. The growls of the creatures on the ground grew louder, and they began to jerk and twitch, dragging themselves upright.

'You heard the lady,' Stanbridge said. 'In the head!'

Rifle bolts clicked back and forth. The men fired again, and this time the creatures stayed down.

Jim allowed more light to flow from his lantern. He moved to the two creatures, the light reflecting from their pale flesh. A few paces behind them, two marines lay dead in the mud. Stanbridge cursed.

'So much for the element of surprise,' Jim said. 'We must find the flanking party and reorganise ourselves. This way.'

The group moved on, two men short. Soon, they were picking their way through rough ground, from which old headstones jutted at awkward angles. They provided some cover for the marines' advance, at least. The sounds of the commotion had ceased, and Jim considered that all of the flanking party had been killed, when a man called out from the dark.

'Halt! Who goes there?'

'Friend,' called Stanbridge.

'Advance, friend, and be seen.'

A lantern flared up, and Stanbridge shook hands with the young sergeant from the *Sparrow*. They stood in the thick of the graveyard, in the shadow of a mausoleum, its great doors sealed shut. Jim shuddered as he recalled what Miss Furnival had told him of Sir Arthur's prophesying.

'What's the trouble?' he asked.

'These things, these are the trouble,' the ensign said, visibly shaken. He waved a hand at the ground, where three ghouls lay dead. 'Bloody lunatics, running about naked. And damned hard to kill.' One of them twitched, and Stanbridge took no chances, stepping forth and ramming his bayonet through its skull.

'Is anyone hurt?' Miss Furnival asked.

The men looked at her oddly, as though the idea of a woman – and an American at that – questioning them in the field was unthinkable.

'Well?' Jim asked, supportively.

'Mackay was bitten,' the ensign said, indicating a man who they now saw sat beside a headstone, nursing his thigh.

'Then he goes back to the boat, immediately,' Miss Furnival said.

Protestations rose up from the men, revealing great resistance to this suggestion.

'Immediately!' Miss Furnival snapped, brooking no argument. She turned to look at Jim. 'Send him away,' she whispered. 'Trust me, if he comes with us, the enemy may see our every move, through his eyes.'

Jim furrowed his brow in disbelief, but in the end complied. He had been urged by Sir Arthur to trust in the woman's expertise, and against these creatures he was out of his depth. 'Do as she says, Lieutenant,' Jim said. 'Send a man with him if you wish, but we can spare no more than one.'

'Aye, sir.'

Miss Furnival smiled at Jim. He thought it was the first time she had looked upon him with real favour since they'd met.

Another man was nominated to help Mackay back to the boats. They had barely begun to hobble away when a great pounding came from the mausoleum, causing the marines to drop at once into firing positions. The doors swelled back and forth, accompanied by frenzied growls and snarls. Jim noticed for the first time that the mausoleum doors were thrice-chained, and padlocked. An unusual measure, and one he was thankful for.

'Trust me when I say we do not need to investigate this place,' Marie said in a low voice. 'I've seen its like before, and we should be thankful for the chains.'

'You don't need to tell me twice,' Jim said. 'We have delayed long enough. Every guard on this island will be heading our way after that ruckus.'

'Why are they not here already?' Miss Furnival asked. 'The island isn't that big.'

'The lady is right,' Stanbridge said. 'Perhaps Osea is not as well guarded as we thought.'

'The wagons...' Jim mused. 'Could they have known we were coming? Have they abandoned this headquarters?'

'What if Colonel Hardwick isn't even here?' Marie asked. 'What if this entire operation is a wild goose chase? Or a trap.'

'There's only one way to find out. Lieutenant, we go directly to the house. No more sneaking about for us. If anyone gets in our way, shoot first and ask questions later.'

NINETEEN

'**G**et out of my head!'

John closed his good eye tight, and pounded his fist on the wall. Plaster crumbled away beneath the blow.

The voices stopped. John opened his eye and looked around, unimaginably grateful for this brief respite, breathing just a little easier. He was still on the landing, at the end of a narrow corridor, where a tight, dark stair led upwards unevenly to an attic.

'Is... is someone there?' A thin voice, foreign, muffled. It came from behind a door John had just passed before becoming overwhelmed by intrusive whispers and visions of past misdeeds. 'Is someone there? Please... answer me.'

John was certain he did not imagine it – or as certain as he could be, given the circumstances. He stepped backwards. He had tried every door on this level – at least a dozen of them – and found them locked.

'Who's in there?' he asked, not daring to call too loudly.

'Oh, thank God. I am prisoner. There is man here, sick, who need help. Are you here to rescue us?'

'Not exactly... I'm rather a prisoner myself.' Silence. 'Look, I can get you out. I don't intend to stay trapped in this house.'

'Thank you!' The voice was tremulous, desperate.

'Stand away from the door. I'm going to break it down.'

John paused for a moment to give the man a chance to comply, and then kicked hard at the lock. It cracked, and the door buckled, but it required a second attempt before finally it succumbed to force and flew open.

The room beyond was small and sparsely furnished. Moonlight cast everything in grey relief; it was the first uncovered window John had seen since entering the house. It was barred.

A man leaned against the far wall, trembling, holding his head in his hands. He was thin and pale, large moustaches poking from behind slender hands, scraggy beard covering a square jaw, and greasy dark hair plastered to his forehead. Beside him was a hard cot-bed, upon which lay a moustached man either asleep or dead, John could not tell which.

'Who are you?' John asked.

The man took his hands away from his face. He looked vaguely familiar. His eyes were quick and clever, and John was not altogether sure he trusted the look of him.

'My name is Tesla,' the man said.

That was how John recognised the man – he had seen an intelligence dossier on him long ago. The noted Serbian scientist, in the real world living in America playing with electricity. On the Otherside, forced to build portals for world powers. John did not know whether this was the real Nikola Tesla, or the Othersider, but either way the mission now took on a new significance. John stepped fully into the room, quickly scanning about for any place where an enemy might hide. Satisfied, he backed towards the window, facing the door at all times. He set down his candlestick and gave the bars a rattle. They held firm.

'It is no use,' Tesla said hoarsely. 'They keep us here for... I know not how long. What day is this?'

John had to pause to think – he had become so disorientated in his short time in the house that he had lost all sense of time. 'October the fifth,' he said at last.

'Dear God,' Tesla muttered. 'A month.'

'You have been confined in here a month?'

'Most of this time, yes. Sometimes they take me out to work for them, then bring me back here.'

'What kind of work?'

Tesla looked at John forlornly. 'You would not believe me if I told you.'

'I very much doubt that, Mr Tesla. Indeed, I believe I know exactly where you came from, if you take my meaning.'

'Ah, now I recognise you!' Tesla said. 'You were much younger when last we met, and you had two eyes. Your pretty sister?'

'Do not speak of her,' John said, and the gleam at once vanished from Tesla's eyes. 'We have never met, Mr Tesla, so my suspicion was correct. How did you come here? Did Tsun Pen bring you?'

Tesla frowned. 'Who?'

'The Artist, did he bring you from the Otherside?'

'Madam Artist did not bring me, no. I come on my own, through Lazarus' Gate, in my *Munjolovac*.' He declared this proudly, and John hadn't the foggiest what he meant.

A faint creaking from outside the room caused John to turn, and both men listened for a moment, until John was sure there was no immediate danger. He needed information from Tesla, but the man's grasp of English seemed a barrier to comprehensive answers.

'You said "Madam Artist". You have dealt with a woman?'

'Yes. A pretty lady, but cruel. A Majestic. She has men, and *wampyr*, and now she has my *Munjolovac*.'

'I'm sorry, what is that?'

'Ah, she is the finest vessel ever built. It is how I come here. But now, the Artist has her, and I may never see her again.'

'So you were captured? And who is this? A friend of yours?'

Tesla looked to the man on the cot. 'No. This is Mr Charrington. This was his house, once.'

Tesla explained, in a jumbled manner, how he had come to be prisoner on the island, and what he had learned from Charrington. The house at Osea was supposed to be a private retreat for those addicted to drink; Frederick Charrington had funded it as a way to atone for his family's long history in the beer trade, which had sent many to their ruin. A month prior, men had arrived on the island – mostly Chinese. They had forced Charrington to send away his patients and staff, under some pretence. More men had arrived shortly afterwards. Charrington had been forced to send away for wagons and labourers to help ferry supplies to and from the island.

'A very strange way of gaining wagons,' John said. 'Unless they specifically needed the Charrington livery. Oh, good Christ, what a fool I've been!'

'A fool?' Tesla said.

John said nothing, but he had a very bad feeling about his prospects. Frederick Charrington was not the proprietor of Charrington's Ales. The only reason to bring the wagons to Osea – to London – would be to connect the Charrington family to the Artist's operation. The wagons alone wouldn't have pointed to Osea, but combined with Sir Arthur's visions of an island – this island – the Order had been led here. It was surely planned, but why?

Tesla went on. He said he was told that the 'master' would be here soon, who would see to it that Tesla and Charrington were rewarded for their part in some great plan. 'But as you can see,' Tesla said bitterly, 'here we are, and there is no reward save that we are not dead.'

'So this "master"… he is here?'

Tesla nodded, and turned his eyes upwards. 'Upstairs, Madam Artist said.'

John frowned. 'If this was a retreat – a clinic? – until a month hence… why is it in such a state of ruin?'

'Ruin? Whatever do you mean?' Tesla looked confused.

'Look around you, man…' John stopped, as he himself looked about. The bare floor upon which he had stood was now carpeted. The walls that had been peeling and cracked moments ago were papered and smooth. He turned to the door. The corridor beyond was now lit by the glow of candles in wall-sconces, and its appearance was similarly transformed. Even the prison-cot in which Charrington had lain was now a normal bed. 'Not possible…' John muttered.

'What kind of rescue is this?' Tesla asked.

'It's not exactly a rescue… What kind of work were you completing for "Madam Artist"?' John could not understand what game Tsun Pen was playing, but he knew for certain it would be a personal attack. With his mind still reeling, he was not entirely sure he was prepared for it.

'I build things. I build what they always want me to build. Gates between worlds. Weapons of war. My submarine…'

'And where are these other things? The weapons, this submarine? Here on the island?'

'The boathouse. That is where they make me work until I fall. But it is gone, I am sure. Madam Artist told me she take the *Munjolovac*. I will never see her again.'

Something occurred to John, and a sense of dread came with the thought. 'What kind of gate precisely were you building?'

'I have made for her several, my friend.'

'How many?' John urged. 'And for what purpose?'

'I give her the knowledge to construct them. I build for her machines to power them. She take them away, I know not where. But what she really want is way to repair Lazarus' Gate. It should have been called "Tesla's Gate", no? She ask me to build device that will power the gate. Generator so powerful it could last for ever.'

'And…' John hesitated even to ask. 'Did you do it?'

'Of course!' Tesla looked proud of himself, in his utter naivety. 'But it is all theoretical, my friend. There are few places in this world with the electrical power required to make it work. The generator require much power to reach capacity. Only then can it become self-sustaining.'

'And if the Artist were to find somewhere with a large power source. Large enough, I mean?'

'Then… Ah. Then she can open big gate. Like Lazarus.'

'Did you stop to consider the evil that could be wrought with such a device?'

Tesla looked at John as though he did not understand the question. John had met his like before – men of science who saw neither good nor evil in their work, but only in the hearts of men who might use that work for personal gain. John had a growing suspicion that the components now headed to London were not wreckage from the Lazarus Gate at all, but something else entirely.

John took a deep breath. 'Look here, something very strange is happening, and I cannot begin to explain it. I believe I know who this "master" is – he and I have some unfinished business. I need to find him and put a stop to his plans, whatever they are. But we are not alone in this house. You know of the *wampyr*, so I presume you know also of these "ghouls"?'

Tesla only nodded.

'Good, then you should know not to go wandering unarmed about this house. They're out there. That's how I got this.' John pointed to his bound shoulder. 'When I leave this room, barricade that door with whatever you can. Look after Mr Charrington as best as you're able. Do not open this door unless I call you, all right? There may be reinforcements on the way, but I cannot count on it. Understand?'

Tesla nodded again.

John turned to leave.

'Wait! I almost forget,' Tesla said. 'Madam Artist, I think she mention you.'

'What did she say?'

'Just that they were waiting for someone, and when he get here, all this will be over.'

'How do you know it was me she meant? Did she give a name?'

'What was it now… yes, she said they wait for "the last honest man in London". I think it must be you. The Hardwick I know, at least, was honest man.' He shrugged. 'She say when this man come, I can go free. I think she mock me.'

John felt sick to his stomach. He did not want any of this. He felt in no state to face Tsun Pen, or this mysterious woman, or more ghouls. But there was no one else. Someone had to make a stand. He knew that attitude had earned him the ridiculous moniker that now haunted him, and he smiled ruefully at that. He thought all of these things, yet said simply, 'Good luck, Mr Tesla.'

John left the Serbian and the sick man in the room, and entered the long corridor which was now completely changed. What had been derelict and mouldy was now restored, a tranquil retreat, with tasteful décor and soft, flickering lanterns. John took a deep breath to steady himself. His mind, so long a fortified gate, bolted and barred, had been compromised from the minute he had set foot in this house. No... from the minute that creature downstairs had wounded him. He felt the intrusion into his mind even now. The Artist was within him, like a disease; in his body, in his thoughts.

The door to Tesla's room closed behind him, and John snapped to attention. John heard furniture being dragged in place, and then silence.

John went to the narrow attic stair, now cast into light by further sconces. At the top was a door, open just a crack, allowing light to flood out.

Red in tooth... red in claw... the Red Lord knocking at your door...

A strong scent of lavender flowers drifted from the room, and John forced aside the painful memories that it instilled. He set down his candle, drew his sword and ascended the stairs.

John pushed the door open, slowly. Chinese lanterns hung from skeletal rafters, casting flickering orange light into a large room. Opulent furnishings stuffed the attic. Oriental silk curtains framed a large leaded window, by which a thin shaft of light strained to enter, dissipating upon drifting smoke.

Opium smoke.

John already felt groggy as the whiff of the hateful pipe assailed his senses. It pulled at his very blood, inexorably as the moon at the tides. A tremor went through his body. He felt it more keenly than any other man might; it had been a long time since he had chased the dragon, but the body never forgets the lure.

He girded himself. Across the room, a man sat at a desk, his back to the door. He wore a fine suit. Dark, lustrous hair fell past his shoulders, poker straight. John had not thought he would really see his enemy. He had not thought it possible that Tsun Pen could have survived. Tesla had assured him that the Artist's mantle had been taken up by a woman. And yet here he sat. The spider himself.

TWENTY

"'Will you walk into my parlour?" said the spider to the fly;
"'Tis the prettiest little parlour that ever you did spy.'"
The voice was more cultured than John remembered,
somewhat pained and rasping. Perhaps a sword through the
chest could do that to a man, even one such as the Artist. "'The
way into my parlour is up a winding stair, and I've a many
curious things to show when you are there.'"

John trod cautiously, silently, around the edge of the room. He
peered out of the window, seeing nothing but the grey radiance
of drifting fog, and turned his gaze once more to his opponent,
circling stealthily, sword readied.

"'O no, no," said the little fly, "to ask me is in vain, for who
goes up your winding stair can ne'er come down again.'"

There was something very wrong about the man at the desk.
He did not sound like the Artist. He resembled the Artist less and
less the closer John drew. He was tall, yes, but not tall enough
for that monster. The cut of his suit was perfectly regular; John
did not think it could hide those dreadful, vestigial arms. Every
instinct told John that he had been played for a fool from the
moment he had set foot in this house. Or from the moment he
had left his home and gone to London.

John was within a few yards of the man now. He took a

step forwards, held the sword out straight, so that its point was inches from his target's neck.

'You are not Tsun Pen,' John said. 'Who are you?'

'Ah, you always were a clever little fly.'

Before John could react, the man was on his feet, sidestepping the blade with astonishing speed. He held John firmly – one hand on the wrist of his sword arm, and one at his throat. The man was deathly pale, features cadaverous, eyes sunken but shining like amethysts. His breath was rank, like meat long turned. He was whip-thin and hunched, a haunted look about his corpse-like features, the tell-tale look of a man who has spent too long a fugitive. A dangerous man. 'You are a fly in a web,' he hissed, 'and I am the spider, come to feast.'

John aimed a stiff kick to the man's crotch, which barely drew a wince. He punched his assailant hard in the kidneys, grunting in pain at the exertion from his own injured shoulder. The man rocked, but his grip was firm. John felt himself turning purple, his throat contracting under the man's cold, vice-like fingers. In desperation, John jumped from the floor, kicking both feet at the dark-haired man, propelling himself backwards and bringing his enemy with him. John hit the floor, landing on his back, the air evacuating his lungs as his opponent finally let go of his throat.

The man laughed, thinly, wheezing. He still had John's wrist in his grasp, and stood quickly, hoisting John up by the arm. John swung his other arm, punching the man in the face once, twice. A great crack opened up in the pallid, dry flesh of the man's cheek, and a pinkish ooze dribbled whence blood should have flowed. John's fourth strike was batted aside, and the man hit him hard in the stomach, lifting him into the air with the force of the blow, sending sharp ripples of pain through John's body. John felt himself drift weightless, registering only when he collided with the far wall that he had been tossed through the air like a rag doll. He could only think that he had dropped his sword. It was the least of his worries. He tried to drag himself to his feet, but only managed to crawl a short distance when he heard footsteps approach, accompanied by cruel laughter.

'Do you know how long I have waited to take my revenge on you, Hardwick?'

John was dazed. 'I... I don't even know you,' he spluttered.

'Not you, exactly. The other you. Your counterpart and his sister cost me everything. Everything! You thought you had killed me, but here I am.'

He was mad. 'Not... me,' John said.

'Oh, did I confuse you again? An easy mistake to make. It does not matter. He is you, you are him. He is dead, and you will follow. I am going to gorge myself on your blood, Hardwick. I am going to leave you a shrivelled husk, like a fly in a web.' He hoisted John up again by his lapels, so that they were eye-to-eye.

'Where is Tsun Pen?' John gasped.

The man laughed. 'What good will that do you? I am lord of Osea now. A new domain, all mine. A fine house, servants, guards... the girl, Elsbet, to warn me of my enemy's plans. My pet intuitionist to build me whatever device I can dream of. The final part of our bargain was you. The Artist wanted you for herself, but I set my price. I want you dead just as much as she. And now, Tsun Pen has gone, and I am master.'

She? John thought of the woman with the strange accent. This creature had passed himself off as Tsun Pen. Who was really pulling the strings? But he thought hard on this man's words – something was not right, and it was something John hoped he could exploit.

'Elsbet?' John asked. His thoughts began to clear; he felt sure the man – the creature – before him was exerting some strange influence over him. He fought. 'If Elsbet is so important, why send her away?'

'What?' The man shook John until his teeth rattled. 'She is mine. The queen of your Nightwatch is now *mine*.'

'She is gone. The gypsies took her.'

John fell unceremoniously to the floor. The man strode to the window, touching a hand to his temple as if in great concentration.

'My guards…' he muttered.

'Xiang's Chinamen? They left on the wagons,' John said, seizing the moment to rattle his enemy.

'Preposterous!'

'Have you been betrayed? Has Tsun Pen double-crossed you also?'

'She would not dare! Not while I have –' He stopped abruptly. 'Oh, she is clever. She has masked her plans from even my power.' He paced, agitated. John saw that the man walked with a slight limp, his foot twisted. 'There is only one thing for it,' the man said. 'Now I shall have to kill you, and find her. It pains me to do it, Hardwick, truly it does. I wanted to make you suffer, as you and your blasted sister made me suffer. But needs must when the Devil drives.'

'And you'd know all about the Devil, de Montfort.' Both John and the man looked to the door, where Marie Furnival now stood. She had John's sword in hand, a pistol in the other. Jim entered the room, revolver trained on the man, de Montfort. There were soldiers outside the door. John took Jim's hand and laughed with sheer relief.

'Take this… creature… away,' John said. The marines stepped forward, but Miss Furnival bade them halt.

'No! Believe me when I say I have more reason for revenge than any man here present. Lord de Montfort is mine.'

'He is a prisoner of the Crown,' John said. 'This man has vital information –'

'This is no man. He is *wampyr*. And I swore to kill him a long time ago. I will not be denied.'

'Could it be?' de Montfort mocked. 'Furnival? The little girl who tracked me across England? Have you followed me across the very veil?'

'Stand down, Miss Furnival,' Jim said. He stepped in front of her, lowering the barrel of her gun with a firm hand. 'De Montfort, would you like to explain what you're doing here? Or would you prefer to be dragged back to London and interrogated… by the Nightwatch, if it pleases you.'

'The Nightwatch?' de Montfort scoffed. 'By now, I would guess the Nightwatch are no longer yours to command, little man. Besides, if your imbecile Majestics were to read my thoughts, their tiny minds would be torn asunder. You do not frighten me.'

'Not ours to command?' John snarled. 'Explain yourself!'

De Montfort laughed; a rolling, rasping sound that tailed off into a hacking cough.

'The Artist has played you for fools, as she has done to me,' de Montfort said. 'The Nightwatch has never truly been a tool of your pathetic order. The Artist has always shown them what she wanted them to see.'

John caught Jim's eye. He, too, looked quizzical at the word 'she'.

'It is not possible for anyone – even the greatest Majestic – to control all of the Nightwatch,' Marie Furnival intervened.

'She did not have to control them all, little girl,' de Montfort crowed. 'Only the most powerful of them – the girl, Elsbet. With her acting as a conduit for the Artist's powers, the others were easily led. Without her, you have nothing but weak-minded animals, whose visions are little more than the nightmares of children. The Artist laid the foundation of this plan years ago. Who do you think provided the etherium for Uncle Arthur's experiments? Where do you suppose it came from?'

'What the hell is he talking about?' John asked, looking to Miss Furnival, then back to de Montfort.

'I am talking about the harvesting of fluid from the brains of Majestics,' de Montfort said, 'to sell to Apollo Lycea. And such an enterprise, rather akin to farming, truth be told, cannot be conducted in this universe on the scale required. An industrial scale – and this girl knows that the *wampyr* rule industry on the Otherside. Your black marketeers make a pretty penny, true enough, but the real value is in the freshest produce. Only that harvested on my side of the veil is of the greatest efficacy.'

'So the Artist has travelled to the Otherside? Recently?' John asked. 'How? Is this the work of Tesla?'

De Montfort looked annoyed at that.

'Tesla?' Miss Furnival snapped. 'What of him?'

'He's downstairs, a prisoner,' John replied.

'Oh no... no! If Tesla is here, the possibilities are endless. Don't you see, Colonel? He built the Lazarus Gate!'

'I know, Miss Furnival.' John turned angrily to de Montfort. 'So you have worked with the Artist to bring etherium to our world? To sell to the Order?'

'Not just the Order. Every major power across the globe. And not just etherium, but the raw materials required to make it. Majestics, Colonel Hardwick. Some sold like cattle, others released into your world as fugitives, so the likes of you may hunt them. The unfortunate few are spared death, and taken to the bosom of the Order of Apollo. They now rest in a secret hospital ward in London, ready to power a gate. Do you understand yet?'

'I think I'm beginning to,' John said. 'You thought the Artist was leaving you the means to bring supplies to Osea from the Otherside. Machinery. Elsbet. And maybe more than that – an army of ghouls, no doubt. Instead, Tesla's devices are by now on a train to London, perhaps already being loaded into our facility, where the Artist plans to activate it, using the Nightwatch. Am I close, sir?'

'Close enough.' De Montfort gave a thin, sly smile, which made John think he had not quite discerned the whole truth.

'I thought I was part of the Artist's plan,' de Montfort said. 'I was ready to take a place in the new world order. To think, I offered her the Iscariot Sanction, the greatest gift my kind could bestow. She would have made a worthy *wampyr* queen. Yet she spurns me! It appears I have indeed been betrayed. She has not reckoned, however, on my wrath being every bit as swift and violent as her own.'

Jim cocked his revolver. 'Your wrath will just have to wait,' he said. 'Men, take him away.'

'I do not think so,' de Montfort smiled. He clicked his

fingers, and at that signal, cries of pain and alarm erupted outside the room.

A great press of bodies flooded into the attic. Guns discharged. Roars and growls mingled with screams; claws and teeth and pale, muscular limbs flailed in all directions. John tumbled forwards, twisting to keep his feet, fending off blows as best he could. Blood flew in great gushes as the creatures tore into those marines who had not reacted quickly enough. The room filled with ghouls, clambering over each other in their frenzy, climbing up walls and across rafters like scurrying insects.

John grabbed a chair, and smashed it over the first beast to come near him, keeping hold of the broken fragments to jab and beat the seemingly endless flow of enemies.

Only once did he look up at the scene of bedlam about him – to see Miss Furnival fighting like the very Devil. She dodged every flailing claw with grace, ducked beneath every clumsy attack, pushing her pistol to the chin of each ghoul and plastering its brains across the ceiling. All the time she moved towards de Montfort, who goaded her, encouraging her every step. She was the only one close enough to kill the *wampyr*. John sensed that if she succeeded, the ghouls would run, for they were somehow under his unspoken command.

Marie sensed the darkness closing in all around her. She could not look at it, for giving in to her fear of death could only make her falter. Instead, she fixed upon de Montfort. He was not what she had expected; the tall, handsome, aristocratic creature that had so long been described to her was now a shrivelled, scarred, corpse-like revenant. He held sway over the ghouls still, yes, but he was but a shadow of a race long since robbed of nobility.

Yet he laughed at her.

Pure instinct guided Marie's sword-arm. With each stroke, a ghoul fell, or staggered back to be swallowed up by the melee. A beast dropped from the ceiling, claws almost catching her, but Marie dodged away, firing her revolver into its mouth. She squeezed off two more shots, this time at de Montfort. He sneered as he stepped aside each time. The leaded window at his back shattered.

'What spirit!' the vampire hissed, delightedly. 'What nerve! I have not seen the like since I fed your uncle to the Hardwick harpy.'

Marie's expression must have belied the truth. She flailed wildly, and de Montfort laughed. He mocked her, and it stung.

'You did not know! You thought I was the one who drained your uncle. No, he was a sacrifice that I might create another. And how she repaid me! Now, come, child! Come to me. Yes...'

All of the years she had hunted de Montfort, all of the hours she had spent training in secret, and now she felt that work being undone as her anger bettered her. Marie's face burned, her blood raced, her limbs shook from sheer rage. Yet she fought, wilder and faster, until she drew within reach of her target. She swung Colonel Hardwick's blade at de Montfort's neck; he stepped aside effortlessly, swatting her hand with a back-hand blow so powerful that she dropped the sword. She tried to raise the pistol, but de Montfort's hand was on hers at once, forcing her arm downwards. She tried to strike him, but his other hand grabbed her wrist, squeezing so tightly she thought her bones might break. Marie felt tears sting at her eyes now – anger overwhelming her as she looked into the eyes of her uncle's killer. It was still his fault, no matter what he said, what lies he told, but by God he was strong. Frustration consumed her at the thought that she had failed, right at the last.

'You know, I did your uncle a favour,' de Montfort said, softly, lips so close to her cheek the words felt like a lover's caress. 'If I hadn't taken him, the Other would. At least for me, Arthur Furnival fulfilled a higher purpose.'

The revolver dropped from Marie's hand, and de Montfort smiled. He released her hand, and instead gripped her throat.

'Yes, you are a lot like Miss Hardwick. Only... weaker,' he sneered.

Her ruse had worked. She slipped a thin blade from her left sleeve. Even as the breath was choked from her, and pinpricks of light sparkled in front of her vision, she focused all the energy she had remaining. She struck flesh, and staggered only a single step before composing herself. She urged her raging senses to calm, as Lillian Hardwick had taught her long ago. De Montfort yowled, groping at his neck. She had been half blind when she'd struck, but had pierced his throat nonetheless. The blade protruded still from the wound. He was hurt. Marie pressed forward, determined to push the blade deeper and end his life once and for all.

De Montfort stumbled as Marie's hand closed upon the knife. She pushed, and he roared in agony. He knocked her arm aside, shoved her away. From the screams and roars about the attic, she guessed the ghouls had already begun to falter, their master's control over them ebbing, their discipline with it. De Montfort grasped at the handle of the blade, and Marie sprang forwards, grabbing his hand and struggling against him to push it deeper.

He crashed back against the window. Marie felt salty air suck at her face, stinging her eyes. De Montfort's other arm was around her neck now, wrestling her away. She kicked and punched, always working the knife, even as the vampire attempted to pull it free. She hooked her leg about his, and twisted him about, trying to bring him to the ground. He was too strong for that, and although he spun around awkwardly, he kept his feet, and hoisting her up, slammed her into the window-frame. She felt it give beneath the force. She grabbed the ledge with one hand, fragments of jagged glass biting into her flesh, hot blood warming her skin, steaming in cold air. She hooked her legs over the edge to stop herself falling, and de Montfort came with her, hanging out of the window with her in a deadly embrace.

He tried to speak, but only a gurgling croak emerged from his lips. Marie twisted the blade at his throat, her hand now slick with his pale blood. De Montfort pulled. He was going to pitch them both through the window. She would likely die, and he would not. She had just one chance to kill him, and she cared not if she lived or died in the attempt.

Marie let go of the window-ledge with her bloodied hand, and flicked her wrist. The Tesla-made derringer – twin of Jim's weapon – sprang into her hand. Even as she levelled it at de Montfort's chest, she felt herself slip. De Montfort's eyes widened. At this range, she would burn them both, but vengeance would be served. Justice, at last.

Something pulled hard at Marie's heels. Her eyes turned upwards to a foggy sky. The derringer flared; an arc of electricity lit the night for the briefest moment. She felt de Montfort slip away, the knife tearing his throat. He was sliding across the tiled roof, into the mist. The world spun about. The vampire's snarling white face shrank into the mist's embrace. A ghost of a smile on his lips.

Then a gunshot from the window above. A dark pit opened up between de Montfort's eyes. Porcelain features cracked. The smile became a look of terror. He vanished into the fog.

In the next instant Marie was bundled back into the room, away from the cold night, and into Captain Denny's embrace. The fighting subsided. Jim held her fast, one arm wrapped around her waist. In his other hand, he held a smoking gun.

She sank into his arms, and consciousness left her.

John smashed the chair-leg against the head of the ghoul again and again, until its skull caved in and it moved no longer. He staggered back, limbs numb from exertion, and saw with surprise that the tide had turned. Several ghouls were slain as they turned tail from the soldiers. Two others leapt from the window, throwing themselves over the huddled forms of Miss Furnival and Jim, who had sunk to the floor in a heap. The last remnants barged from the room, fleeing like wounded animals. The beleaguered soldiers let them go with little resistance. Bodies littered the floor of the attic room – dark-jacketed marines and naked, ape-like ghouls alike.

John's ears rang from the tumult of gunfire in such a confined space. The blows he had taken to the head did not help. Men were helping each other to their feet, taking stock of their injuries. More gunshots echoed from downstairs, probably other marines firing at the fleeing ghouls. He became slowly aware of Miss Furnival remonstrating angrily with Jim; of blood dripping from her hand. He limped over to them, picking his sword from the floor as he went.

'What's going on?' he asked. 'Miss Furnival, are you all right?'

'No!' Miss Furnival replied. She looked as though she'd been through the wars, but the glare she now gave Jim suggested that wasn't the cause for her vehemence.

'Where is de Montfort?'

'Gone. Out the window.'

'Dead?'

'Yes,' Jim interrupted. 'I got him.'

'You can't be sure of that.' Miss Furnival looked crestfallen. John knew how she felt. He'd wanted to take his anger out on Tsun Pen, but had been denied. Miss Furnival had desired revenge on de Montfort for far longer, by all accounts, and Jim had taken that from her.

'We'd better get outside and check,' John said.

'Is that it?' asked Jim. 'Straight back to work.'

John looked at Jim for a second. Did he want thanks? An explanation? 'Is there something more important you need to do?' he asked.

Only when he pushed through the group of marines, and heard Jim's footsteps on the stairs behind him, did John allow himself a wry smile.

'I should have done it. He was mine.' Miss Furnival kicked gravel across the path.

'I suppose you'd rather I let you tumble from the window with him?' Jim asked. 'You'd have been burned alive, or at least broken your ruddy neck.' Jim could not understand her. Her manner was one of remorse, and regret, yet here lay her enemy, dead.

'We'd have gone together. Do you know what it's like to dedicate your life to a cause, Captain, only to never realise your goal?'

'No, I don't,' Jim said. 'I've never had a cause worth dying for, and I'm not sure I want one if this is what it does. De Montfort is dead, Miss Furnival, and you are not. I'd say that was a fine result. I thought you'd be happy.'

Miss Furnival looked down at de Montfort's broken body, spread-eagled upon the gravel drive. 'So did I,' she said.

More marines filed out of the house, supporting the walking wounded. Tesla limped behind, his arm around Stanbridge's shoulders. Fred Charrington was carried on a makeshift stretcher.

'Colonel Hardwick,' Tesla said, hobbling over. 'We must get to the boathouse. I must know what she has taken.'

'No time, Mr Tesla,' Hardwick replied. 'We must return to London post-haste. Whatever is left on this island will have to wait.'

'No, no, Colonel, it cannot. She already have the *Munjolovac*, and the generator. If I can visit my workshop, maybe I can find what I need to help you stop her, no? It is the least I can do. You rescue me, after all.'

'So it's true,' Marie said, her temper flaring again. 'Your fabled submarine. It was you who brought de Montfort to this universe.'

'Not by choice, dear lady, I swear. We do not all possess the ability to fight, like you. Some of us have other talents.'

'To the boathouse then,' John said, 'but we'd best be quick about it.'

As they marched along the path, John took hold of Marie's arm. She glared at him for the indelicacy.

'You and I need to talk,' John said. 'You knew an awful lot about this de Montfort fellow, not to mention Tesla. And if my ears did not deceive me, there was some mention of your Uncle Arthur being killed once before. Is there anything you would care to tell me, Miss Furnival?'

235

'There's no time for that now,' she said angrily.

'John, old boy,' Jim said, placing his hand on John's arm, coaxing him to release his grip on Miss Furnival. 'She's right. And… I should have mentioned it earlier. But trust me when I say that none of that matters right at this moment. She's with me, and I vouch for her.'

Both John and Marie looked at Jim with raised eyebrows, then at each other. John nodded grimly. Miss Furnival shrugged her arm away from John and strode off down the path, muttering, 'Men…'

They had barely made it halfway to the boathouse when they had seen the great orange glow, a hazy sun in the gauzy fog. As they drew closer, acrid oil-smoke thickened the salty air, creating a miasma to rival a London particular. The boathouse was in flames. One final order from Tsun Pen, John guessed, executed by some agent skulking about the island.

As the wooden frame of the structure fell away, great struts of some outlandish machinery were revealed; thick cables sparked with crackling electricity as their integrity diminished. Huge gouts of flame spiralled into the night air as oil ignited, plumes of crimson and orange spiralling upwards, roaring against the sea wind.

Attracted by the blaze, the *Daphne* had come about to the north-east side of the island, its lights visible through the murk. Captain Abrams would not be aware that he should be looking out for a submarine. If such a vessel truly had existed here, it was gone.

Tesla sank theatrically to his knees. 'My work… my designs. All gone,' he whimpered.

'Mr Tesla, compose yourself,' John said. 'We must away. The Artist has escaped us, and we've played into her hands. It is time to end this game.'

'What's all this about "her", anyway?' Jim asked. 'What has happened to Tsun Pen?'

'Tsun Pen is dead,' said John. 'Some woman has taken up his

work where he left off; the same woman you encountered at that hospital, I'd wager.'

'But who?'

'If it were not so impossible, so wretchedly impossible, I would hazard a guess,' John said, solemnity threatening to overwhelm him. He could not admit his suspicions out loud. He could not admit them to himself. It was absurd. 'As it stands, we need to gather our men and get aboard that ship. Our enemies have a head start over us, and God only knows what havoc they wreak even as we stand here.'

'John?' Jim was hesitant.

'This was a distraction,' John said. 'We were brought here to tie up all of the loose ends of our new Artist's plan. Elsbet has been sent to safety, probably out of the country. De Montfort was to kill me, or we were to kill each other. You, the other agents… you were sent here to get you out of the way, but also to ensure Tesla's equipment would be delivered to its destination. Those "gifts" the celestials gave us were little more than a Trojan horse. I don't think she really cared what happened to the vampires, as long as we were detained long enough here.'

'Long enough for what?'

'I think she is heading for St Katharine Docks. I believe she plans to open a gate to the Otherside, beneath London, and we have paved the way for it.'

TWENTY-ONE

Friday, 6th October 1893, 2.45 a.m.

THAMES ESTUARY

The *Daphne* had made good time, and was signalling the Coalhouse Fort on the north bank of the Thames. For the last half an hour, John had stood alone on deck, trying his best to make sense of everything. Jim had explained Miss Furnival's status as a refugee from the Otherside, and how she had come in search of de Montfort. Miss Furnival, for her part, had barely spoken a word since they had boarded. When she emerged on deck and made a beeline for John, it came as some surprise. She stood beside him at the gunwale, looking out across the broad Thames, lights reflecting from its black surface. Even now, even though they had fought side-by-side, John had little wish to speak with the American. Jim was right – he really wasn't one to give his trust easily. He cursed himself inwardly, and cursed Jim for getting the measure of him so astutely.

'I'll take one of those cigars, if you've got any left,' Miss Furnival said. She turned her eyes from the river.

John smiled despite himself, shook his head at his own foolishness, and offered a cigar. She took it, and he lit it for her.

She should have looked ridiculous smoking it, but somehow her casual manner and boyish dress made it seem perfectly natural.

'Not very ladylike,' John said.

'You mean the pants, or the stogie?' she grinned. 'Perhaps they just don't breed fine ladies where I'm from.'

'You mean America, or...' John stopped himself from saying it, and tensed. He found himself thinking of another woman he had met from the Otherside. An assassin, with a strength and martial prowess the equal of any man he'd ever known.

'I knew her... your sister,' Miss Furnival said.

'What?' he asked, realising he had drifted into some bitter reverie, and now snapping back to reality.

'Not really your sister, but you know what I mean. She and my Uncle Arthur were close. They were together when she... when he was killed.'

'Lillian Hardwick was not my sister. She was a murderess. She was the cruellest creature I have ever met.'

'It wasn't always so,' Miss Furnival said. 'I was only a girl when I first met her, visiting England for the first time. She was nice. Pretty. I think the death of my uncle changed her, in more ways than one. I think she loved him, you know?'

John paused. 'Was she not too young for him?' In many ways he had no wish to learn anything about his imposter family, and yet he could not deny that he had often wondered about Lillian; what had made her so callous, and whether there was anything of the sweet girl he had known in the real world in her.

'Uncle Arthur isn't quite as old as he looks. But yes, many people thought so. Her father especially – the real one, not your... oh, this is confusing. Look, I hardly knew her, but I looked up to her because she was an agent. An agent! Can you imagine what it's like being a tomboy, growing up on an old plantation, riding trails with cowboys, and then being told one day you have to go to England and dress like a lady and marry a rich gentleman? Of course you can't. But Lillian Hardwick, well, she sure bucked the rules, so why couldn't I?'

'You sound like you admire her,' John said, suspiciously.

'I think we're kinda alike, her and me. All alone in the world, but not ready to stop fighting just yet; it's just that maybe we're fighting for different reasons. What happened to her wasn't fair. What she became isn't who she was meant to be. I think she made a lot of wrong choices after my uncle died, and maybe it was easier to let them eat her up than try to atone. Does that make sense?'

John hung his head, and took a deep breath. 'It makes all the sense in the world.' He rolled his shoulder, wincing at the pain. The cold had almost made it seize up.

'It'll take some time to heal,' Miss Furnival said. 'That's how he got into your head, you know. De Montfort. I can only guess what that was like.'

'I've had worse,' John said, though he was not certain he meant it. He remembered all too clearly the things de Montfort had whispered in his mind; the things that creature knew about him that no one else in the world knew. Almost no one. 'This de Montfort... he killed your uncle? And this is why you hated him so?'

'It was something more.' Marie turned away, staring out over the river, exhaling a plume of cigar smoke. 'He was partly responsible for... well, for everything. For the world – my world – toppling over the brink.'

'How?' John could scarce believe that the petty revenant he had fought on Osea could have done so great a misdeed.

'He tried to hold Britain to ransom. He found the means to create other *wampyr* – to transform humans into vampires for the first time in two thousand years. And not mindless ghouls, but true vampires – powerful nobles, even stronger than he, and twice as cruel. He threatened to unleash a plague of vampirism upon the world, and when he was opposed he attacked London. In doing so he killed the world's most powerful Majestic, the only woman capable of holding the Riftborn at bay. From there on, everything went to hell.'

John took a moment to make sense of it all. 'Did de Montfort succeed? At creating more of these… "*wampyr*", I mean?'

Miss Furnival looked at John, and there was sadness in her eyes. Or perhaps pity. 'Yes.'

'Ah. The "Iscariot Sanction",' he muttered. John felt gooseflesh rise as a memory forced itself upon him, unbidden and unwelcome. He thought back to when he had encountered Lillian Hardwick three years prior. The woman who was his sister in another reality, a mockery of sweet Lilly. Had she not moved with exquisite grace? Had she not displayed great feats of strength and speed? Had her eyes not sparkled in the night like distant stars?

The death of my uncle changed her, in more ways than one.

'How's the hand?' John asked, desperate to change the subject.

'I won't be sewing needlepoint anytime soon, but I can still pull a trigger.'

'Good,' he said. 'That's all you will need it for in the hours to come. Did you keep my rifle for me?'

'In the hold. Say, why do you have a Winchester anyhow? It's a fine weapon, but not the gun of an English soldier.'

'I'm ashamed to say it is the fulfilment of a boyhood wish, Miss Furnival. An affectation I have indulged. My father…' John cleared his throat. 'He bought me many books when I was a boy; that is, before he ruled that they were filling my head full of daydreams. He came by a stack of your "dime novels" once, and a big map of the Americas. I used to dream of life on the plains, where a man could ride free and carve his own destiny. And like you, I was instead forced into a very different life. A life of duty, military service, and managing tedious financial affairs.'

'So I guess you know what it's like… to not belong?'

'You could say that. Would you return home, had you the chance?'

'I always wondered if I'd go back, once de Montfort was gone, but now… I don't know what's left. Maybe I've been fighting so long that I don't have anything else to do once the fighting is over. On the Otherside there's always a war, just to survive.'

'And if you do not survive?'

'Maybe that's not so bad. I mean, as long as you do what you got to do. Figure I've played my hand, now I've just got to cash my chips.'

John nodded at that. 'Jim… Captain Denny… he was trying to save you. He thought he was doing you a service. You know that.'

Miss Furnival's colour rose. 'Maybe I didn't need saving.'

'Not from de Montfort, no. But from yourself? You are reckless, Miss Furnival. You are too driven by your anger, and if you are not careful, it will be the end of you before you can take your revenge.'

'And if Ambrose Hanlocke was here now, would you counsel him so? You men seem awful concerned for my wellbeing, all things considered,' she said.

'Not really. I just don't want to be killed as part of your death-wish.'

She scowled at John, and then her eyes softened. She laughed. 'You know what, Colonel? I don't think we are so very different after all.'

'Oh, I think we are very different indeed, Miss Furnival, though perhaps not quite in the way I had imagined.'

They stood in silence for a while, watching the gaslights of Gravesend and Dartford blink into view, yellow stars revealing themselves as finally the sloop left behind the thinning mist and steamed along the river.

The hatch opened behind them, and Denny appeared, looking more than a little awkward when he saw John and Marie together.

Miss Furnival stubbed out her cigar. She rubbed at her arms and shivered. 'Well, much as I'd love to stand out here and gas all night, it's a mite cold. And I reckon you boys need to talk.' She nodded to John, and took her leave, pausing before she reached Jim.

'Colonel Hardwick,' she said. 'I think you would have made an excellent cowboy, for what it's worth.'

John smiled to himself. Having an Othersider as an ally would take some getting used to, but if indeed Sir Toby had trusted her… He gritted his teeth. He had almost forgotten about the old man. He wondered how much Sir Toby had known about this predicament. John had known for a long time that the Order was experimenting with more Otherside equipment than they told the common agent. He knew also about the etherium, although de Montfort's revelations had shocked even him. But a gate? Would Sir Toby really have sanctioned the building of a gate? And to what end? It had more the stamp of Cherleten. And James Denny, John reminded himself, was Cherleten's man.

Jim took Miss Furnival's place beside John at the gunwale. 'You and Marie have reached an understanding, then?' Jim asked.

'Marie now, is it?' John raised an eyebrow. 'I thought you hated Othersiders to distraction?'

Jim looked away. John knew that was mean. He offered Jim a cigar as some inadequate way to atone, but Jim refused it, and so the two men stood in silence for a time.

'What's on your mind, Captain?' John said, when Jim's dithering had become unbearable.

'Are you going to share your theory?' Jim said.

John took a draw on his cigar. 'What about?'

'You know very well. The Artist, or, rather, the imposter. You know who she is, don't you?'

'No.'

'That's not what you said earlier.'

'What I said was that I had a theory, but it was impossible. Therefore, my theory is irrelevant.'

'You said something else earlier, too. Well, not tonight – back in Kent when I came to get you.'

'Oh?'

'You said…' Jim hesitated. He looked nervous. 'You said that you would have taken Elsbet from the Nightwatch, had you anywhere to take her where she would not be found. That seems to have worked out rather well, all told.'

John turned to Jim in disbelief. 'What are you trying to say?'

'Just that… I don't know. You've been away a long time, old boy. You're involved in whatever is happening now, more than anyone can guess. And you've been rather ahead of the game up to now.'

'How? I was almost killed on Osea. I walked into a trap.'

'I do not think it was a trap for us. It was a trap for de Montfort. You know Carr said he spotted some gypsies on the road to the coast, with a Charrington's Ale wagon amongst their caravans. Anyone you know?'

John sighed. 'As it happens, yes, although the men in question have no love for me. If it weren't for that celestial, I'd probably have had a knife buried in my gut by the roadside. They took Elsbet, and I'm not sorry they did. But if you are suggesting collusion… Good Christ, what has the Order done to you? Are you now as cynical as me? Trust me when I say it is no way to live.'

'It wasn't the order that taught me to trust no one. It was you.'

They held each other's gaze for a moment. It was not in John to back down, and he saw the same stubbornness in Jim. But everything John had seen, and what he suspected, made him wonder if this hostility was worth the trouble. There would be plenty of that ahead, and John needed an ally, not another adversary.

'I am not your enemy, Jim,' he said. 'It is not my place to pass judgment on you for your mistakes, to offer forgiveness, or anything else. I would wish that you extend me that same courtesy, for are we not both haunted by the ghosts of our pasts? And we can never escape their judgment, can we? I have come to think, however, that perhaps their presence could become more tolerable if… if they could be faced with a friend.'

Jim's hard face at once transformed into an expression of surprise, and John could well understand why. He had made himself a man of uncompromising standards, unsentimental and ruthless. He knew this. And in doing so, he realised he was not simply manipulating Jim, but he believed what he was saying.

John surprised himself as much as he surprised Jim when he realised he truly did need a friend. And what a fool he felt that he had so long denied himself this simple truth.

'I...' Jim struggled for words. He looked deeply affected by John's sudden attempt at burying the hatchet. 'We've been through a lot, old boy. And that's just tonight.' He smiled. John returned it; the old James Denny, always ready to lighten the mood whether or not it was called for. 'Maybe it's best that some things remain unsaid,' he went on. 'Just as it is best they remain in the past, where they belong. You're right, John, we've both erred. Maybe I forgot that I owe you my life.'

'No, do not reconcile out of obligation. I would not have escaped de Montfort had you not come back for me, so we are even on that score. It was good to see you disobey orders, though. I was beginning to think you were too much like me.'

Jim laughed. 'So was I. Perhaps we may both yet be redeemed, if we deserve it.'

'Redemption is for romantics,' John said. 'I'd take a little justice over redemption right now.' John was wary of talking more, lest memories be recounted, and old wounds reopened. He exercised his shoulder again, and called up to the foredeck. 'How long before we reach St Katharine's?'

'Less than half an hour, sir,' an ensign replied. 'Coming up on the Isle of Dogs now.'

At those words, John felt as though he had swallowed a block of ice. Sure enough, the sloop was already bearing around the Greenwich Peninsula, and before them the East India Docks stretched from the elbow of the Thames to the banks of the Isle of Dogs itself; and the isle was dark, silent and ominous. The last time John had been there was when he had slain Tsun Pen.

They pushed on through the inky water, London opening up before them, vast constellations of lamps, which would burn through the night even though only rogues were about to benefit from them. John gazed north, and squinted as something caught his eye. He frowned; every yard the ship drew closer to their destination brought something disconcerting clearer into view.

'Ensign, what is that?' John pointed across the banks of Rotherhithe, at something on the northern horizon. Though all of the East End and the City was obscured still by the protrusion of Greenwich, something was clearly amiss. The ensign at once took up his telescope, and muttered, 'Good Lord,' before handing it to John.

For one, heart-stopping moment, John saw movement against the sky, and in his mind's eye he saw the great, claw-like shadow of the Otherside, reaching up to the heavens. He shook away the vision of the thing. This was no terror from the Rift, but smoke. Black, roiling smoke, towering over the city, creating dark pillars against an indigo sky, blotting out the stars. Only as they passed Rotherhithe, and the glow of Limehouse revealed itself, could John even begin to pinpoint the source of this disturbance. Or, rather, sources. He counted five great black plumes, rising hundreds of feet into the air. Three were close together, near the centre of London. Two were closer, not far ahead of them in fact, either side of the scaffolded silhouette of Tower Bridge. He did not need to see it to know that St Katharine Docks were ablaze. And now the ringing of distant bells began to drift towards the *Daphne*. An uncommon number of people moved about the banks of the Thames on either side, like little black ants scurrying from a flooded nest.

The ship's own bells began to ring; a great, monotonous warning. Men appeared on deck within seconds; Miss Furnival followed. The ensign pointed out the smoke to the ship's mate, who in turn shouted for Captain Abrams.

They were too late. London was under attack.

'Blimey, the bloody Navy are 'ere now.' The red-faced policeman paused at the edge of the *Daphne*'s gangplank, holding his ribs, panting heavily.

'Captain Denny, Apollo Lycea. What's happening here, Constable?'

'A what now?' the policeman asked between ragged breaths.

'Never mind.' Jim looked at the blaze, the fire tenders, the debris. Flames licked from the windows of the Apollo Lycea facility, which to most people was simply the office of a shipping company. A great rent in the side of the building now billowed with acrid smoke. It was as though the Othersiders were back.

'Stand down, Constable,' a gruff voice commanded, the accent Irish. From the press of police and onlookers, a stern, white-haired man approached, dressed all in black. It took a moment for Jim to recognise the formidable presence of William Melville, now superintendent of Special Branch. 'Captain Denny? Saw the signals from the ship there. Where is Hardwick? Ah, here he comes.'

John appeared at Jim's back, and nodded to the Irishman somewhat curtly. They had a grudging mutual respect, but Jim recalled how Melville had been made to look rather foolish once, at his flat refusal to acknowledge the existence of the Otherside. The wily old government agent had lived to regret that mistake.

'You are to come with me,' Melville said. 'Lord Cherleten is waiting.'

'Waiting?' Jim asked. 'How did he know we were coming?'

'We've known you were coming since you passed Canvey,' he replied, already walking away. 'The fact that you aren't dead is fortuitous.'

Jim followed, checking that John and Miss Furnival were in tow. They left the steamboat wharf where the *Daphne* had moored, bypassed the primary dock, and cut across Little Tower Hill. For a man in his senior years, Melville set quite the pace. At his approach, several officers fell into line, clearing a path through the melee of onlookers as Melville headed straight for the Tower of London. It was a stone's throw away, this great monument to the monarchy – the flames of the dockland blaze could still be seen behind them, glowing angrily above the rooftops.

They marched across an expanse of gravel that was once a moat, the tower guards, stern and well armed, waving them through the defensive lines. As the little entourage approached the dark walls, a narrow door swung slowly open and, without missing a stride, Melville led them inside.

'A little ostentatious for a secret meeting, don't you think?' John asked. They had entered a large chamber on the first floor of the Develin Tower, where Cherleten awaited the agents at the head of a great oak table. Men stood on guard at each of the exits. The chair that Cherleten had chosen resembled a throne.

'No, Colonel Hardwick,' Cherleten replied. 'It is secure. And this is not a meeting, it is a council of war.' Cherleten indicated the chairs and bade everyone sit. He gave a fleeting look of disapproval to Miss Furnival, and a similar glare to Tesla, but said nothing. John noted Cherleten did not appear surprised at Tesla's presence, only irked.

Spread upon the table was a large map of the City of London, and several other large rolled sheets. Melville did not sit, but instead stood in the shadows with his men.

'Five bombs have been detonated in the city this night,' Cherleten said, 'of a magnitude far greater than anything the Othersiders ever unleashed during the Lazarus campaign. I am afraid to report several key locations around London have been targeted, doubtless to cause the maximum disruption, and to stretch our resources as thin as possible. The death toll is mercifully low, but the destruction is considerable.'

'The club?' Jim asked.

'Thankfully not. Whitehall was not unscathed, however.'

'Horse Guards?' John interrupted, drawing an annoyed glare from Cherleten.

'No. Why does that concern you particularly?'

'My dog is at Horse Guards,' John said, flatly. It gave him some satisfaction to see Cherleten look at him rather stupidly.

A loud crunch came from across the table. Cherleten glared at Tesla with some annoyance, though the Serbian appeared oblivious. Tesla munched at a pile of hard ship's biscuits donated to him by the bemused crew of the *Daphne*. He poured himself a third cup of tea, from the pot that had been brought in specially. John had insisted the scientist's request be granted, saying that the man had been a prisoner of the Artist, and ill-treated. Now he was a valuable ally, and would be extended every courtesy.

Cherleten shook his head at the distractions. 'The bombs were delivered on the backs of wagons late last night. Beer wagons, we believe.'

'They can't be the same wagons we saw leaving Osea,' John said. 'They must have been planning this for some time.'

'Entry to the docks facility was gained through strong-arm tactics,' Cherleten went on. 'Dynamite was thrown inside when our security staff attempted to assist what they believed to be a wounded man on the street outside. We think some of the enemy died in the initial blast, before detonating a cart-load of explosives on the west side offices. Armed men were seen entering the facility by the police. We do not know how many are inside, or how many of our own people are hostage within.'

'Were you inside at the time, sir?' Jim asked.

'No. I was meeting with the Prime Minister, as it happens, discussing what was to be done about the Artist in light of Sir Toby's passing.'

'Is there any word about my uncle?' Miss Furnival interjected. This prompted another irritated glower.

'Physically, Sir Arthur is doing well. Mentally... he is enfeebled. The doctors are treating his condition as a brain fever; that is all they can do. I would recommend you go to him, Miss Furnival – there is nothing you can do here.'

'Oh no, Lord Cherleten,' she said. 'I wouldn't miss this for the world.'

'*Hmmph.*' Cherleten turned away from the woman. 'As we speak, a small team of hand-picked men is assembling outside. Colonel Hardwick, Captain Denny – you are tasked with leading them inside the facility and dealing with this threat. The resources therein are too valuable to lose.'

'Lord Cherleten,' John said. 'It is my suspicion that the enemy knows more about the facility than you realise. I think they intend to use some of the Otherside machinery that you have down there to wreak havoc on this city. Some of the... most secret machinery.'

Cherleten's features drained of all character. John could not say in the presence of all those assembled what precisely lay in the armoury's vaults. He did not himself know the entire catalogue of Otherside technology therein, or how many of its secrets had been unlocked by the Order's scientists, but he knew that it would be terrible beyond imagining if it was activated.

'How does the enemy propose to use it, Colonel?' Cherleten asked, incredulously.

'They sent the means to make it work ahead. The armoury took delivery of a shipment supposedly from Tsun Pen just hours ago, yes? Precisely. That shipment was purported to contain wreckage from the Lazarus Gate, but was instead the missing components of a portal. A very powerful one.'

Cherleten's fingers arched, nails scratching against the aged oak tabletop. 'It does not change our course of action,' he said. 'Indeed, it makes it all the more imperative that we launch a counter-attack immediately.'

'How many men do we face?' Jim asked.

'Uncertain. Our intelligence suggests there are Russian soldiers among their number, however.'

'Ahh, Russians!' Tesla moaned, before returning to his biscuits.

Cherleten ignored him. 'They will be well armed, and well drilled. The primary entrances to the facility are nigh-impossible to approach – they have not only been barricaded, but are guarded by snipers located on the upper floors. It is likely there are hostages inside, not to mention a great deal that is of value to the Order, or else I would shell the blackguards and be damned.'

'Our point of entry, then? The sluice-gate?' The most secret entrance to the facility lay on the riverside: a sluice-gate that provided access to a private dock.

'It is already compromised,' Cherleten explained. 'The gates are impervious to bombardment. They can only be opened from the inside, but when we sent agents in to operate the controls, we heard gunfire. They did not return.'

'How could this happen again?' Jim muttered.

'No one could have predicted such an audacious attack on the city,' Cherleten said. 'We have one of the largest police forces in the world; soldiers galore. And yet their job is to respond to danger, not anticipate it. For that duty, we have only the few good men of Special Branch and, of course, ourselves. And yet it seems the enemy's intelligence is more comprehensive than our own.'

'I disagree, Lord Cherleten,' Melville interrupted. 'With so many agencies working so tirelessly, and such secure locations affected by these attacks... all I can say is that they are too well orchestrated for the work of a criminal gang, even if the Russians are aiding them.'

'The Artist is no ordinary criminal,' Cherleten said. 'The truth is that to combat her we have relied increasingly on more esoteric means. That, in itself, has been our downfall.'

'The Nightwatch is officially deemed a failure, then?' John said.

'Sir Arthur may never recover from his experiments. And Sir Toby... well, he paid the price for our over-reliance on mysticism. If the Prime Minister sees fit to assign me permanent command of the Order, then I assure you I shall entertain no thought of psychics ever again. After this night, Colonel Hardwick, the Nightwatch is finished.' The gleam in Cherleten's eye as he spoke did not escape John's notice. Cherleten had lusted for control of the Order for so long that his anticipation of that goal betrayed him. He enjoyed the moment, even at this great cost. And that made John suspicious.

'Now,' Cherleten said. 'Time is of the essence. Colonel Hardwick, I would have you select what men you wish to take into the lion's den. We have agents, police, guards... pick the best. I would advise a small party of capable fighters – too many, and you will be detected and fired upon before you even cross the street. Take what you need from the Tower armoury – Melville will show you. And this plan, here, is of the facility. Study it well, for most of the rooms on the lower levels have never been accessed by agents of your rank. If Miss Furnival insists on going along, take her with you. Mr Tesla, you will remain here under guard. You are now our –'

'No,' John interrupted.

'I beg your pardon?'

'I said no. Tesla comes with us. If there is any way to sabotage the Artist's portal, then he will know how. What hope do the rest of us have?'

'That is out of the question. Mr Tesla's status as a citizen of the Otherside makes it quite impossible –'

'I'd listen to the colonel, Lord Cherleten,' William Melville interjected. John was surprised to see a twinkle in the Irishman's eye; perhaps he too disliked Cherleten. 'As you were saying earlier, the threat is an esoteric one. Sending in men to shoot at the problem might not be the best strategy. But sending in a supposed genius like Mr Tesla…'

'Supposed?' Tesla said over a loud slurp of tea.

'No offence, sir,' Melville smirked. To Cherleten he said, 'We should not send our men in there under-equipped.'

Cherleten sighed, exasperated. 'Have it your way, but on your own heads be it. Captain Denny, I must speak with you in private while the others prepare. Come now, it will only take a minute.'

Jim and Cherleten emerged onto the east curtain wall of the Tower, the vast pillar of smoke before them; flames, men scurrying to and fro like worker ants.

'Sir, Colonel Hardwick is still the most senior-ranking agent present. Surely he –'

'He is not my concern, and he is not my man,' Cherleten snapped. 'Think on it, Captain Denny. Hardwick has been in self-imposed exile for over a year. He did not answer our missives regarding Bertrand. He could have been a rogue agent for all we know.'

'Sir, I really think not. He –'

'Listen to me. Colonel Hardwick is compromised, or at least he will be when he finds out what the Artist has in store.'

'And what would that be, sir?' Jim eyed Cherleten with suspicion.

'There is no time to go into all that. Just know that we are in the business of intelligence, Captain, and that sometimes intelligence must be withheld for good reason.'

'Like the full extent of the Otherside devices in the armoury?'

Cherleten gave Jim a sharp look. 'Sir Toby is gone. Sir Arthur insensible. I have spoken to the Prime Minister, and he has endorsed my plans for the future of the Order. For all intents and purposes, I *am* the Order, Captain Denny, and you are my man. Can I depend on you to do your duty?'

Jim did not trust Cherleten to play him straight. And yet he did not believe Cherleten would endanger England with his plots and schemes. In fact, for all his brashness, Cherleten had actually been right all along – certainly more so than Sir Arthur, who had got more than one of Jim's men killed for his errors of judgment. And the wily old devil always knew things that mere agents did not. 'Devil' sounded about right, and better the devil you know. 'Always, sir,' Jim said, finally.

Cherleten held Jim's gaze for a moment too long, then seemed to accept the reply. 'Very good. Now, somewhere in that facility, there is a man. Dr Crookes – do you remember him? Good. If he is alive, it is vital you rescue him, for he has knowledge that is invaluable to us, and must not fall into the wrong hands. If it becomes impossible to see him safe, or if the Artist's gate threatens to flood our world with horrors, then I am afraid there will be only one avenue open to you if you are to avoid disaster.' Cherleten handed Jim a large bunch of keys. 'The larger keys will admit you to areas of the facility that were previously off-limits. If possible, you will enter those areas alone, for they contain secrets not intended for the likes of the Furnival girl, and certainly not for the eyes of common soldiers. Each of the smaller keys opens a secure box, located at each of the six security checkpoints within the facility. You know four of them. The others are located in the centre of the facility, one outside the engineering lab, and one at the north entrance to the Nightwatch ward. Within each box is an explosive charge, which you must prime.'

Jim looked at Cherleten in disbelief.

'Pay attention! There is technology in that facility that you could only dream of. Much of it we barely understand ourselves. It cannot be allowed to fall into the hands of the enemy. You must prime all six, make sure of it. Then take the red key to the wet dock. The detonator is located beside the sluice-gate controls. The key activates the electric circuit that will detonate the bombs and destroy the facility. Once turned, you will have only five minutes to evacuate via the lifeboats. Five minutes exactly, so do not tarry. The sequence cannot be reversed, so be sure of your course of action before turning that key.'

'Is this my mission, sir? To destroy the dock facility?'

'No, of course not. Your mission is to kill the Artist, and wrest control of this facility from her.'

'That is the second time you said "her", sir. So you already know...'

'You are being dashed insubordinate today, Captain Denny. Your priority is to stop the Artist, and save the facility at all costs. But if it transpires that you cannot – if the Artist's forces are too great – then use the keys. Destroy everything.'

'But sir – the facility staff. Agents, scientists, nurses, engineers...'

'You will be pleased to hear the facility is operating with a skeleton crew, although how many of them live still is anyone's guess. In any case, it is not your concern.'

'I cannot just let them die!'

Cherleten fixed Jim with a glare halfway between supreme

annoyance and seething rage. 'If it comes to it, Captain, it will already be too late for them, and for us. By the time you make the decision to turn those keys, believe me when I say the choice will be clear. Destroy the facility, or see everything you hold dear destroyed in kind. Is that clear?'

'Perfectly.' Jim almost choked on the words.

'Do not trust Hardwick. He will not see this act done – it was not out of charity that Sir Toby allowed him to go on a long leave of absence, and it was not gladly that I agreed to his reinstatement. Hardwick's insistence on bringing Tesla along is suspicious at best. And as for the Furnival girl… she has done what she came here to do. With de Montfort dead, her bonds of loyalty to the Order are severed. She would be as like to abscond this world at the first opportunity as help you further.'

'What do you mean, sir?'

'I mean, she is not quite what we would call a refugee. Oh, her loyalty is not to our Otherside counterparts, but neither is it fully to us. She works for herself. She rids our world of vampires. But the only man on our side to whom she lends any affection is Sir Arthur, and he, it seems, is little more than an imbecile for the foreseeable future. She has no place here. She belongs on the Otherside, and she knows it.'

Cherleten, as ever, adopted the least charitable view of the situation. But was he right? 'Whatever Miss Furnival or even Colonel Hardwick might wish,' Jim said at last, 'I shall do my duty.'

A familiar deviousness played across Cherleten's freckled features. 'That's my boy.'

TWENTY-TWO

There was but one entrance to the docks facility that had escaped the attentions of the enemy, and John now oversaw its opening for the first time in many a year.

There were eighteen men in all – or, rather, seventeen and Miss Furnival. John had selected mostly policemen and Special Branch operatives, with a few riflemen for support. He had ignored Cherleten's recommendations in favour of seasoned officers with experience of fighting in confined spaces, such as rookeries and warrens. To that end, he had ordered the majority to arm themselves with shotguns, pistols, truncheons and sabres. Once within the facility, John expected the fighting to be close and bloody.

They stood in a tiny, tree-filled square opposite the walls of the Royal Mint. Behind a nondescript monument – a crumbling obelisk unadorned but for the small carved seal of Apollo Lycea – three burly Coldstream Guards prised a large, heavy drain cover from the ground. Beneath lay not a drain at all, nor a ladder to some Roman sewer, but instead a steep flight of steps, leading to a metal door. An emergency exit, forgotten by all but Cherleten.

Jim stepped forth with a set of old iron keys that looked as though they belonged back in the Tower of London. He opened three locks with three separate keys, and swung open the door carefully, wincing as hinges squealed and metal dragged on stone.

Silence within. John stepped up and dared shine a lantern inside. A short corridor, bare brick, terminating at more steps leading down. Cobwebs draped brick pillars, floor to ceiling, and water trickled down the walls.

Down the steps, through the door, into a square room long emptied. John flicked a lever and a dull electric light pulsed weakly, giving Jim a little illumination as he opened the locks on another thick metal door.

Only the faint echo of a drawn rifle-bolt alerted John to danger. He yanked Jim aside. The bullet hit the door, ringing loud, sparks flying. Jim dropped to one knee, firing a pistol into darkness, deafening. Brickwork exploded into plumes of dust. John hit the floor, belly down in the grime, Winchester blazing away. The enemy fire lessened; John guessed there weren't many of them. A small patrol maybe – a few men sent to watch this disused section of the facility.

The enemy shrank away, their shadows growing smaller, curses in a foreign tongue audible only when the firing paused for a second. John's soldiers took up positions in pairs, firing their rifles as the next pair stepped over John and advanced. So they moved, two men covering the next two, until John was able to get to his feet and hurry forward, down the centre of the lines. The broad corridor in which he found himself opened ahead into a storeroom, sectioned into aisles defined by bare shelves.

As John emerged, a large rack toppled towards him. He leapt away as it plummeted into the adjacent unit with a deafening crash. The man behind it had a gun ready. John did not have time to think; at such close range he barely had time to lash out with his rifle butt, knocking the man's hand aside. The enemy's pistol discharged, striking the floor. Miss Furnival leapt past him, kicking the enemy hard in the stomach. The man swung at her, she ducked the blow effortlessly and took hold of his arm, wrenching it sharply and catapulting him away from her.

The man staggered back, and John shot him dead.

Movement in the shadows. Miss Furnival drew a pistol, a swift, fluid motion ending in three gunshots. A man cried out in pain. There was a loud curse, which John recognised as Russian. The enemy were retreating as the soldiers and policemen filed into the room.

'Secure the area!' John shouted. 'Kill those men; don't let them call for reinforcements.'

The soldiers obeyed, dashing after the enemy. More shots rang out as John surveyed the room, Jim and Marie by his side.

Jim shone a light on the man John had killed. 'Russian?' Marie asked.

'Aye,' John said. He patted the man down, but found nothing other than pocket-change and spare cartridges.

Jim unfolded his map. The facility was substantial, stretching beneath an entire row of large office buildings. Thick-walled tunnels formed something of a labyrinth; the 'armoury', named for the famous weapons store, was the jewel in the Order's crown – Cherleten had made sure of it. 'Outside this room there's a maze of corridors,' he said. 'We must not let the enemy get behind us.'

'We shall need a lookout on each junction as we advance,' John replied, 'and call them back gradually as we clear the way ahead.'

'The storage room is here,' Jim pointed to a large room on the map, which he'd marked with an X. 'That must be where the Artist is.'

'No, that is just one storeroom. The real prize is here.' John pointed at another room, larger still.

'What's there?' Jim asked.

'The things you have never been shown. This is where Otherside technology recovered from the Thames is studied, to see if it can be used. If the Artist plans to open a gate, she'll find what she needs there.'

'Then that is where my generator is taken,' Tesla said.

'It has to be,' John said. 'It is the only storeroom with access tunnels large enough for such deliveries, although the main approach is likely buried under rubble now. We shall have to use the side tunnels, or perhaps the ventilation shafts.'

'We won't all fit through there,' Miss Furnival said, looking up at a metal grille above, which covered one such shaft.

'It will of course take you from your secondary mission,' John said to Jim. Denny shifted uncomfortably – he had not wanted to tell John about Cherleten's fall-back plan of destroying the facility but, as he had put it, 'there should be no secrets between comrades-in-arms'. That openness did not extend, however, to the soldiers, who remained in the dark about the whole affair.

'Don't you worry about that,' Jim said, glancing at the men furtively. 'Just magic up a route past the enemy if you'd be so kind.'

'Here,' said John, tapping on the map. 'This is the experimental weapons room. If it has not been compromised, we can find enough Tesla pistols to put the fear into the Russians.'

'Except I don't believe Cherleten gave me a key for that,' Jim said.

'It is a combination lock, known only to the quartermaster, and a select few agents,' John replied. 'As long as the combination hasn't been changed, I am the key.'

Another shot rang out. Jim shone his lantern in the direction of the broad passage that led out of the storeroom. One of the soldiers – a hardy Coldstream Guard – signalled in the air.

'Looks like the way is clear, old boy,' Jim said. 'Lead on.'

We are one.

The words rattled John as surely as a blow to the head. A harsh whisper inside his mind. He stopped in his tracks.

'Something wrong, old boy?' Jim asked, when he saw that John was not hurrying along with the rest of them.

'I… I don't know.' It was difficult to admit. He did not want to show weakness, not now, and not to Jim. And yet, he sensed something he could not explain. He knew he had been compromised at Osea, where de Montfort had rifled through his thoughts like a callous burglar. But de Montfort was gone now. That meant either some other force was exerting influence over him, or perhaps an all-too-familiar spirit was not yet done with him.

They stood at a crossroads between corridors. The bodies of white-coated engineers and suited armoury stewards littered the floor. Most were clean kills – gunshots, blades. Most, but not all. And that meant the threat of vampires was not yet over. The electric lighting – Cherleten's pride and joy – flickered on and off at intervals, broken lamps cascading intermittently with orange sparks and a smell like sulphur.

We are one.

John knew they had been led here. Or, perhaps, whoever read his thoughts had predicted his movements and set up an ambush. Their progress so far had been dogged periodically by harrying soldiers. Echoed shouts in Russian, and sporadic coughs of rifle-fire, had shepherded them here.

'John!' Jim hissed.

John snapped to attention. 'Something is not right. We need to come up with another plan.'

'We're almost there,' Jim protested.

'I think –'

A scream. Wet, gargled, tailing off into an agonised yelp, ending abruptly. It came from the right-hand corridor.

Gunfire echoed through the tunnels. More screams, and throaty growls.

One by one, the lights above the party blinked out, leaving darkness in their wake. From all four points of the junction, the darkness approached, advancing as a black curtain, until the last, flickering light failed.

A tapping sound came from the darkness, growing faster, closer. Scraping, scurrying, like a great mass of rats scampering across the hard tiles of the facility floor at first; then something very definitely larger than rats. Pinpricks of violet light advanced, bobbing in the black voids to left and right. Growls and low whines came with them. The men at John's side breathed hard.

He could smell the fear on them, and so could the things that came from the dark.

'Lanterns!' It was Miss Furnival who shouted.

The ghouls drew nearer, rancid breath carrying on the air, eyes sparkling.

Matches were struck, lanterns lit.

In the yellow lamplight, the ghouls shrank back. They dropped from the ceiling like spiders; they shielded their eyes.

'Fire!' Miss Furnival shouted.

Rifles rattled. Volley after volley boomed in the confines of the corridors. A cacophony of screeches almost drowned out the reports. Then the shooting stopped, and the sounds of gunfire were replaced with the wet hacking of flesh beneath blades, the crunching of bones under truncheons and rifle-butts, the snapping of jaws and the agonised cries of men.

John looked about in desperation, seeing the mission slipping away. A sudden flare of brilliant light flashed, electricity arcing from Jim's derringer. Sickly white flesh blackened and charred, and gave John an idea.

He smashed a lantern against the wall, and tossed it into the left-hand corridor. Oil ignited, ghastly faces glowed orange for just a second, before flames licked up around them. The ghouls began to clamber over each other in their bid to escape the fire. John drew his sword, slashing and thrusting at any creature that came close. Miss Furnival darted low, two curved knives held in a backhand grip, whirling amidst the creatures as they fled, slicing throats and severing limbs. She fought like the devil. Worse, she fought like Lillian.

Soon, the last screeching, naked monster vanished from the amber glow of the flames, back the way they had come. John could not count how many there had been. He counted four dead men at his feet, torn apart; heard only the testimony of ragged breaths and stumbling soldiers that they had been in a hard fight. Men beat at the flames, and the corridor slowly darkened. John's shoulder throbbed. He slumped against the wall, struggling to catch a breath.

'What just happened?' Jim gasped. 'Where did they come from?'

'The Artist must have smuggled them into the facility somehow,' John said. 'But such numbers... I'd say Melville was right when he suspected there were greater forces at play. Just how big is this submarine vessel?'

'Not big enough for this,' Tesla answered. The Serbian had kept well out of the way so far, and held his tongue. 'The *Munjolovac* can carry ten men perhaps, though not comfortably. I think Madam Artist would not share space with such creatures.'

'It's not in their nature to launch a coordinated attack like this – not unless their master commands them,' Miss Furnival said. 'Maybe the Artist controls de Montfort's ghouls. Maybe the Russians brought them. Who knows?'

'They had those brand-marks on them, did you see?' Jim noted. 'Army markings, perhaps? Maybe it is the Russians after all.'

'It sounded as though the Russians were fighting them too,' John said. 'I'd wager those ghouls are not under the full control of the enemy, and that can only be good for us.'

The fire burned still down one corridor. Jim shone his lantern along the others. There was no sign of movement.

'We have no choice but to continue,' Jim said.

'Begging your pardon, sir,' one of the men spoke up, somewhat angrily, 'but what about the wounded? We can't leave them here for them... things!'

John rubbed at his forehead; he felt peculiar. He needed to get on with the mission. The more he delayed, the more he felt the malign influence infiltrating his thoughts. 'If they cannot find their way out, then I suggest they fortify this position as best as they are able and form a rear-guard,' John said, feeling far more irritable than he ought. 'The rest of us will damn well follow our orders and press on.'

The man stepped forward, face a deep shade of burgundy by the dying firelight. The stripes on his arm showed his rank of sergeant, Coldstream Guards. Burly, moustached and insubordinate. 'With all due respect, sir –'

John was prepared to shout the man down, but Jim stepped between them, interrupting the soldier's flow. 'In my experience, Sergeant,' Jim said, 'those words are usually followed with a distinct lack of respect.'

John recognised those words at once, as a favourite saying of Sir Toby. Hearing them caused his anger to subside. He was not feeling himself. He stepped back.

'What's your name, Sergeant?' Jim asked.

'Carruthers, sir.'

'Well, Sergeant Carruthers,' Jim said, 'the *colonel* here has given an order.' Jim stressed John's rank. 'I for one intend to follow my orders, regardless of where they lead. And do you know why? Because down that tunnel are weapons so powerful they could wipe this city off the map. Weapons gathered here by the Crown because no nation on earth can be trusted with their use. And right now, they are being stolen by enemy soldiers. Enemy soldiers! Here, on the sovereign soil of England. I don't know about you lads, but I'd rather die than let the Russians, the Chinese, or anyone else get away with that. Because if they succeed, they could kill every man, woman and child in London. So are we going to stand here and argue all day, or are we going to show them what British steel is all about?'

Carruthers nodded, his emotions writ large across his lined face, until finally he hoisted his rifle and cried, 'Aye, sir!' This brought a round of 'ayes' from the other men.

The group was soon on the move again, now in near darkness. They hurried to the next junction, trying every door as they went to ensure no one could ambush them from the side-rooms. At the end of the corridor was a T-junction. To the right, the corridor terminated at a reinforced door, bloody handprints slapped onto its surface, smearing down to the floor where a dead guard lay. To the left, a light flickered, illuminating a stretch of passage that curved right.

'That's the weapon store,' Jim said. 'The guard must have been trying to arm himself.'

'Or find a secure place to hide,' John said. 'Come on, we need to arm ourselves, too.'

John set about the combination locks – there were three, each of which had to be set in turn. He worked quickly, hoping that Cherleten hadn't changed the combination. When the third sequence was dialled, the door clicked, and John swung it open. He flicked a lever on the wall beside the door, and electric lights blinked on. And they revealed a room almost entirely empty. A few pistols and boxes of ammunition lay on otherwise bare racks. Some were strewn about the floor, but where once hundreds of guns, knives and explosives had been kept, only empty space remained.

'Dear God,' Jim said. 'They've raided the armoury. The Russians have Tesla weapons now.'

'No,' John said. 'The door was locked.'

Jim stared at him dumbly. 'Does it lock itself when closed?'

'No. The dials must be spun for the locks to engage. No one would raid an armoury, turn off the lights and lock the door, unless they were doing it legitimately.'

'The security forces?'

'Let's hope so,' John said. 'We might find some lying about, that being the case. Best take what is left. Arm yourselves.'

Jim and Marie did as instructed. When they were done, John looked both ways along the corridor.

'These passages form a loop,' John said. He pointed back the way they had come. 'That way is the most direct path to the stores, but it's where the sounds of fighting came from. Ahead leads to the Nightwatch.' He glanced at Miss Furnival to gauge her reaction, and was relieved that she let it pass. 'There are other experimental wards – another level below this one. Even I don't know what's there. We should set the charges first, and double back if –'

A great rumble came from the bowels of the facility. The floor shook. The walls vibrated, and the rumbling intensified.

'What the devil?' Jim said.

The rumble became a low whine, slowly increasing in volume

and pitch. Soon it was a nauseating squeal. Men held their heads, and covered their ears, but it was of little use. The lights above them, previously dead, began to flash again. Bulbs popped, showering fragments of glass and sparks below. Luminous motes of dust began to drift all around in the darkened space, amber-gold. The walls themselves began to shimmer like a desert mirage, their surfaces patterned with the faintest impressions of green and purple glow.

The last honest man in London has come. A fitting tribute.

The words jabbed into John's mind. He gasped with pain, bunching his fists.

'What's happening?' Jim shouted over the squeal, but John could not answer.

'It's a gate,' Marie shouted. 'A big one.'

Jim wore an expression first of disbelief, then of horror. John knew what he was afraid of. The thought of passing through another gate was enough to unman him still. All who had seen the Otherside had nightmares of the many-tentacled thing that surveyed the world from its lofty height in the burning sky. None desired ever to cross through again.

As the frequency of the fearful trilling reached fever pitch, John felt complete stillness. All around him, Jim, Marie, the men – all of them grimaced at the noise, but John tuned it out. He could hear nothing but muffled cries and a distant rumbling, as though he were submerged in deep water. Something called to him, pulled at him.

John turned, looking down the left-hand corridor. And there she was. Elsbet, pale and delicate in death, staring into the next passage. She turned her head to look at John over her shoulder. Dark hair drifted across a wasted face like the tendrils of some deep-sea creature. Her eyes, black and glassy, pierced John's heart for the briefest moment, before she turned that fearful gaze away once more, and walked away. Her bare feet trod lightly across broken glass. Her white shroud floated out behind her, caught on some ethereal current. She vanished around the corner.

John knew what awaited him, and he knew what he had to do. Elsbet had guided him before, and was doing so again; whether to his doom, or to his salvation, it hardly mattered. Before he even knew what he was doing, he found himself walking away from the men, towards the spirit. He was dimly aware of being followed – Tesla. The Serbian stuck to him like glue.

The sound returned violently, shaking John to his senses.

'John! Where are you going?' Jim called out, not for the first time.

John saw the look of puzzlement on Jim's and Marie's faces, and was about to return to the group when a deep rumble shook the ground, rattling his teeth. John felt a hand on his arm. Tesla yanked him back, as a great crack opened up in the walls, across the ceiling. Lintels fell, missing John by inches. He scrambled away as a cascade of bricks and timbers spilled from the fault-line, filling the corridor with choking dust.

Some moments passed before John realised what had happened. He staggered to his feet, helped Tesla up. He heard Jim's voice from the other side of the debris, muffled.

'Jim!' he cried, before coughing up a lungful of brick-dust.

'I hear you,' came the reply. 'We're going to dig through.'

'There's no time, Jim. Go on ahead. Prime the explosives.'

'No, not until there is no other choice.'

'There is no other choice! Prime them. I'm going to finish this.'

'John, what –'

'There's a gate opening underneath London, Jim. You know what that means. Tesla is with me, he can stop it. Prime the bombs. If we succeed, I'll meet you at the sluice-gate. If we fail… you have your orders from Cherleten.'

'Cherleten be damned,' Jim called.

'That's the spirit! But I fear he's right this time. Let me save you a tricky decision, Captain,' John said, in his most commanding tone. 'Go on ahead and prime those explosives. My last order is a simple one: if I do not make it out before you, do your duty and detonate those bombs.'

Jim said nothing.

'Captain Denny, every second lost is a second that the gate grows more powerful. You know what comes next.'

'We hear you, Colonel,' Marie answered for Jim. 'We're going. God be with you.'

'And you, Miss Furnival. And you.'

TWENTY-THREE

'**W**e should not have let him go alone.' Jim turned the key in the detonator control panel. The device within began to tick rhythmically, audible even over the relentless drone.

'The colonel knows what he's doing,' Marie said. 'I figured that much about him.'

'He doesn't even have the keys. How far can he get?' Jim closed the panel and locked it again.

'He seemed to suggest he knew this place better than either of us, though Lord knows how. Anyway, if he gets stuck, I'm sure he'll head for the sluice-gate. He won't just wait for the tunnels to flood. Now come on, where next?'

Jim could not help but worry. 'This way,' he said. He led the way to a set of double doors as he sorted through the ring of keys. As he tried one in the lock, Jim frowned, and placed the palm of his other hand on the door.

'What is it?' Marie asked.

'Still warm. We're close to where they set off their explosion now. Just overhead. Alright, everyone, be careful – parts of the facility may be unsafe.'

'Tell us something we don't know,' Carruthers quipped, drawing forced laughter from the others.

'Very good. Now, brace yourselves.'

The men with rifles pressed their backs against the wall opposite the door, and took aim. Marie cranked the Tesla pistol she'd retrieved from the stores. The other men positioned themselves either side of the doors, weapons readied, lanterns raised.

Jim pulled the doors open. No one fired. He hurried into the room, lantern shining ahead of him, followed by the others, two at a time. Jim slipped on something, kept his feet, and shone the light down to reveal great smears of blood across the tiled floor.

The room was large, mostly in darkness, save for the flickering of small fires here and there. Cupboards and tables were overturned; the floor was strewn with rubble and large pieces of mechanical equipment, mostly mangled and smashed. Amongst the debris, bodies lay scattered or buried, not all of them in one piece.

Those tables that remained upright were still covered in machinery, large and small, some connected by chains, others topped in great rods coiled about with wire, all silhouetted in the gloom. On the right-hand side of the room, beams of reinforced concrete had half-fallen into the basement from above, twisted steel rods protruding from their sides like so much wickerwork. Wooden joists had fallen with them, and lay burning and charred atop piles of bricks. Smoke drifted hazily into the room, clinging to the ceiling like storm clouds.

'Sir, over here!' A Special Branch constable dashed across to a left-hand aisle, stooping to the floor, and Jim saw movement where he crouched. Someone was alive.

Jim gave the order to secure the room, and was by the constable's side in an instant. The policeman cradled the head of a gaunt man, face a mask of blood, light hair now red and matted. He groaned, and reached up to his saviours.

'I know you,' Jim said. 'Amworth, isn't it? What happened here?'

'I... there was an explosion,' the man said. 'And then men came; soldiers. We hid. But... when they left... oh, God!'

Jim placed a hand on the man's shoulder and tried to hush

him. 'Do not worry, we're here now. If the soldiers did not do this to you, then who?'

The man grasped Jim's arm, and stared at him, eyes wide. 'Monsters,' he hissed.

Jim looked at Miss Furnival, who gritted her teeth.

Jim frowned. 'What were you doing here so late, Doctor?' he asked. 'And all these others?'

The man took some heavy breaths, stertorous and croaking. 'We were... told to report for... duty. All hands who... worked today.'

'I don't understand. Everyone who worked today was asked to report here, late at night?' Jim was answered with a nod. 'By whom? For what purpose?'

'It is a matter classified,' he said.

Jim rattled the keys that were hung about his neck. 'I am Captain James Denny,' he said, 'and Lord Cherleten has given me full jurisdiction. Now, explain to me what happened here.'

Amworth considered this, and answered only reluctantly. 'There was... a woman. She took a drug from us. You know it?'

'Etherium.'

Amworth nodded. 'She used it. Too much... and she had power. Power over our subjects, and over us. She... said things. *Showed* me things. In my mind.'

'Wait – your subjects? The Nightwatch?'

Amworth nodded again.

'The last time I saw you, Mr Amworth, you were attending the Nightwatch. But this... What exactly is it you do here?'

'I... No. I cannot say.'

Marie stood, and looked around the room with intense scrutiny. 'I can,' she said at last. 'He's not nurturing psychics for the Nightwatch. He's testing them, to see if they can power a gate.'

'What?' Jim asked. But he only had to look at the shock – and fear – on Amworth's face to know that Marie had hit upon the truth. 'You're stockpiling etherium. You're using this equipment. This mysterious woman – she stole some of it, right?'

Amworth nodded; he looked tearful.

'And your "monsters". What of them?'

'They... they went after her.'

'After her?' Jim asked. 'Were they with this woman, or not?'

'No. They came from... there.' Amworth pointed feebly towards a large bulkhead door, on the other side of the room. It was open only a crack, but it should have been sealed. 'The monsters – some kind of degenerate inbreds, perhaps – they killed my team. After I was injured, I feigned death. I think perhaps they would have...' his words tailed away into a spluttered, hacking cough.

'Mr Amworth, that door leads to the lower levels, does it not? This woman surely came from the sluice-gate – she would have entered via the east door.'

'She did.'

Jim was starting to build a picture in his mind. A flash of insight struck him, and he hoped his instinct was wrong. 'Mr Amworth, I am going to get you to safety, but first you must answer me. This is of the matter critical. This facility has been attacked tonight by several detonations. Did these monsters attack before or after the bombs went off?'

Marie looked to Jim in puzzlement.

'Before,' he said. 'They rampaged through the laboratory. Then the explosion... the facility shook, much was destroyed. Just as I thought... all was quiet... the woman came. That is when I knew my... sleeping Majestics, my lambs... were in grave danger.'

Jim got to his feet. He had not quite pieced together the puzzle, but what he guessed so far gave him more cause for worry than all the events of the past week combined.

'What's all this about?' Marie whispered, looking furtively at the men around them.

'You remember when I made those accusations against you?' Jim asked.

'This is hardly the time for apologies –'

'No, you misunderstand. I accused you of being an informant. Cherleten and Sir Toby assured me that the Artist's intelligence

271

came not from you, or any other, but from the minds of the Nightwatch through esoteric means. But what if they were wrong? What if there is a man on the inside? Someone who oversaw the clearing of the weapons store? Someone who released vampires into the facility to kill those men who had performed those tasks *before* the bombs went off.'

'Who could have done such a thing?'

'That's what I'd like to know. Maybe the answer lies down there.' Jim nodded towards the vault door.

'I don't know, Captain. We've delayed long enough as it is, and with Colonel Hardwick and Tesla lost... Perhaps we should get on with the mission, and worry about traitors afterwards.'

'Uncovering this traitor, should he exist, is the mission as far as I am concerned,' Jim said. He knew he was becoming distracted by this new line of thinking, but he also had a feeling in his gut that he was right. He could not – would not – let it go.

John crawled awkwardly through a narrow vent, hot from exertion, shoulder prickling with pain as he dragged himself along on his elbows. An ignominious way to get about the facility, certainly, but a necessary one. Tesla grunted and groaned behind him. More than once John had to pause so the scientist could catch up, and urge him to be quieter.

At last John reached the metal grille which he was certain fed into the small office beside the old evidence room. It had been some time since he had visited this part of the facility, and then it had been in much more formal circumstances.

As he pulled himself up to the grate, knees and elbows scraping against rough-hewn bricks, he froze. He heard voices below, gruff. Chinese. John managed to signal Tesla to stop, and was glad that the Serbian heeded him. John held his breath, and eased himself forward an inch at a time, for fear that the dragging noise he made would alert whoever was below. The brickwork all around him seemed to resonate with the high-pitched hum, tuned to the key of another world.

John peered through the grille. Two celestials stood in the room below, sharing a joke. One held a long pipe, which gave off a pungent aroma of the east. The second man stroked the hilt of a knife at his belt as if it were a much-loved pet. Two rifles leaned against a desk. There was a door behind the men, which led to a room that had long been off-limits, having been sequestered by Cherleten for some secret project or other. The door was ajar, but there was little to see from here but flickering lights.

John squeezed an arm back to his belt and pulled out a knife. This was his best chance, if he was quick and quiet. He certainly could not risk a gun going off. He regretted now leaving his Winchester and cane-sword behind when he entered the vents, but he had been sure they would be a severe hindrance in the tight space. They were prized possessions both. It suddenly occurred to him that he had not asked Jim to take care of his dog should he not make it out of the facility. John pushed that thought aside; he could not be distracted now.

John moved over the grate, as carefully as he could, pulling up his legs as much as he was able, and finally kicked down hard at the metal. He dropped through, landing harder than he would have liked. He briefly registered a look of shock on the faces of the two celestials, and threw himself at the nearest man, smashing him against the wall with his good shoulder. The second man withdrew the dagger from his belt. John spun away from the first celestial and slashed his knife hard against the throat of the second. The man dropped the dagger and fell to the floor, clutching his throat as if to stem the torrential flow of blood. The other man reached a rifle, but John was on him quickly. He grabbed the celestial from behind, an arm around the man's throat, and stabbed upwards through the ribs and into the lungs. John kept his grip tight, his own wounded arm aching, but he maintained the hold until his enemy's struggles ceased.

John lowered the man to the floor. He grabbed a rifle, checked its load, and slung it over his shoulder. He wiped his knife, and retrieved the dagger. It was ten inches long, straight, ornate; bone-carved handle, bronze pommel. He tucked both into his belt and crept to the door. Peering through the gap, John saw two men wheel a huge chunk of strange machinery through the double doors at the far end of the room. Along the floor, weaving between dead bodies, thick cables trailed the room's length, some of them sparking dangerously with electrical current, attached to all manner of generators, from familiar oil-fired contraptions that rumbled and rattled, to strange Otherside devices, which arced with power. Fewer than half the room's electric lights were working now, and those blinked on and off fitfully. Whatever was drawing power from the generators appeared to be leeching energy from the entire facility; perhaps from the city beyond for all John knew.

A guard swung open the double doors to let the men with the trolley pass. Even when John had been one of the Order's most trusted agents, he had not been permitted access to this inner sanctum. Now, the locks were blasted away, and the enemy entered freely. Beyond the doors, an intense amber light flashed. Shadowy figures moved back and forth. And then the doors swung shut, leaving a lone guard. By the flickering light, John saw that he was a large man, light of skin, with fair, close-cropped stubble for hair. He wore a khaki shirt, sleeves rolled up to reveal bulging arms. A military man by his bearing, Russian by the silhouette of his rifle and the cut of his uniform.

John remembered that the doors at the opposite end of the room led to a broad corridor, wide enough for heavy goods to be brought down from the docks. John expected most of the security would be stationed in the corridors, for there was only one way in or out of this area. John took a breath and calculated his approach. He knew of no vent that could take him past this point. He would have to tackle the guard and try to slip into the room beyond unnoticed. He had weapons enough; if the men inside were working, unprepared for a fight, he could feasibly cause considerable damage before they could retaliate. If the guards outside were alerted, however…

'Psst!' Tesla hissed from above.

John had almost forgotten the Serbian. Tesla would make it difficult to infiltrate the area. With little choice, however, John helped Tesla down from the shaft, and quickly explained his plan.

'Is there nothing in there we can use?' Tesla asked, peeking through the door.

'I have no idea,' John whispered. 'Do not wander off. As soon as I'm certain that guard is alone, I make my move, and I need you close.'

John watched the guard, waiting to see if there was any further activity, and prepared to move out.

The hairs on the back of his neck stood on end. He felt his breath misting on the air. John closed his eyes, composed himself, and then looked back into the office, past the puzzled face of Tesla.

Elsbet stood in the shadows. Her hair clung glossy and lank to her pale, dead face. Her eyes were mercifully closed. John turned away, and shuddered.

Without a word to Tesla, John moved out. He had no wish to stay in that office with the spirit. He had even less desire to consider once more if he was mad, and if the ghost of Elsbet was simply his own guilty conscience come to haunt him. He needed solitude and a plentiful supply of good Irish whiskey for those particular philosophical questions, neither of which he had the luxury of right now. And so he focused on the next best thing: the mission – on avoiding certain death once again.

He stole around tables, benches and long units of shelving, staying close to the wall, stepping over debris and the corpses of armoury staff with sure-footed ease. Even were John's approach not covered by the ululating sonic assault, he would have been silent as a cat on the hunt. He closed in on his prey, one step at a time, eyes never leaving the target. He took out both knives. Stealth was his only asset now.

John reached the end of a long bank of workbenches, and

carefully set down the rifle. He had only ten feet to cover. The soldier looked on edge, holding his rifle just a little too tightly.

When the soldier looked away, John closed the distance to his quarry, lightly, swiftly. At the last second, the man turned. He saw John too late, and almost fumbled his rifle in surprise. John stabbed the soldier in the gut, caught a blow to the shoulder in the process that jolted him to the core, before thrusting upwards with the Chinese dagger. The blade pierced the man's throat, under the chin. The man's eyes rolled back into his head, blood flowed over the hilt of the blade, over John's hand, warm and sticky. John lowered the man to the floor before withdrawing the dagger with some distaste.

John grimaced, and rolled his shoulder. Spots of blood were already seeping through the dressing. He wiped the blade clean, and considered how to approach the door.

Behind him, someone clapped, slowly, sardonically. John's blood froze in his veins. He couldn't remember the last time someone had sneaked up on him.

John spun around. A celestial stood only four or five yards away. His approach had gone unnoticed. John recognised the man at once. Xiang. The man who had defeated him at the gypsy camp. The man who had killed Bertrand.

'You fight well, Agent,' the celestial said. 'Shall we see how well?' He adopted a fighting stance, legs wide apart, body turned sideways to John, one arm outstretched in invitation to attack.

'How the devil did you get here?' John asked.

'Ah, my mistress has her ways. Now, prepare yourself.'

John glanced over his shoulder. The doors were still shut. He looked about the room. Tesla had disobeyed him and slunk off behind a row of tables, and now peered over at John and this new foe. At least he was keeping quiet. There was no one else in the room.

John sighed heavily, shoulders sagging, feigning only a fraction more exhaustion and resignation than his weary bones felt.

And then he struck, adder-swift, the dagger an extension of

his arm, whipping towards the Chinaman's face. And yet if John was a snake, Xiang was a mongoose. The man moved barely an inch, but it was enough to see John fly past him, the dagger missing its mark. John's insides bunched up as a knee drove into his ribs. He spun, delivering a backhand slash with his own knife. Xiang swiped it away with a palm, barely showing concern for the cut he received, but he had clearly not expected the strike. John twisted to face his opponent; he had learned the formal fighting styles of the east – he had practised them further since encountering Tsun Pen's men at the Isle of Dogs three years past. He knew never to turn one's back on a skilled opponent.

It hardly mattered. John had never fought anyone so fast, and now found himself slashing wildly, the celestial ducking low, then punching. Fast hands, striking five times in combination, shaking John's ribs. A roundhouse punch to the head, and John was turned about, spitting blood. He dropped his knives involuntarily, staggered backwards towards the doors. Xiang grinned wickedly, and ran at John. The man took flight, both feet connecting with John's chest, and the world collapsed around John's ears.

John crashed through the door, flailing backwards, struggling to keep his feet. He was dimly aware of men all around him, of flickering amber lights, of strange phenomena crackling in the air. The celestial marched towards him. John already knew he had failed in his mission – he was uncovered, whatever hopeful plan he had was dashed. If he were to achieve anything now, it would be to kill this accursed celestial, and take as many of the man's allies with him as he could.

The celestial aimed a kick at John's head. John knocked it aside, and lunged at his foe. Daggers of pain coursed through him as Xiang grabbed his shoulder, hard fingers digging into torn flesh. John grunted, but did not cry out. He would not give his enemy the satisfaction. Instead, he let the pain wash over him, going limp, stumbling. The celestial yanked back John's head.

For a moment, the room spun into focus. Faces leered at him, lit by pulsating waves of light. Voices urged the Chinaman to kill him. A great, circular portal flashed, striving to become a solid wall of energy, like a baby struggling to take a first breath; to live.

John lifted his head to face his foe. The celestial had drawn back his arm, hand held palm outwards, ready to deliver the killing blow. He afforded himself a smile at John's expense.

Movement behind the celestial. A metallic ringing. Xiang staggered sideways, and Tesla was there, metal pipe in his hands, looking terribly apologetic. The onlookers went quiet, but were caught flat-footed. John reacted quickest, relieving Tesla of the pipe and shoving the Serbian out of the room. With throbbing head and aching limbs he turned on Xiang again, single-minded, blanking out everything else around him. The celestial lunged at him, but John struck first. The pipe connected hard with Xiang's shoulder. Xiang stumbled sideways, but still managed to flash a kick to John's ankle, trying to trip him. John was ready for that; he sidestepped, pressed forward, before raising a knee hard into Xiang's crotch. John had long learned how to fight in the Chinese style. But he'd also been a soldier, and a prisoner, fighting in the pits of Burma for the amusement of his gaolers. He had not won many of those fights by sticking to the martial code.

He saw the shock and pain in the celestial's eyes. John followed with a head-butt to the bridge of the man's nose, a stiff jab of the pipe to the stomach, a spinning heel-kick to the temple. The celestial went down.

Someone grabbed John by the left arm. Again, his shoulder burned, and it awoke in John a bloodlust he had long thought buried. He spun, shifting his assailant's grip into an arm-lock, throwing him to the ground. The man had a pistol in his other hand. John dropped the pipe and took the gun, swinging the man upwards as a human shield, squeezing off two rounds into an advancing figure he could barely see clearly for the sweat, tears and blood in his one eye. He staggered backwards from the room, the man in his grip shouting obscenities in Russian. John almost fell backwards over Xiang, who even now had managed to right himself. The celestial stood, a gaping wound in his head. He tried to adopt a fighting stance.

For a moment their eyes met. John admired his tenacity. But this was the man who had hanged his most trusted lieutenant. He deserved no honourable death. John raised the pistol and shot the man in the forehead. A promise was a promise.

And now John's vision cleared, and his mind also. Who had he been fooling, to deny his nature? This was what he was; this was John Hardwick.

The Russian shouted again, and John twisted the man's arm so tight the wrist almost broke. The man screamed in pain. Soldiers were approaching slowly, cautiously, rifles readied, dark silhouettes before the large gate that nigh filled the room – an irregular circle of steel, brass and copper panels, entangled in wires and cables. Yellow light ebbed and flowed from its boundary, sometimes haphazardly, sometimes rhythmically. Something dark scratched at John's mind – something lurking behind the stuttering gateway, ravening for ingress, waiting impatiently for the energy to coalesce and the gate to become stable. John felt Tesla's breath at his back, the scientist cowering behind him. The plan, such as it was, was in tatters.

The Russians took aim. John pointed his pistol first at the head of his hostage and then, when the others did not slow their approach, he aimed at the closest soldier instead. This was it; he would go out fighting.

And then he stopped. Everything, the very world, seemed to stop. The soldiers had parted. A figure came from their ranks, walking slowly, assuredly towards him; a woman, beautiful and dusky, framed in the light of the gate. At first, for a fleeting moment, John thought it was Elsbet – if not the ghost, then the real girl, the Otherside double, returned to London after all. And then with growing agony, with horror, with elation, and everything in between, he knew who it was who now approached him. The strength drained from his body, the fight left him. He could do nothing in the face of his greatest triumph, his greatest defeat, his greatest regret.

Rosanna stood only three feet away from him, swathed in a long flowing dress of yellow. She stared at him with such antipathy that John's heart broke all over again.

He let the Russian go. The man stumbled away, and turned angrily, only to shrink back at a wave of Rosanna's hand.

John had suspected. He had *known*. But he had not been able to admit it until he had seen the truth of it with his own eyes. Rosanna was the Artist.

'You have returned to me at last, John Hardwick,' she said, her voice stronger than ever, full of steel and ice. 'I never doubted that you would, despite the obstacles in your path. It was foreseen.'

John tried to speak, to move, but no words would come from his lips, and his feet remained rooted resolutely to the floor. The soldiers stepped past Rosanna, and even as one of them raised a rifle-butt ready to strike, John could do nothing. He watched the weapon fall upon him as though the world had stopped turning and time itself had slowed. He felt some small relief as blackness descended.

TWENTY-FOUR

J im led the way down aged stairs, into cellars that were surely far older than the dock facility. Low, vaulted ceilings made the dark warren all the more claustrophobic. Rough-hewn stone and slippery brickwork brought the smell of damp to Jim's nose. This area was well below the level of the Thames, little more than an overlarge damp-cellar, used for some secret purpose.

They filed through a narrow corridor, and into another large room, like a hospital ward, though in conditions surely unsanitary. Jim noted that this area must lie directly beneath the Nightwatch ward – the one he knew about, at least. He noted also that the doors should have been locked and barred, but were instead wide open.

Jim tried to ignore the gasps of his men as flickering electric lights illuminated perhaps twenty unfortunate souls, strapped to metal gurneys that flanked the room, sited between thick pillars. Jim advanced down the aisle, disgusted by what he saw and heard, what he could smell. Low groans, from poor creatures so weak they could barely cry out. Eyes stared at the ceiling from sunken sockets. Susurrating machinery and hissing bellows assisted the subjects' breathing. Etherium dripped into their veins through long tubes. Worse still, several subjects were attached to large pieces of machinery coiled about with wires, which trailed to wicked-looking coronets embedded in the skulls of the unfortunate Majestics. Jim was certain that not all of the subjects were alive.

'My God,' one man said. 'That smell...'

Jim glared at Amworth, who had limped along with the group, too frightened to be left alone upstairs. 'You leave them like this?'

'They know no better,' the man said. 'In their etherium-addled state, they are inured to their body's discomfort. It is a mercy.'

'A mercy!' Miss Furnival snapped. 'Look at them!' Amworth instead looked at the floor. Miss Furnival grabbed him by the chin and turned his head to a gurney, upon which lay a callow youth, with a bruised and sunken face, most surely dead, stinking like a latrine. 'I said look!' she said.

Jim pulled her away, for Amworth looked in a terrible way himself.

'The machines that keep them alive... they are powered by electricity,' the man said, in a small, childlike voice. 'The attack shorted the circuits. We could not have known. They would have felt nothing. Nothing at all.'

Jim looked away in disgust, and put an arm around Marie to stop her from striking the fellow.

'Mr Amworth,' Jim said. 'Where does that lead?' He pointed to a large set of double doors at the far end of the room.

'Back to the wards,' Amworth said, sullenly.

'We can reach the sluice-gate from there,' Jim said. 'And these side-rooms?' The dingy, irregular chamber was punctuated by heavy, iron-shod doors on either side.

'Stores mainly. Most are out of bounds to us.' He gave Jim a grave look. 'We do not ask.'

'Our own people have done this,' Miss Furnival hissed at Jim, ignoring Amworth now. 'Did you suspect?'

Jim shook his head.

'You provided these subjects,' she seethed. 'You and the colonel.'

'Not willingly. I did my duty, as did John, but not for this. Never for this.'

'Captain Denny... James... if these experiments are successful, the Order will be able to open gates, just like the Othersiders. And you know the danger that poses. They think they're advancing science. They think they can find riches beyond imagining, and technology, and maybe capture some Majestics and Intuitionists. But you know what else may come through those portals. You've seen it.'

Jim cringed at the thought, for he knew all too well. He saw it in his nightmares each time he slept. He snapped from his reverie at once, abruptly aware that the men were listening to every word, with revulsion and confusion both. He was about to suggest that he and Marie go on alone, when he heard a noise up ahead, prompting the men to raise their weapons in readiness.

A figure hurried across the far end of the room towards the main exit. Jim caught a glimpse of a white coat and silver hair.

'Who goes there?' Jim shouted. 'Answer me, or we'll shoot.'

'No, don't shoot!' came a frightened voice. A man stepped forward into the light, fearful, hands raised. 'Captain Denny... is that you? Oh, thank God! It is I, Dr Crookes.'

'Doctor, what the devil are you doing down here?'

'I'm in charge, for my sins. I was overseeing some late deliveries when we came under attack.'

'Dr William Crookes?' Marie asked, as the old man came fully into the light.

Crookes looked at her as though seeing her for the first time, and nodded warily.

Marie whispered into Jim's ear. 'On the Otherside, this man's double discovered etherium. This cannot be coincidence.'

'You!' Crookes said, coming nearer, squinting. 'Sir Arthur's niece.'

'The same,' Miss Furnival replied.

'Dr Crookes,' Jim said, 'I am happy to have found you. We are on our way to the sluice-gate, and all survivors of the attack are to come with us.'

'I am grateful, Captain,' the old man said. 'We should make haste.'

'Wait.' Marie looked deeply suspicious. 'You look in good shape, Dr Crookes, considering all your men are dead.'

'I managed to lock myself in the office when I heard the commotion.'

'Really? That office over there?' Marie marched over to the far corner of the room, from where Crookes had emerged. Jim was taken aback, but as soon as he saw Crookes' nervous manner, the way the man hurried after the American in protest, Jim knew she was on to something. He followed at once, waving his men with him.

'This door is locked, Doctor,' Marie said. 'How conscientious of you. Care to open up, and let us see what's inside?'

'That is quite out of the question. This facility contains research of the utmost secrecy, and you are not even an agent.'

'But I am,' Jim said. 'Open the door, please, Doctor.'

'I will not.' He glared at Amworth, who limped along, holding on to a constable as though for dear life. 'Amworth, you simpering idiot. Why have you brought these men down here?'

'Because I ordered him to, sir,' Jim intervened. 'Because Lord Cherleten has vested the authority of this installation in me.'

'In my absence, Captain. But now I am here, and you are relieved of such weighty responsibility. Despite this chaos, there is still a hierarchy within the Order, is there not?'

'There is.'

'Then follow it! Perhaps it is time you stopped listening to this woman and did your duty!'

That gave Jim pause. Something felt wrong, but then, the most secret installation in the Order was under attack by a psychic, foreign agents, and vampires. Perhaps, Jim thought, it was time to follow orders. Perhaps Crookes was right.

'Damn you men and your duty,' Marie snapped, pulling Jim out of his thoughts. 'Look where duty got Hardwick. Look where it's got you. Do you think these half-dead nobodies here will thank you for doing your duty? You think this coward here – ' she waved a hand at Crookes, who gasped at the affront, '– gives a damn for your duty, beyond you bringin' him grist for his mill? It's your damned duty that got us in this mess, Captain Denny. When're you going to stop doing what you're told, and think about doin' what's right instead?'

Jim knew he was about to attract a world of trouble; he could feel it in his marrow. He worked his stiff hand, making a fist, untangling the aches as he untangled his thoughts. Finally, he set his jaw and turned to Crookes. 'There is still a hierarchy within the Order, Dr Crookes. You are quite correct. But your role within the Order has ever been kept secret. As such, I do not know you; I do not know your rank; and I have the keys.'

Jim cycled through the bunch, trying each one in the door, doing his best not to smile at Crookes' growing protests. When at last he found a key that fitted the lock, he swung open the door, surprised to see that it was two inches thick, heavily reinforced. Beyond it, a passage sloped downwards, floor slick with green-brown ooze. A smell like rancid meat drifted upwards from the darkness.

'Hid in your office, you said?' Jim asked. 'Strange-looking office. Perhaps Cherleten doesn't like you very much.'

'Captain Denny, I warn you,' Crookes said. 'Do not go down there if you value your position within this order.'

'That's the thing about spies,' Jim said. 'You never can tell when they're telling the truth, or when they're bluffing. Makes them damned good at cards. That's why I don't game at the Apollonian. Miss Furnival, shall we?'

Marie smiled deviously. 'Oh, Captain Denny, you know how to treat a girl.'

We are one.

John opened his eyes – did he have two eyes now? – and looked about at the faces all around him. Five sisters clad in yellow save for one, all dark of eye and hair, faces still as though carved from rock. The odd one out, the girl in white, stood slowly, and as she did the other four faded away into shadow. The girl's eyes were closed. She did John a mercy, for he did not wish to see those eyes again. She turned away and pointed.

Footsteps echoed in the darkness. Someone drew near. A man. He came into view, tufts of grey hair beneath a black hat. Face stern and eyes cold.

'It seems as though you have been blessed with the nine lives of a cat.' John recognized the voice, and the words. The first words his father had spoken to him that fateful day, when he had returned from the grave to shoot his own son and leave John for dead.

'No...' It was all John could say.

'You have been on a journey which is given to so few men to make.'

John felt powerless. He could not move. His father's words filled him with fear, as though he might be killed once more at the hands of Lazarus. But they were just words. This was not real. How could it be?

'Can you understand what it is to lose everything dear to you, for nothing?' Marcus Hardwick asked. Echoes; just echoes of words spoken in anger, long ago.

'You are not real!' John cried.

Before his eyes, Marcus Hardwick was transformed, shadows shifting, face melting and forming features anew, until Sir Toby Fitzwilliam stood before him. Then came the shot, ringing out, and the old man convulsed. He spat blood.

'We do what we must for the good of the Empire...' he gasped. He fell.

John tried to stand, but could not. His feet were as lead, his hands clasped to something – the arms of a chair perhaps, as though he were manacled, but shadows clung to him and he could not see. But he sensed something in the dark, from the black outline of Sir Toby's crumpled body, a pool of something oily and wet spread across an indiscernible floor. John knew it rather than saw it. Some distant light reflected from it, the growing pool of blood, forming a shape.

It came closer to John's feet, and he could not move them, though he felt that allowing the blood to touch him would be the worst of all things.

The pool spread into a body, wings, claws, and a great crested head. The dragon of John's oldest nightmares stretched out before him, a heraldic mosaic formed from the blood of his mentor.

Something approached from the long dark; a circle of golden light, distant, but drawing nearer, like the lamp of an approaching train through a tunnel. Soon, John was forced to squint against its brilliance. He could not turn away.

Elsbet appeared at his side. John felt the freezing aura about her, the sweep of wet, lank hair across his shoulder. He sensed her cracked, blue lips near his ear, and she whispered familiar words to him, words he had heard in a prophecy years ago.

He is the destroyer of worlds and the healer of worlds. He has seen his realm burn, and seeks to burn ours and everyone within it. Only the young dragon can stop him, but he does not have the strength.

Her breath formed ice upon John's cheek. Her words had once prophesied the coming of Lazarus... or had they? They seemed now more poignant than ever.

Elsbet stood, and walked away from John, her slender figure silhouetted in the onrushing amber glow. The light flickered as shadows pawed and pushed at it from the other side, with sharp claws and hungry mouths. Smoky waves rippled across its surface. Shadowy hands reached from the heart of the glow to embrace their sister. Elsbet did not stop. She walked on and on, through the blood-dragon upon the floor, until the light consumed her, and she was gone, leaving only a trail of bloody footprints flickering in the yellow light.

'The power, it stabilise.' The voice was muffled, swimming into John's consciousness like the remnant of a dream. He blinked, light attacking his eye immediately. Through a mist-like blur, he watched dark figures move all around. Slowly, they coalesced into solid forms. Soldiers – the Russians. Chinese guards. All laboured as one, cranking handles, tightening metal fittings, lugging machinery about the room. All of them united in one great endeavour: the gate.

John was sitting upright on a hard chair. His head ached. He could barely make out what was going on around him. But he was near the gate. He could feel its warmth, its energy. He felt electrified. His hair lifted towards the pulsating amber light.

'Better hurry, Tesla,' a man said, his voice a thickly accented growl. 'You are almost out of time.'

'If I am out of time, all of us are out of time, no?'

'But you go first, *kozyol.*' The first man laughed.

'Russians,' Tesla moaned. 'It does not matter which universe, it is always Russians.'

Slowly, John developed an awareness of his wider surroundings. He tried to stand, but was tied to his chair, the rope wrapping about his waist and binding his wrists. A tall, wiry man glowered at him. It took a moment to recognise the soldier who had knocked him unconscious... how long ago? John's stomach clenched as everything flooded back to him. He had always prided himself on his ability to observe details, to compartmentalise every fact in order to use them later. But now the thought of Rosanna had come back to him, as though it had all been a dream, and he was struck once more by the feeling of utter helplessness and... grief... that had consumed him. It was only now that he looked about, senses pricked to alertness, and saw her.

She was one with the light, her yellow dress melding with the crackling portal, whose amber glow seemed to flow into the room like a sentient liquid, some oleaginous form of life, before shrinking back into the ramshackle gateway that framed it, then blinking out altogether, before the pattern started again. With each cycle, it remained stable just a few seconds more. And with each flux, the fearful tuneless trilling became less adequate to mask the other sounds beneath. The scratching, the chittering. The noises that John felt were at once in his head, and behind the light.

She must have sensed John was awake. She stood there, bathing in the light, and her eyes fixed upon him. Finally, she stepped from the pedestal at the foot of the great circular gate, and approached. The smell of lavender assailed John's senses. It had so long been a scent he associated with Rosanna, but now it was overpowering.

'I wondered, over the years, if I would ever see you again,' she said. Her voice was strange. Gone was the exotic warmth of the Romani accent. Instead she sounded stilted, too measured for the hot, passionate woman John had known before. 'Slowly, it became not a matter of "if", but "when".'

John tried to speak, but the words stuck in his craw. Rosanna saw this, and smiled. It was a smile John recognised, but it was not Rosanna's.

'I told you not to return unless it was with my sister. But now you have handed Elsbet to my people, so perhaps you are a man of your word after all. The last honest man in London.'

'Why?' John finally formed the word, though he felt stupefied. 'Why the Artist? How?'

'So many questions, Colonel Hardwick,' she said. She turned her face from John, and when she looked back, she was changed. Her features were hard as stone, beautiful as a sculpture, and yet malign. 'How could I be anything else? I *am* the Artist.'

'What? You have taken his empire?'

'You really are a fool. I have rebuilt *my* empire from the ashes in which you left them. I have taken this form, this power, as I foresaw three years past.' She leaned forwards. 'Look into my eyes, John Hardwick. I am Rosanna. I am Tsun Pen. *We are one.*'

John felt his head spin. Had he not seen wonders and terrors unimaginable, he would give no credence to such madness. But he had seen more than he ever wished to, and thus he could do nothing but believe. He felt sick. 'It is not possible,' he said. He denied it. He denied it because he loved her. But he saw more than Rosanna behind those eyes. He saw evil.

'You killed me, Hardwick. You plunged a sword through my heart. You watched me die, and then you burned my house to the ground. And when you did these things, you freed me. I had known all along that my spirit was too powerful to be constrained by mortal tethers, and had even foreseen the object of my salvation: this Rosanna. But I lacked the proper… motivation… to risk leaving it. I had clung for too long to a monstrous form, convinced that from my lair I could hide away from the world, and yet manipulate it. How much more can I achieve now? I am beautiful. I am free. Rosanna was possessed of a power so immense, so pure, and yet for the most part untapped. The two Tsun Pens had power, and ambition, but no freedom. Our souls cried out to each other, reached through the Eternal Night, and became as one. Now, we three, together… we no longer require solitude. We do not hide. We do not even need to peddle prophesies. We see into the future for our own ends. We create the future. And instead of paying the Artist to avert the course of destiny, the governments of the world will pay us not to destroy them.'

'Pay you…'

'What you see before you, John Hardwick, is a demonstration. I have already brought the Order of Apollo to its knees, and they will beg forgiveness before I am done. They betrayed me. They reneged on our blood-pact, and sent you, a useless whelp, to assassinate me. And I let it happen, because I had already foreseen that death was only the start of the journey. I have lived three lives, and in each I was an outcast, a wanderer, a pauper. Now, I shall be a queen. Perhaps I should thank you, but I am not so magnanimous. My goals may be far-ranging, by ambition limitless, but I have chosen this place for a very personal reason.'

'Elsbet?'

Rosanna tossed back her head and laughed. Now she sounded like the gypsy woman whom John had loved. Her laughter was music and light, but even so, it ended with a hollow timbre.

'No, John Hardwick. The agony that Elsbet endured was only a motivation. It gave him a foothold into my mind. It helped convince me to let him in. *You* are the cause of it all.'

'Me?' John had not felt such dismay since he had signed the order that had condemned Rosanna's people to capture. But something sparked within him – she'd said 'let him in'. This was Rosanna talking, not Tsun Pen, unless they truly were of one mind.

'Always you! You slew Tsun Pen. You betrayed me! Do you know what became of Nadya, and Gregor? I can see from your eyes that you do know, and yet somehow you live with yourself! Do you know that Esme died of fever because of the life of hardship you inflicted on us? Do you know what happened to Drina when they came for her? Drina, the very best of us all!'

'She was, and she was nothing but light!' John said. He was desperate, but he recognised fully the voice of Rosanna, and it gave him hope. She was in there still, two – or three – personalities, each with a voice. Only one of them mattered to John. 'Drina would not want this. She would counsel against such madness.'

'The Five Sisters are no more, John Hardwick. I am the last, and I will make you pay.' A strange expression crossed her features. The outburst was unmistakeably Rosanna, but there was an instant look of regret, or perhaps inner chastisement, as though she were giving something away; some weakness.

John tried to cling to reason, to observe this strange enemy and examine her faults, but all he could see was Rosanna; all he could think of was what he had driven her to, what had become of her sisters because of him, and he was heartsick for it.

'What I do now, John Hardwick,' she went on, more coolly, 'I do for power, and wealth, and legacy, yes. But I do it also for revenge. I cannot deny that I am glad you escaped de Montfort. There was some pleasure in the thought of you being drained of life by him. But now… seeing your face, your dismay at what your own pathetic sense of honour has wrought upon the world… this is worth more to me than all the jewels in your empire.'

'Stop your gloating and get on with it,' the wiry Russian interrupted, glaring at Rosanna – at 'the Artist'.

She returned that look in kind. 'Do not presume to instruct me, Orlov.'

'I am paying you. I am protecting you. Perform your tricks and be done, or we leave you here with nothing.'

'Where will you go? Every soldier in London is ready to kill you. There is only one way out of here, and it is through that gate. Tesla provided the science, but I provide the magic, no? Without me, you have nothing but a very large generator, which will quickly become a very large bomb. Now help Mr Tesla, and hold your tongue.'

Orlov looked as though he might strike Rosanna for the slight, but in the end he gritted his teeth and stepped away.

'Hardwick,' she said. 'This gentleman is Dmitri Orlov. He is much like you. Soldier, assassin, spy. He is an excellent shot, also like you. I hope you can find it in your heart to forgive him for the death of Sir Toby Fitzwilliam?'

'Sir Toby,' John gasped. 'You really did want him dead? And for me?'

'He gave the order that destroyed my people!' she snapped. For a brief moment again, it was Rosanna, the hot gypsy blood in her veins giving rise to a display of emotion. Then her face became a mask once more, wearing an expression so similar to Tsun Pen's sardonic sneer that it made John shudder. 'That it weakened the Order was a considerable bonus. That it made you all act so rashly, to enter my web with insufficient men, with Tesla at your side, and no solid plan… that was all to the good. But yes; truthfully, I did it for you. Now, if you will excuse me, I must tend to matters. You, John Hardwick, can watch.'

'Wait!' John said. His mind spun with the possibilities of all he had learned. But he grasped for something – anything – to distract Rosanna. To buy time for… he knew not what, but there had to be a way out of this nightmare. He looked about, taking in every detail of his surroundings. Could he move fast enough to disarm a soldier? What then?

'Yes?' The Artist cocked her head, a bemused smile upon her lips.

'The gate. How can you escape through it? You'll be trapped on the Otherside, which is surely now in ruin.'

'No, foolish man. Do you think this is the only work Nikola Tesla has performed for me in these years? I have other gates at my disposal, on both sides of the veil. I have travelled far, and seen much since last we met.'

John looked to Tesla, who avoided his gaze and busied himself with the machinery. The Serbian had mentioned no such developments. 'How? How did Mr Tesla come into your possession?'

'Possession...' Tesla muttered, loud enough to draw an irked look from the Artist.

'Mr Tesla attempted to flee the Otherside in his ingenious submarine, during the battle of London Bridge,' the Artist said. 'He brought de Montfort with him, though not through choice. I saw it, naturally. I painted it. I knew at once I must have him. Tesla was the true genius behind the Lazarus Gate, after all. He has already built several portals for me, to increase my supplies, to provide my followers safe passage whenever they need it. My arrangements with de Montfort meant that I had to leave Tesla behind – I should thank you for bringing him to me, for with his help my plan will be all the simpler. Look at this, John Hardwick! None of Mr Tesla's gates were ever as powerful as this one, powered by the handsome supply of electrical energy to this facility. And the Nightwatch, of course.' She indicated the machinery where Tesla worked. John saw now that more cables and tubes snaked away from it, over into a shadowed corner of the room, where sleeping Majestics lay on steel gurneys, eyelids flickering to the rhythmic pattern of the gate.

'You went to great pains to rescue Elsbet from this fate, yet you are quite happy to shackle these poor wretches for your gain.'

'A necessary evil. They serve a greater purpose now.'

'But this... Why go to such lengths if you do not need to?'

'I have always admired your inquiring mind, even if you do not use it to its potential. I need to provide proof of my true power for the Russians, so that they never again question me. In doing so, I shall make an example of Great Britain, and your precious order. This gate is unique. It was constructed from the Lazarus Gate, and it draws upon my own power as well as Mr Tesla's electricity. It can be used from both sides. And it can do more than that. Mr Tesla discovered how to tune the gate to an infinite number of worlds, and things that cannot strictly be called worlds at all. Once we have left, with every resource we can strip from this "armoury" of yours, we shall open up the gate. By the time this power supply is consumed, who knows what horrors will have found their way into this world?

'This facility will be the epicentre of the greatest catastrophe the world has ever known. For this secret, and others like it, the Russians will make me a queen, and no one will ever dare raise a hand to them – or to me – ever again. This is the ultimate weapon, John Hardwick. A weapon so powerful it will end the prospect of war in our time. Is that not worth any price? Unfortunately, like any such weapon, it must be used, just once, as a demonstration of its efficacy.'

'Surely you know that what happened to the Otherside will happen here,' John spluttered. 'It is madness! It cannot be controlled.'

'Tell that to your own Lord Cherleten,' Rosanna – no, Tsun Pen – scoffed. 'You know that this gate was almost operational before we even came here? Mr Tesla's generator merely gave it the power that your scientists could not. We would not have had sufficient time to build an entire gate from its component parts. Apollo Lycea has been trying to activate it themselves for some time. They have been buying etherium from me because they were unable to harvest enough themselves, and they sought a way to find a fresh supply. Etherium, and more besides! They did not ask where it came from, as long as it came.'

There it was. Cherleten had known about the Artist all along – or at least about someone posing as the Artist. It stood to reason that Sir Toby must have known too. John had always suspected that his retirement to the country had not been challenged robustly enough. Now he knew why.

The Artist laughed again, this time with pure malevolence. 'Perhaps you now know what it is like to be betrayed, John Hardwick. Were your masters really worthy of your loyalty? I think not. But do not worry, they shall soon be taught a lesson. The power of the Lazarus Gate is the greatest in the world. It is not for Britain to control.'

'No. It is for the highest bidder,' John said.

'And still you judge me! You really are priceless. Listen to me, John Hardwick – there is a catastrophe coming. You know of the Riftborn? Of course you do. They have seen this world. They lust for it. They want nothing more than to tear every man, woman and child limb from limb. I am going to provide just a taste of what that means, and when I am done, your government will beg for my aid. Furnival thought the Nightwatch could make me obsolete, but I have been able to mask my plans from those simple-minded unfortunates from the beginning. If I control the gates, I control the flow of etherium. I will strip the Otherside clean of weapons to combat the Riftborn. And I will bring forth my own soldiers, using monsters to fight monsters.'

'The ghouls? De Montfort?'

'De Montfort was useful, yes, but his secrets are now mine. With my mercenary army I –'

'Enough of this!' Orlov snapped. 'Look.'

The Artist turned as Orlov pointed. The great amber light was finally coalescing into something else – a solid, juddering mirror, rippling all over its surface like water being vibrated. The pitch of the hateful noise changed subtly. Tesla pounded a fist on the side of one of his machines.

'Mr Tesla,' the Artist said. 'Is it ready?'

'Almost, Madam Artist,' he said, with a sideways look that spoke of fear and loathing both.

'Almost is not good enough, Mr Tesla. I have already foreseen the enemy's plans. They seek to destroy this facility rather than allow us to hold it. If you do not work faster, you will be here when it is swallowed up by the river.'

'What?' Orlov said. 'You never tell us this, witch.'

'Would you have escorted me to an underground facility had you known it would soon fall on our heads, Orlov? As I said, the only way out of here is through this gate. Fear not, I have seen the future. I have seen my deliverance on the Otherside. It is known.'

TWENTY-FIVE

Jim put a handkerchief to his mouth. There was a vile smell from the cellar, somewhere between a sewer and an abattoir. Crookes chuntered the whole way; Jim ignored him.

Only two of the men had accompanied Marie, Jim and Crookes this far – Poynton and Sykes, two capable-looking Special Branch constables. Jim suspected that they might find something 'top secret' in the sub-cellar, and as such he needed only men who could keep their mouths shut – William Melville was their chief, and so discretion was guaranteed. The remaining eight stayed back, under Carruthers' command, keeping an eye on Amworth and maintaining a rear-guard. Carruthers seemed happy with being left in charge, and it kept the man out of Jim's hair for the time being.

Jim knew he was delaying his mission unforgivably. For as much as he was curious about Crookes' motives, in truth he was allowing himself to be led by the wilfully rebellious Miss Furnival. He knew this, and let it happen regardless, for John. By delaying his mission, he could buy more time for Colonel Hardwick, and for all he knew it was wrong, he felt it was the least he could do.

They came to an iron-barred gate, like a cell door, which no key of Jim's would unlock.

'Open it, Dr Crookes,' Jim said.

The old man shook his head, huffing in his aristocratic way, as though never in his life had he been spoken to so insolently.

'Do it, sir, or you will be forced to.'

'I do not have a key. These are Lord Cherleten's private stores. I hid here, in this corridor, and was unable to go further.'

Jim shook his head. 'You may work in service of the Order, Dr Crookes, but you are a man of science, not subterfuge. You're a bad liar.'

Jim patted the man down, and Crookes uttered oaths and curses at the indignity. Finally, he found what he was looking for – a key ring. He was about to pluck it from its chain when Crookes snatched them back angrily.

'Very well, Captain, I shall do it. But this is your last warning – what you might find in these rooms is not for your eyes, and will guarantee a court martial.'

Jim nodded towards the gate, and with a sigh Crookes complied, unlocked it, and swung it open.

Jim shone a lantern inside, seeing little more than piles of crates in a dank, low-ceilinged room, with a few doors leading off. He nudged Crookes inside, and bade the others follow.

A pile of perhaps twelve crates lay to the left side of the room. Jim noted Chinese characters on the nearest, but saw that all were nailed shut. He had neither the tools nor the time to open them, and could already guess at their contents. Marie's expression showed that she followed his thinking.

'What's in here?' Jim asked, indicating the nearest door.

'Just an office,' Crookes said. 'Lord Cherleten's office.'

'He has two offices?'

'This one is not the most comfortable, but it is the most secure. Do not go in there, boy, or he'll have your head.'

'Boy?' Jim raised an eyebrow. 'Dr Crookes, you really know how to pique a chap's curiosity. Key?'

'I really do not have it. This is Lord Cherleten's office, as I said. Only he has the key.'

Jim considered this. He didn't know what he expected to find. All he knew was that Crookes had lied repeatedly, that there was like to be some kind of informant within the Order, and that John even now was probably in dire straits. He really should leave this be and set about his mission. But then, what if Crookes was the traitor? If Jim was forced to destroy the facility, any evidence would be lost also. Jim would never have another opportunity to uncover the truth.

There was a deafening roar in the confined chamber as Marie fired her six-gun, punching a hole in the door's lock. She kicked it open. 'Time for talking is done,' she snapped.

The constables stepped away. An unpredictable, gun-toting American woman was clearly beyond their expertise.

'Subtle as ever,' Jim said.

'You want to know what's in there, and we don't have much time. I don't trust this man as far as I can spit, so let's look around and get out of here.'

Jim agreed wholeheartedly, and stepped into the office.

It appeared as though Crookes was telling the truth. Jim's lantern at once shone upon a desk opposite the door, exactly like the one in Cherleten's office upstairs, down to the fastidious arrangement of his cigar box and decanters. Above it, however, in a gilt frame, was a large oil painting. Jim knew the hand of the piece at once, though it took him a moment for the significance to sink in. It was incredibly similar to one that he had seen recently, in the hospital theatre on Fulham Road. He had never seen this particular painting before, but he had heard it described, by John, a few years prior.

He stepped closer. The painting depicted the aftermath of a battle between monsters: a dragon and a gigantic spider, in the shadow of some crumbling Gothic manse. The spider was slain, sliced open by the dragon's claws. From the great rent in its abdomen, thousands of its tiny progeny swarmed towards the figure of a woman caught in a tangle of webs. She was dark of features, wearing a yellow dress. The paint around her had been smudged, as though by clumsy fingers. Jim frowned; he felt this was significant, though he could not place how.

'Jim…' Marie said.

He turned around. Marie was looking at more canvases, most under sheets. Jim had been so engrossed in the one on the wall he had been oblivious to all else. Now he pulled a cloth away, revealing dozens upon dozens of paintings, of all shapes and sizes, stood neatly in rows. And the one nearest Jim now came into stark focus. He trembled, anger building inside him. The painting was small, a cityscape, London in flames. St Paul's ruined, demons in the streets, madness and death. He had seen it before, this exact painting. He picked it up, hands shaking. He threw it aside. There behind it was another familiar piece: Paris. Behind that, Moscow.

Jim spun on his heels and marched from the room. He hoisted Crookes from his feet, pushing him against the crates. The two constables made a half-hearted show of pulling Jim away.

'Where did those paintings come from? When?' Jim spat. He remembered Constable Dakin, nervously poking around that dark hospital. He remembered keeping the frightened lad alive, only for him to be killed senselessly later, for those same paintings.

'Paintings?' Crookes wheezed. 'I have no idea what –'

'Do not lie to me! Good men died for them. Innocent men! You will tell me –'

Jim stopped as a low cry, like some tortured soul, echoed from the furthest door. He dropped the doctor, who spluttered and dusted himself down, muttering unconvincing threats.

Marie was already at the door. 'There's someone in there. More Nightwatch?'

'Down here?' Jim asked, although he doubted nothing now.

The heavy iron door was not locked, but barred. Marie lifted the bar and drew back a pair of latches. Without pause, she entered the room. Jim shoved Crookes aside, and followed Marie, bringing up light quickly. Poynton and Sykes came after, Crookes swept along with them.

The stench was unbearable. Bile rose in Jim's throat.

It was a dark, unsanitary room. Butcher's blocks sat alongside workbenches and desks, which looked singularly out of place. Meat-hooks hung from the walls. Chemical apparatus and distillation tubes bubbled and dripped. Strange electrical devices lay on one bench, inert, but surely of Tesla design. The walls were lined with reinforced cell doors. In what looked like a medieval crow's cage, the body of a dead ghoul rotted. Parts of it were cut away like so much meat. Its neck was branded with a number: 72.

'What is this?' Jim asked, though the words came like a croak. Just speaking made him want to be sick.

Marie, by contrast, walked slowly past the benches and desks, taking in every bottle and tube, every instrument, until finally she reached a rack of phials and notebooks.

'You should not be in here. Go now, and perhaps we can forget this...' Crookes managed.

Marie was flipping the pages of a notebook, her face darkening like thunder.

'This is *wampyr* blood,' she said, with quiet rage.

'What? Why would they drain these creatures of blood?' Jim asked. 'What kind of study are they –'

'No, James, you misunderstand. This is taken from what they call Purebloods. It is what de Montfort collected from the Otherside. We believe it is what he used to create more of his kind from living humans.'

'The Iscariot Sanction?' Jim asked, agog.

Marie nodded. 'It seems as though the Order is trying to replicate de Montfort's experiments,' she said. 'Crookes, what are you –'

She stopped. Crookes had moved, quietly, unnoticed in the shadows. He now stood beside a cell door, a strange device in his hand, a rod coiled about with copper and brass. The device sparked blue. His other hand was on the door-bolt.

'Put it down,' Jim said.

'This... this scientific endeavour is for the good of all,' Crookes said.

'How do you figure that?' Marie snarled.

'I was warned about you – of your lack of ambition and vision. If your people had learned to control these things, you would never have had to fear the Riftborn. The ghouls are foot soldiers in a war against hell. They are our defence against the things that destroyed your world. And you would dare deny us.'

'You think you can control them? You?'

'After a fashion, perhaps. Our methods are crude, for now, but we will learn.' He glanced to the racks of blood.

'And the ones who escaped?' Marie said, unable to hide the anger in her voice. 'Oh... they were set free, weren't they? To see what they'd do? You have no idea what you do here. No idea of the cost...'

'Crookes,' Jim said. 'Put that thing down.' Jim reached to his holster.

Crookes glared at Jim and then at Marie. And then he swung open the door.

Marie fired first. A bestial scream echoed around the chamber. Three ghouls scrambled from the cell, like racehorses from the traps. Jim darted back, shouting commands at the constables. Crookes threw open another door, and another. A ghoul darted at the doctor, who held up the strange rod, crackling bright with electricity; the ghoul shrieked and shrank away from him.

Jim tried to intercept Crookes, but his path was barred at once. He shot a ghoul in the head, another barrelled into him. Jim ducked and lunged, trying desperately to avoid whipping claws. He saw Crookes race through the door. Poynton went after him. Sykes heaved a ghoul off Jim, but two more leapt onto the man's back, biting and tearing until their own snarls were drowned out by Sykes' screams.

Blue lightning flashed. Jim found some breathing room, and flicked his pocket-pistol into his hand. Another ghoul died wreathed in energy, pale skin turning black. Marie was by Jim's side. In the confusion she had picked up one of the same strange rods that Crookes had found. She squeezed the handle, and electricity arced across the upper parts of the rod. The ghouls cowered away from her, expecting pain, and Jim knew from their reaction that they had been conditioned thus. He got behind her as she directed them back. He found another rod, copied Marie to activate it, and joined her. The ghouls screeched and shielded their eyes, cowering timidly as the rods sparked. Together, Jim and Marie herded the creatures into a cell, and slammed the door fast, bolting it behind them.

Jim could not bring himself to look at Sykes' body. Instead, he snatched up the lantern, and ran out of the room, in the hope that Poynton had fared better than his comrade.

Outside, he saw the constable nursing his arm, his jacket singed and smoking.

'Bloody burned me!' Poynton moaned.

Jim raced to the iron-barred gate, rattling it ineffectually. Crookes had locked it, and fled.

'Sykesy?' Poynton said.

Jim put a hand on the man's shoulder, and shook his head. 'Don't go in there, lad, it's not pretty.'

Poynton slumped to the floor, forlorn.

'Maybe Carruthers got Crookes,' Marie said.

'Let's hope so. I suppose we'd better shout for help.'

'No need,' Marie said. She delved into her pockets, and withdrew a set of keys.

'Where did you get those?'

'Uncle Arthur.'

'You really could have said before I threatened my superior…'

'There's nothing superior about that wretch,' Marie said, keys jangling at the lock. 'Besides, you looked like you were havin' fun for once. Only thing is… if one of these fits, it'll prove Uncle Arthur knew more than he was letting on. I… I kind of hope they don't fit.'

She tried several in the lock, and her shoulders sank when one of them clicked. She swung the gate open, sniffed, and left the room in silence. Jim helped Poynton up, and followed.

Wednesday, 30th December 1891
SANDRINGHAM

The prince's hand trembled as he flicked his cigarette over the ashtray. He looked at Crookes with rheumy eyes, singularly out of place in a man approaching his twenty-eighth year.

'So you see,' the prince's physician said, 'we have explored every avenue. Though Lord Cherleten led us to believe that there was but one more course open to us.'

'Indeed there is, Dr Roche,' Crookes said. He beheld first Albert Victor, then Roche, and only briefly did his eyes flicker to the figure in the corner, enfolded in shadow. 'The treatment, however, is of a most exotic and... powerful kind. If it works as we hope, its efficacy will be regarded in no small part as miraculous. If not... I am afraid it could be dangerous. Deadly, even.'

'Given the alternative, Dr Crookes, I am sure you can understand why His Royal Highness is willing to take the risk. The prince's ailments are of a most sensitive nature, and were they to become known, his betrothal to the Duchess of Teck, as joyous a surprise as it was to the Royal Household of course, would be thrown in some considerable doubt. This is grave indeed. His Royal Highness therefore requests –'

'Enough!' the prince snapped. He tried to punctuate his command by standing, but his legs buckled and he slumped back into his seat. A pained expression crossed his wan features; beads of perspiration formed on his brow. 'This protocol is tiresome. As I am still, for the time being, amongst the living, I shall speak for myself.'

Dr Roche bowed, and averted his eyes.

Crookes saw now the impetuousness in the young prince – a reckless streak that had caused much gossip at court and beyond.

It had led the prince to propose to the lovely Princess Mary despite being afflicted with various ailments – venereal and otherwise. He was prone to outbursts and impulsive acts. From the look of him, Crookes suspected the prince suffered the same haemophilia that had plagued his late uncle Leopold to the grave.

'Your Highness,' Crookes said. 'I understand that Lord Cherleten explained to you a great deal about the process when last you spoke. I am here to explain to you the potential side-effects, should you truly choose this course of action.'

'Side-effects be damned,' the prince said, his voice rasping and weak. 'Roche here has me on every pill imaginable. I have the damned gleet, Dr Crookes, and it persists for all of these treatments. There is something in my very blood. I sicken for everything. I am dying. What, then, have I to fear from your "Iscariot Sanction"?'

'Your Highness, this treatment carries with it the risk of madness – to lose one's own personality. We have yet to find a suitable subject for the final tests.'

'You have found one, Dr Crookes. Am I not of royal blood? Am I not granted my status by God Himself? You will find none other as worthy to receive the gift of vitality. Of immortality.'

'Immortality at a price, Your Highness. You will require… procedures, regularly, if you are to prosper in your position. If you are to lead a normal life. And there is the other condition.'

'Yes, yes. I accept it gladly. Make me whole again, Crookes. Make me whole and I shall take command of Cherleten's little army, be assured of it.'

'Very well, Your Highness.'

'We have conditions of our own.' The figure at the back of the room stood now, and from the dark stepped the Queen, stern-faced and dressed as ever in her afflictions.

'I… yes, of course, Your Majesty.' Flustered at the sudden interjection, Crookes stood and bowed.

'I have your guarantee that my grandson can sire children after the treatment is done?'

'As much as these things may be guaranteed, then it is my understanding that male recipients of these… gifts… at least, are fertile still.'

'And the child would be normal?'

Crookes felt himself reddening, for in truth he was uncertain. And yet he recalled the stories he had heard of Lord Cherleten's doppelganger on the Otherside. Normal? Perhaps not. But normal *enough*? Yes, that was a story he would be willing to sell. 'The child would be… special, Your Majesty. Blessed, some might say.'

Or cursed, would say others, he thought.

The Queen seemed to consider this for a moment, then nodded. 'And Princess Alexandra must never know,' she said. 'Never.'

'I swear it, Your Majesty.'

'Then you have your answer. Go now, and tell Lord Cherleten that we look forward to his next visit. If we are successful, his position in the eyes of the Crown is assured.'

'I shall convey your message at once, Your Majesty.'

Dr Crookes bowed low, and smiled.

Friday, 6th October 1893

'We wasn't to know,' Carruthers protested. 'He's in charge, ain't he? This fella said so.' He pointed at Amworth.

Jim sighed. 'Which way did he go?'

Carruthers pointed to the far doors, which led to the Nightwatch wards.

'The sluice-gates, perhaps?' Jim muttered. 'But why?'

'Tesla's submarine?' Marie asked. 'Maybe that was always the plan. Perhaps he was to escape in the submarine, and leave this place to be destroyed.'

'I think it's worse than that,' Jim said. He pulled Marie by the arm, away from the men, and spoke quietly. 'This mess goes deeper than we could have realised. Dr Crookes could not have orchestrated this alone. Your uncle had at least limited access to this area, so he must have suspected something even if he wasn't involved. But Cherleten must be in it up to his neck, because he knows everything that goes on down here.'

'Don't you drag my uncle into this. You've worked for Cherleten for what? Three years? Are you saying that he's crooked?'

'I have always known he was crooked, Marie. I just didn't think he would go this far.'

'Is this because of the paintings? You think Cherleten sanctioned the killing of those policemen to get the paintings? Why?'

'To give him some advantage over Sir Toby, perhaps. Who knows? Dakin was killed for those paintings. Maybe Cherleten came by them afterwards, but I doubt it, otherwise they'd be in the evidence room upstairs. Just like those ghouls down there aren't in the dead-room. They're hidden, in a place that even Hardwick didn't know existed. And don't forget the weapon stores. Emptied before we got here. The other stores are likely to have been similarly emptied; they must have worked all day, and the staff left behind who did the work were left to die first at the hands of the ghouls, then the Artist's men.'

'Why? Doesn't he need them? And what about the Nightwatch?'

'Cherleten knows the facility is going to be destroyed one way or another. I'd guess he's removed essential equipment, so that he can continue his experiments after the facility is gone. Where he's moved it to, however, is another question. I imagine essential personnel were not scheduled to work tonight – he told me himself that the facility was staffed by a "skeleton crew" tonight, as if he'd expected something to happen. And as for the Nightwatch… Cherleten never trusted them, and never trusted your uncle. He's always wanted nothing more than to militarise the Order with Otherside weapons. It's all an arms race for him, Marie.'

'Hold your horses, James,' Marie said. 'I know you're sore about Dakin, but that's a big leap. You're the one Cherleten entrusted with the explosives. Why do that if he's part of some conspiracy? Why not just get Crookes to do it?'

'Honestly, I don't know. Maybe things moved too fast. Maybe Crookes didn't have the key to the bombs, or couldn't reach them because it wasn't safe. Maybe he got delayed down here, and just didn't make it out before the Artist arrived. If he was in here, it must have been something to do with the vampires – Cherleten certainly wouldn't trust just anyone with that particular dirty secret. For all we know, he might have been told to wait so he could steal that submarine we've heard so much about.

'But look, Cherleten might not care if Crookes lives or dies. By openly putting trust in me, it looks good for him – he needs people like Melville on his side. I don't think Cherleten is planning to overthrow the Empire or anything. I think he wants to destabilise things, start a war, make a rift in London – or make it clear to the Prime Minister that the Russians have attempted to do just that. Sir Toby said it himself – the Prime Minister wouldn't allow the militarism of Apollo Lycea. Well, Cherleten has damned well made certain that will change.'

'Everyone is racing to build the ultimate weapon,' Marie said, her voice cracked. 'They don't care about the risks, as long as they're the first to get there.'

Jim nodded. 'When our people are killed by Riftborn, and the Russians are blamed for all of this, Gladstone will think Cherleten was right all along. He'll be placed in charge of the Order, for a start, and who knows where he goes from there. Maybe that's enough for him – the most senior spymaster in England. People have killed for far less power than that.'

'So now... Crookes gets out of here in the submarine, which Cherleten wants for himself. That means either we fail, in which case the Rift destroys all of this, and us with it. Or we succeed, in which case only a few of us escape, and Cherleten deals with us later.'

'I'd say that's a fairly safe bet,' Jim said.

'Or a fairy story. But let's say I believe it. What do we do?'

'First, we go back into that lab and gather what evidence we can. Then... we help John. Because the only way we win is if we prevent both of those outcomes. This is why Cherleten didn't want Tesla to come along. He could shut down the gate, or sail off in that submarine of his, or both.'

'A frontal assault on trained enemy soldiers. I don't like those odds,' Marie said.

A great rumble erupted all around. Dust fell from the ceiling. Carruthers and the men scattered for cover. The low vibration from the distant portal had become so ever-present that Jim had grown used to it. Now, however, something had changed.

'It doesn't sound like John has been very successful,' Jim said. 'If we're going to act, it must be now. Damn; it feels like suicide.'

'Wait a minute...' Marie said. She held up the baton, and squeezed the handle until the prongs sparked with electricity. 'I have an idea. But trust me, you aren't going to like it.'

TWENTY-SIX

'The gate it is almost ready, Madam Artist,' Tesla said.

The Artist did not so much as look at John again. She brushed Orlov aside, leaving him fuming in her wake. She approached the gate, beside which stood a strange device, crackling with power, with long leather-strapped rods protruding from it like horns. The Artist moved quickly, rolling up the sleeve of her dress, tapping at the vein of her arm. From the bank of instruments beside the gate, she withdrew a long tube, with a needle at one end, and inserted it into her arm, before strapping the needle in place. Almost at once, a pale brown fluid began to travel along the tube, and into the Artist's veins. John saw now that the tube was attached to a small machine, which used a system of pumps to force etherium into the Artist.

'This is madness…' John gasped.

The Artist stepped towards the machine with the tall rods, and took one in each hand. She nodded to Tesla, who threw a great switch. Coruscating arcs of lightning flashed around the gate, the machinery, and the Artist. John saw now only Rosanna, in pain, crying out as she was wreathed in electricity. Every light in the room flickered and died. All that was left was silence, and the steady amber glow of the gate. It was almost still now, a polished mirror of gold, reflecting the stunned faces in the room.

In the reflection, John saw himself. And he saw that his guards had turned away from him to witness this great spectacle for themselves.

John had been working at the bonds behind his back since he had awoken. It had been instinct more than anything, for he certainly struggled to conjure up an ounce of fight in the face of the Artist. But the Russians – Orlov in particular – that was different. John had killed the leader of the celestials, and that had been to his advantage. Xiang had seen first-hand John's knack for working loose common knots, and may have bound him more securely. As it stood, he finally had a hand free. He glanced about as surreptitiously as he could. He used the mirrored surface of the portal to select his target. Orlov was just out of reach, and another Russian stood between John and he, but closer still was a Chinaman with a rifle, a knife tucked into his boot. He would be first. It occurred to John that Rosanna – the Artist, whatever she was – may have foreseen his escape attempt. But she appeared otherwise occupied, slumped over Tesla's machinery, struggling for breath.

John knew he had to secure the scientist. If anyone could stop this madness, it was Tesla.

A dark shape brushed the surface of the gate from the other side, causing ripples to flow across the pool of light. It was gone as quickly as it appeared, but not before several men had flinched away from the formless thing, despite the shadow's fleeting appearance. John had received an impression of it, a squamous tendril, a claw; perhaps both, perhaps neither. A predatory thing, seeking a way in and through. There was no more time to think.

John leapt to his feet, grabbing his chair, hurling it at the Russian in front of him, while throwing himself at the Chinese guard to his left. John was unsteady on his feet. There were more guards than he had at first thought, and workers too, around the peripheries of the room.

No time. Stop thinking. Act.

John hit the Chinaman hard, upending him, grabbing the

knife from the man's boot and jamming it into his heart in one smooth movement. A shot rang out; masonry exploded behind John's head. He rolled forward, bringing the dying celestial with him, the body taking a bullet. John snatched up a rifle and shot the gunman dead. He leapt to his feet, and ran for cover.

Orlov was after him. Men stood ahead. John swept low, jabbing the butt of the rifle into the ribs of the first man, swinging up and around to crack the skull of the second before he could react. John dropped to one knee and squeezed off a round at Orlov. The Russian had pre-empted the attack, and had already swung one of his own men in front of him. John's bullet struck the man's shoulder. Orlov pushed his human shield forward, full-tilt, roaring curses in his mother tongue. John sensed movement all around, though no one would risk opening fire with their commander bearing down upon John like a raging bull.

John darted aside, staying low to the ground, kicking out at the wounded man's knee. He tumbled. Orlov dropped him to avoid toppling over with the man he'd sacrificed. John jumped up, struggling with the bolt-action rifle, which felt like a heavy, ill-maintained antique. He could not work the bolt quickly enough, and Orlov pounced. He hit John with a powerful left hand, and only the glint of yellow light from a blade forewarned John of the incoming right. John dodged backwards. The knife cut the air an inch from his nose. Another Russian appeared behind John; a hand grabbed his wounded shoulder.

John rammed the rifle-butt into the new man's stomach, finally sliding the bolt into place. John fired from the hip at the same time that Orlov kicked at the barrel, and the shot went wide, striking the golden surface of the gate, causing a brief, brilliant flare of light. Orlov slashed again with his knife. John brandished the rifle like a club, parrying the blow.

'Give it up, English,' Orlov said. 'Look around you. If we wanted you dead, we would have killed you already.'

Orlov was right. John glanced over his shoulder and saw three men, ready to set upon him. Two more waited behind Orlov.

Rosanna was nowhere in sight – perhaps she had seen the bullets flying and fled to safety. John knew Orlov was right. He could not win this. But when had that ever stopped him?

'Come on, English,' Orlov said, catching his breath. 'We don't want to kill you, eh.'

John thought of Sir Toby. He thought of all the death and chaos caused by Orlov, for without the Russians, the Artist would never have come so far. He thought of the terror that was about to be unleashed on London. His one good eye narrowed. 'Your mistake,' he growled.

John dashed forward, ignoring Orlov's surprised counter-strike, ignoring the pain as the Russian's blade bit into his side. He cracked Orlov hard on the bridge of the nose with the rifle. The Russian staggered back, leaving his knife dangling beneath John's ribs. John pulled it out, roared with pain and rage, all of the sorrow and anger at this dire predicament manifesting in one herculean effort. Orlov tried to recover, but John pressed. Even as other hands grabbed at him, John tore away, and plunged the knife into Orlov's gut.

The tall Russian staggered, a look of utter disbelief on his face. Someone struck John, and he slashed wildly with the knife, swinging about in a deadly arc, wounded and tired, but dangerous as a cornered beast.

The knife was knocked from John's hand by a stinging blow. Men leapt upon him from all sides, and he struggled, until he felt a cold hand on his throat, and looked up into Rosanna's brown eyes. His vision blurred, his bones and muscles sang a chorus of pain. He could not fight her; he knew he must, but he could not.

'That was not foreseen,' she hissed. 'You really do have a habit of disrupting one's plans. I was rather hoping that Orlov would see what is about to come through that gate, but you have robbed me of that small pleasure. Still, it makes no difference in the grand scheme of things.'

John wanted to ask what she meant, but he could say nothing as she squeezed his throat. He almost wished she would strangle the life from him, and make the nightmare end. All he could hear was the serene hum of the gate. His head swam.

Then a great flash of light half-blinded him. A scream. Gunshots – how many? Something struck Rosanna's shoulder, spinning her around. Her blood sprayed onto John's face. He fell to the floor as the men released him and scattered. More gunshots reverberated around the room. Soldiers crouched low, returning fire at some new enemy. Another flash of light. Electrical energy streamed across the room in an arc, searing a Russian soldier, blistering his flesh instantaneously. John followed the source of the blast.

Marie Furnival. The young American leapt behind an overturned table as return fire thudded around her. Bullets ricocheted off Otherside machinery. Sparks flew. Smoke filled the room like grey fog. John crawled for cover as soldiers on both sides dashed to and fro, or hit the ground writhing in agony from bullet-wounds.

There was more. Ghouls. They were a procession of deformity – one with a nose torn off, or rotted away; one with skin so wasted that its ribcage protruded externally over its chest; another with no ears; yet another with a bulbous head like the worst-affected victim of syphilis imaginable. Each was branded with a number, like cattle. They tore across the room, uncoordinated, wild, throwing themselves at anything that moved. Teeth snapped at throats. Claws ripped limbs and faces. The chamber was not large enough for such a battle – the roar of gunfire was deafening, the stench of scorched flesh and spilt blood overwhelming.

Jim was near the doors, crouching behind a large oak desk, one hand on Tesla's head, keeping the Serbian in cover. John counted too few men for this task. They must have come headlong through the corridors, through the stiffest resistance of the Russian soldiers and Chinese gangsters. Stupid. Brave, but stupid. But what of the ghouls? Where had they appeared from?

At last, John's legs submitted to his will, and he scrabbled across the debris-strewn floor, past a fallen soldier – one of his own, a man he had picked from the Tower garrison, and brought to his death. John rolled over the desk, and found himself side-by-side with Jim.

'Sorry we're late, old boy,' Jim shouted over the din.

'What the –'

John could not finish. The light from the gate grew abruptly brighter, and hotter, and the low humming sound intensified. The golden light ebbed away, turning first crimson, then purple.

'This not good!' Tesla said.

'What's happening?' John called.

The noise grew louder. The gate shimmered, faded waves of purplish ghost-lights flickered all about the room. The ceiling all but vanished, replaced by a night sky, half-real. In that sky were constellations that John did not recognise. Wind began to whip around the room, thunder rumbled, an unnatural storm brewing.

'She has tuned the gate to another universe,' Tesla cried. 'She brings the Riftborn!'

'How do we stop it?'

'We cannot! Only Madam Artist can stop it, but not from here. On Otherside, she have device, the twin of this one. She can use it to close the gate. But not now – now the portal is open to a different world, yes?'

John understood. The gate no longer led to the Otherside, but to the 'Rift'. To hell itself.

'Can you put it back? Can you make it lead to the Otherside?' he asked Tesla, desperation growing.

'Perhaps, friend Hardwick. But she will not close it. She mean to let it absorb all power, to reach critical mass. Only when there is no more energy to drain, no more Majestics to consume, will the gate close.'

The gate now pulsated with energy that made the ground rumble and debris fall from the walls, and then came the chittering. An insectoid clacking as of huge mandibles; a scratching, intrusion of claws and fingernails, picking inside John's head. The smell of brimstone filled the air. Shadowy tendrils passed across the surface of the gate. Sparks flew as something indistinct, but sharp-taloned, tested the shimmering portal.

They came. Formless, unfathomable. The Riftborn. They were shadows one moment, demons the next. They were huge and tiny both. John could not get a fix on them, and nor did he wish to. Reason would not allow him to look upon them, or make any sense of them. They were wraiths, their unknowable aspects cloaked in shadow, and motes of floating witch-light. Faces leered from the spaces between realities, as though the very air parted at the presence of these stalking horrors.

Tendrils of shadow probed about the room, now slicing like razors, then caressing like a lover's touch. John could barely fathom what was happening, but he knew these were the things that Sir Arthur called the Other. More came, their number announced only by flickering shadows or, rather, an absence of light.

The gunfire began again, and screaming. This time, terrible screams, almost inhuman. One Russian flew backwards through the air, bleeding from his eyes, nose and mouth, bones cracking as he went. John received an impression of a monstrous black shape carrying the man, with thousands of appendages snaking about him; it may have been all in his mind. He prayed it was.

Ghouls shrieked, and flailed at the intangible Riftborn. They fought, where mere men could not, but these were no pureblood *wampyr*. John suspected the ghouls were prey for the demons, just as the rest of them were, but they provided a distraction at least. Over it all, upon the pedestal of the gate, Rosanna stood. The wind lifted her from her feet, whipped her hair about her face like smoke, and she laughed. The Riftborn flew about her, but in her etherium-glutted state, she appeared to be their match.

'What can we do?' Jim shouted as the noise rose to unbearable levels.

'The gate has become a self-sustaining circuit,' Tesla replied. 'The Artist's power it provide a greater catalyst than I anticipate.

A rare miscalculation on my part, Captain, and one that has costing me dear, no?'

'I'm sure I don't understand,' John said. 'Can we not cut these cables?'

Tesla looked at John as though he were an imbecile. 'Cut the cables? My dear colonel, my devices are not so easily manipulated.'

John stared at Tesla agog. 'We cannot turn off the power? What lunacy is this? Who would design such a thing?'

Tesla frowned, pulling in his chin indignantly. 'My design; it is flawless and just as I intend. The power this facility provide allow the gate to reach critical mass, no? And the Artist, she open the conduit to worlds beyond, where energy and matter work as one, with the third element, aether. The electricity, it no longer fuels the gate. This is my life's work. This is a perfect model of the gravity of directory.'

'What the devil are you talking about?'

Marie dragged herself over, staying low as broken bodies and scrambling ghouls flew past them. 'He's saying,' she yelled, 'that the gate powers itself now. We can't turn it off. Pretty soon it will absorb so much power from the multiverse that anything could come through. Or maybe all of London could get sucked in. Who knows?'

John exchanged an appalled glance with Jim.

'What if we kill her?' Jim shouted.

Tesla shrugged. 'It is too late for that, Captain. Unfortunately now the only way to close the gate is from the other side, and for that... I am afraid we need her.'

'Then I shall distract her,' John said. 'And you, Mr. Tesla, will alter the frequency and rid us of these demons.'

'Here, you'll need these,' Jim said. He handed over John's cane. He beckoned to Miss Furnival, who passed him the Winchester, and Jim handed that over too.

'Where did you get these?' John asked.

'We came back to look for you, and found them in a

317

storeroom. That is how we knew you had gone into the air ducts, and realised you must have come here.'

'You were foolish to come back for me. You should have flooded the facility.'

'Then you would be dead, and Rosanna with you,' Jim replied, quietly so that only John could hear.

'Precisely my point.' John could scarce admit it to himself, but he half wished to have died by Rosanna's side.

'We'll cover you,' Marie said, priming her Tesla pistol.

'On the count of three…' Jim shouted.

But John was already gone.

TWENTY-SEVEN

The wind threw debris about the room. John held up a hand to shield his face. Impish claws plucked at him, tearing his skin. His ears rang with the screeches of incorporeal Riftborn. He looked up at the dais. Rosanna floated inches from the ground, staring balefully at John's approach, purple and green lights flickering behind her, like the *aurora borealis*.

Miss Furnival was at John's back. The American had followed unbidden, blazing away at ghoul and demon alike. John admired her spirit. He hoped it would not get her killed.

Rosanna descended lightly to her feet. Tendrils of smoke coalesced all about her. Lightning crackled. She looked at those who opposed her with the arrogance that only Tsun Pen could possess.

'To fight me is folly,' the Artist said. 'You might as well try to turn back the tides. What are you, compared to one who has cheated death not once, but twice? Look about you! Do you see the power I wield? Even the Riftborn cannot touch me. I can summon them here at will, to bring an end to everyone in London, and create a city of madness. Is that what you want? Lay down your weapons, and I may yet spare you.'

'Who the hell are you?' Miss Furnival shouted, defiant to the last.

'Hell?' The Artist tossed back her tousled hair and laughed. 'How apt. Perhaps it is hell that brought me here. Brought us here. And if it be so, then my name is Legion, for we are many. We are the Artist – Tsun Pen of two worlds. We are Rosanna, of the Romani, as your friend Colonel Hardwick has already discovered. We are reborn.'

'You talk too much,' Miss Furnival said. John saw that the American was about to fire upon Rosanna. He raised a hand to stop her, but even before she could pull the trigger, a great shadow erupted from the gate, momentarily forming a grasping, clawed hand. It swiped at Marie, passing clean through her; she fell to the floor, screaming. John leapt backwards as the shadow swept in front of him. For a second, he saw a pair of blazing eyes, and the face of a Chinese dragon shimmer in the black smoke, and then the whole thing vanished back into the abyss.

'Do not test me,' the Artist snarled, her voice strong over the howling winds. 'Drop your weapon, Hardwick. Do it!'

John relented. Marie writhed in agony upon the floor.

'You shall not rob me of simple revenge, John Hardwick. Your end will come at my hands. It is foreseen.'

John tried to conjure the strength to fight, though he could see no way out. Each time the Artist spoke with Rosanna's lips, in a voice that was not Rosanna's, John felt such a wave of sorrow and despair that he could scarce act.

And then John sensed movement beside him, and for the briefest moment saw a swish of a white dress vanish into the smoke. He felt a familiar chill, like death. This was what Elsbet had been leading him towards. It was always Elsbet who had foreseen the end – not of London, not of John Hardwick, but of her people. John did not know for certain what she was trying to tell him, but some glimmer of hope filled him.

'Perhaps I will spare your friends,' the Artist was saying. 'They can tell their master that the balance of power has tilted. But you, John Hardwick, stay with me. This is the price Rosanna insisted upon for letting me in, and I never renege upon a bargain.'

'And did Rosanna also agree to turn her back on her people, forever?' John said, finally forcing himself to his feet. It was all he could do to stand as the wind buffeted him. He knew strange figures stalked all about him. He dared not look upon them.

The Artist's eyes narrowed. 'Her people are already gone, Colonel Hardwick. You saw to that.'

'That is not true, and if she believes it is so, it is because hatred has clouded her mind. Her people live still. Some travel with Andre – I saw them with my own eyes. The Elsbet of the Otherside travels with them. Some are incarcerated here in London, and will be first in line for destruction when this insane plan comes to fruition. What of them?'

'She knew the price!' the Artist snapped.

'Did she?' John took a step closer, the Artist's anger emboldening him. He felt the eyes of the Riftborn turn upon him hungrily. Was she keeping them at bay? 'Did she understand that her sisters would die for the price of an imposter, a double? No, I do not think Rosanna would have agreed to that at all. I do not believe for a moment that she understood the consequences.'

'Her… her people…' the Artist faltered, squinting her eyes as though the words would not come. 'Our people… some may be sacrificed, yes, but others live on, across the sea. I sent them away. It was the bargain.'

'Again, only a few, and only for the sake of Elsbet's doppelganger. But where do they go? What safety is there for them once this hell is unleashed? The real Elsbet – her soul, her spirit – remains trapped here in our world, waiting to be consumed by these monsters? Monsters that you will unleash in Rosanna's name!'

'What do you know of souls and spirits? Are you a Majestic now? Do you seek to counsel *me* on the afterlife?'

'I have seen her,' John said, solemnly. 'She has haunted me for my sins these past three years. I have never known peace, because she has never known peace. And she led me here. Listen to me, Rosanna – *Elsbet led me here*. For you. To save you.'

Some change came across the Artist's countenance. She closed her eyes and shook her head as though on the brink of some momentous decision.

'Rosanna, listen to me,' John said, daring another step closer. 'What passed between us is not reason enough to unleash this terror upon the world. I broke a promise to you – a vow – and I have regretted that ever since, and always shall. Do you think I do not wish to see the Order of Apollo burn? I have thought on it often for what they did. But I urge you now to think of the innocent lives at stake. Tsun Pen cares only for personal gain at the expense of queens and kings and prime ministers. He does not reckon the human tally – but you do. At least, you always did. Your people, my people – they are one! And they all face extinction if the Riftborn come through that gate.'

'I...' The woman's eyes opened, and John saw something vulnerable, and human, within. She was there, he knew it – Rosanna. 'It is too late,' she said, though her voice was little more than a whisper. 'It is... foreseen.'

John cast a glance to the machinery, where Tesla toiled with dials and switches, Jim whispering in his ear.

The gate changed hue, flashing briefly back to amber, then flame-red. The resonance squealed so loud that everyone who still lived within the chamber doubled over in pain, clutching at their ears, and none more so than Rosanna. As John struggled against the noise and the whipping gale, he saw Rosanna crouch to the floor. She screamed in agony. John reached out to her, though it was a struggle to do so. Now he knew she was in there still, and he could not bear to see her harmed, in spite of everything. But he stopped, as he saw something more.

The Riftborn were sucked back into the portal, howling. A few smoke-like wraiths grabbed at John as they went, trying to drag him with them. But the worst of their attentions focused on the Artist. John leapt to her side, and tried to pull her away from the shadows that engulfed her, then dissipated, then came again, pulsing in time with the portal's endless thrumming. She pushed John away, and thrashed at the shadows, which John could now barely see.

'Rosanna!' John cried. 'Let me help you.'

She looked up at John, face full of anguish. Shadowy fingers pulled at her hair, at her clothes. Blue veins bulged at the side of her head as the psychical assault took its toll. She held out a hand, finally beseeching John silently for aid, lips moving wordlessly. But something held John back from her, some invisible force would not allow him to intervene.

Then abruptly, something in Rosanna's eyes changed. She at once pushed upright, throwing off the wraith-like forms that assailed her like a robe.

'I need no help! Only I bear the will of two worlds in one form, and only I can control this gate!'

With that, the Artist held her hands out as though performing a conjuring trick, and the gate changed colour to a deep orange, flecked with crimson spume. The surface became agitated, the ripples growing stronger, until the liquid energy of the portal lapped over the sides of the gate, casting weird lights across the room. From behind the portal, something screeched; tortured faces pushed against the rippling veil, like tortured souls fleeing the fires of hell. The Artist held up a hand, and the things beyond screamed louder, and then were gone.

'"Much have I seen and known; cities of men, and manners, climates, councils, governments, myself not least, but honour'd of them all,"' the Artist gloated.

Tesla was wrestling frantically with his controls. He shouted to Jim. John made out 'Too strong!' and 'She'll kill us!'

'This was once the Lazarus Gate,' the Artist said, as John stepped away from her, 'but now it dances to my tune. I can summon forth the denizens of infinite worlds, or travel between them with impunity. And on the Otherside, treasures lie forgotten in the streets as the world's powers descend into madness. Now, time is fleeting, and these games have run their course. Can you hear that? Can you hear the resonance of the gate? That is the sound of the world changing for ever.'

'Stop this!' John shouted.

The noise of the gate reached fever pitch. Lights danced all about the room, lightning flashed in long tendrils to every corner of the chamber. Rosanna basked in a supernatural gale, like some Gothic heroine glaring at her foes from a rugged clifftop. The wind whipped at her yellow dress, and before John's eyes Rosanna levitated once more, now laughing as intangible forces lifted her into their embrace. The shadows that slid about the room formed great clawed fingers, or strange, scuttling forms. They yanked at John's clothes, his hair. They buffeted him like a ship in a storm. Warm air thickened about him. He felt himself caught in the warping veil, his stomach lurching as though he were falling endlessly. He had felt this before. He knew what came next.

John shook the clouds from his mind. He clutched a hand to his bloody shoulder, using the pain to focus his thoughts. Miss Furnival was hoisted into the air, her eyes rolled back into her head. Jim was curled up on the floor near Tesla's machinery, clutching his head, raving like a man in a fever-dream. Was Rosanna in his mind? Or was it the things at the gate, scratching and pushing at the veil?

Tesla reached for a lever; a great shadowy tendril whipped towards him, directed by the Artist. It coiled about the Serbian's arm, snapping it audibly. The scientist cried out and fell beside Jim as the shadow retreated.

'Stop this madness!' John shouted again, perhaps as much at the storm of psychical turbulence about him as at Rosanna. 'You have the gate, your revenge is here for the taking. Kill me if you must, but release them.'

'I am surprised to find someone you care about, John Hardwick,' Rosanna said. 'Do you care more for them than your precious honour, I wonder?' A high-pitched squeal came from the gate, setting John's teeth on edge. He gasped as the sound sliced through his thoughts. Rosanna only laughed. 'What chaos. What power. Is it not wonderful?'

John looked up. Everything was distorted as though viewed through aged glass. Behind Rosanna, something moved. A girl, dark of hair, wearing a soaking wet dress of white linen. She stood, silently, and John felt his blood run cold. Rosanna seemed unaware of the ghostly presence at her back.

'Perhaps you are right,' Rosanna said at last, with a laugh.

John dropped to one knee as the resistance of the fierce wind ceased without warning. Miss Furnival fell to the floor with a sickening thud.

The Artist raised her arms, and at her gesture the portal calmed, glowing amber once more. The strange sensations subsided, and the lightning became little more than a blue arc sporadically circling the gate. Rosanna waved a hand, and Jim ceased his convulsions.

'I have seen the future many times,' Rosanna said. 'The art of foretelling is never exact, but it has steered me here, for what end I do not know. And yet that is half the fun, is it not? I have seen you three many times. I have painted your futures. Captain James Denny, who must watch for the coming storm. He is a man out of time – his fate is woven so completely in the dark events to come that I could not stop it if I wanted to. And then there is Miss Furnival, who has already seen more than you and Denny combined. She does not belong to this world, and if she stays she will know only betrayal from those for whom she cares. That sounds familiar, don't you think?

'I will leave here, John Hardwick, as you suggest. But I will let this portal ravage your world. I will leave you alive to see it, and know that I am out there, and that I hate you. This is revenge enough, I see that now. Your future is foretold. It is written in stone. Everything you touch will wither and die. You shall not know peace for the rest of your days, knowing that somewhere, in some world, I live. And one day, I shall return to destroy everything you hold dear. You should have killed me when you had the chance, but you are weak.'

She turned to the portal, tracing a luminous hand across its shimmering surface. She bowed her head solemnly. For all her words of vengeance, John sensed that Rosanna – or maybe even Tsun Pen – was filled with regret. The ruination of her plan to arm the Russians, perhaps? Or something more?

The destroyer of worlds and the healer of worlds. A fitting tribute.

The whisper forced its way into John's thoughts, an icy draught finding ingress through a casement. Words spoken long ago at a séance in a gypsy camp, where five sisters had shown John what lay beyond the veil.

The wraith was at his side. Everything was still, and cold, and grey, as though all warmth and colour had been sucked from the world. John knew, somehow, that this was the moment Elsbet had prepared him for. He stepped forward.

'Rosanna, I know you can hear me,' John said.

She turned but slightly, to look at John over her shoulder from the corner of her eye. Even so, John saw her sneer, so reminiscent of Tsun Pen.

'Part of you exists still,' John persisted. 'I saw it earlier, and that is why I could not kill you. It was not weakness – you know what I have done these past years. You know that I would never shy from killing without good reason. It was love stayed my hand, Rosanna. It is love that stays my hand still.'

Rosanna spun about fully, anger in her face. Passionate, Romani anger. 'Then it is love that shall kill you!'

'Your prophecy is wrong,' John said. 'I do not have to spend the rest of my days alone. And neither do you. We can all change our destiny.'

Rosanna began to speak, but the words did not form. Instead, she froze. Her expression changed to one of surprise, and then grief. Perhaps even fear. 'Impossible,' she whispered.

The shade that was Elsbet approached her, incorporeal hands outstretched, which Rosanna tried to take in her own. Elsbet was on the dais now, speaking to her sister without words.

Rosanna nodded, understanding whatever psychic message passed between them, and trembled. Soon, the ghost faded, vanishing completely, and Rosanna was left alone on the plinth, tears dripping from her cheeks.

John had never truly felt alone these past three years; he had felt watched, always. Now, a great weight was lifted from his shoulders. Elsbet had gone, perhaps for ever. John looked to Marie, only now starting to move weakly. He looked to Jim, dragging himself to all fours, blinking in utter confusion. Tesla alone was lucid, one hand on the machinery, pulling himself to the control panel, looking to John for some signal, some order. Had any of them seen Elsbet? John did not know, and it did not matter.

'This ends now,' he said softly to Jim. 'Goodbye, old friend.'

Jim looked up at John, eyes widening.

John nodded. Jim tried to stand, but doubled over in agony at the effort, clutching his ribs. He understood what John was going to do. That was good; it meant that the damage to his mind was not permanent. Jim would recover.

John stepped onto the dais beside Rosanna, without fear. She looked at him, so conflicted, so full of grief, and she did not struggle when he put his arms around her. He whispered into Rosanna's ear all the things he had wanted to say three years before, but was never given chance to. He held her close until finally she looked up at him and blinked, as though clearing the other personality entirely from her mind. Now it was Rosanna; just for that instant, John saw that she was back, though for how long who could say.

'John Hardwick... What have I...?'

'Shh,' John whispered. 'I love you. Which is why this is the only way.'

'What do you mean? No!'

A hardness crossed her features – the expression of Tsun Pen perhaps. She was about to push John away; he felt the resistance well up in her. But it was too late.

She barely knew what was happening. Her eyes widened; she struggled to no avail.

'We are one," John whispered. He closed his eyes, and let himself fall into the light, Rosanna in his arms.

TWENTY-EIGHT

'**N**o!' Jim cried, head pounding with the effort.

For a moment, the chamber flashed bright, and there was silence – a momentary lull in the crescendo of violent phenomena that had preceded John and Rosanna's disappearance. It was an eerie stillness, as though everything – time itself – had slowed to witness the Artist's fall. It did not last.

Jim tried to stand once more as the trill of the gate erupted again. He was near lifted from his feet by swirling shadows, which coalesced into strange forms all about him, before shrinking back from the light of the portal in rapid, pulsating waves. Jim choked back nausea.

He pulled away from the shadows, and scrambled to Miss Furnival. Tesla was struggling manfully to activate his unfathomable devices with only one functioning arm.

'Tesla!' Jim shouted. 'What's happening?'

'This is bad. Very very bad,' Tesla replied, looking more wild-eyed than ever. 'I tell you, Captain, Madam Artist she control the gate. Not its full power, but she regulate the gravitational waves, and –' Tesla saw Jim's expression, and took a breath before continuing. 'Without Madam Artist, the gate it draw power to itself, exponentially. It will continue until there is none left to absorb, and then... whatever is on other side when it stop, it come through, unbidden.'

Jim thought he understood. The gate was warping and changing with every passing second. The ever-changing gate would soon become a passage to other worlds, other places, with denizens only too eager to cross the veil. A merry-go-round of potential destroyers of the world.

'Will destroying the facility stop it? All we need to do is get to the sluice-gate and blow it. The Thames will come crashing in, the dockside buildings will collapse – if the gate is not crushed by debris, it will at least be submerged.'

'Perhaps,' Tesla said. He paused, lips moving as he pondered the variables. He nodded. 'It break my heart. But yes. I think it work. The volume of water entering this area should be greater than the gravitational capacity of the portal. The pounds of pressure per inch, combined with the enervated –'

'English please, Mr Tesla!' Jim snapped.

'I… ah… the river it extinguish the portal like candle flame. Yes?' Tesla's expression suggested that the explanation was wholly inadequate, but that he saw no point in going into detail.

'Then we must get out of here,' Jim said. Miss Furnival was gaining strength, and Jim tried his best to help her up, trying not to let his own pain show.

'Not yet,' Tesla said. 'Your friend the colonel, he may yet stop this.'

'How?'

'Madam Artist has travelled between the worlds many times. She have her *wampyr* allies on what you call the Otherside, yes? And that is where I build my gravitational resonator. It is sister to this one. Everything else, it already here, left behind from the Lazarus Gate. But the resonator is the key. Madam Artist control it, from this side, or that side. If she deactivate it, then the gate it close.'

'And what then? Will John be trapped?'

'Without this gate, then yes. You leave the gate here, it can be controlled from the Otherside. You destroy it, and your friend, he gone forever. He know what it is he does, I think.'

'He know. I mean, yes, he knows,' Jim said, giving a rueful shake of his head.

Finally, Marie steadied herself, and Jim gave a quiet grunt of relief when she stopped leaning on him. She dusted herself down, embarrassed to have required his help.

'We... we have to wait for Colonel Hardwick,' she said.

Jim wanted nothing more than for John to come dashing back through the gate, but as the kaleidoscopic range of the portal swirled and changed, Jim could see little hope.

'How long do we delay before there is no turning back?' Jim called to Tesla, who had now managed to get a large pair of his eponymous coils crackling with energy.

'A few minutes... half an hour. I cannot be certain. Without Madam Artist, the gate it has become more unstable than ever. It is fascinating! It teach me things that I could not possibly have learned from merely –'

'Mr Tesla, please!'

'It is your choice, Captain. Only Madam Artist have the strength to close the gate. Her power is great, and the etherium she consume is too much even for the best Majestic here. It would be fatal for a mere mortal to use this device.' Tesla indicated the two large levers that Rosanna had activated earlier. 'The colonel... he would have to persuade her, no? Or force her.'

Jim hung his head. 'Unlikely,' he said. He looked into Marie's eyes. She pleaded silently for him to delay, but Jim knew she cared little for the world at large. She had done what she came to do, and would be willing to risk all to save John. Jim had no such luxury – he had a duty to the Crown. He would see to it that there was a Crown still to serve when this day was done. 'If we wait much longer there may not be time enough to set the explosives. We have to leave him.'

There was a momentary look of defiance from Miss Furnival, but finally she nodded acceptance, and hung her head. Tesla waited patiently for them to make a decision, even as lightning flickered all around and unnatural shadows congregated in every corner of the chamber.

'Mr Tesla, you will come with us to the lifeboat, of course,' Jim said.

'But my *Munjolovac* is here, Captain,' Tesla said. 'I shall make my own way, yes?'

'I am afraid not, sir. You must come with us – every courtesy will be extended to you of course, but given the circumstances you are now a prisoner of the British Crown. I hereby commandeer your... um... Munjo-vat... under the terms of the Lazarus Act.'

'*Munjolovac*,' Tesla corrected, only half-heartedly. The Serbian looked crestfallen. Jim felt for him, but the man was the most brilliant scientist of the Otherside, and had participated, however unwillingly, in an unprecedented attack on Apollo Lycea. Even if Cherleten had betrayed the Crown, Jim still had a duty to perform. Cherleten and Crookes would face justice soon enough, and it was left to Jim to see that justice done.

A great crash came from the gate, and the entire chamber flooded with light. A deep rumble shook the chamber so violently that Jim almost lost his footing, his cracked ribs jangled within his chest painfully, and a pressure built behind his eyes so suddenly that he thought his head might burst.

'Come on!' he grunted. 'There's no time to discuss this.'

Miss Furnival held her own head, and blood trickled from her nose. She looked as though she might be violently ill, and it was all she could do to nod acquiescence.

Jim picked up John's cane and Winchester almost reverently, and then the three of them made for the exit as fast as they could. They had no sooner reached the doors than the sound of the gate reached fever pitch, and then cut out completely, the sudden silence more deafening in the wake of the constant noise that had preceded it. The light blinked out, leaving just one or two weak electric lamps flickering as illumination. The pain in Jim's head subsided almost instantly, leaving only a prickling sensation across his scalp. The three strange companions stopped and turned, eyes blinking in bewilderment at the sudden relief they felt.

The gate had closed. Before them was a large ring of steel and brass and copper cable. No lights, no mirrored pool. The shadows did not writhe and crawl. The floor no longer vibrated.

'He... he did it,' Marie said.

'He's gone,' Jim added.

The silence was broken by a groaning noise. Jim and Marie looked about, and found beneath a pile of debris and overturned tables one of their men, in a bad way, but alive. Poynton.

'Good lord, Poynton,' Jim said. 'But you've got nine lives!'

'Reckon they're all used up, guv,' the man said. Jim looked him over. A few broken bones perhaps, and more superficial wounds than he could count. But Jim was delighted that anyone had survived the fight – more delighted still when Poynton clearly had no idea exactly what had transpired in the chamber. There would be no difficult conversations to have about Riftborn, on top of everything else.

'So what now?' Marie asked. 'I suppose we don't need to blow this place sky-high any more. We just... walk out the front door?'

'I suppose so,' Jim said. He had been in such a state of anxiety that the relief of this sudden and unexpected reprieve had not sunk in. 'First we need to go back and get Amworth. I'll have that man testify under oath, if it's the last thing I do. Mr Tesla, I...'

Jim turned, and Tesla was gone. He looked at Marie, and she at him.

'He's gone for the submarine,' she said.

Together, they dashed from the chamber in pursuit of Tesla, as fast as their beleaguered bodies would allow. They crossed the dark storehouse, and through the doors that led back into the heart of the complex. Jim tried not to look at the bodies that littered the floor. The battle had been brutal. Now Chinese lay alongside Russians, and ghouls, and too many of Jim's men for his liking. All to save John, against orders.

Jim tossed the Winchester to Marie, and stooped to pick up a lantern from among the dead. As he did, something crashed into him from behind, sending him sprawling over a pair of corpses that were locked in an eternal struggle. He heard a scuffle, sprang to his feet, and turned to see a large Russian wrench the rifle from Miss Furnival's grasp and throw her to the floor. Poynton tried to struggle too, but was struck hard, and fell down. Jim stared down the barrel of the gun, and then looked up into the eyes of Orlov.

'Thought you were dead,' Jim wheezed. He felt weaker by the second.

'You think it because I want it so,' Orlov said, sounding every bit as weary as Jim. The lower portions of his grey shirt glistened dark with blood. 'I find this submarine that you talk about, and I take this Tesla back to the motherland. No hard feelings, *Kapitan*.'

The rifle lever clicked. A shot rang out. But it was not the Winchester that had fired.

Orlov dropped the rifle, and slapped a hand to his neck. Blood oozed between his fingers. His eyes glazed, and he fell.

Miss Furnival grabbed the rifle. Jim scrambled for the lantern, and shone it along the corridor, in the direction of the shot. Four men, ragged and war-torn, shielded their eyes from the light. Jim recognised them as the wounded from the crossroads. He shuttered the lamp, and laughed with relief.

'Beggin' your pardon, Captain,' one of the men said, 'but things was all quiet back there. Some of the lads made a break for home. When we heard the commotion, the rest of us decided to come find you, but it was slow goin' on account of us being torn up a bit, and us gettin' lost and all. Sorry we didn't make it sooner, sir.'

Jim knew the men had seen the bodies. They would feel guilty for not playing their part. He ceased smiling, and nodded in sympathy at the fallen.

'You have nothing to apologise for,' Jim said. 'What's your name, lad?'

'Butterfield, sir.'

The man wore the remnants of a police uniform. Jim had called him 'lad', though Butterfield was not much younger than he was, in truth. Maybe the Order had aged Jim unduly. Now, he forced his most winning smile, tried to conjure some words of encouragement. One last push. 'There's work yet to be done, lads, if you have it in you. And as true blue bloody heroes I'm sure you do. Fall in, and look lively.'

Jim took Miss Furnival by the arm, and limped off towards the dock, knowing that those four men would follow. It was their duty.

TWENTY-NINE

The area that everyone called the 'sluice-gate' was somewhat more grand than the name might have suggested. The gates themselves were large, metal sliding doors which, when open, allowed access to the Thames beyond. From the river they looked like just another industrialised feature of the waterway – few would suspect that behind them lay a secret installation.

Jim and Marie stood now in a wet-dock, some hundred feet long and fifty across, with a high, raftered ceiling within whose eaves a few pigeons huddled together. A walkway covered three sides of the chamber, extending almost as far as the gates themselves on the two longer sides. Between these raised stone platforms was a deep dock, large enough for perhaps a schooner to make deliveries direct into the heart of the facility. Overhead, iron stairs and grated walkways criss-crossed the dock, leading off to the overground offices and dockside warehouses. A bitter wind whistled through the rafters and skeletal gantries. Jim fancied he saw a flickering orange glow overhead where the chamber was exposed to the elements, and the fires outside still raged.

Fires burned within, too. Smoke drifted idly across the water. Dust and debris lay in piles on the left-hand platform, alongside dislodged sheets of corrugated iron and metal struts from the roof. Bodies lay scattered around. Chinese, Russians, facility guards, and emaciated ghouls that looked in death like unearthed corpses. Who had fought on which side was unclear, for the dead littered the floor haphazardly, some torn by tooth and claw, others shot, or hacked to pieces by blades. Jim's men stepped cautiously onto the platform, almost dragging Amworth along, who quailed at the sight of more bloodshed.

The controls for the gates were sited at the far ends of the lower walkways, but they were not needed now. The gates were open. Along the right-hand side of the docking bay, four life vessels were moored – long boats, equipped with steam motors and oars; none had been taken. But it was something else in the water that drew Jim's full attention.

The upper hatches of a great ironclad submarine were visible above the murky waterline. What part of the vessel's armoured hull could be seen was elegantly curved, segmented plates interlocking like the scales of some exotic sea-creature. Upon the cupola, a silver-grey plaque was inscribed with a single word in Cyrillic script.

Муњоловац

Jim bent double, clutching at his sides. Miss Furnival ran ahead of him towards the submarine, her energy seemingly boundless.

'Crookes!' Marie exclaimed.

Jim struggled to catch up, and saw where Marie pointed. Sure enough, at the foot of a short gangplank beside the submarine, Dr Crookes lay spread-eagled on the platform. Jim checked for a pulse.

'He's alive, but only just. What the devil happened to him? Why didn't he take the submarine?'

'Because, Captain Denny, it is defended, no?' Tesla stared down at them from the top hatch of the vessel, beaming. 'Madam Artist remember to set the counter-measures. Clever lady.'

'Mr Tesla, come down from there this instant,' Marie said.

'Miss Furnival, I am glad you make it. I was afraid you would be too late, no?'

'Too late for what?'

'To come with me.'

'What? Why would I –'

'No need to be pretending, madam. You are not one of them, I know this. You do me the greatest turn in removing first de Montfort, and then Madam Artist, who make my life so miserable. And now I am reunited with my '*Lovac*, my greatest treasure, the queen of the oceans! I can go anywhere, do anything... but it is a lonely life I face, no? I think it must be lonely for you, and so I hope that you would be here. I hope you might accompany me, on a so-great adventure.'

'I...' Marie paused, sounding most unsure of herself. 'No, Mr Tesla, I cannot. I'm afraid I must ask you to step down from there, and surrender yourself and your vessel to us.'

'No, no, that is quite impossible. I have too-important work to do. I have a world – many worlds – to save, and many terrible wrongs to set right. You have nothing here, my dear lady. You who are without a home, and without a cause. Yes, I see it in your eyes. You have follow de Montfort for so long. He talk of you once. He never would have admitted, but he know that you are a shadow to him for many years, and it scare him. Trust in me, dear lady, I know what it is to devote one's life to a single cause, at the exclusion of all else that is dear. And when that work is over, what then? I offer to you a new cause. Better to tread a righteous path, than to follow the orders of the unrighteous, no?'

'What cause?'

'The noblest! And if I am right, you will see again your uncle, your real uncle, and all who have been lost.'

'Impossible!' Marie gasped.

'Nothing is impossible, dear lady, if it lay with realm of science. Not to me.'

Jim dragged himself to Marie's side. He saw her falter. She

looked so very sad. He took out a revolver and aimed it at Tesla. 'Mr Tesla, the lady requested politely that you turn yourself over to our custody. I am not so polite.'

'Ridiculous!' said Tesla. 'You will not shoot me.'

Jim pulled the trigger, firing a warning shot at the armoured cupola just a few inches below Tesla's waist, ringing the submarine's hull like a bell.

Tesla barely flinched. 'If there is one thing I learn from the long years of captivity, Captain,' Tesla said, his tone now very sincere, 'it is that I am worth more alive than dead. I am – what you say? – commodity? To you, and more so to your employers. Cherleten, is it? I know him from the Otherside. I wonder if your version is as mean of spirit? Ah, I see from that look that he is; and yet you are loyal to him! Oh, you military men are all the same, only your flag it change.'

'That is not so,' Jim said. 'My association with Lord Cherleten is about to come to an end. Look, Mr Tesla, you have my word that you will be treated as a gentleman.'

'But I am not gentleman, Captain Denny. I am a poor boy from Smiljan, too long locked away from the world I was born to change. If Miss Furnival not change her mind about coming with me, then I must bid you both farewell.'

'You have forced my hand, sir,' Jim said. He gave the nod to Butterfield, who made his way to the gangplank and hesitantly climbed across towards the *Munjolovac*'s hatch.

'I would not do that...' Tesla said.

Butterfield put his hands on the hull to steady himself, and let out a cry as his arms were pushed violently away from the vessel by some unseen force. The man was thrown to the ground, where he crumpled in a heap.

'I warn you,' Tesla said. 'Counter-measures. The *'Lovac* is jealous mistress, no? She not allowing any to put hands on me ever again. Now, Miss Furnival – will you come?'

Marie looked to Tesla, then to Jim, and back. 'No,' she said. 'Whatever fate may lie in wait for me, Mr Tesla, it will be my own. I think your destiny lies elsewhere. Perhaps our paths shall cross again someday.'

Jim hobbled to the gangplank and helped Butterfield back to the platform. He looked across the water, where the gates were now open to reveal the Thames beyond, and a paling sky overhung with black clouds. An electrical storm raged outside, wind howling, lightning forking. Jim looked up at Tesla once more.

'You can do more good here,' Jim said. 'You can work with our scientists, to protect us against the Riftborn, and whatever else lies out there.'

'I cannot stay, Captain Denny. Your government does not want to protect itself – it wish to build weapons. The Nightwatch, the gates, the guns – all of it to grow powerful. They court disaster, and they think it wisdom. I cannot work for your government, or be the puppet of any other. I have spent too-long time in captivity, peddling wares for those who threaten me. I have use my genius for nothing more than destruction. I can produce such devices that would make the Riftborn pale in comparison. No more! Believe me, Captain – if I stay, you may live to see man-made horrors beyond your comprehension. I will not be responsible. I go now, back to where all this began, to find a way of my own, far from the madness of lesser men.'

Tesla popped his head inside the submarine, and the vessel sprang to life with a judder. He reappeared, waving with surprising cheer. Even as he did so, the storm beyond the sluice-gate grew louder. Thunder rumbled overhead, and a fell wind blew into the dock, which smelled of smoke.

'What is happening out there?' Jim shouted over the noise of thunder and the submarine's engines.

'The gate, when it awaken, it draw power from the very heavens. Aha! That is why this ship get its name, Captain Denny. *Munjolovac*. It mean "storm hunter". Most apt, no? Now we go to find the greatest storm of all – the very first storm, where it begin, and where maybe it end. Perhaps that is my destiny, Miss Furnival. I think you are right. Farewell, Miss Furnival, the bravest lady I ever know. May you find the peace that you are deserving. Farewell, Captain Denny.'

And with that, Tesla closed the hatch. Moments later, the segmented armour plates of the *Munjolovac* rippled like the scales of a living creature, and the vessel snaked eel-like beneath the surface of the water, a trail of dark bubbles marking its path through the sluice-gate, and out into the Thames, where the silhouettes of Royal Navy vessels waited silently, for a foe they could not see.

'That's that, I guess,' Marie said, regret clear in her voice.

Jim said nothing. Now that he'd finally stopped, and had the time to consider all that had happened, he felt empty inside. John Hardwick was gone. After everything they had been through, he was gone. Jim clenched his fists. The old wound in his hand was playing up, making it hard to close his fingers. It sent pain shooting up Jim's arm, and he savoured it. He did not know whether to laugh or cry, to shout out or simply walk away into the dark tunnels to be alone with his thoughts. He closed his eyes, and when he did he saw the shadow on the sky, and heard it pricking at the corners of his mind, peeling away at his nerves bit by bit. When he opened his eyes, he fancied he could still see the shadow, out there across the river. Marie was looking at him expectantly. The survivors were, too. They'd seen enough horrors for one lifetime. Jim had seen enough for several.

And that was what plagued his thoughts. The power that the Artist had wielded but briefly could still be harnessed. Even if Cherleten and Dr Crookes were stopped, there would be others. And the shadow would watch, and bide its time.

'Captain Denny? James?' Marie said, frowning concern.

The only person who ever called him James before he'd met Miss Furnival had been Jane.

Jim took a deep breath. For a moment he asked himself what John would do. There was a time not so long ago that he knew exactly what the answer would be. John would have taken to the boats as Miss Furnival suggested, and reported to Cherleten.

He'd probably have shot Tesla, too, as a matter of national security. But that had been the old John Hardwick. If he was here now, knowing everything that his actions had wrought, what would he do? If he had a chance to be the man he wanted to be, rather than the one moulded by a tyrannical father and a life of war, what then?

In the end, Jim knew he could not compare himself to John Hardwick any longer. Instead, he closed his eyes and pictured Jane. His greatest failing as a man of honour. She had always been proud of her dashing cavalryman, because she had never truly seen into his heart. Only now did Jim realise how much he wanted to be the man Jane Pennyforth had thought he was.

Jim made his decision. In silence, he marched away from his group, towards the sluice-gate controls – towards the detonator. He took the ring of keys from around his neck, and sorted the red key from its fellows. He heard footsteps behind him. When he reached the box, Miss Furnival was by his side. As he held up the key to the detonator panel, she placed a hand gently over his.

'Jim… what are you doing?'

'What's right,' he said. He looked her straight in the eye. 'The Lazarus Gate is back there, stronger than ever. Tesla's machinery can't fall into the wrong hands – Cherleten's hands. I'm done standing by while the power-hungry steer us towards destruction. I'm done hunting down desperate men, women and children – killing them – for… for this.'

She nodded slowly. Jim swore her mouth turned upwards at the corners, just a fraction. Her large eyes sparkled. 'There'll be hell to pay,' she said.

'Hell be damned,' Jim said. Now they both smiled.

Miss Furnival took away her hand. Jim pushed the key into position, turned it, and stepped away as something clunked, followed by a light, rhythmic ticking.

'We have five minutes.' Jim turned and shouted, 'All hands to the lifeboats. At the double! Someone get Butterfield. And don't forget Crookes – mustn't deny the gallows-men their due.'

Soon they were underway, slipping through the sluice-gate and out of the shadow of the docks.

Overhead, lightning flashed again against tumultuous clouds that glowed with a red rind heralding dawn. A jagged streak lit up the sky, striking the great scaffolds that encased Tower Bridge. For a second, perhaps even as the Serbian's remarkable submarine passed beneath, electricity snaked between the twin towers of the bridge.

Like Tesla coils.

THIRTY

Jim and Melville marched side-by-side up the broad path to the Tower of London. Ten Special Branch constables strode alongside them. Dr Crookes was dragged in tow. They had watched half of St Katharine's collapse into the Thames, gouts of flame extinguished by the onrushing river, leaving a smouldering pit in its wake.

They had made no secret of their intent since Jim's lifeboat had landed. Jim had reported directly to Melville, handing over what scant evidence they had collected, and extracting a statement from Amworth. Crookes had remained tight-lipped, but he would break. Jim and Melville had held a council of war, and now intended to enact the will of that council.

The Prime Minister was informed. Queen Victoria was informed. Lord Cherleten was to be arrested.

The Tower guards waved them through the gates. They ascended the steps of the Develin Tower, and rapped loudly on the door to the first-floor chamber. When no response came they attempted entry, but found the door barricaded. Soldiers were called to break down the door, and laboured hard to push through the pile of heavy medieval furniture behind it. It must have taken no small endeavour for the single occupant of the room. Finally, Jim squeezed through.

Cherleten was dead.

He sat in a great carved chair, like a throne. His brains were dashed over the stone of an ancient fireplace. Blood trickled from his mouth. A small pistol lay beside him on the floor. A few feet away, upon the ledge of the room's only window, was a note. It read simply:

Ever have I sought to further the strength of our great nation, and this most exalted Order, and ever has that strength come through great sacrifice. It pains me to leave Apollo Lycea in the hands of those lesser men who lack the strength to do what is necessary. This latest foe has faltered at the last. But there will be other enemies, stronger ones, in the years to come. And there will be none amongst my peers with the foresight or fortitude to defeat them.

If I have one regret, it is the death of one Sir Toby Fitzwilliam. His demise came about because I allowed an enemy to blame him for my own deeds, and that was a failure of courage on my part. What Sir Toby lacked in vision, he compensated for in honour. Prince Albert Victor begged for the Iscariot Sanction, that he might be cured of his ills – that he might serve his Empire as commander of the wampyr. He knew the risks full well, and unfortunately the process was unsuccessful. What we learned from said process, however, was invaluable.

And yet, we could not abandon our work, not even for the prince's sake. The Russians – already known to be buying black-market Otherside artefacts – were implicated, by my testimony, and it was Sir Toby who signed the sanctions against the Russian czar. His assassination was a direct consequence of this action, and one that I had not foreseen. As some small recompense, I bestowed upon my men the means to avenge this injustice, at the expense of the Order's St Katharine Dock facility. I see now, at the end, that justice was served.

With my one sin duly confessed, I go now to a place where I shall be judged not by men of lesser ambition, but by God, our Great Architect. I go safe in the knowledge that I shall not be found wanting.

For God, Queen & Country,
AC

Monday, 9th October 1893, 9.00 a.m.
GOWER STREET, LONDON

Jim's fingers jabbed away at the keys of the typewriter. He had never quite got to grips with the thing, but hand-written reports were a thing of the past.

He barely noticed when Mrs Whitinger entered with a tray of tea things, and he turned around at once as she set them down, noting the look of surprise on his landlady's face as she saw the mess around the room.

'Captain Denny, these cases… Are you taking a trip?'

'Ah. I was going to speak with you about that, Mrs Whitinger, but I'm afraid it's all happened rather quickly. As it happens, yes, I am taking a trip, and I expect it will be a lengthy one. Should I return –'

'You think you may not?' she asked, anxiety writ upon her. She had been in a mind to fuss ever since Jim had returned home injured – there was no other reason she would play housemaid and wait upon her lodgers, even ones as favoured as Jim.

'I did not mean to sound so dramatic, Mrs Whitinger. But you know how it is. I shall send word, of course.'

'When do you leave?'

'Today, I expect. I must finish packing, and I have some business to attend to here first, but then I put out to sea.'

'Might I ask where you are going, in case anyone asks?'

'If anyone asks, I would hope you tell them to mind their

own business. I cannot say for certain in any case. To start with, north, to colder climes I think. After that… wherever the fates deign to take me.'

'Another adventure, Captain, and you so frail… Is it to do with those terrible bombs the other night?'

'In a manner of speaking, but I doubt I'll be blown up any time soon. Do not fret on my account, dear lady. A few more scars merely adds to my already prodigious reputation.' He winked at her, and she shook her head disapprovingly.

'Never change, Captain Denny.'

'Never, Mrs Whitinger.'

As soon as the landlady had left, Jim turned back to his typewriter, a bittersweet smile on his lips, and concluded his report.

On the subject of Colonel John Hardwick, it is my belief that, although he may yet survive on the Otherside, the chance of him returning to us in any fit state is negligible. Therefore, it is with regret that I must recommend Colonel Hardwick be presumed dead at this time, and his heroism unto death, which saved my life and the lives of several allies, be marked with a posthumous commendation.

Jim leaned back in his chair. He considered, even now, whether to confess what he knew about Tesla. He thought on Tesla's words at the end: 'Now we go to find the greatest storm of all – the very first storm, where it begin, and where maybe it end.'

Alaska. It had to be. The place where William James had first seen the phenomenon that would become a portal; where he had slipped through the veil accidentally, causing the Othersiders to begin their research into gates in earnest. Jim knew he was inviting a world of trouble by withholding the information. But whatever Tesla was up to, Jim knew one thing only: it was not for Apollo Lycea to know. The Order was all but over. Even now, shadowy conclaves discussed whether to reinstate Apollo Lycea, or let it die with its inner circle.

Men of ambition clamoured to assume command. Other agencies argued for the Order's demise. Bad enough that somewhere out there was the equipment that Cherleten had smuggled out of the docks facility. It still had not been found.

No. Better that these faceless bureaucrats and spymasters who picked the bones of the Order's carcass knew nothing of Tesla. He could be presumed dead also.

And so Jim bound up his report, addressed it to William Melville, and continued his packing. Other arrangements had already been made. Other loyalties secured, or paid for. Other avenues investigated. Jim rather liked the idea of becoming a wanted man; now that certainly would add to his prodigious reputation.

Jim's first port of call that morning was Hampstead, to his old home that had more in common with a modest country house than a London abode. He had not returned to it for over a year. Not since Jane.

He alighted from his cab and made his way to the ivy-covered house. He leaned heavily on Hardwick's cane as he went. He found it reassuring.

The servants admitted him with warmth in their smiles, and directed him to the library. Jim ascended the stairs, across a long landing, from whose walls his advance was monitored by the portraits of great heroes, and beady eyes of mounted stag's heads. He stopped outside the door of the library, took a deep breath, and was about to knock when he heard a voice from within.

'Enter, Captain.'

Jim muttered a small prayer, and swung open the door.

Colonel Denny stood beside his bookshelves, a great tome in his hands, squinting at rows of old volumes of military history, many signed by heroes of war, Nelson among them. The colonel turned to regard his son with eyes that had lost none of their steel through age.

'The prodigal returns,' Colonel Denny said, voice a rumble due to a lifelong predilection for brandy and cigars.

'But briefly, Father,' Jim said.

'Run out of money have you? I see you have spent last month's allowance as quickly as it was paid. Hope you're not at the gambling houses again.'

'No, Father… though my financial provision is not quite adequate for –'

'– For the lifestyle to which you have become accustomed?' The old man beheld Jim with a look of great disapproval.

'No, Father, as it happens. That is not why I'm here. Not exactly, anyway.'

'Not exactly, eh? So it is about money.'

'No. That is, it is more about why I'm spending it.'

The colonel slammed shut the book he was holding, and put it down on a table beside him. 'Do I want to know?' he asked.

'I am sure I could not disclose the full details. You know how it is.'

'Yes, I know. That bloody club and its bloody rules. No fit occupation for an honest man.'

'Father, we have exchanged harsh words on this matter in the past, and I am here to tell you that you were right. That you are still right.'

'Eh?' The old man looked decidedly off-guard. That was the colonel – always ready for a fight; always out of his depth when one was not forthcoming.

'Father, I apologise unreservedly for the pain I have caused you, and I shall send apologies again to the Pennyforths, should they wish to hear them. I apologise also for not listening to you on certain matters surrounding my… secondment… to a certain organisation, and the way I left Horse Guards. I did what I thought was right at the time, and I have learned the hard way that I should have regarded your wisdom on the subject more highly.'

'Oh. Well… yes, you should.'

'Father, the true reason I am here is that I am going away for a while. There is a possibility that I may not return.'

'What? Where are you going?'

'I am not at liberty to say. I came here today to offer my most sincere apologies for what transpired between us. I know that I have proven, in many respects, a disappointment to you. Perhaps, through toil and duty, I have learned how to be the man you wanted me to be. I know that I have no right to ask anything of you, but regardless: I ask that we might part company today on good terms, so that neither of us may have cause to regret our parting, at the end.'

Colonel Denny had frowned throughout, but at those words, 'at the end', his great brows untied themselves. He looked as though he might respond in kind, but checked himself. He turned back to his books.

'Stuff and nonsense,' he said at last. 'Not sure what manner of youth I raised.'

There was an uncomfortable pause. Jim sighed, turned, and made his way to the door, cane tapping on the parquet floor.

'Send your things over before you go,' the colonel said. Jim looked over his shoulder – his father had not turned away from his books, nor would he. Instead, the old man said, 'I'll not have a son of mine living for ever in some Bloomsbury boarding house. Your old room will be ready for you, when you return.'

Colonel Denny was not a man for displays of affection, either giving or receiving them. Those words, however, were more than Jim could have hoped for. It was all he could do to say, 'Thank you,' and leave the house with his head held high.

A couple of hours later, Jim strode across Horse Guards Parade, collar turned up against the morning chill, the clicking of John's cane echoing from the flagstones. He made his way to the barracks of the Blues, where a few men still saluted him as they recognised him, looking on respectfully at their war-wounded former officer. They could not know how he'd come by his injuries, but it was moot. Animosity was for now set aside for a wounded cavalryman.

Jim passed through the stables, and out to the kennels. He exchanged pleasantries with the kennel-master, before taking ownership of the dog, Gregor. The brute was somewhat reluctant to go with Jim, and the kennel-master informed him that Gregor had quickly established his seniority in the pecking order of the regimental hounds. Jim doubted this not. The dog licked at John's cane, and seemed satisfied after doing so that Jim was a friend, finally ceasing its straining at the leash. Perhaps, Jim thought, the dog was worthy of its namesake after all, for Gregor, though a powerful and assertive man, had been slow to anger and loyal to a fault; qualities that had proven his downfall.

Jim wondered if perhaps the dog would be better off in the kennels for a time longer, and certainly the kennel-master seemed rather taken with Gregor, for all the dog's faults. But Jim had made a promise to himself – for good or ill, he would keep the dog with him from now on.

With a thanks and farewell, he returned once more to his cab, tossing the driver an extra coin for the inconvenience of transporting a dog that was clearly larger than he had anticipated. Gregor hopped into the carriage with surprising agility, where he bundled himself onto the waiting Miss Furnival, and showered her face with licks as she giggled. Jim climbed into the cab, surprised at the sudden show of affection from both of his unlikely companions.

'He's magnificent!' she said.

'Glad you like him – he will be a companion for some time to come.'

'There's still time to change your mind,' Marie said.

'And you. Your Uncle Arthur needs you.'

'No,' she said, smiling sadly. 'He'll be just fine without me. But... this isn't going to be easy.'

'Nothing ever is, Miss Furnival,' Jim smiled. He leaned out of the window and called up to the cabbie. 'The Victoria Dock, my good man. We have a ship to catch.'

EPILOGUE

Friday, 6th October 1893, 5.00 a.m.

THE OTHERSIDE

John woke slowly, almost reluctantly, a great amber glow stinging his eyes. His vision blurred. He lay on a cold floor, slime slipping between his fingers when he tried to move. He could smell old loam and rust. He thought perhaps he was at the St Katharine facility still, although the room would not stop spinning long enough for him to tell. Every part of him ached.

He remembered some detail, like a long-forgotten dream. He remembered the warmth of golden liquid, a membranous barrier through which he had half-fallen, half-fought, never wanting to emerge from its womb-like embrace. He had not been alone. He remembered staring into a pair of dark, beautiful eyes, in which was reflected… fear? Happiness? Rage?

Rosanna.

The recollection of her name pierced his thoughts like a dagger to the heart. It cleared away the fug of the dream, and John remembered what had happened all too clearly. The fierce aches of his many wounds came into focus along with the dark room in which he lay. He was staring up at a vaulted ceiling.

353

A low, steady hum rang upon the stones, unsettling powdery mortar, which rained upon his face.

John had peripheral vision only on his right side. Something lay near to him, pale and unmoving. He did not want to look. He knew it was a corpse, and could not bear it if Rosanna was gone. At last, he forced himself to turn, pain shooting through his body at the simple act of moving his neck. What stared back at him was not Rosanna, but a ghoul, its dead flesh a patchwork of puckered scars, its once-bright eyes dark and lifeless. In its forehead was a clean bullet-hole. Small-calibre pistol. The observation of detail steadied him. He squinted. More of the creatures lay beyond the first – four, as far as he could see by the soft golden light.

The portal! John now came fully to wakefulness. He had come here to shut down the portal. Where was Rosanna? He had to find her. He struggled to move, coughing up blood with the effort of rising to his elbows. And then he heard a noise – sharp boot-heels on stone.

With a great effort, John turned over, towards the light, and saw the gate. It was not the same portal; it was contained not within a ring of metal, but instead a stone archway. Beside it, singularly out of place, a tall stack of strange instruments and machinery whirred and clicked quietly. A woman, her slender form silhouetted against the light of the gateway, wrestled with controls. She heaved upon two levers, large as a railwayman's switches, which creaked and clicked as they resisted.

'R... Rosanna...' John croaked. He rolled onto his front, and pushed himself up, almost falling on his face as his left shoulder buckled.

The woman finally, with great effort, heaved both switches back fully. The sound of the gate deepened, growing quieter. The machinery stopped its whirring. The light blinked once, twice, and then the portal was gone, leaving almost total darkness.

'Rosanna...' John said again. His head spun. He wasn't sure if he was awake or dreaming.

Two pinpricks of light appeared in the gloom. Violet eyes turned upon John, and came towards him.

'She is not here, this "Rosanna" of yours,' a woman's voice said. 'You should have let me kill her years ago. I was trying to do you a favour.'

'What?' John was confused. The voice was familiar, the eyes fearsome.

A match lit, and was put to a lantern. A warm glow filled the chamber. John stared up in disbelief at Lillian Hardwick.

'Surprised to see me alive?' she asked.

John could not summon words; he could barely move. He heard footsteps on the stone behind him.

'Any sign?' Lillian asked.

'No, miss. She kicked the clouds sharpish. Scarpered. Bloody 'ell, is that…?'

'It is.'

John turned to see the man who approached. The stranger stepped forward. Hunched shoulders and bowler hat at first concealed the scarred face beneath, but the man stepped into the light and John recognised an old ally; a taciturn policeman who he had long thought dead at the hands of Tsun Pen.

'Ecclestone? Larry Ecclestone?'

'The very same, guv. I'll be blowed.'

John tried once more to stand, twisting to face Lillian, eyeing her warily as he struggled.

She sighed, and held out a hand to him. 'A lot has changed since last we met,' she said. 'Give me your hand… brother.'

And John Hardwick took it.

AUTHOR'S NOTE

A few very kind souls, in praising the Apollonian Casefiles, have referenced their 'authenticity'. That's a peculiar word when talking about a twenty-first century book set in the nineteenth century, but it's rather gratifying to know that the book feels authentic, as I (and my editors) put a lot of work into making it that way. The Apollonian Casefiles are by no stretch historical novels, but at times they're close – I wanted to conjure the idea that, if you removed the supernatural and SF elements, you'd end up with a fairly authentic-feeling Victorian thriller. To this end I set aside specific stages of the editing process to remove anachronistic language, and to check for Americanisms and idioms that have changed meaning between then and now. Some characters are based on real historical figures – you can look them up. You'll find places mentioned in these books that don't exist any longer, but did at the time. Some events really did happen, although not always as described. I worry about details, such as 'could you really take a train to Maldon East on a Friday afternoon in 1893?', and whether or not tube lines existed around Fulham Road at the time.

In this book, however, I've taken a liberty. I was so inspired by the story of Frederick Charrington, and his conversion from ale magnate to temperance supporter, that I brought his purchase of

Osea Island forward in time by about ten years. This is probably the wildest flourish of artistic license in any of the three books, for which I hope you, dear reader, can forgive me. If it's any consolation, St Katharine Dock didn't blow up in 1893 either, so maybe we've simply slipped into an alternate timeline whilst meddling with portals and etherium.

ACKNOWLEDGEMENTS

And so we come to the third book in a trilogy. A bittersweet moment for a writer, and the culmination of a lot of work. Thanks must be given to Titan Books for giving me the opportunity to bring the Apollonian Casefiles to print, and for helping make these books the best that they could be.

For this book, particular thanks must go to my trusted 'alpha readers', my friend Mat Ward and my dear wife Alison – my harshest critics and loudest cheerleaders. Also, special thanks to Predrag Vasiljevic, for helping me with my Serbian – Mr Tesla owes you much.

As we close the door on the Apollonian Club, I can't help but wonder what exactly becomes of Tesla, and Jim, and of course John Hardwick. That, friends, is a story for another day.

ABOUT THE AUTHOR

Mark A. Latham is a writer, editor, history nerd, frustrated grunge singer and amateur baker from Staffordshire, UK. A recent immigrant to rural Nottinghamshire, he lives in a very old house (sadly not haunted), and is still regarded in the village as a foreigner.

Formerly the editor of Games Workshop's *White Dwarf* magazine, Mark dabbled in tabletop games design before becoming a full-time author of strange, fantastical and macabre tales, mostly set in the nineteenth century, a period for which his obsession knows no bounds. He is the author of *The Lazarus Gate*, published by Titan Books.

Follow Mark on Twitter: @aLostVictorian

THE LAZARUS GATE

MARK A. LATHAM

London, 1890. Captain John Hardwick, an embittered army veteran and opium addict, is released from captivity in Burma and returns home, only to be recruited by a mysterious gentlemen's club to combat a supernatural threat to the British Empire. This is the tale of a secret war between parallel universes, between reality and the supernatural; a war waged relentlessly by an elite group of agents; unsung heroes, whose efforts can never be acknowledged, but by whose sacrifice we are all kept safe.

'Steeped in rich fantasy and Victorian authenticity'
GEORGE MANN

'A splendid start to what promises to be terrific series'
JAMES LOVEGROVE

'A powerful Victorian esoteric fantasia'
GAVIN THORPE

THE ISCARIOT SANCTION

MARK A. LATHAM

In an alternate reality, the world is in peril. The sky burns with a supernatural fire, demonic entities run amok in the streets, and in the north of England, sinister beings plot to claim a part of the Empire for their own. Young Apollo Lycea agent Lillian Hardwick, and her Majestic partner Sir Arthur Furnival, are sent to expose this plot. To complete their mission they must overcome foes both mundane and supernatural, uncover a Royal conspiracy, and unlock the secret of the Iscariot Sanction. And yet what they find in the industrial cities and windswept moors of the north is a danger unlike anything they have faced before; a threat that will leave them – and the Empire – changed forever.

'Exemplary entertainment'

LOVE READING

'Highly entertaining and original'

RISING SHADOW

'A thrilling mystery'

MUGGLENET

TITANBOOKS.COM

SHERLOCK HOLMES: A BETRAYAL IN BLOOD

MARK A. LATHAM

Count Dracula: monster, murderer, vampire. This is what we have been told. This is what they want us to believe. When Sherlock Holmes acquires the fabled 'Dracula Papers', the stage is set for one of the greatest battles of wits since Reichenbach. Why did five men really pursue a Transylvanian nobleman to the ends of the earth? Who was really behind the series of murders that would have every man, woman and child in England whispering 'vampire' for years to come? The world's greatest detective would have the truth, though he must overcome the brilliant genius of Abraham Van Helsing to get it.

PRAISE FOR THE AUTHOR

'Fans of Bram Stoker's *Dracula* will like this one'

KIRKUS

'One of my favorite science fiction reads all year'

GEEK DAD

'The reader will become ensnared in Latham's setting'

FANTASY BOOK REVIEW

For more fantastic fiction, author events, exclusive
excerpts, competitions, limited editions and more

VISIT OUR WEBSITE
titanbooks.com

LIKE US ON FACEBOOK
facebook.com/titanbooks

FOLLOW US ON TWITTER
@TitanBooks

EMAIL US
readerfeedback@titanemail.com